IRON
TIGERS

Michael Farmer

A SIGNET BOOK

SIGNET
Published by New American Library, a division of
Penguin Group (USA) Inc., 375 Hudson Street,
New York, New York 10014, U.S.A.
Penguin Books Ltd, 80 Strand,
London WC2R 0RL, England
Penguin Books Australia Ltd, 250 Camberwell Road,
Camberwell, Victoria 3124, Australia
Penguin Books Canada Ltd, 10 Alcorn Avenue,
Toronto, Ontario, Canada M4V 3B2
Penguin Books (NZ), cnr Airborne and Rosedale Roads,
Albany, Auckland 1310, New Zealand

Penguin Books Ltd, Registered Offices:
80 Strand, London WC2R 0RL, England

First published by Signet, an imprint of New American Library,
a division of Penguin Group (USA) Inc.

First Printing, August 2004
10 9 8 7 6 5 4 3 2 1

FLAMES AGAINST THE NIGHT SKY.
A CITY ON FIRE.
CIVILIANS CORRALED AND EXTERMINATED.

MOSCOW: THE DAY AFTER TOMORROW.
STAY TUNED. . . .

The American television correspondent's face—well known to the viewing public from reports in Kuwait, Bosnia, Afghanistan, and Iraq—conveyed a sense of urgency that was palpable to his global audience.

The live feed darkened as a gloved hand appeared and covered the camera. A harsh Russian voice said, "All equipment now belongs to the Russian government."

The cameraman broke away from his captors to continue filming. Simultaneously audiences heard a rapid series of shots. The picture tilted sideways as the camera fell to the ground. The reporter's voice, now verging on hysteria, was clear over the street noise. "Tommy . . . Tommy!" As audiences watched, bright red arterial blood pooled around Italian leather. *"You bastards!"*

More shots sounded and the feed went blank.

Iron Tigers is dedicated to the precious ladies of my life: my daughters, Meagan, Dylan, Logan, and Carson. Few things in this world are certain, my angels, but one thing you can count on is that you hold your father's heart in your hands. With love . . . Daddy

ACKNOWLEDGMENTS

It is impossible to thank all the people who made *Iron Tigers* possible, but I'll try. If I miss someone, let me know and you'll receive a free signed copy.

First, to my editor at Signet, Ron Martirano—thanks for making the publishing process, if not pleasurable, at least tolerable. Ron learned that it's much tougher dealing with a globetrotting full-time soldier/author, methinks.

To my agent, Jake Elwell, of Wieser and Elwell, Inc.— thanks as always for the sage counsel . . . and for the Sergeant Rock graphic novel. *Make War No More,* baby.

To my friends and colleagues who provided technical assistance and/or took the time to scrub the manuscript and provide their input (some good, some not so good, all appreciated): Matt Wloczewski (aka "Little Man"), Mark Stoller, Kit Carson, Sean Dehlinger, Cookie Sewell, Jim Webster, Melinda Britt-Farmer and Greg Valloch. Special thanks to Paul "pk" Kelley for dual-hatting it as an armor and Russian expert; sorry I couldn't write fast enough for you, pk (and no, the next chapter of book three isn't ready). Any mistakes, as ever, are my own.

Kit Carson, former scout and current master knife maker, extraordinaire—thanks for proofing *Iron Tigers* with a tactical eye and for providing Rolf Krieger's "Carson M16" knife to the story—it's a thing of wicked beauty. Special thanks also to Paul Gillespie of Columbia River Knife and Tool (http://www.crkt.com) for the loan of your M16 and M18 series knives for research. You and your staff are a class act.

My Web master, Bill Park of Parker Information Resources in Houston (http://www.parkerinfo.com)—you're a harsh taskmaster, Billy; thanks.

To Lieutenant Colonel Costas . . . thanks for all of the useful background details you "couldn't" tell me about the CIA. I'd have probed deeper, but I'd hate for you to disappear in the middle of the night.

To Scout, a Jack Russell with lots of heart (and attitude), for providing the inspiration for one of the more colorful characters ever to grace a military novel. Try to remember you don't weigh a hundred pounds, big boy.

To Jean . . . thanks for providing a calm place in this world following one of the stormier periods of my life. All is good once again, in large part thanks to you.

And finally to my daughters—you are my touchstones. Never forget that. When deployments, work, and a chaotic year made focus difficult and writing impossible, you always brought me home . . . thanks. You'll always be Daddy's girls.

FOREWORD

I'd like to thank all of you who have written courtesy of my Web site regarding *Tin Soldiers*. It was a novel conceived by a young captain sitting in the middle of the Kuwaiti desert way back in 1996. I can't tell you how happy the book's reception has made me. Again, many thanks.

Moving to the work at hand, *Iron Tigers*. As I finish this novel it is early 2004. I'm a senior major now and sitting in a very different geographic location—Baghdad, Iraq. And many things have changed in this world since 1996. It has gone from a relatively peaceful place (from the American perspective) with just a few assholes we had well under control to a madhouse in which a few fanatics have attempted to change our very way of life. A world in which planes full of innocent civilians are used as weapons against civilian and government targets. But as I write we have these "terrorists" on the run. When they speak, they have to climb from under a rock. They may be alive, but they ain't happy.

Iron Tigers has taken the events of the 2003 war against Iraq and blended them with the conclusion of *Tin Soldiers* in an attempt to keep the story line current. Hopefully the faithful will understand. And I hope you all enjoy reading this tale as much as I enjoyed writing it. Scouts out!

—Michael Farmer
Major, Armor
U.S. Army
Baghdad, Iraq
14 January 2004

Once more unto the breach, dear friends, once more;
Or close the wall up with our English dead.
In peace there's nothing so becomes a man
As modest stillness and humility:
But when the blast of war blows in our ears,
Then imitate the action of the tiger;
Stiffen the sinews, summon up the blood,
Disguise fair nature with hard-favour'd rage . . .

—William Shakespeare
Henry V, act III, scene I

Prologue

_____

_____

_____

Fires lit the night sky. Though dozens of Moscow streets were in flames, no emergency sirens could be heard— not above the rumble of armored vehicles and marching boots over cobblestones. Earlier in the evening angry citizens had lined the city's major thoroughfares. Now soldiers with bayonet-tipped rifles corralled knots of protesters at intersections. Canvas-topped military vehicles circulated through the streets, picking up the now meek and silent citizens. No one knew where the protesters were taken, but within an hour the trucks would return empty, prepared to take on fresh cargo.

The American television correspondent's face—well known to the viewing public from reports in Kuwait, Bosnia, Afghanistan, and Iraq—conveyed a sense of urgency that was palpable to his global audience. He gestured at the streets behind him as the video camera rolled. "As you can see, it hasn't taken Konstantin Khartukov long to crack down on what the new government calls 'subversive elements' here in Moscow. We're told that similar roundups are occurring in St. Petersburg and other major Russian population centers."

Khartukov's photo appeared in the left corner of the network picture—a handsome man, dark-haired, mid-fifties. Baseball scores crawled across the bottom of the screen. The foreign correspondent's live feed from Moscow continued on the right side of the picture. "As we all know, after years of economic woes Khartukov won the recent presidential election in a landslide by campaigning on a platform of military reform and the resurrection of Russia as a world power. The former KGB officer and hard-line member of the Communist Party was expected to tighten down on many of the individual liberties the Russian people have enjoyed since Boris Yeltsin's ascension to power over a decade ago. It is safe to say, however, that these actions"—the reporter paused to turn and gesture at a T-80 tank as it rumbled past—"have taken the entire world by surprise. Before sunrise this morning, Russian troops conducted a coordinated sweep, rounding up all non–Communist Party officials from the Federation Council, the Russian parliament's upper house, and the Duma, the parliament's lower house. Leftists loyal to Khartukov, many key members of the Politburo under the Soviet regime, replaced these elected officials.

"The violence you're seeing now is the result of citizens taking to the streets in protest of these actions. The speed with which the military swept down to crush the protesters makes it clear that the government was not only prepared for the rioting, but expected it. Within hours the Russian government seized control of all media—television, radio, newspaper, Internet Service Providers—and declared martial law. . . ."

The reporter disappeared from view as the cameraman instinctively turned toward the sound of nearby gunfire. Within seconds he jogged back into view, motioning for the cameraman to follow. Audiences sat riveted as a group of Russian youths, refusing to be led away by the troops, filled their screens. A squad of soldiers separated the group at rifle point. One of the young protesters, a young man in his late teens or early twenties, spit into the face of the soldier nearest him and yelled something in Russian. On the direction of their senior NCO, two soldiers grabbed the protester and threw him against the nearest wall with enough force to knock the breath from him and then stepped quickly away. The news crew's boom mike picked up a distinct series of pops. The camera tightened on the youngster as his body pirouetted and slid to the sidewalk, eyes already glazing over. The camera panned once more to the newsman. A veteran of global hot spots, he was nonetheless stunned into silence by the display of violence.

The network anchor's voice cut in from New York. "Carl, are you and your crew safe?"

Regaining his composure, the reporter nodded. "I believe we are for the moment, but this is obviously a volatile situation. . . ."

The live feed darkened as a gloved hand appeared and covered the camera. The sound rolled on. A harsh Russian voice addressed the American news team in broken English, "You leave immediately. All equipment now belongs to the Russian government. My men will collect, then escort you and crew to airport."

The reporter's voice rose in anger. "What are you talking about? We have a permit to . . ."

For a brief moment the audience saw a Russian major confronting the American newsman as the cameraman broke away from his captors to continue filming. Simultaneously audiences heard a rapid series of shots. The picture tilted sideways as the camera fell to the ground. After a moment the American newsman's shoes appeared in the picture as he moved to his cameraman. The reporter's voice, now verging on hysteria, was clear over the street noise. "Tommy . . . Tommy!" As audiences watched, bright red arterial blood pooled around Italian leather. *"You bastards!"*

More shots sounded and the feed went back.

Riyadh (*London Times*)—Postwar tensions between Saudi Arabia and the West reached new heights today. Saudi Arabia, which forced the United States to withdraw its military hardware and personnel from Saudi soil last year before the start of the Second Gulf War, has seen a dramatic decline in demand for its crude oil exports to the U.S. and other Western nations. In retaliation the kingdom is now pressuring fellow OPEC nations to raise crude prices by fifty percent.

Kuwait City (Reuters)—In a move expected for weeks the emir of Kuwait, Sheikh Jaber al-Ahmad al-Jaber Al Sabah, and Iraqi president Ali Abunimah announced in an early-morning press conference that their nations would sign a joint-protection treaty later today. Both leaders expressed a desire to further Iraq's role as a democratic leader in the region.

Baghdad (*Christian Science Monitor*)—In a stunning development the governments of Iraq and Kuwait, along with the United Arab Emirates, Qatar, and Venezuela, have announced their withdrawal from OPEC and the establishment of a new petroleum cartel, the Arab Oil League, or AOL. The AOL nations will account for forty percent of world crude reserves and almost half of former OPEC reserves. Initial reports from Riyadh indicate the Saudi government is surprised and angered by the development. OPEC's past strength stemmed from its ownership of eighty percent of world oil reserves. The loss of so many of its members and such a large percentage of the world's production capacity strikes a hard blow to the OPEC power base.

Moscow (AP)—Russian president Konstantin Khartukov and the Saudi crown prince announced Russia's entrance as OPEC's newest member. While the addition of Russia does not fully compensate for the loss of former OPEC nations last month, the union is what one White House official has called "a match made in hell." Khartukov has made significant gains over the past six months in retooling the Russian military back to superpower status, but his efforts have slowed recently due to lack of funds. Cash will no longer be an issue as oil revenues begin to flow into Moscow.

Riyadh (Reuters)—The Saudi military today announced new contracts with Russian arms manufacturers for the immediate purchase of military hardware ranging from rifles and tanks to surface-to-surface and surface-to-air missiles. The West had provided the majority of Saudi arms in the past, but the total collapse of relations between the kingdom and Western nations has made replenishment of spare parts extremely difficult in recent days. It was also announced that a series of joint exercises is planned between Russian and Saudi forces in the near future, likely to coincide with the U.S. exercises in Iraq scheduled for the spring.

Chapter 1

One If by Land

Desert Lion was the first of a series of biennial defense exercises involving Iraq, Kuwait, and the United States. It was entering its second week and proceeding smoothly. The first iteration primarily involved ground forces. Plans for subsequent exercises in the years to follow called for the full mix—ground, sea, and air. Before recent hostilities in the Middle East, maneuvers of this scale and mix were unimaginable. Things were different now. A friendly Iraqi government had replaced a regime that had been the United States' chief source of concern in the region since before Operation Desert Storm.

It hadn't been easy. Once the United States and a few allies won a short but hard-fought ground campaign, the Western forces found their work had only just begun. Separatist elements wanting the government turned over to the locals immediately made life hell for coalition troops safeguarding the budding nation. External forces from bordering nations—primarily Islamic fundamentalists—had also inflamed Iraqi believers, who had been suppressed for decades.

But the time for Iraqi rule of Iraq finally came. It came in the form of free elections. Iran and other fundamentalist states hoping to build their sphere of influence by having a friendly ear in the "new Iraq" were disappointed with the candidate selected president, the former leader of Iraq's military forces, General Ali Abunimah. Abunimah had risked his life to bring the ground war to a quick end when Iraq's leader gave the order to unleash chemical munitions—munitions whose existence had been vehemently denied for years—on American forces in theater. Before Abunimah's intervention, the United States had been within a razor's edge of unleashing nuclear hell on deployed Iraqi forces, world opinion be damned. Despite embedded reporters with heretofore unheard-of access to the military being present throughout the war, news of the near miss never became public.

The 2nd Corps' logistics site was a hive of activity despite the early hour. Iraq, Kuwait, and the United States were one week into Desert Lion and the fuel for the majority of the armored and wheeled vehicles of all three armies was dispersed from the central facility.

An Iraqi soldier on guard duty stopped beside a burning barrel and slung his AK-47 assault rifle over his shoulder. Reaching into his pocket, the guard pulled out a pack of cigarettes and lit one. It was three o'clock in the morning and he paid little attention to his mission of guarding the fuel depot—this was a peacetime exercise, after all. Instead he savored his temporary respite from the desert night's chill. A movement on the perimeter caught his attention. The soldier turned but saw nothing. His break had warmed him but the barrel's flames had significantly impacted his night vision. Reluctantly, he crushed the cigarette beneath his boot and trudged into the darkness on the off chance that the exercise planners had decided to introduce opposing forces into the scenario. A blur was all he saw as a gloved hand shot across his mouth and a blackened combat knife slammed into his jugular.

Two hours later the sergeant of the guard discovered the soldier was missing. As nothing appeared amiss within the perimeter, it was assumed the guard had found a warm spot and gone to sleep. The next morning, when he'd still not reported in, the missing soldier was reported AWOL. Desert Lion continued per the exercise directive and the Iraqi guard became an ancillary administrative footnote.

2nd Brigade, 1st Cavalry Division Headquarters
Southern Iraq, Vicinity the Saudi Border

The U.S. Army officer, a full colonel, nodded his head slowly. His eyes were closed as he held the field phone to his ear, a study in patience. "Yes, I understand that." The colonel nodded again. "I understand that as well. Now let me ask you a question," he continued in a reasonable tone. "Do you understand that I'm a *goddamned brigade commander* looking at Russians—I say again, *Russians* of all things—creeping along the border, and that I want some air support over this area right *fucking* now?!"

The lieutenant colonel standing nearby winced. As the 2nd Brigade XO, it would be his job to play nice and de-fuck things with the Air Force once his boss finished his tirade.

Mac Colts, the 2nd Brigade commander, calmed himself with a visible effort. "Look, I really don't care where the birds come from but I need them ASAP. Ivan's been playing footsies with us for the past two weeks, but this is different. We've got American M1A2-SEP tanks and Russian T-80Us looking at each other across less than five kilometers of desert—and there's a lot more T-80s than M1s. Am I being clear? If the shit hits the fan, we're going to need close air support."

After signing off Colts turned to his XO. "Sorry, Roger. I know I just made your job a little tougher, but those pukes piss me off sometimes."

Roger Boreman nodded. "Not a problem, sir."

"So have we heard anything else from the boys at the front?" Colts asked.

Boreman shook his head. "No change as of the last situation report."

Colts walked to the map mounted on the tactical operation center, or TOC, wall. The confusing combination of blue and red icons arrayed along the Iraq-Saudi border added up to one thing—there were a lot of Russians nearby.

For the past month Colts's brigade, one of three 1st Cavalry Division brigades participating in Desert Lion, had run simulated battles with Iraqi and Kuwaiti forces. As the exercises had been winding down two weeks earlier, imagery from national sources began indicating that the Saudi-Russian exercises under way through northern and northeastern Saudi Arabia were beginning to look less like exercises and more like prepositioning movements for an attack. Saudi and Russian forces were inching closer and closer to the borders of former OPEC nations Iraq and Kuwait. To a lesser extent the same was true along the borders of Qatar and the UAE.

The 1st Cav had deployed to cover a large piece of border real estate, one of its three brigades in Kuwait, two in Iraq because of the northern nation's longer border. Iraq was rushing to backfill the 1st Cavalry brigades in its country. While their T-72 tanks and BMP-2 infantry fighting vehicles were older than those of their potential adversaries to the west, they'd been upgraded with thermal sights and were loaded with high-grade depleted-uranium-tipped ammunition. Kuwait, Qatar, and the UAE, along with U.S. Marine Corps forces, were preparing hasty positions along the borders. Word was that the 4th Infantry had been alerted and was preparing to move into the theater from the United States, as was the 75th Rangers and other units, both standard and special operations capable.

As Colts scrutinized the array of forces building in Saudi Arabia, he had a gut feeling that these units weren't going to make it in time to do him and his men a great deal of good. Turning back to his XO, he pointed at the blue icons representing the 1st Cav's tank and mechanized infantry forces. "Roger, make sure all tracks are topped off ASAP, then move the fuelers back a few kilometers. Tell them to be ready to come forward again when we need them. If the Ruskies are serious, we're not going to have time to dick around waiting for gas."

Boreman nodded. He knew his boss was correct, especially where the Abramses were concerned—the tanks held five hundred gallons of fuel, but the consumption was measured in gallons to the mile rather than vice versa. "Roger, sir. Most of the units are reporting they've already topped off. Our tankers are getting kinda dry, but I'm expecting a convoy of fuelers from the depot at Najaf any time now."

Even as the men turned back to the map the convoy was entering the 2nd Brigade's lines, dust billowing behind it.

Chapter 2

Sweet Home Alabama

C Company, 2-77 Armor Headquarters
Fort Carson, Colorado

The four new soldiers had only just arrived at Fort Carson earlier in the day. Fresh from their Advanced Individual Training, where they had learned anything and everything there was to know about the M1 series tank, they took a collective deep breath as the small but extremely vocal man momentarily ceased shouting.

Assigned to C Company, 2-77 Armor, they now stood in front of the assembled soldiers and NCOs of their new unit. Most of the troops watching the four new recruits were seasoned veterans. The newbies felt trained eyes looking them over from every direction, measuring them.

The drill sergeants they'd left behind at Fort Knox, Kentucky, seemed mild in comparison to their new first sergeant. While not much over five and a half feet tall, the veteran soldier appeared carved from a single piece of thin flexible steel. As First Sergeant John Rider caught his second wind, the four soldiers squinted in self-defense against the close-quarters verbal assault as it continued.

"Look around you, shitbirds!" Rider yelled, waving a hand westward toward the Front Range of the Rocky

Mountains. He paused, smiling, and his voice calmed. "Could you have asked to be posted to a more scenic spot?"

One of the privates cocked his head and examined the looming peaks. The private's name was Boggs and he was from Alabama. This was the first time in his nineteen years on this earth that Boggs had seen such natural grandeur. He smiled and spoke in a low voice, more to himself than anyone else. "They're mighty nice, all right."

Rider was on the young troop in a heartbeat. "What was that, Private? You already talking out of turn in my formation? Don't need to treat old Top Rider with the respect due him, is that what you think? You think I'm your *bitch*, Private?"

Boggs snapped to the position of attention and back to reality in the same instant. "Yes . . . uh . . . no. I . . . I . . . I meant, yes, First Sergeant—the mountains are mighty pretty."

Rider stared at the soldier a moment longer, memorizing every line of his face for future reference. "Well don't get too used to the sights, shitbird," the crusty NCO said in a quiet voice. "The bad thing about this company is we don't seem to hang around home too much."

"Top's on a roll, isn't he?" said the captain standing next to the back door of C Company's training room. He watched the proceedings with a bemused expression. While it may not have been the way corporate America would indoctrinate new recruits, the captain knew his senior NCO was attempting to ensure the company's new troops, most fresh from high school, stepped off on the right foot.

The lanky lieutenant standing next to the captain nodded. "Yes, sir. He is that."

The captain rolled a soggy toothpick in his mouth. "Yep. That's some grade-A shit, all right."

Looking to his commander, the lieutenant watched the toothpick dance back and forth. "Still having oral fixation issues, sir?"

The more senior officer nodded disgustedly. "Yeah," he said, pulling the soggy piece of wood from his mouth. He held the toothpick several inches from his face and stared at it with a frown. "These things are freakin' nasty."

The lieutenant stared at his boss. "Sir, you started the toothpick thing to get over the Copenhagen addiction. Now *that* was a nasty habit."

"Doc," said the captain, shifting his gaze from the toothpick to his charge.

"Yes, sir?"

"When I want your opinion, I'll give it to you." The toothpick went back into the captain's mouth with a wet plop. "And if I didn't tell you before, now hear this—shut the fuck up."

The lieutenant smiled and turned back to Rider's show. "That's why I'm going to hate to see you go, sir. I'll miss listening to your uncanny command of the English language. Speaking of which, have you received a date yet?"

Both men knew the date the lieutenant referred to—the captain's change of command date, the date he formally handed over the company's reins to a new commander and moved on to his next assignment.

The captain nodded, smiling. "Three weeks and five days, Doc, but who's counting? After that, on to Eglin Air Force Base and a joint assignment on the beach in Florida." He frowned. "I hate to leave C Company, but Melissa and the girls have earned this one." A shadow passed over his features as he recalled the pain and uncertainty his family had been through during the previous year's war. "And then some."

"Finally, gentlemen," said Rider, winding down, "you are now members of the finest military organization in which it has been my privilege to serve in fifteen years of military service. You are men of Cold Steel. Not too long ago, this company distinguished itself in some of the toughest fighting of the Second Gulf War."

The privates turned their heads to the front as one and looked at the company guidon—a flag signifying the unit's type and designation. It was mounted atop a long wooden staff. A unit's guidon is always stationed at the front of its formation and is held by one of the unit's best soldiers. Pennants signifying the unit's awards would trail from the top of the staff.

A tall, lean sergeant named Almo held Cold Steel's guidon. It looked basically the same as the ones they'd seen in basic training at Fort Knox, a green M-26 series tank superimposed over green cavalry sabers on a bright field of yellow. The Middle East's desert sun had faded C Company's colors almost white. At Fort Knox the edges of the flags were crisp and sharp; their new unit's standard was tattered and frayed from time and weather. And a pennant none of the soldiers had seen before dangled atop the C Company staff—a small red, white, green, and black scrap of material whose bright colors contrasted sharply with the guidon itself. It was a battle streamer from the recent war made in the colors of Kuwait, the country their new unit had been instrumental in saving. The new soldiers knew some of them were filling spots left vacant by men who were casualties of that war, who'd died earning a colorful scrap of material that cost less than a dollar. But the men of C Company wouldn't have taken any amount for the streamer; it represented what they stood for, what they were willing to lay down their lives for.

"You shitbirds will learn to live up to the legacy of the men who have served this unit in combat, or I'll send you next door to B Company. Is that clear?"

"Clear, First Sergeant!" the four yelled in unison.

The first sergeant stood centered in front of the group,

hands on his hips. "Good. The Black Knights ain't bad people, not by a long shot . . . but they ain't Steel. Now I want to introduce you to your new commander, Captain Dillon. When I call you to attention, you *will* respond with a resounding *Cold Steel, sir!*"

The company's senior NCO came to attention, feet together, arms at his sides, and bellowed, "Company, atten-*chun*!"

Each of the troopers snapped to the position of attention, feet locked together, hands straight at their sides, head and eyes to the front. *"Cold Steel, sir!"*

As the soldiers' cries rang out, Rider executed a crisp about-face, turning his back on the group. Standing rigidly at attention, he waited.

Taking his cue, Captain Patrick Dillon stuffed the toothpick into his pocket and moved smartly toward the assembled soldiers. He slowed down and turned, calling softly over his shoulder, "Doc, it's about quitting time. Why don't you make yourself useful and go buy some beer . . . preferably Newcastle." Without waiting for a response, he faced forward again and continued toward his new troops.

As Dillon moved out, Doc Hancock looked to the right, toward C Company's billets. A large figure stood in a second-floor window. Hancock moved his hand slowly up, touching his index finger to his nose and nodding; understanding, the big man sent the lieutenant a thumbs-up and a smile, then disappeared from sight.

Dillon was halfway to Rider and the group of soldiers when the music began. From the billets area "The Imperial March" track from the original *Star Wars* movie blasted across the quadrangle. The martial notes beat the air and Dillon found himself unconsciously walking in step with the music for a moment, much the same as Darth Vader had. Shaking his head to clear it of the tune's heady effect, he and Rider sent simultaneous scowls in the direction of the billets. The music abruptly shut off.

As Dillon stopped in front of him, Rider raised an arm in salute—and put forth a supreme effort not to laugh in front of the new soldiers. "Sir! The company is formed."

Dillon returned the salute and spoke softly. "Thanks, Top. Find Bluto . . . you can bet your ass he was behind that musical interlude. But grill Doc first. He's just fresh enough that he'll squeal like a stuck pig."

Rider nodded and stepped off smartly, moving with a purpose toward the empty spot where Lieutenant Doc Hancock had been standing moments earlier.

Dillon moved forward two steps and stopped in front of the young group. "At ease."

The company's newest soldiers immediately spread their feet and popped their arms behind their backs in a rigid parade rest position. They hadn't had much experience with officers in their short military careers, much less with combat veterans who held the potential to command them in life-and-death situations. They saw the 4th Infantry Division patch that Dillon, like First Sergeant Rider, wore on his right shoulder—a diamond-shaped piece of cloth with four ivy leaves pointing in the cardinal directions of north, south, east, and west. Centered between the leaves was a gun sight. The young recruits wore the patch on their left shoulders, as did Dillon and Rider, indicating that the 4th Infantry Division was their current unit of assignment, but the fact that the captain and first sergeant—not to mention over half of their new unit—also wore it on their right shoulders indicated they'd served in combat with the 4th Infantry Division (Mechanized).

Most of the new soldiers had just begun basic training when the war began. Their drill sergeants had given them hourly updates on the fighting. During their downtime—of which there had been precious little—

they'd congregated around the day room's single television, focused on news reports from the field. As they'd watched the bullets fly, they all wondered if they'd be equal to the task should they find themselves in the same situation. They *knew* the men before them with combat patches had been equal, because they were alive.

Patrick Dillon looked at his new charges and remembered how intimidating this moment had been for him years ago. He'd served his time as a private, moving up through the ranks until he'd attained the rank of sergeant before deciding to seek a commission. He looked behind the new soldiers at the rest of his men. Unlike the stiffly postured soldiers to their front, the men who'd served under him in combat stood in relaxed stances. Never one for formality, Dillon said, "Okay, everybody but the new guys, get the hell out of here and go home. If I see you hanging around five minutes from now we'll find something for you to do down at the motor pool."

From fifty throats there issued a chorus of broken responses such as "hoo-ah," "roger that, sir," "you don't have to tell us twice," and "hurry up before he changes his mind." The voices were overridden by the sound of boot leather slapping concrete as the men exfiltrated the area.

Dillon waited until only the four new men remained within earshot. "I said 'at ease.' You guys are going to pull some muscles if you don't loosen up." His voice broke into a stage whisper so Rider, currently chasing Doc Hancock down a nearby sidewalk, couldn't hear. "And then how are you going to be able to get away from Top Rider?"

The remark had the desired effect. A few quiet laughs, the easing of shoulder muscles, the slight shuffling of feet to loosen stances. As the captain turned and began walking slowly in front of them, the men sized up their new commander.

At five feet nine, Dillon wasn't tall, but he was thick

through the neck, back, arms, and shoulders. At the moment he was wearing the Army's black beret. The soldiers who had seen him when they'd initially reported to the C Company's orderly room on arrival knew that beneath the beret his hair was almost pure silver. What they didn't know was that before the Second Gulf War, only months ago, there'd been only a few strands of silver mixed in with a full head of brown hair. His eyes were a pale blue. Combined with his white hair and windburned skin, they looked like chips of ice. Other than the combat patch on his right sleeve, the only difference between his uniform and theirs was his boots. Rather than black leather combat boots with laces, Dillon's were hand-tooled with straps that wound their way up his legs almost to the knees. Tanker boots. The recruits knew only soldiers who entered battle on sixty-eight-ton monsters had the privilege of wearing them, and then only after qualifying their tank in gunnery for the first time. Each silently vowed that it wouldn't be long before he possessed a similar pair.

Dillon paced in front of the small group. "Gentlemen, I'm not big on speeches. You've been assigned to my company. I love it almost as much as I love my own family. Hell, to me, my company *is* part of my family." He paused, thinking of the men he'd lost during his watch. "I won't be here much longer. It's time for me to move on. But remember this . . . the company comes first. It will survive long after all of us have left it. And it is what we make of it. The company's other soldiers are your brothers. Just like real brothers, you'll have disagreements. But when the chips are down, these brothers are the ones that will be willing to lay down their lives for you. If you can accept that, then welcome. Anyone who can't, come by my office later this evening. We'll quietly move you to another unit." Dillon could see in the newcomers' eyes that he'd be alone in the office tonight.

As he was about to dismiss the new troopers, a white sport utility vehicle wheeled into a parking spot twenty feet away. The men, not long back in "the world" following their months of isolation at Fort Knox as they'd trained for their new profession, watched with dropped jaws as a striking auburn-haired woman climbed from the truck. A simple skirt and blouse did little to hide what was one of the lovelier figures any of them had ever seen. As they watched, the woman walked in their general direction, allowing more time for appreciative stares. Their new commander, understanding their interest, joined them.

Boggs leaned toward the soldier next to him and winked. "Now, Bryant . . . *that* is a fine-looking woman. That's just how we grow 'em back in 'Bama."

Private Bryant did his best to ignore his new companion.

Boggs continued, undaunted. His southern accent thickened as he warmed to his topic. "Matter of fact, I wouldn't be surprised if she *is* from 'Bama, Bryant. Our women are known *worldwide* for the suppleness of their skin and the sweetness of their hips—hips made to both bear children with ease and with a delicious curve that can drive any man who happens to observe them as she strolls down the avenue of an evening insane with lust."

The private continued watching the woman as she approached, fascinated by his own observations. "Yeah," he said, now more to himself than anyone, "I'll just bet ya she's a 'Bama gull."

Dillon walked down the line of troops toward the voice he'd been listening to with interest. He placed a casual hand on Boggs's shoulder and turned to the woman. "Melissa, I believe Private"—he paused to read the soldier's name tag—"Boggs has a question for you."

The soldier realized he'd gotten a little carried away and had been talking louder than intended. He blushed and stammered, "Why, no suh. That won't be necessary, Captain Dillon, suh."

The woman of Boggs's dreams had stopped next to Dillon. The captain wrapped a proprietary arm around her. "Honey, this is Private Boggs. Private Boggs, this is my wife, Melissa. Boggs was wondering if you're from Alabama, sweetheart."

Boggs felt his heart melting as the woman looked his way and smiled. "Why, no. I'm a Carolina girl, born and bred, Private Boggs. Why do you ask?"

The red cast of Boggs's face deepened. He pulled his black beret from his head and wrung it in his hands. "No reason, Missus Dillon, ma'am . . . you favor some of the girls from back home is all."

Melissa Dillon had seen puppy love a time or two. She smiled at the young soldier as a burst of maternal affection spread through her. "Why, thank you. I assume that's a compliment. What's your first name, Private?"

"Beauregard, ma'am, but my friends call me Bo. And I *assure* you I meant no disrespect, Missus Dillon. . . ." This last was delivered more to Dillon than his wife.

The woman smiled again and sent a meaningful glance her husband's way. "Thank you, Bo. I'm sure you didn't."

The new men headed toward the billets after the formation broke up, ready to relax for the first time all day. Bo Boggs pulled off a combat boot wearily and dropped it to the tile floor with a thunk next to its mate. Hearing a knock on the door, the private looked up with a *what now* expression and resignedly got up.

A sergeant stood in the hallway. It was the Charge of Quarters, or CQ, the NCO in charge of the company area during off-duty hours. "You Boggs?"

"Yes, Sergeant."

"Top wants to see you. Now." With that the NCO turned and made his way back down the hallway.

Boggs's spirits spiraled downward. This really wasn't stacking up to be his day. Grabbing the nearest boot, he pulled it on and began hastily lacing it. Something told him showing up at Top Rider's desk sans boot wouldn't make things any better.

As he entered the company's building, Boggs noticed two men cleaning out the conference room. He figured them for fellow privates until he glanced at the rank on their collars. One, a huge monster of a man, was a first lieutenant. The big man was berating another lieutenant cleaning alongside him. The smaller officer, he noted, was the same lieutenant Boggs had seen standing behind the company with Captain Dillon before the earlier formation.

The big lieutenant was animated. "Damn it, Doc, Rider's an old man . . . thirty-five if a day. All you had to do was exfiltrate quietly from the A.O. How the hell could you let him catch you?" The big man paused in his sweeping and leaned on his broom. "Then you sing like a freakin' canary. Where's the loyalty in that, man, huh? Where's the love?"

The other lieutenant paused in his task of waxing the company's trophy case. "You weren't there, Bluto. That man is like a cobra. Fucking hypnotic." He renewed his wax-on, wax-off routine. "I'd have told him my mother's cup size if he'd asked."

The big lieutenant cocked his head. "You . . . you know your mother's cup size?"

Private Bo Boggs continued moving and left the lieutenants to their work. Even at this early stage in his career he knew there were conversations that he just didn't need—or want—to hear. Stopping outside of Rider's door, he knocked once loudly.

"Come!"

Moving into the office, Boggs stopped short of the

desk behind which First Sergeant Rider was scribbling out paperwork. Coming to parade rest, he waited.

Rider didn't look up. "At ease, shitbird. I'll be with you in a minute."

Boggs relaxed slightly and looked around the office, taking in the memorabilia that Rider had collected throughout his years in the Army. Awards, photos . . . and was that an Iraqi battle flag?

Rider looked up as he set his pen aside. "Okay, troop, what happened with Captain Dillon?"

Lost for a moment in his study of the room, Boggs looked to his first sergeant and shook his head. Rider was staring at him from behind steepled fingers. "I'm sorry, First Sergeant, I don't understand," he drawled with an accent that made Rider hungry for a bowl of grits and a side of red-eye gravy.

"Well *something* happened, son."

Boggs shook his head. "First Sergeant, if I in some way offended the commander . . ."

Rider waved off the remark. "Boggs, what in the hell are you talking about? Never mind. Here's the bottom line. Captain Dillon's loader just transferred out. He told me *you* were going to be the man's replacement." Rider paused. "Let me spell it out for you, Boggs. The old man can handpick his crew from all of the soldiers in the company. That usually means the most experienced and squared-away troops are in his crew. He's away from the tank a lot, which means the other three crew members have to be able to accomplish the work of four men. It's *extremely* unusual for him to ask for a 'cruit to fill a spot. So I'll ask you one more time . . . what happened?"

Relieved, Boggs relaxed. "Well, First Sergeant, it could have been my natural charm and charisma were just too much for the captain to ignore." The private leaned forward conspiratorially. "He does seem to be an insightful man. And my instructors at Fort Knox said I showed great potential. . . ."

Rider jumped from behind the desk and pointed toward the door. "Get the hell out of my office, Private!"

Boggs scrambled to the safety of the hallway.

John Rider, no longer able to keep from laughing, sat down once more behind the desk and listened to the sound of receding boots in the corridor. Dillon had told him of Boggs's encounter with Melissa Dillon. Dillon had told him that any man with that kind of taste in women showed real potential. Rider thought the commander just might have his hands full with this one.

Remembering his two charges, Rider stood from his desk. Walking from the office, he proceeded to the conference room. "How are you stooges—I'm sorry, *gentlemen*—coming along?"

Both men continued working and sounded out in unison, "Fine, First Sergeant."

Chapter 3

Bonds Forged

Captain Bob "Muddy" Waters stood stiffly outside of the battalion commander's office, not quite yet ready to knock. He had no idea what this summons was about. The door opened suddenly as he'd just worked up the nerve to lift his hand. Lieutenant Colonel Rob Estes, the 2-77 Armor commander, smiled. "Hey, Muddy! You ready to talk?"

Waters looked cynically at his commander. "I'm not really sure, sir."

Estes moved back into the office and waved the captain in. He sat behind his desk and gestured for his newest company commander to take a seat. Once Waters was settled, Estes got straight to the point. "Muddy, let's talk jobs."

Muddy Waters didn't like the implications of the statement. "Sir, I have a job. Anvil commander, remember?"

From Estes's troubled expression Waters knew whatever was coming couldn't be good. "Muddy, there's not an easy way to tell you this. I've got to remove you from command. The Department of the Army has decided that you weren't a lieutenant long enough to rate promotion to captain—battlefield performance notwithstanding. Carrying that thought forward, they also feel you're too junior to hold down a company command slot when we have so many captains waiting for command billets." He leaned forward. "For what it's worth, I think you proved yourself more than ready and have done a helluva job."

Waters had started the war as Alpha, a.k.a. Anvil, Company's executive officer. He had taken charge of the unit when his company commander suffered a nervous breakdown under fire. After reorganizing Anvil, Waters fought alongside Estes and destroyed a large number of Republican Guard tanks that had located a seam in 3rd Brigade's flank. The action earned Waters and his tank crew the Silver Star. For his part, the brigade commander had been so impressed with the lieutenant that he'd given Waters a battlefield promotion and the reins to Anvil full-time.

Muddy Waters looked distraught. "Who's taking over Anvil, sir?"

Estes knew how his subordinate felt. A good commander feels like a father to his men after a time. It was hard enough turning them over to someone after a normal command time frame of twelve to eighteen months. To have them suddenly ripped away was even tougher. "We're not bringing in anyone new, Muddy. Captain Rose from the Dealers will take over. He needs another six months or so of command time anyway."

The D Company "Death Dealers" had deactivated two weeks earlier; 2-77 Armor had executed the restructuring plan that called for them, along with all of the other tank battalions in the active army, to give up one of their four tank companies. The powers that be figured that with the M1A1 tanks being replaced by M1A2-SEP tanks and M1A1 digitized tanks in the near future, forty-four tanks organized into three companies could do the same job as fifty-eight of the older tanks organized into four companies. The new tanks would boast twenty-five-

and fifty-power second-generation forward-looking infra-red, or FLIR, sights that, in conjunction with improved tank munitions, would allow the smaller tank battalions to close with and kill the enemy more efficiently than the older and larger battalions could. The cuts didn't stop in the armor battalions. All of the mechanized infantry battalions were going through the same downsizing for the same reasons and losing a company of Bradley Fighting Vehicles.

What the bureaucrats hadn't explained was why, even though the fielding of the new equipment was behind schedule, the battalions had been stripped of 25 percent of their primary combat systems. Most of the Army's officers and NCOs knew the driving reasons: for one, recent conflicts saw that even older M1s and Bradleys more than held their own against superior numbers. The bean counters in Washington kept harkening to the latter and took it as a green light to continue the cost cuts and modernization plans despite schedule delays in receiving the newer combat systems. Committees and subcommittees decided the current force, the majority of which were still equipped with the older combat equipment, could handle any threat that popped up on the screen in the near future.

"Captain Rose is a pretty good commander," said Waters quietly after a few moments.

Estes merely nodded, giving his subordinate whatever time he needed to digest the bombshell that had been dropped on him.

In the ensuing silence Muddy Waters came to terms with the loss of his command. He knew Estes wouldn't have given him the bad news until after he'd fought the decision—which meant his commander had lost. As there was nothing he could do about the situation the former captain, now once more a first lieutenant, sat straighter in his chair and looked up to meet his boss's gaze. "So, sir, what have you got in mind for me? I don't think moving into the XO position at Anvil would be such a hot idea—I'm sure Captain Rose feels the same way."

Estes shook his head. "Having old and new commanders together in the same company is a situation ripe for disaster, no matter how well-meaning both are." He sat back in his chair. "No, I've got something else in mind."

Waters raised an eyebrow in curiosity.

"I told you I'd been thinking about this." His eyes twinkled. "I need a scout platoon leader. Interested?"

No platoon leader job compared with commanding a tank company, but an assignment with the scouts was close. The scouts often found themselves working well forward of all the other friendly units, snooping and pooping to get their battalion commander the firsthand intelligence he needed on the enemy in order to make good decisions. If the scouts failed people died and battles were lost. Until recently, the tank battalion scout platoons consisted of ten Hummers—half with .50 caliber machine guns up top, half with Mark-19 automatic grenade launchers. When the Army cut the mechanized battalions to three companies, they'd also sliced four of the scouts' Hummers and handed them over to the newly formed brigade recon troops.

All of these thoughts had run through Waters's mind in the split second he took before giving his decision. While tanks were the shit, scouting definitely rocked. "I'm your man, sir."

"I thought that might be your answer," said Estes. "Have you met your new platoon sergeant before?"

Waters shook his head. "No, sir."

Estes put his boots on his desk, leaned back in his chair, and grinned. "Muddy, let me tell you about Rolf Krieger."

Krieger's parents were German-born, barely escaping East Berlin before the Soviets closed the Iron Curtain.

His grandparents had not been as fortunate—they'd died facedown in the snow two months later, mowed down by East German border guards within an arm's length of the barbed-wire fence separating east and west.

The Kriegers, their grand escape accomplished, had not been certain where to go. They'd decided to head to the United States as Frau Krieger's sister had settled in Chicago five years earlier. Herr Krieger had been an engineer in Germany, but found that post–World War II anti-German sentiments continued running high in America's heartland when he attempted to find work in that field. Engineering jobs advertised as available were suddenly not needed—and that had been the polite rejections. The need to place food on the table for his expectant wife forced him to take a series of blue-collar jobs for which he was vastly overqualified. But the Kriegers didn't complain—they were free. More importantly, their children would be free, would never know the feeling of a jackboot on their throat.

Rolf's mother and father had spoken poor English and thus his first spoken language was German. Still, being raised in Chicago, he learned English from his friends before starting grade school. This did not save him from a slight Germanic accent that he carried to this day.

The accent, combined with his six-feet-three, two-hundred-forty-pound chiseled frame, led his men to call him Arnold—but never to his face. Rolf Krieger lived for two things: training his scouts for success and personal improvement. The latter included both body and mind. Krieger didn't joke. If asked why not, he would say he simply did not have the time. There were too many important tasks to be accomplished to waste energy on frivolous activities.

On graduating from high school, Krieger had been offered full-ride football scholarships by Notre Dame, Michigan, and Ohio State. His eighteen solo tackles per game were still a state record and the stuff of local legend in his old neighborhood. To his parents' dismay, Krieger had declined the scholarships and enlisted in the Army.

Rolf had been a quiet child and his moody silences continued into adolescence. His parents didn't realize how deeply he'd been affected by their stories of the horrors surrounding their escape from East Germany and the loss of his grandparents. He'd never discussed it growing up. True to his nature, he instead devised a plan to deal with those he blamed for his family's misfortunes—the Soviets. If and when the balloon went up in Europe, he wanted a piece of the action.

Within a week of graduation the burly teen had wandered into his local recruiting station. The recruiter sitting behind the old government-issue wooden desk, an Army staff sergeant, had stared at Krieger's test scores in amazement. While it wasn't unusual to see physically or mentally gifted recruits walk through his door, rarely did he see men or women who combined both of the attributes to the extent Rolf Krieger did.

"Son, what do you want to do in this man's Army?" the NCO had asked as he looked through Krieger's paperwork. "I see here that you're fluent in German. We can refine that skill at the language school in Monterey, California." The sergeant had winked conspiratorially at that point. "Sweet duty, Monterey. On graduation you'd be shipped to a military intelligence billet. Those slots are hard to qualify for, but you've got the scores. Matter of fact, I think we're offering a sizable enlistment bonus for linguists. How does ten thousand dollars grab you?"

The young giant sat quietly in his chair, hands folded in his lap. While his parents were not poor, he knew that ten thousand dollars would be a gold mine to them. After a few moments, he asked one question. "Will I get to fight?"

The NCO frowned. The majority of recruits who came

through his office wanted into the Army for the educational benefits—"three or four years of service and then back to civilian life for me, thank you, Sergeant." As they signed their names on the dotted line, you could almost hear their silent prayers that they'd see no combat during their brief military careers. The assignments of choice for these men and women were as far removed as possible from potential action on a battlefield. Most of them would kill for the chance he'd just offered this kid.

At last the recruiter shook his head and answered Krieger's question. "Linguists don't fight, son."

"Then it is not the job for me. I want to fight. What else do you have?"

The sergeant pulled a computer printout off of his desk and scanned the available combat arms slots. "We've got infantry—mechanized, airborne, and walking flavored—tanks, artillery, and a few more." He handed the list to Krieger.

Krieger stared at the sheet of paper. Something caught his eye and he fixated on the word. "What is a scout?"

The recruiter shrugged. "Well, you have your ash and trash in the rear—the support pukes. You have your tanks and infantry at the front, along with the artillery— the fighters. If you keep going forward past the fighters, you'll run into the scouts. They're on, or behind, enemy lines determining the enemy's location, disposition, and composition." The recruiter stared hard at Krieger. This seemed like a good kid and he didn't want to bullshit him. "Son, the scouts' asses are generally in the wind. They operate on their own, live by their wits. In war, their first mistake is generally their last."

Krieger looked into the NCO's eyes. "So. They are the best."

The staff sergeant returned the stare evenly and straightened his back in an unconscious movement. On one of the lapels of his Class A dress uniform was a gold "U.S." emblem. On the other was a round disk embossed with crossed sabers, the insignia of the cavalry. "Some would say so, yeah."

"Can I be assigned duty in Germany? On the border?"

The NCO sat back and laughed. It was the mid-1980s and the Cold War was in full bloom. "I don't think that'll be a problem, kid."

Satisfied, Krieger relaxed. "Where do I sign?"

Private Krieger had excelled at both basic training and the tough 19 Delta scout training at Fort Knox. On arriving in Germany, he'd been assigned to the 11th Armored Cavalry Regiment and duty on the border dividing the two Germanys. He lived for the day that the Soviet horde would make their move through the Fulda Gap, the avenue of approach that all military planners foresaw the Red Horde utilizing and across which was stationed the Blackhorse troopers of the 11th Armored Cavalry Regiment. The Blackhorse was the first line of defense, the force responsible for slowing down the Soviets and East Germans long enough for the rest of NATO's heavy forces to mobilize behind them. Most considered it a die-in-place mission. The troops of the 11th Cavalry looked at it as the ultimate challenge.

When the wall came down and peace broke out four years later, Rolf Krieger had taken it as a personal affront. He'd joined the Army to avenge his family and now his chance was lost. In the years that followed, Krieger had continued to hone his military skills. After the Gulf War was over and the Soviet Union dissolved, the Russians were the last threat on anyone's mind— except the big German's. His parents' stories were still fresh in his mind. He bided his time.

Waters sat quietly until Estes finished, and then raised a skeptical eyebrow. "So he thinks the Russians are coming?"

Estes stared at the junior officer. "I'd have said he was a little . . . eccentric . . . myself until the events of the past few months. But with the new Russian president, who's to say he's wrong?"

Waters nodded. "Yes, sir, but I'd have to say Russia is still a long way from being a threat to us."

Estes considered the remark and shook his head. "I disagree—large army; they've been modernizing their equipment and accelerating training levels of late; oh, and they have nukes."

"Yes, sir, but . . ."

Estes continued. "Did I mention that, while consistently attaining evaluations as the best NCO in every unit he's been assigned, along with never missing a training exercise or deployment, Sergeant Krieger has completed a master's degree in political science, the base work for a Ph.D. in international relations, and is close to completing his dissertation? Straight A's in all the course work, by the way."

Waters's eyes bulged.

The lieutenant colonel leaned forward. "Muddy, the *experts* you see on the cable news channels trying to predict world events could learn a thing or two from our good sergeant."

"Jesus," Waters muttered. "How the hell did he manage that and still keep up with his military career?"

The Iron Tiger commander shrugged, tapping a pencil on his desk. "He'd tell you discipline was the key." The pencil stopped abruptly. "Here's the scary part. In the two years I've known him, I've never known Krieger to be wrong. *Never.* You think about that when you look at the reports of Russians on the Saudi border."

The newly demoted lieutenant thought that one over a few seconds and then stood.

"Guess you'd better go over and meet Arnold."

"Arnold?"

Estes rose and walked to the door, holding it open for

Waters. He smiled. "That's what some of his men call him, but I recommend you don't. He really doesn't like it."

Waters nodded with a frown, beginning to wonder what he'd gotten himself into.

As Waters entered the office he was to share with Rolf Krieger the room grew darker. A gulping sound escaped from the lieutenant as he realized the loss of lighting was caused by the giant behind the computer rising to greet him, his bulk smothering the overhead lighting's rays.

A massive hand reached out to shake Waters's. "Captain Waters, I presume," said Krieger with just the faintest trace of a German accent.

Waters took the proffered hand, praying the blond giant wouldn't squeeze his own into a pulp. "Not anymore. It's Lieutenant Waters now."

The NCO nodded. "I have spoken with the colonel regarding your demotion. I told him it would not change my decision as obviously it was through no fault of your own."

"Your decision?" asked Waters in confusion.

The big blond nodded. "Of whether or not to accept you as my platoon leader."

"You had a choice?"

The sergeant stared at his new lieutenant a moment, then moved on with the conversation. "I have looked over your record, sir. While it is exemplary, I could not help but note that you have not attended the Scout Leader's Course." The Scout Leader's Course was an intense three-week course at Fort Knox designed to train young officers and senior scout noncoms to lead reconnaissance platoons. The attendees were all lieutenants handpicked for assignment to cavalry units or senior scout NCOs; nonetheless, there was a large failure rate by Army standards, which spoke highly for the course's standards.

Waters nodded. "I couldn't get a slot when I was at Knox since I wasn't—"

"Going to be assigned to a cavalry squadron," finished Krieger. "Yes, I am aware of that policy. One option is to send you on temporary duty to Fort Knox for three weeks to attend the course. I know some people and could get you in on short notice. Lieutenant Colonel Estes has already agreed to this, should it be the route that we decide to take."

Waters was surprised. "He has? He didn't mention it to me."

The big NCO smiled for the first time. It was a frightening sight.

"That is because I offered him a better solution, should you agree," said Krieger.

Waters was intrigued despite himself. "Which is?"

"I will train you. We would begin"—Krieger glanced at his watch—"at nineteen hundred hours tonight."

"Tonight?"

Krieger nodded. "Yes. We will conduct your training much like the scout course at Fort Knox, but concentrate on what you need to know in order to lead *this* platoon. You'll learn the basics first . . . threat models, intelligence preparation of the battlefield, various methods of reconnaissance and surveillance, demolitions—I've laid on the live demolitions range and some explosives for this phase of your training—field expedient antennas, and conclude with a field training exercise with the platoon to bring all of the training together for you."

"Sounds . . . good," said Waters. *And daunting,* he added silently.

"I knew you would think so, Lieutenant."

Waters began to warm to the idea of training under the big German American. If nothing else, he was clearly competent. "So, what's on for tonight? Threat analyses? Map board training maybe?"

Krieger shook his head as he examined his new platoon leader from head to foot. He stroked his jaw. "The gym, I think."

Waters felt like a bug under examination by a skilled entomologist. He looked down his six-feet-one-inch body that weighed a whopping one hundred seventy pounds and then back up at Krieger. "Why the gym?"

"You do quite a bit of cardiovascular work, *ja?*"

Waters couldn't help himself. *"Ja."*

"Distance running? Biking?"

Waters nodded. *"Ja, ja."*

Krieger narrowed his eyes. Was this lieutenant being sarcastic? He looked closer at Waters's chest and arms, nodding to himself.

"What?" asked Waters, feeling even more self-conscious.

"Turn around," said Krieger simply.

"Why . . . oh, forget it." He turned a slow three hundred sixty degrees. "Satisfied?"

The NCO nodded again as if confirming a diagnosis. "Yes. Definitely the gym."

"What are you trying to say?"

"Sir, you have demonstrated that you can lead troops and are in most respects an outstanding soldier. I will maximize your overall potential by bringing your body up to the same high standards you have set for yourself in the other areas of your life." Krieger crossed his arms over his large chest. "Besides, you want to keep up with your men, don't you? Set the example?"

Muddy shrugged, giving up. He was beginning to feel like a girly-man. "Sure. Nineteen hundred at the fitness center it is."

Krieger nodded. "Very good." He walked to his desk and resumed typing on his laptop computer as if he'd never been interrupted.

Waters walked over out of curiosity. "What are you working on, Sergeant Krieger? Everyone else in the battalion cleared out a long time ago."

The big man kept typing. "My dissertation."

"The colonel mentioned you were finishing up your Ph.D." The lieutenant leaned over the desk to take a look. "What's the topic?"

Krieger continued typing. "The Russian threat to Middle Eastern oil reserves—their current exercises dovetail nicely into my hypothesis. I've been working on it for six months, but the draft is almost complete."

Waters looked at the NCO incredulously. "Six months? But the Russians only moved into Saudi a few weeks ago."

Sergeant Krieger looked up dismissively and shook his head. "The signs were there. People simply chose not to see them."

Dillon Home
Colorado Springs, Colorado

Patrick Dillon hung up the telephone and walked into the living room. Melissa sat on the couch, legs curled under her, looking at him expectantly. "Well?"

Dillon sat next to her and smiled. "It's a done deal. We close on the house in Florida five weeks from today."

Melissa Dillon squealed with delight and hugged her husband. "Oh, Pat, it finally seems real," she breathed into his shoulder. "After all of the time you've spent away the past few years . . . I feel like we're starting a whole new life, one that I don't have to worry about midnight calls telling us you're deploying to some godforsaken place where people will be shooting at you."

Dillon smiled softly and stroked his wife's hair. "I know."

Dillon's youngest daughter, Carson, ran through the

living room. Her blond hair bounced up and down beneath a set of Mickey Mouse ears. "Flor-i-da—Flor-i-da. Mi-ckey, Mi-ckey, Mi-ckey!" she chanted.

Melissa smiled. "I think she's just a little excited about the Disney stopover."

Dillon grinned. "Do ya think?" He flipped on the television. Both he and Melissa automatically tuned out the children as they watched the special report in progress. As if on cue, the phone rang.

Still watching the report, Dillon picked up the phone. "Hello." As he listened to the caller his gaze shifted from the news to his wife's face. "All right," he said. "Alert the company. I want all personnel present with full gear in one hour."

The conversation wasn't lost on Melissa. She sat quietly watching her husband, her best friend and lover. The father of her children. Tears rolled slowly down her cheeks. "We were so close, Pat," she whispered. "So close."

Mountain Fitness Center
Fort Carson, Colorado

Waters's arms felt rubbery as the Antichrist—a.k.a. Rolf Krieger—pulled the barbells off of his chest with ease and returned them to their ready position on the bench.

Sweat poured from the lieutenant as he struggled to a sitting position. Krieger squatted next to his new platoon leader. "Can you feel the burn yet?"

Waters stared at the NCO without smiling. "Oh yeah."

The blond giant clapped his hands. "Good. This is the point of the workout where we begin to make real gains."

Krieger's pager sounded. He looked at the number and frowned. "It is the staff duty NCO. One of our soldiers must have had a spirited evening. I will call and check in. You take the opportunity to stretch and get some water. Hydration is critical. When I return, we will finish your last sets of bench presses, then move on to some arm work."

The lieutenant threw his hands in the air in frustration. "Sets? As in plural? Oh, come on, Arno—" Waters clamped his lips together before he could complete the mistake cycle, but it was too late.

Krieger folded his arms across his chest. "What did you call me? Do I remind you of someone, Lieutenant? Do you perhaps confuse me with someone who works out in order to look pretty for movie cameras?"

Waters shrugged in helplessness. "Noooo. You misunderstood. . . ."

The NCO nodded as he walked away. "I was thinking two sets. Four will be even better."

Waters groaned. "Sure, Sarge. Great. Can't wait." He stood and stretched, angry more at himself than Krieger. He hadn't been to the gym in a long time, too long. While he stayed in good shape, he obviously had neglected the strength aspect. Now he was paying the price.

Krieger or no Krieger, the lieutenant was ready to end the pain as soon as possible. He lay down on the bench beneath the barbells, ignoring Krieger's directions to wait until his return. Grasping the bar, he pushed upward and cleared it from the bench. Blowing quickly three times, Waters lowered the weight to his chest, breathing out deeply as he threw the bar up. Blowing quickly again, he pumped out another rep.

On the third repetition events began taking a turn for the worse. First, the young officer noted that he didn't so much lower the bar to his chest as gravity gave him a fuck you. This observation was confirmed when he attempted to push the weight off. It went nowhere. Blowing rapidly three times, Waters strained again. Nothing. He closed his eyes as black spots spread across his field of vision.

"Need a hand, soldier?" asked a husky female voice.

Waters opened his eyes. His upside-down view revealed a set of supple and muscular tanned calves two inches from his face. He craned his neck, following the curves upward; the rest of the legs remained a mystery as round two of the black spots began.

Muddy panted, trying to catch his breath. "Uh . . . no. I'm . . . okay," he croaked in embarrassment. *God, just let me die now,* he thought.

The woman ignored Waters's words. She grasped the bar in the middle with both hands and jerked it upward, returning it to the bench support arms.

Waters sat up shakily. As he tried to catch his breath the woman walked to the front of the bench and faced him. She was tall, the lieutenant noted, at least five ten. He continued his observations in a rapid scan that would make his gunnery instructors proud: early twenties, long black hair pulled into a ponytail, deep brown eyes, and drop-dead gorgeous. He glanced at the woman's left hand out of habit—no ring. There was a God in heaven and all was good.

Just my luck, he thought. One of the best-looking women I've seen in ages and I've got to meet her like this. I wonder what the odds are that she has a fetish for skinny morons?

It dawned on Waters that she was speaking to him. "I'm sorry. What did you say?"

"Are you sure you're all right?" asked the woman dubiously.

Waters could only nod.

"I *said* you really shouldn't be benching without a spotter."

"Yeah, I figured that out the hard way," said Waters.

A small frown creased the pretty woman's brow. "I've got to run, if you're *sure* you're okay?"

Waters nodded again. "Yeah. And thanks."

She smiled. "Okay, then. Nice meeting you. . . ."

Waters reached out a hand. "Bob. Bob Waters."

"Shelly Simitis," she said, taking his hand and smiling.

"Greek?" he asked.

Her smiled broadened. "Very good. Second generation on both sides."

Waters grinned. "See? I'm not a total loser."

Laughing, she headed for the door. "Sure you're gonna be okay without me?"

Waters waved. *No,* he thought, his heart melting. *I'm not sure of that at all.* "Sure thing. Nice meeting you."

Krieger entered the weight room and met Shelly Simitis halfway to Waters. "Hello, Sergeant Krieger."

The big NCO kept walking. A frown crossed Simitis's face before she turned toward the exit and left the room.

"What was that about?" asked Waters.

"What?"

"Do you know her?" the lieutenant asked, nodding in the direction of the exit.

"We have met," said Krieger. He didn't offer further explanation. "And what have you been doing? Judging by your breathless state and shakier-than-usual arms, I would venture you were lifting alone?"

Waters smiled. "Finished up the benches already. Ready to move to the arm work?"

Rolf Krieger shook his head. "No, there has been a change in plans. Your current physique will have to sustain you for what is coming." Grabbing Waters by an arm, he hustled the lieutenant toward the door.

"What's up? I thought—"

"Do you remember the platoon training plan we discussed this afternoon, Lieutenant?"

"Yeah."

The big German smiled, visions of Russians dancing in his head. "We are accelerating it."

Chapter 4

Point, Counterpoint

White House Situation Room
Washington, D.C.

Jonathan Drake, the first Independent candidate elected president, the ex-senator, the ex-teacher, and the recently blooded chief executive of the American people, tilted his chair back and stared at the Situation Room's ceiling, fingers laced behind his head.

Though the clock behind Drake was digital, its time automatically updated by the Naval Observatory's nuclear clock every thirty seconds, his staff encircling the table could almost hear it tick in the room's booming silence. They watched three minutes count off—it seemed like ten to them.

"Sir," said the CIA director.

"Yes, Chris?" answered Drake, eyes still staring toward the ceiling.

"Everything all right?"

"Yes, Chris. Everything is fine," answered the president quietly.

Chris Dodd and Angela Bennett, Drake's national security advisor, exchanged glances. Dodd shook his head imperceptibly. He had been with Jonathan Drake since the former senator and college professor took office and knew his moods.

"Maybe I can provide some insight, Mr. President?" asked Bennett.

Drake eased his chair down and looked at Bennett. She had only recently joined his cabinet following the unexpected death of her predecessor. While he didn't know her as well as he'd have liked, she'd been by far the most qualified of the applicants.

Drake gave a slight nod. "Very well, Dr. Bennett. Please explain to me why after over a decade of peace, Russia is suddenly in a rush to bring two nations with more than sufficient nuclear weapons to annihilate one another and a nice chunk of the globe into a cross-border confrontation?"

At forty-five Angela Bennett could easily pass for ten years younger. More than once in her career adversaries had misjudged her to their detriment. It never occurred to the fallen that the statuesque beauty with straw-blond hair could be anything more than a civil servant who had used her looks to climb to the top—despite an impressive background that included Georgetown Law, staff time with two secretaries of defense, and starting and running with precision one of the most successful think tanks in Washington.

The national security advisor's polished nails danced over the keyboard in front of her. Bennett pointed to the electronic world map Dodd had briefed from minutes earlier. Lights began illuminating all over it: Eastern Europe, large sections of Asia, portions of the Caribbean and South America. "Sir, this was the Soviet Union's empire, its sphere of influence and satellites, up until the early 1990s."

After a few more keystrokes Eastern Europe went dark. Likewise Cuba. Other lights dimmed and went out. The sole remaining light, Russia, looked small and insignificant after the previous array. "As its influence has deteriorated, so has Russian pride. Early thoughts that democracy and a free-market economy, combined with abundant natural resources, would catapult them once more into prominence as a world power proved overly optimistic."

She turned her full attention on Drake, her blue eyes fixing him. "Pride, Mr. President. This is all about pride."

Drake looked doubtful. "They'd risk a nuclear war out of *pride*?"

Bennett nodded. "Yes, Mr. President. But they don't think it's much of a risk." She stared at Drake. Not knowing him as well as the other cabinet members, she wasn't sure how far she could go. Bennett gave an inward shrug and went on. If she were fired she could still go back into business for herself and quadruple her current income. "Most of the world is ignorant of our near nuclear release during the war. But grant me that countries with robust intelligence networks got wind of it."

The president nodded. "I'm sure they're aware of what happened. Go on."

"If the Russians had been in your position—facing an enemy that had already used chemical weapons on the Red Army—they'd have gone with a tactical nuclear response. Particularly since the opposing force did not have a nuclear retaliatory capability."

The president said nothing but continued observing Bennett.

"They don't think you have the stones to press the button, sir," she said finally. "That's the bottom line."

"Watch it, little lady," crackled a baritone voice behind Bennett. "Whether you realize it or not that's the President of the United States of Fucking America you're talking to. And I don't like your tone."

Angela Bennett looked down the table to the speaker. It was the chairman of the Joint Chiefs of Staff, Army General Tom Werner. A smile danced around the edges of her mouth as she looked at the gruff tanker. "I'd heard you had a mouth on you, General. I had no idea,

though . . . the United States of *Fucking* America?" She
shook her blond head. "Really."

Werner, one of the few people who knew just how
close Jonathan Drake had been to unleashing nuclear
hell on Iraq the previous year, began to rise from his
seat.

"Steady, Tom," said a hard but quiet voice. Heads
turned to the president. "Let her finish."

With an effort the old warhorse lowered himself.

"As I was saying, Mr. President," said Bennett, throwing an unsaid *before I was so rudely interrupted* look at
Werner, "they do not think you'd go that far. If you
wouldn't go nuclear to protect your forces who were in
harm's way when the enemy couldn't even retaliate in
kind, you surely wouldn't risk the Russians targeting
America's population with ICBMs. In their minds it becomes simple: Can their forces in Saudi Arabia, along
with their Saudi allies, defeat the combined forces of
Iraq and Kuwait, plus one American heavy division?"

No one said anything, so Bennett went on. "If they
accomplish that, can they overcome whatever forces are
then brought into theater to reinforce their opponents?
They know we wouldn't enjoy unopposed resupply
routes as we did during previous wars in the Middle
East." Bennett looked around the table, fixing all of
the cabinet members with her stare. She stopped when
her gaze once more rested on Drake. "If they could do
that, they'd be part of the richest and most powerful
alliance on the face of the earth. The new OPEC would
control over *three-quarters* of the planet's oil. That's
almost the same reserves the old OPEC controlled.
But—and this is critical to the equation—the old OPEC
was relatively friendly to U.S. interests. This OPEC
definitely would not be. They'd have their foot on the
neck of the industrial West. And Russia would be their
strong right arm."

She gave the room's members one last look. "Oil and

other natural resources flowing out of Mother Russia, new markets open to them across the board, cash flowing in, prestige regained . . . *pride restored*."

Angela Bennett retook her seat, slowly crossed one long leg over the other and steepled her fingers in front of her on the table.

That's one cold bitch, thought Chris Dodd.

Jonathan Drake sat quietly for a few moments and then looked to his advisors. "Dissenters?"

No one spoke.

"Very well. Recommendations." Drake turned to the chairman. "You first, General."

General Werner stood. "Yes, Mr. President. Three of our Interim Brigades and the Eighty-second Airborne are already loaded and preparing to fly as we speak. Per your directive the Fourth Infantry Division, the Rangers, and select Special Forces are also mobilizing." Werner paused. "We're trying to reinforce the First Cavalry and the Marines already on the ground as quickly as possible, sir, but it doesn't look good. The Russians are poised all along the border, outnumbering us more than two to one. Our best hope, should they attack, is to make them pay for every foot of desert they cross with blood. If we can do that, bloody them, make it hurt, we can slow them down . . . hopefully long enough to bring in our reinforcements."

Drake smiled wanly. "We've been here before, haven't we, Tom?"

The big general nodded, recalling his words to the president when multiple divisions had massed against a single American brigade in Kuwait only months earlier. Ironically, that same brigade would be part of the 4th Infantry contingent even now boarding planes for the Middle East. The poor bastards couldn't buy a break. "We'll do our damnedest to ensure we have the same end result, sir."

*   *   *

When the meeting adjourned Angela Bennett left the Situation Room and took the elevator to the ground floor. She exited the elevator and moved down the hallway, her shoes making no noise on the thick blue carpet. After a few feet, she stopped at a glass door opening onto an inner garden the public never saw. She walked out, sat on a stone bench, and pulled a pack of Marlboro Lights from her purse. As she flicked her lighter, a shadow fell over Bennett.

"Don't underestimate him," said Christopher Dodd.

Bennett looked up, startled. "Who?"

"Drake. He's not as simple—or nutless—as you think."

Angela Bennett took a long pull from the cigarette and exhaled slowly. "Is that why you followed me out? Concerned I might be making waves? Don't want me to rock the presidential barge?"

Dodd smiled. "You want me, don't you?"

Surprised by the remark and unsure she'd heard accurately, Bennett coughed out a plume of smoke. "*What* did you say?"

"I said he's a good man. And tougher than you think."

"That is *not* what you said. You said I wanted you."

Dodd looked at her seriously. "You've made it. You're the national security advisor for the President of the United States. You've got nothing to prove here, Doctor."

"That's not what I was trying to do in there. . . ."

"Yes it was, unless you were just trying to turn me on," said Dodd.

A well-manicured hand flew toward Chris Dodd's cheek. At the last moment he stopped it in an iron grip, close enough to his face that he could smell the fragrance of body lotion Bennett had used earlier in the morning.

Smiling slightly, Dodd released the hand, turned, and walked back toward the White House. A moment later she heard his voice float from the doorway through which he'd entered. "If that's the case, though, mission accomplished."

Bennett, usually careful of where she discarded her butts, threw the half-finished cigarette into the stones at her feet. Forcing herself to relax, she took a deep cleansing breath and leaned back on the bench. Was he right? Maybe. She knew Christopher Dodd had a reputation for being a sharp cookie. Hell, he had a reputation for *lots* of things, one of which he'd just confirmed in his comments to her . . . male-chauvinist-pig-womanizer. Reminded of his none-too-thinly-veiled interest in her, Bennett tried to regain her righteous indignation. For some reason she was having a hard time doing so. Rising, she smiled thoughtfully and walked back toward the White House.

Presidential Dacha
North of Moscow, Russia

Konstantin Khartukov sat before a roaring fire swirling a large snifter of brandy. He stared into the flames reflecting on how far removed the dacha was from the chaos of the capital only a few miles away.

Moscow was becoming a city of distinct blacks and whites once more, much the same as Russia itself. His country had tried in vain to become like Western nations, giving each man the same opportunities to improve himself and his lot in life as his neighbors. But it wasn't meant to be. Russia was, as Rudyard Kipling had once said, the most westerly of eastern nations, not the most easterly of western.

The czars had understood the most fundamental fact of Russian life: the common man needed to be subjugated. Vladimir Ilyich Lenin and Iosif Vissarionovich Dzhugashvili—known to his people as Koba, or "Stalin" in English, for "man of steel"—had sought to change this, raising "the worker" to an exalted status. After a few years of Soviet government they unfortunately found that the czars had been correct. A hungry People's Party worker secure in the knowledge that he and his family would not be allowed to starve during the harsh Russian winters was willing to put up with anything. After glasnost, perestroika, and their recent doomed attempt at democracy, it had once more become clear that Russians wanted a firm guiding hand even in the twenty-first century. Konstantin Khartukov was now that hand.

"If I did not know that you Communists were godless, I'd say you were communing with Allah," said his visitor, watching the Russian president stare silently into the flames.

Khartukov had almost forgotten he was not alone. He now looked to his guest and smiled. "Your Highness, Russian atheism is a myth. After more than a half century of suppression, churches sprang up overnight."

"So you believe in God?" asked the Saudi crown prince, crossing his legs at the knee and looking to his host with a curious gaze.

Khartukov looked at the man sitting opposite him in an overstuffed leather chair. By his bearing alone an observer would know the man was educated and well-to-do. His suit, a two-piece cashmere affair, was obviously custom tailored. Having attended graduate school at Oxford himself, the Russian guessed Gordon Carter of London. The prince looked not so much like a member of the Saudi royal family as he did a rich European, rested and well tanned after a monthlong holiday on the French Riviera.

Khartukov arched an eyebrow. "Believe in God? Me?" Before answering, he looked to his guest's needs. "More vodka, Prince?" he asked, indicating the chilled bottle sitting in an iced bucket.

"Please, call me Ali. Not at the moment. But I must say your Russian vodka is *excellent*. I have never tasted its equal."

The Russian barked a laugh. "Sorry. I'm afraid the superiority of our vodka is also a myth. It's Polish."

"Polish?"

"Yes. Belvedere to be specific." When he was a young field agent it would have surprised Khartukov to see a Saudi drinking alcohol. No more. The Russian knew that the strict Islamic conventions were much more steadfastly adhered to inside their homeland. It was party time—sex, drugs, and alcohol—once many crossed the royal kingdom's borders and ventured into Infidel Land.

The prince held the glass at arm's length. "Polish. How divinely *wicked*." He smiled. "Now, back to your beliefs—or nonbeliefs, as it were. . . ."

"I'm afraid it is something I do not often dwell on," said Khartukov. "Growing up the State was God. My mother, on the other hand, still practiced her Greek Orthodox faith whenever my father was not watching too closely, so I have some familiarity with the topic."

He was silent for a moment. "I concede the possibility of his existence. Let's leave it at that."

A commotion at the room's edge drew their attention. "*Unhand* me, you lout," said a high-pitched voice. The Russian words sounded strange when combined with the speaker's mild French accent.

"My personal chef," said Khartukov, indicating with his glass a tall, lean man with wild black hair who had just entered the room. Currently the chief of the president's security detail was detaining him to check the contents of a covered platter.

The Frenchman was working himself into a lather. "How many times have I served President Khartukov?" he hissed. "I have been with him longer than you, *cyka*. If my soufflé falls, it will be on *your* head."

The prince, who had a working knowledge of Russian, was clearly entertained. "What did he call your guard?"

"A bitch," the president said with a smile. "Claude has a way with words."

The big security man smiled, but it wasn't a pleasant expression. "Easy, my pretty," he said, finished with his inspection. "Your precious soufflé is fine."

"I found him in a small bistro off of Leningradsky Prospekt last year." Khartukov reached down and grasped the beginnings of a small belly between thumb and forefinger. "I have a bit of a weakness for pastries. One taste of Claude's strawberry macaroon tart and I knew I had to have him full-time in my employ."

The prince looked over the chef, pursing his lips appreciatively. Though lean, the Frenchman was broad through the shoulders. "He does look . . . capable."

"Oleg," he called to the security chief, "it is all right. Claude has had sufficient opportunity to poison me in the past if he had so wished."

Somewhat mollified, the Frenchman approached in short quick steps. Removing the dish's cover, he waved his hand over the dessert with a flourish. "Sir, you are in fine fortune tonight. Fresh cherries were available at that little open-air market off of Arbat, so I was able to prepare a fine compote." Still upset, his hands shook slightly as he served the president and his guest. "It may be too late to appreciate the dish's full effect. It is supposed to be served immediately out of the oven, but—"

Khartukov held up a hand as he removed his fork from his mouth. "Do not concern yourself, Claude. It is delicious, as always. Once more you have outdone yourself."

The chef was beside himself with delight. "Thank you, sir. I do my best." He stepped back, busying himself in preparing cups, saucers, cream, and sugar for the urn of coffee that had just arrived.

The men sat in companionable silence for a few minutes, enjoying the dessert and using the opportunity to
gather their thoughts regarding the reason for their
meeting.

"So have you considered my offer?" Khartukov said
after what he considered an appropriate amount of time
in which to change the topic.

Prince Ali looked toward the chef, who was busy a
few feet away berating the unfortunate Oleg for only
narrowly avoiding being responsible for a culinary disaster. The security man, accustomed to the cook's quirks,
was taking the browbeating in stride.

"Do not worry about Claude," said Khartukov. "I
have checked his background extensively, as I have all
of my staff. His parents were both practicing members
of France's Communist Party. He shared their beliefs
and applied at an early age, with their blessings, to study
in Russia." The president laughed. "Our nation may
miss many of the creature comforts of the West, but for
decades we were the crown jewel of communism."

The prince, with a personal staff of his own in the
royal palace in Riyadh, nodded his understanding and
then moved back to the original question. "Yes, I have
discussed your proposal with my brother, the king. In
his opinion your demands are excessive."

The Russian continued to relax back into his chair.
"Then his answer is no?"

The prince smiled. "Why do I have the feeling that
you are not overly concerned at the response?"

"Because, Ali," Khartukov said, "I know how badly
you need my support. Without it our military exercises
will remain just that—exercises."

The prince was no longer smiling. "Are you willing
to negotiate?"

"No."

The Saudi held a master's of business administration
from Stanford and had put the schooling to good use

for his kingdom over the years. He knew when an opponent was bluffing. And when he was not. "Very well. It will be as you ask. Once we have our renegade brothers' lands under control you will receive a double portion of the profits from their fields."

"And the military aspects of the agreement?"

The Arab scowled. "We have only recently removed the Americans from our soil. Our people had demanded it for years. But with an ever-present threat from Iraq, we had no choice but to allow U.S. forces to occupy our land and air bases. How do you think my people will respond to, forgive the language, replacing one infidel with another?"

Khartukov smiled. Both he and the Saudi royal house's representative knew he had already won. These negotiations were a mere formality. Without Russia Saudi Arabia's oil profits, their sole source of real revenue, would dry to a trickle. "Prince, forgive my language, but I do not give a rat's ass how your people respond to Russian forces in their beloved homelands."

A tense silence ensued.

The Russian leaned near Prince Ali and whispered, "Tell the king that it comes down to this: will he find it easier convincing his people that the Russians are their friends or telling the royal family that they will have to give up the luxuries that Saudi oil profits have allowed them to become accustomed to over the past three decades."

Both men knew the answer. And both knew there was no need to bother the Saudi king with the question.

"Very well," Ali said. The resignation in his voice could not be missed.

"And the military hardware contracts?"

The Arab closed his eyes and rubbed them slowly. Reaching for the vodka, he helped himself to another glass. "Done," he said, waving one hand in a vague circle.

"Very good. I can see the stories I have heard regarding your people's bargaining abilities are not unfounded."

For the first time that evening the prince looked completely serious. "One thing I learned in America while studying business, Konstantin. When you get the better of a deal, do not rub the other party's face in it. Memories are long . . . especially when dealing with Arabs."

"I did not mean to offend," said Khartukov, pouring himself a glass of vodka. "It was but a poor choice of words." He raised the glass to his guest. "To victory."

"To victory," echoed Prince Ali, smiling once more.

Settling back in his chair, Ali recrossed his legs. "So we will adhere to the original timeline?"

"There is no reason not to," replied the Russian. "My Spetsnaz did their job at the fuel depot with textbook precision. That action alone should ensure a successful first phase." A shadow crossed his features and he appeared to want to say more.

"Are you having second thoughts yourself, Konstantin?" asked the Saudi.

The Russian shook his head absently. "No. We will be successful. It is only that the American reinforcements are arriving much more quickly than I had thought possible."

Prince Ali had worked with the American military for over a decade in his own country. He had even studied with them at the United States Air Force's Air Command and Staff College. "For all of the trouble they've caused us, I must admit I admire their tenacity. When they decide to do something it is, as they say, full throttle."

Khartukov smirked at the irony of the statement. *All the trouble the Americans caused them,* indeed. If it weren't for the Americans Saudi Arabia would have been Saddam Hussein's next objective after Kuwait in 1990.

"Do you feel we should wait until a better opportunity presents itself?" Ali asked. "The American division will be gone in a few months, leaving Iraq, Kuwait, and the smaller nations to the south on their own."

Konstantin Khartukov gave a quick shake of his head. "No. We must strike now. We took the American division into account when we planned this operation. The only reinforcements they've added thus far have been their vaunted airborne troops from Fort Bragg. In all honesty very well trained soldiers, but mere distractions when involved in armored, open-desert operations."

The Russian continued after a few moments. "It is the men trickling in to man their heavy equipment that has me a bit concerned. They will have to draw their tanks and other heavy equipment from the prepositioned stocks in Qatar and Kuwait. These men could make a difference if we do not neutralize those equipment sites during our initial air and missile strikes."

"This is so," said Ali. "I am no longer sure how much equipment they have in Kuwait or Qatar. They learned their lesson when the sites were pounded by Iraq at the beginning of the last war. All of the armor and artillery is now under cover and they only move the equipment at night. They know that despite being in friendly country, it only takes one spy or terrorist to supply their enemies with information that could seriously damage them."

Khartukov smiled. "Well, they will find the task of defending against Russian jets and tanks a bit more difficult than their fight a year ago with Iraq's ancient ground forces and inaccurate SCUD missiles."

"Enshallah," said the prince. *Allah willing.*

"Yes, if it is God's will," mused the Russian. "And God's will starts tomorrow."

They discussed the details of the upcoming campaign for over an hour until both felt comfortable with the details and timing.

"Pardon me, Mr. President," said a quiet voice from his elbow. "Will you require me further this evening? Some fresh coffee perhaps? Or a nightcap?"

Khartukov shook his head. "By all means, Claude, you have earned the rest of the night off. Tell Nikolai I said he is a very lucky man."

Claude blushed and smoothed his white apron. "I will, sir. Good night," he said, departing.

"You are very kind to him," observed Prince Ali.

The Russian shook his head. "If it were up to me—and to a large degree it is—I would string up every homosexual in Moscow by their balls. Give their family jewels a useful purpose for a change. But I will have to find Claude's equal in the kitchen before I can do that."

The Arab looked a bit disappointed as he watched the chef's receding figure. Noting this, Khartukov signaled the security man. Oleg disappeared into a side room for a moment and then reappeared with two young women. Neither was dressed for the Moscow weather.

Ali's spirits rose once more. "Ah, Konstantin, you are a fine host and a good friend. They are truly beauties." He turned conspiratorially to Khartukov. "But tell me, is Oleg . . ."

White House
Washington, D.C.

Angela Bennett stepped out of her office and was almost overrun by Chris Dodd. "Come on, beautiful, hustle it up," he said, grabbing her wrist and resuming his previous jog down the corridor toward the Situation Room.

"I could have you charged with sexual harassment, you know," she said, trying to keep pace with the CIA chief.

Dodd smiled over his shoulder. "But you won't."

"The *hell* I won't. You and I are going to come to an understanding, *Mr. Director,* and quickly." Despite her anger Bennett sensed that something big was afoot. She picked up her pace to match Dodd's as she yanked her arm from his grip.

They skidded around a corner and almost bowled over a secretary. "Sorry!" he called, not slowing down.

When they were within fifty feet of the Situation Room Dodd transitioned to a rapid walk.

"So what's the rush?" Bennett asked, trying to catch her breath. "I was already on my way."

Dodd stopped just outside the door and faced her, all business now. "We've confirmed the attack."

"When?"

"Tomorrow. Across the board . . . Iraq, Kuwait, the UAE, Bahrain, Qatar."

This was Bennett's first experience as part of a team involved in a national crisis. Her previous efforts had been in analyzing potential points of crises as head of her think tank or Monday-morning quarterbacking the actions of others—others holding positions like she herself now held. "How good is your intelligence?"

"The man who sent it is the best field officer I've ever run," Dodd said without batting an eye. "Bar none. It's solid."

"How close to Khartukov?"

Dodd hesitated. As a former field agent, he was reluctant to divulge information that could harm his people. It could take months, even years, to get the right agent in the right place to be of use at the right time. The stars had aligned on this one. Archangel was the best field officer Dodd had ever run. And now he was in the eye of the hurricane. "Close. Let's leave it at that."

"Hey, that's not good enough," said Bennett. "I'm the president's national security advisor, for Christ's sake. If my clearance isn't good enough, whose is? Damn it, I've got to know that the recommendations I'm making are based on solid information. Am I being clear for you?"

Dodd ran a hand through his hair and leaned his back

against the wall. "Yeah, you're being clear enough. But until you've had body parts of people you're responsible for mailed to you one at a time over a period of months after some bureaucrat—intentionally or unintentionally—has blown his cover, I don't think you can understand."

Dodd didn't see the momentary look of sympathy cross Angela Bennett's face. It disappeared quickly, replaced by one of stony resolve. "Who is he?" she asked quietly. "Where is he placed that you're so certain of the information?"

Dodd stood silently for a few more moments, hands in his pockets, looking at the hall floor. "His code name is Archangel . . . and that's all I'll give *anyone* on that score. And he's a member of Khartukov's personal staff."

Bennett's face softened. "There. Was that so bad?"

"Yeah. Yeah, it was," said Dodd, pushing off of the wall and heading into the Situation Room. The woman had no idea how tough it was.

As they walked into the room Bennett smiled to herself. She had the feeling that Chris Dodd's attitude was a mask designed to hide his softer side in a testosterone-filled world. Time would tell.

Chapter 5

_____

_____

_____

If You Ain't Cav . . .

1st Cavalry Division TOC
Southwestern Iraq Border

"Status on unit moves," said Major General Jack Jeffries to the one-star general standing beside him. Jeffries—known as Pegasus 6 to his men—commanded the First Cavalry Division. The general next to him was Kirk Shillings, the Assistant Division Commander (Maneuver), or "M."

Tall and thin, Kirk Shillings wasn't a physically intimidating specimen; a second glance, however, usually gave observers pause. Shillings possessed an intensity that transmitted a silent "don't screw with me" message to the world. He now turned to his boss and removed the radio handsets he'd been holding next to each ear. The M shook his head and grimaced, answering in a slow drawl picked up during his formative years on a south Texas ranch. "Not looking good, sir."

Shillings moved from the radio to the electronic display mounted to the side of the division's tactical operation center. "We have Russian and Saudi armor positioning at points starting along the western Iraq border adjacent to Jordan, running south all the way to the UAE."

The 1st Cavalry Division had been notified only minutes before that an attack against them was imminent.
While Washington had only just figured this out, the
division had had a pretty good idea for the past week
that hostilities were about to be initiated from the west.
Russian movements along the borders of friendly Middle
East nations had not looked anything like the exercises
they were billed as. They were prepositioning movements, pure and simple.

When Russian and Saudi units began inching toward
the border, the 1st Cav's three maneuver brigades—
brigades composed primarily of M1A2-SEP tanks, the
most high-tech tank in the world, and digitized M2
Bradley Fighting Vehicles, or BFVs—had been participating in Operation Desert Lion with Iraqi and Kuwaiti
troops. When the division staff had gotten word of the
Russian and Saudi troop movements along the border
they'd thrown together an ad hoc defense plan. For the
past few days the troops of the 1st Cav and their allies
had been preparing to move to defensive positions in
accordance with that plan.

Tired of waiting for word from Washington, Jack Jeffries, the 1st Cav commander, had issued the order earlier in the day for all units to begin moving toward their
assigned sectors. While technically there were many
Iraqi and Kuwaiti generals who outranked him, none
argued that he was the best qualified to organize their
combined forces. Truth be known, they were damned
glad Jeffries was there and had picked up the ball.

General Jeffries had moved two of his three maneuver brigades into positions along the Iraq–Saudi Arabia
border. His third brigade straddled the Iraq-Kuwait
border adjoining Saudi Arabia. He'd pulled them
within a few kilometers two days ago. Now they were
supposed to be moving up to the border and into their
actual fighting positions.

"What's the problem?" asked Jeffries.

"You remember that company of tanks that went down last night? All of their engines started going dead on them?" asked Shillings.

"Yeah."

"We're starting to see it across the board," said the M.

Jeffries was thoughtful. "When you say 'across the board,' do you mean within that company's battalion, within that brigade, or—"

"Across the entire division, sir," finished Shillings. "It gets worse. It's not only our division. The Kuwaitis and Iraqis are also reporting higher and higher numbers of vehicles that are just, for lack of a better phrase, dying in place. The hydraulics and guns are in working order. Electronics check out fine. It's only the engines. They're seizing up. Lots of reports of fuel line damage as well."

"Fucking Ruskies," muttered Jeffries. He hadn't gotten where he was because he was slow on the uptake. "They sabotaged the fuel stocks."

Shillings nodded. "That's my guess. None of the units south of us are reporting problems, so my guess is that Ivan got into the Second Corps fuel depot at An Najaf. I've already pulled samples from our fuel trucks and have sent them south for analyses. I also took the liberty of grounding our aviation assets until we can guarantee their fuel is good."

"Smart move, Kirk," said Jeffries. The last thing they needed were Apaches falling out of the sky. "Call the Kuwaitis and see if they can fly in some fuel bladders. Our tanks and Brads are nothing but pillboxes as it stands. And the second one of our howitzers or MLRS rocket systems fire, their goose is cooked." The standard operating procedure for artillery was to fire and move, fire and move. The cannon cockers knew that as soon as one of their massive 155mm shells arced into the sky there would be fire-finder radars triangulating their position and sending counterfires their way. If they were still there when those counterfires impacted . . . well, it wasn't pretty.

"Wilco, sir. Already made the call an hour ago when I thought bad fuel might be the problem."

"By God, Kirk, now I know why I keep you around," said the general. "Until we see if the fuel's gonna get here in time to do us any good, scrounge what we can and push it to the reconnaissance units. I've got to get some eyes moving forward ASAP."

At that moment a white-and-brown blur jumped on the table next to the map. "What do you think, Phantom?" asked Jeffries. The Jack Russell terrier issued a single throaty bark. Jeffries stroked the animal's short, white coat. Phantom accompanied the general everywhere, including the Middle East. He was considered the division's good luck charm. Jeffries nodded at the dog's bark. "I agree. We could be well and truly fucked."

Jeffries looked all along the borders of the display. He inwardly fumed at the number of Russian and Saudi divisions he saw reflected there. Someone in Washington had botched this one badly when they'd merely echoed the explanations of Russian and Saudi Arabian officials . . . nothing but large-scale exercises. The government intelligence agencies hadn't thought the new Russian president had been on board long enough to even consider a play this big. Now he and his men might have to pay for that miscalculation.

The general looked at his own force's disposition. The 1st Cavalry had men and equipment scattered across two countries. And most of the equipment was running out of fuel. That was the downside. The upside? He was in command of the most modern warfighting organization the world had ever seen. The U.S. Army spent a lot of research and development dollars after Desert Storm. The equipment held in his men's hands was the fruit of that effort. He might not be mobile, but *by God* he'd give the Russians a fight they'd remember.

Looking to Phantom, Jeffries smiled. The dog had walked across the table and started sniffing the red lights indicating the enemy's last reported locations. He growled, deep in his throat.

"That's right, boy. They think they want to play with the Cav." Jeffries smiled thinly and looked at the red lights. "All right, you bastards, come get some."

Saudi Arabia-Iraq Border
2nd Brigade Combat Team (Blackjacks) Security Zone
Twelve Hours Later

As the sun set over an isolated stretch of desert, nothing moved save the sands. The Russian sergeant commanding the BRDM-2 armored reconnaissance vehicle moved slowly east. A few kilometers behind him, Russian tanks, infantry fighting vehicles, and artillery were unwinding to begin their attack against the American positions in southwestern Iraq.

The BRDM was part of the initial fight—the recon battle. If he could find the Americans and report their positions quickly enough that the tanks and other armor behind him could maneuver into the enemy's flanks, the battle would be half over. On the other hand, if he missed the American positions or died without reporting them, his comrades could stumble blindly into an ambush. For all of these reasons—and because he valued his skin—Sergeant Aleksei Oblov moved slowly and carefully, checking each terrain feature ahead of him before proceeding.

"This is Two-Three. Currently at Checkpoint Five. Negative contact, over."

A voice filled with static came through his armored

crewman's helmet ear cups. *"This is base. Proceed to Checkpoint Eight, over."*

"Two-Three, proceeding to Checkpoint Eight, out."

Oblov gave his driver instructions to move out. The sun was almost down now. This would both help and hinder their efforts. While the darkness would help cover their movement, none of the Russians tried to fool themselves. The Americans owned the night. Their thermal sights were far superior to the 1970s technology incorporated in the BRDM-2's infrared driving and searchlights. Worse, their IR lights would call the attention of every American with night-vision goggles. Their best bet was to depend on stealth and leave all lights, including the IRs, extinguished.

As the Russian NCO mulled over these thoughts, beneath him, unheard, soldiers cursed.

"I really wish those guys would move out," whispered Specialist Don Delauder, dust raining down on his Kevlar in the darkness.

"Take it easy, Don," said his NCO, Sergeant Matt Harmon. "And you don't have to whisper. Trust me, they can't hear anything in that track that's not coming over their radio."

That the Russians were in their area was no surprise to the two battalion scouts. The brigade recon team, seven kilometers to the west, had made the call hours ago . . . the Russians were coming, and they were coming in force.

"Yeah, yeah, I know," replied Delauder tightly. "It just seems natural to bitch when you have a seven-ton armored vehicle stopped on top of your head."

As they sat in the darkness of the small hidden position, both waited. Delauder put his lips to Harmon's ear. "Hey, Sarge, how much did you say they're paying us for being in a hostile fire zone?"

Harmon smiled. "So far as I know, no one's declared this a hostile fire zone, so you're not making jack."

Delauder grimaced as more dust rained down on his head from above as the armored scout car finally moved off, diesel engine rumbling loudly. "Well, for argument's sake, let's say someone declares that we are indeed in a hostile fire zone. How much?"

Sergeant Harmon shifted, lifting the cover of their hide position slightly and peering out into the twilight. "One hundred and fifty bucks a month."

The young scout beside him slapped the stock of his rifle. "Well that's just fucking great. Now I can afford the payments on that used Hyundai I've been eye-balling."

Harmon looked down. "I wish to hell you'd quit complaining, Delauder."

"And I wish I had a big dick," said the specialist, pointing toward his crotch. "But here we are, Sarge."

"All right, all right." Harmon knew the time to start worrying was when a soldier stopped griping. "How many Javelins do we have . . . and don't say not enough. I know that already."

Delauder didn't need to count. "I've got one missile attached to the command launch unit, plus three additional missiles ready for reload."

The Javelin was the best shoulder-fired antiarmor missile in the U.S. arsenal. A man-portable antitank missile, the Javelin's range of twenty-five hundred meters was three times that of its predecessor, the Dragon. On top of that, the Javelin was a fire-and-forget munition—the gunner could loose a missile on an enemy tank and drop behind cover. Earlier-generation tank killers like the Dragon were wire-guided, meaning the gunner had to fire the missile and keep the sight on the target until impact. This was not generally a healthy way of doing business. Add to this the fact that the Javelin was a top-attack munition; it departed its launch unit and looped up, gaining elevation, then zeroed in on its target where the armor was thinnest—on top.

"Roger, stand by," said Harmon. Harmon hadn't heard any engine noise for the past couple of minutes, so he deemed it safe to slide the cover off of their spider hole and get some fresh air. Plus the radio had much better reception when the aerial was above ground. To an onlooker, it would have appeared that a portion of the desert floor was opening up.

Harmon stood a bit, bringing only his eyes above ground level. He could see the BRDM moving off to the east. Automatically, he looked west with his night-vision goggles. Seeing nothing, but knowing more Russians were out there, he called to Delauder, "Don, pass up the LRAS."

The Long-Range Advanced Scout Surveillance System, or LRAS3, was cutting-edge night-vision technology. Similar Russian equipment amounted to nothing more than ugly stepsisters. The system, fielded to battalion and brigade recon units only since 2001, provided scouts a real-time capability to detect, recognize, identify, and pinpoint far-target locations up to fifty kilometers—over thirty miles—distant.

In the old days, circa Desert Storm, scouts had to find their own locations on a map, find the enemy using binoculars or night-vision devices, then calculate, based on their training and experience, exactly what the enemy's location was. They would call this information in to their commanders or ask for indirect fires on the enemy. As many times as not the fires weren't even close to the intended target. God help them if the enemy was moving quickly, at which point the artillery would likely not authorize the fires because the odds of hitting anything were so poor. No longer. The LRAS's GPS, combined with its laser range finder, allowed the scouts to determine far-target position locations to a ten-digit grid coordinate in the blink of an eye. And they could update the data every second if necessary. At ten kilometers the circular error probability on the reported position was sixty meters, much lower at closer distances. Because the LRAS interfaced with the other digital systems of the digitized army units such as the 1st Cavalry, the scouts could determine a far target's grid coordinate location, dump the enemy position information into a spot report, and forward the report to the headquarters in seconds. The location information could also be sent directly to supporting artillery units. A far leap from 1990 . . . see the enemy at a much farther distance than he could see you, send a digital spot report and request for fire, watch the enemy go boom. Simple. Beautiful. *Definitely* good shit.

Harmon and Delauder were 19 Deltas—cavalry scouts. While they'd have liked to put a Javelin up the BRDM's Russian ass, that wasn't their mission tonight. The plan that had come down from the division headquarters at noon was clear. Push out the recon as far as possible, hide their vehicles, and go to ground.

"*Ghost Six, Ghost Two-Three, over,*" said Harmon over the radio handset.

"*This is Ghost Six, go,*" came the scout platoon leader's voice.

"*This is Two-Three. We have one enemy PC, one kilometer east of our position and continuing on Avenue of Approach Two, over.*"

"*Roger, will advise counter-recon team. Out.*"

The scouts figured the counter-recon tanks and Bradleys behind them were already tracking the enemy reconnaissance vehicle. The friendlies had the same FLIR systems the scouts were using, after all. But it never hurt to be careful.

Once more stillness settled over the desert. Harmon could hear the moan of the wind. It always seemed to pick up this time of day, no matter what patch of desert it was in what corner of the globe. Looking into his hole, Harmon called his partner. "Don, better warm up the IR system on the Javelin. I think we'll have company soon enough and it's getting dark."

"Roger," said Delauder, popping above ground level for a breath of fresh air.

Behind their position a sonic crack split the night. Both soldiers turned and saw the BRDM burning. "That 120mm depleted uranium is a beautiful thing," observed Delauder with a dreamy smile.

"Yep," replied Harmon. "I thank God every day that the Russians don't have M1s." A thoughtful look crossed the NCO's face. "I guess that's the first shot fired in a new war. Funny, after all those years of watching each other across walls and through the barbed wire of the Iron Curtain, we've never had a shooting war with the bastards. When I was a kid, everyone knew it was gonna happen, just a matter of time. But it never did. Until now."

Delauder put the Javelin's night sight to his eye. "How do you think our M1s stack up against the Russian T-80s?" he asked.

Harmon thought about the advantages and disadvantages of the two tanks. "The T-80 is lighter and has a lower profile, but it doesn't have the survivability or lethality of an M1. It falls way short of the M1A2s our guys have." Harmon smiled. "Then again, most of our A2s are dead in the water and can't move. I'd say that turns the tide in the T-80s' favor in this particular situation."

Delauder nodded, frowning at the black humor his boss used at the worst possible times. Did he really think it helped to settle his nerves? He continued to observe west. "Here they come," he almost whispered.

Harmon threw his binos to his face. Despite the fading light, the picture was clear enough. To his front he saw three tanks. The three tanks turned into nine tanks as the enemy platoons came on line. The nine tanks turned into over thirty tanks as the Russian companies came on line. Both men knew that the battalion in front of them was merely the spearhead of a combined Saudi-Russo force that was much larger.

"Whoa Nellie," said Harmon under his breath.

Delauder continued observing west through his Javelin's IR sight. "My sentiments exactly."

"Ghost Six, Ghost Six, this is Ghost Two-Three. We have approximately three-zero T-80 tanks moving west, vicinity TRP Alpha Four-Four. They have moved into a line formation. Sending digital report and request for fires now."

Soviet doctrine taught that the Russians would stay in columns as long as possible to make better time. They only deployed into a line formation when moving into the attack. The fact that they were deploying into a line meant they knew, at least roughly, where the American forces were located. And they also knew there was no way the Americans were going anywhere, except on foot. As it became clear to the division's leadership that their fuel supply had been sabotaged, and that the sabotaged fuel was even now running through almost every one of their vehicles, units had been given fragmentary orders, or FRAGOs, to find the best defendable pieces of ground in their immediate vicinity and to prepare for battle. Units had done so and shut down their engines, hoping that if they absolutely had to move, they might be good for a few extra miles before breaking down.

"Understand three-zero T-80s," said the scout platoon leader. *"Stand by."*

As the two scouts watched the Russian armor lumber toward them the ground began to vibrate. The sand around the outer edge of their position trickled onto their gear in the bottom of the hole.

"Two-Three, this is Six . . . artillery fires denied by higher. Continue to observe and report."

Harmon looked at the handset unbelievingly. *"Say again, Ghost Six?"*

The sympathy from the distant station was clear, but the voice remained firm. *"Sergeant Harmon . . . if our artillery units fire, the enemy will know the location of our tubes within seconds. They would be targeted by Russian counterfire units."* Ghost Six paused for a long heartbeat. *"They would die, Sergeant Harmon."*

The NCO continued watching the approaching Russians. He knew many of his fellow NCOs in the artillery battery that supported their battalion. If they weren't firing it wasn't because they were afraid to die. Those men's hands would even now be wrapped around lanyards, waiting to unleash 155mm shells on the approaching formation. Knowing the men behind the tubes, Harmon would bet his stripes they were *begging* for permission to fire. But the time for that apparently hadn't yet come. But Harmon knew that the time was rapidly approaching. The tanks in front of him made the fact abundantly clear.

"This is Two-Three. Acknowledged."

"Roger. Good luck. Six out."

When the radio spooled down and quieted, the night enveloped the soldiers. They were trained to operate on their own, independent of their unit's main body. But rarely did they feel alone. They always knew that if worse came to worst, tanks could come forward and assist, or they could call for tons of hot steel from the artillery batteries to buy the time necessary to exfiltrate an area. Neither of those options were a choice tonight.

"You know, Sergeant Harmon," said Delauder, watching the approaching Russians, "I don't think the Hyundai's worth it."

Harmon snorted, seeing two more groups of tanks and mechanized infantry move east over the distant horizon, looking like large green insects through the PVS-7s. "Piece of Jap shit anyway . . . *Ghost Six, Two-Three. Spot report follows . . .*"

Airborne Aboard C-5 Galaxy
Twenty Miles North of Kuwait City

Patrick Dillon turned to Rob Estes for at least the tenth
time in their trip from Colorado Springs and uttered
the same words. "Sir, this is bullshit."

Estes's Kevlar helmet was pulled low over his eyes.
He lifted the forward edge and peered out sleepily.
"Damn, Pat, I was hoping all that bitching was just a
bad dream and I'd be waking up at home with a view
of the Rockies from my bedroom."

"I should be with my troops, sir," Dillon said in a
low voice, staring outside into the darkness. "That's
my place."

"Yeah, yeah," said Estes. "Don't you think I told
Jones the same thing? Don't you think I'd also like to
be with the boys?"

Colonel Bill Jones, commander of the 3rd Brigade,
4th Infantry Division (Mechanized) Strikers, had left
word that he wanted a handful of his experienced combat leaders to take part in a teleconference prior to the
brigade deploying for Kuwait. Unfortunately someone
forgot to tell Ma Bell and the trunk line supporting
the videoconference was accidentally pulled offline for
maintenance just as the CENTCOM commander in
Tampa had appeared on their monitor. It had taken the
better part of three hours to switch the feed to an alternate line, get all the participants from across the country up and complete the teleconference. The delay
meant that Estes and Dillon had departed a couple of
hours after their troops were already in the air. They'd
received word an hour earlier that their battalion, the
2-77 Armor Silver Lions, and most of the Striker Brigade were on the ground in Kuwait City awaiting
their arrival.

"Besides," continued Estes, "you've got Bluto Wyatt

and First Sergeant Rider with your men. Not only are they both extremely competent, but they've been through this before. I'd be surprised if they weren't wheeling and dealing as we speak to get you the best tanks of the mothballed brigade sets at Doha."

The Strikers were drawing their equipment from stocks in Kuwait. Previously another set had been pre-positioned in Qatar, but U.S. Central Command's move to the Qatar peninsula meant there was no room at the inn. Now all of the tanks, Bradleys, and other war stocks for the region were maintained in Kuwait. And Dillon's men were already there—without him.

Dillon nodded. "You're right. Guess I'm just a little nervous about the new guys in the company. They *haven't* been through something like this and were nervous enough without seeing the old man pulled from the aircraft just as it was about to go wheels up."

"It wasn't a total waste of time," said Estes. "Or did you already know that the Russians had T-90s in service already, much less in Saudi?"

The silver-haired captain shook his head. "No. I have to admit that one took me by surprise as well. Too bad they couldn't tell us how many."

Both men were silent for a few moments. "They really put some effort into that baby," said Dillon, thinking of the new Russian tank.

Estes nodded. "I still think the A2-SEPs are more than a match for them," he said, referring to the 1st Cavalry Division's M1A2-SEP tanks.

Dillon grimaced. "Yeah, but how will our fifteen-year-old M1A1s stand up against them?"

Estes threw a piece of bubble gum in his mouth. "We'll do okay."

Both of the tankers were seasoned and knew that might not be the case. They had faith in the steel beast that had seen them through Desert Storm and the Second Gulf War, but now they would be facing cutting-edge Russian technology. And as a general rule, Russian troops were better trained than the Iraqis they'd faced in the previous two wars.

Dillon sat forward and reached into the back left pocket of his pants, a look of disappointment crossing his face when he realized it was empty.

Estes offered him a piece of bubble gum. "Still holding on to old habits? How long has it been now?"

Dill took the gum and popped it in his mouth. "Three months."

"Have you tried nicotine patches?"

Dillon lifted the left sleeve of his desert-colored Battle Dress Uniform shirt, exposing his biceps. Two small patches adhered to the arm. "The shit's overrated," he said, popping a bubble.

As the men gathered their gear for the landing a streak of light flashed by the window immediately to Dillon's right. The plane plunged toward the ground and the interior lights went out as their pilot began evasive maneuvers.

"Oh fuck," said Dillon, reaching down to ensure his seat belt was buckled and tight.

"Roger that," said Estes, doing the same.

The C-5 leveled out and made a change in course heading.

Estes gave his protégé a conspiratorial wink. "Guess we don't have full air superiority in this one."

While neither of them had spoken of it, they'd both been worried about getting their men safely on the ground. Their job was to man the tanks and Bradleys stored in Kuwait and get to the fight; to do that they had to arrive in one piece. Although they gave every Air Force officer they saw hell, particularly the pilots, it was good-natured jibing for the most part. Both men had a great deal of respect for their brothers in blue. They knew that the Russian and Saudi Air Forces were significantly better armed and trained than the Iraqis they'd faced over the past decade. For the most part the Saudis flew American aircraft and their pilots had been trained at the same schools as their American counterparts. Ruling the skies for any given amount of time would be tough. The two Iron Tiger leaders had felt better about their odds when word had come down that their men were on the ground at Kuwait International Airport, but now their fears were being justified.

Dillon looked out his window. There was a new moon and illumination was good enough that he clearly saw the jet fighter that flashed past. He didn't recognize it as a MiG-31 Foxhound, Russia's most capable air defense interceptor, but he knew it wasn't a friendly.

The American aircraft banked hard. The C-5, as long as a football field and six stories high, was powered by four General Electric turbofan engines, each capable of forty-one thousand pounds of thrust. The pilot was red-lining all four, coaxing every ounce of power he could get in a vain effort to outrace the swift Russian fighter—or to at least throw off his aim. There were almost one hundred service members on board the C-5 plus a lot of equipment desperately needed by the men on the ground. The aircraft commander knew that without a little help from his friends, the U.S. fighters that had to be in the vicinity, this was going to be a short and one-sided effort.

As the pressure of the turn eased, Dillon was once more able to look out the window. He saw the Russian jet silhouetted against the moon as it completed a turn and aligned itself on them once more. As the fighter flew closer, rapidly closing the distance between itself and the lumbering transport, Patrick Dillon saw death reach out for him.

The MiG pilot was in so close that he had decided not to waste one of his precious AA-9 Amos air-to-air missiles—he might need those to fight his way out of the area. Instead he selected his cannon and began the methodical procedure of walking his rounds into the target before him.

"Sir, we could be fucked," said Dillon, straining to be heard as he watched the MiG's cannon rounds fly high as the American aircraft abruptly dropped five hundred feet. "That was damned close."

Estes, also straining, said through gritted teeth, "No, Pat, God wouldn't do that to us. We're tankers. He wouldn't let us die on the threshold of battle riding around in a flying bus."

The C-5 leveled out. Dillon looked through the window. The sky appeared to be clear of aircraft attempting to end the Irishman's life. But he couldn't see the MiG hurtling toward him from above. When the C-5 dropped the Russian had gained altitude and swung around in order to get a fresh line on his kill. Now he opened with cannons for the killing pass. The Russian was ready to be finished with this business—it was rather embarrassing that it had taken him this long to drop one defenseless transport aircraft—and to head back toward Saudi airspace before the American defense fighters arrived.

The first clue Patrick Dillon had of their fate was a shrieking sound as the MiG's armored rounds peeled back the fuselage above his head. He swung toward Estes. As he did so his commander disintegrated in front of his eyes, struck by three of the MiG's large-caliber shells. Before Dillon had time to react to this horror a blinding pain washed over the left side of his face. When he opened his eyes moments later he couldn't see. Reaching to his face he felt blood—lots of blood. Whether it was his or Estes's he had no idea. He could see a little better after wiping his eyes with his hands. Flames danced around the passenger compartment. As his world spun into darkness Dillon heard the C-5's crewmen rushing frantically to get the damage under control and their aircraft on the ground.

None aboard the flaming craft saw the F-16 Falcon that was their savior. As the MiG swung around to strafe the length of the C-5 the American fighter was already firing his own guns. He downed the MiG . . . but not in time to keep the Russian from firing those few fateful rounds.

The Falcon pilot could do nothing but watch as the large transport hurtled toward the ground. *"This is Snowman flight lead . . . we have an aircraft going down,"* he yelled into the radio. After reporting the doomed bird's location and direction, the pilot stayed close. He shook his head savagely as he clung to the C-5 like a shadow. He couldn't save the plane—that was now in the hands of Fate and the bus driver piloting it—but by *God* no Russian would touch it.

Watching the C-5 illuminate the night skies with its trail of flames, Snowman smiled. *You might just make it, you son of a bitch,* he thought. As a professional aviator, he knew that the big transport's pilot was above standard. Despite what was surely a frantic cockpit and systems that were dropping out on him by the second, he was now lined up for a landing at the Kuwait International airfield.

Snowman was slightly aft of the big aircraft. The flames illuminated the exterior well enough for him to get a good visual beneath the fuselage. *Shit.* The landing gear had lowered only slightly and was deploying no further. The Falcon pilot pulled forward such that he could see his counterpart in the C-5 crew compartment. The man appeared calm and had an iron grip on his controls.

As the C-5 pilot looked out of his windscreen, he saw Snowman gesturing wildly beneath the injured aircraft. Giving Snowman a thumbs-up, he smiled grimly. Hydraulics shot, he knew he had no landing gear. Looking forward, he finished final preparations for an emergency landing. "Okay, fighter jock, let me show you how the big boys handle their toys. . . ."

Seconds later Snowman watched as the C-5 made contact—dead fucking center and lined up beautifully. Hurtling down the runway, its tail began to turn, a shower of sparks one hundred feet high marking its passage.

1st Cavalry Division TOC
Southwestern Iraq Border

Jack Jeffries looked at his display once more. How things could change in twelve hours. He listened to the reports coming from his division's reconnaissance assets—brigade recon teams, battalion–task force scout platoons, even some Army Special Forces teams were reporting in by the second. The enemy was moving east at a deliberate pace. History had never seen anything like the massive mechanized fight building in this godforsaken piece of desert. And unlike previous armored battles it would be fought in near total darkness. When the sun came up, the world would be a different place.

Beside Jeffries Phantom began doing circles on the floor, chasing his stub of a tail. *For a smart dog,* thought the general, *he could be a real nimrod.* He turned to Kirk Shillings. "All of the recon elements in place, Kirk?"

The M nodded. "For the most part." He pointed out the blue lights on the map marking scout and recon troop locations. Their position-location information was automatically updated through the division's digitized systems. The 1st Cavalry, or the First Team, as they liked to call themselves, was a twenty-first-century fighting team. Unlike less modern units who knew subordinate unit locations only by what was reported over the radio, determining enemy locations only when they found them or vice versa, every soldier on every combat system on the First Team knew where he was, where his friends were, and where the bad guys were. If one scout, tanker, or grunt could see an enemy vehicle or soldier, everyone in the division knew where it was.

"Looks like they're going to hit the Blackjacks first," said Jeffries, indicating the forces rapidly approaching his 2nd Brigade.

"Yes, sir," said Shillings. "We're not going to be able to wait much longer, sir."

Jeffries was thinking the same thing. He knew that Russian maneuver forces, by doctrine, would rain down artillery and rockets on their enemies just prior to their attack. Preparatory fires, these firestorms were called. They were meant to make the men defending the position button up and go to ground. While the defenders tried to ride out the massive strike, the Russian tanks and mechanized infantry increased their speed, rapidly closing on the position. That was the situation now in the Blackjack area of operations. There was little doubt the artillery would start hitting the 2nd Brigade any moment. One thing could be counted on—the Russians were suckers for doctrine.

"Still don't think they'll throw chem at us?"

Kirk Shillings shook his head. "Reports are solid that no chemical units or munitions are in close enough range to be of use for the initial fight." Shillings smiled. "Of course, that report's subject to change should our chemical alarms sound when the first artillery impacts."

For this reason, the two men, like their soldiers, wore camouflaged Nuclear, Biological, Chemical, or NBC, suits over their field uniforms. And their protective masks were close at hand.

Jeffries nodded to himself. Time to put the game face on. His self-propelled artillery and multiple launch rocket systems would have one chance and then their collective wads would be blown. He picked up the radio handset linking him to his subordinate commanders. *"Broken Arrow, acknowledge."*

In Vietnam, units called "broken arrow" when they were about to be overrun. Every aircraft in range with bombs or bullets converged on the area in a last-ditch effort to prevent American troops from dying. While the situation might not be exactly the same, for some reason the code word had seemed right to Pegasus 6.

Across the huge expanse of desert real estate that the 1st Cavalry was responsible for, scouts and recon teams began lighting up every Russian formation they saw with LRAS. Artillery combat observation lazing teams, or COLTs, operating forward in the security area did the same. Confirmed enemy locations for thousands of Russian combat systems poured into the 1st Cav's targeting centers.

Saudi Arabia-Iraq Border
2nd Brigade Combat Team (Blackjacks) Security Zone

"Acknowledged," said Matt Harmon into his radio. He tapped Specialist Delauder on the shoulder. "Get down, Don."

Delauder continued tracking the progress of the approaching tanks and mechanized infantry to the west through his LRAS. "There are more of them now, Sergeant Harmon."

"Don," said Harmon, "get down *now.*" With that the older NCO grabbed the young scout and threw him into the bottom of their position. He quickly handed down the LRAS, covered their position with the thick plywood once more, and huddled down next to his partner.

"What the *fuck* was that about, Sarge? You almost broke my neck. . . ."

Delauder broke off as all hell broke loose outside. The interior of the small position, nothing more than a hastily dug hole of five feet, just large enough for both men and their equipment, shook and threatened to collapse.

Harmon turned on a blue-lensed flashlight. The interior of the position glowed eerily. As portions of their shelter's sand walls threatened to collapse, Delauder saw his NCO grinning evilly.

"Why the hell are you smiling? If that Russian artillery gets any closer—"

"It ain't Russian," Harmon yelled to be heard over the tumult. "And it ain't that close!"

"What do you mean it ain't that close?! It's right the fuck on top of us!"

"It's ours and it's hitting those tanks and BMPs you were watching. It's landing a few kilometers away."

The hole shook again. The concussion from multiple rocket strikes lifted the five-pound plywood covering their position into the air. Sand cascaded into Delauder's face as it thudded back into position. Huddling into a ball and pulling his Kevlar helmet tightly onto his head he looked into Harmon's face. "Thanks for the info. I feel much better now that I know they're not after me."

Five kilometers west of the two scouts Russian armor and American technology met in the desert night. As the armor rolled east in anticipation of fighting a degraded adversary, U.S. Army Tactical Missile System rounds, ATACMS for short, arched skyward into the stratosphere. Within seconds Russian fire-finder radars were calculating the position of the American MLRS launch vehicles, but it was too late to do anything about the rounds and missiles already fired and the hell they would wreak on the Russians for the next several minutes.

The ATACMS carried Block II Brilliant Antiarmor Technology, or BAT, submunitions. Designed to defeat moving armor deep before it could engage American forces, the ATACMS missiles reached the apex of their

trajectory and turned gracefully earthward. Missiles were
fired at every enemy formation within seventy kilometers. Each of the ATACMS deployed thirteen of the
BAT munitions into the night sky as their nose cones
opened high above the earth, each of the submunitions
gliding to a preprogrammed target area. Thousands of
the lethal BATs were in the air, sensing the fast-
approaching earth for sound and heat signatures. Once
in its area, each BAT selected a discrete target within
its acoustic segment of the formation. Terminal infrared
seekers locked on moving tanks and BMPs, guiding the
BATs to terminal impact on the thinly armored tops of
their victims. A tandem shaped-charge warhead drove
the BATs into the Russian war machines. The fortunate
crews experienced only mobility or firepower kills. Most
of the hits, however, were catastrophic, the BATs driving into the vehicles' interiors, exploding and killing the
crews instantly. Onboard munitions added to the destruction. All along the border Russia's lead echelons
ground to a halt.

"I want reports. Now," said Jack Jeffries calmly.
"It looks like they're stopped, sir, at least for now,"
said the M. Shillings had a handset in one ear, was reading electronic reports, and looking at the situation display all at the same time. "Initial indications are that
there are some survivors, but not many. While the BATs
were hitting the armored formation, we had Block One
BATs hitting their identified air defense units and
MLRS and one-five-five fires across the board."
"By *God* those cannon cockers earned their money
tonight," said Jeffries, referring to the artillerymen responsible for the massed fires. "Did the Russians get any
counterfires off against them?"
Shillings set the handset down and nodded toward it.
"I was getting some reports in just now."

Pegasus 6 frowned. "And?"

"Yes. And some of the firing units were hit hard, despite your orders."

Jeffries merely nodded. He'd known when he'd told the cannon and rocket crews to fire three volleys and then abandon their weapons to seek shelter that many of them would disobey the order, instead continuing to send steel downrange.

"A number of the crews still had a little fuel remaining and displaced. Not many, but it's something."

"Okay. Target them against any Russian air defenses still remaining. The Air Force isn't going to be happy with us if they get their peckers shot off."

When the Army defends, it breaks its area of operations into zones. The main battle area, or MBA, is the terrain the tanks, Bradleys, and dismounted infantry dig into and kill the enemy within. The goal of the counter-recon is to not allow enemy reconnaissance into this area. When the enemy main body rolls into the MBA, the goal is for them to know nothing—not where obstacle belts are emplaced, not where units are located, not where the best avenues of approach run—nothing.

The battalion–task force scouts, along with the counter-recon company team composed of heavy combat vehicles, operate forward of the main battle area. They are the counter-recon specialists and operate in what is known as the security zone; the imaginary line separating the MBA and security zone is the forward edge of the battle area, or FEBA.

Farther into the security zone are the brigade recon teams, COLTs, and ETACs. ETACs are enlisted tactical air controllers, highly trained and organized Air Force airmen who go forward with Army units, assisting them in calling in close air support aircraft. The farthest point on the map where these men are found is the forward line of troops, or FLOT.

Operations conducted within the MBA and security

zone are considered close operations. Operations past the FLOT are deep. Other than ATACMS, the Army doesn't have many options to strike deep. That's where air support comes in.

While the artillerymen of the 1st Cavalry struck throughout the close area, numerous flights of F-15s, F-16s, and A-10s closed from Turkey and Kuwait. To the south Navy F/A-18s and Harriers supported as well. American ground forces had pounded the lead elements; American air power would slam the trailing echelons.

"Battle damage assessment from the air strikes against the rear?" asked Jeffries.

"They did some damage," answered the M. "Still a lot of steel rolling this way. And the Air Force took some air-to-air losses. They stacked up well against their Russian and Saudi counterparts, but we knew we couldn't expect clear skies."

"Battle damage assessment against the Russians?"

Shillings shook his head, a strange look on his face. "You know, sir, despite the fact that I've been working around this digitized Force Twenty-one equipment for a couple of years, I'd never have believed . . ." He stopped speaking a moment, then continued. "In just over ten minutes, we destroyed roughly three divisions: *three divisions* of Russian armor and Russian men in *ten minutes*."

Though he knew that he and his men were far from out of the woods, that there was a lot more left to do in this fight before it was over, he took pause to consider Shillings' words. Three divisions. The casualties would have to be in the thousands. Perhaps in the tens of thousands. Plus the casualties inflicted on the second echelon by the Air Force, Navy, and Marine pilots and aviators. *Good Lord,* he thought.

"Okay, Kirk," said General Jeffries slowly, "what would you do now if you were in the Russians' position?"

Shillings didn't say anything at first. He instead looked

at the display. He thought about the reports received regarding enemy casualties and his own division's capabilities. Then he looked Jeffries in the eye. "I'd launch everything I had. Unlike us, the Russians have never shied away from throwing unit after unit into the fire. They know that sooner or later a breach will be opened through which they can force more men and equipment. Yes, sir, I'd hit us now and hit us hard if I were them."

Jeffries nodded. "As would I."

Chapter 6

Doctor, My Eyes

Field Hospital
Kuwait International Airport

Patrick Dillon's first act on waking was to lean to his left and vomit violently.

"That's okay, Captain," said a deep but gentle voice. "That's the anesthesia talking."

Dillon lifted his head, a head that felt as though it weighed a hundred pounds. He saw an Army doctor, a full colonel, standing at the foot of his bed. Like most military doctors the man didn't exude the authority of his rank. But he seemed friendly enough. "Thanks, sir. I feel much better knowing that it wasn't the oysters."

The doctor smiled. "Do you remember what happened? Why you're here?"

For the first time, Dillon thought about his circumstances. He looked around. A military shelter of some kind and the place smelled of alcohol and antiseptic. If that weren't enough, the doctor was a dead giveaway. Memories caught hold in his lethargic brain. The flight to Kuwait. The MiG.

"Colonel Estes? How's he doing?"

More memories kicked in. The aluminum skin of the C-5 being punctured by the MiG's cannon. Estes's body writhing next to him like a puppet.

After a few moments, the doctor spoke. "You've been out for a while."

Dillon noted suddenly that his vision was . . . different. "Colonel? My eyes . . ." As he spoke, he raised a hand to his face. As the hand passed over his right eye, darkness. He moved it away and his sight returned to its former state. He moved the hand over his left eye and there was no change; but he felt the bandages.

"Doc?" he said.

"Your left eye received some damage during the accident. Small slivers of aluminum from the aircraft."

"How long will I have to wear the bandages?"

"If you're up to it, we can see how your eye's doing now." The colonel hesitated. "With this type of injury it's hard to say what the long-term effects will be. You could see fine now. Then again, your vision might not be what it was, but gradually return later. Or . . ."

"I might never have the use of the eye again?" finished Dillon.

The colonel nodded, glad he didn't have to say the words. "If you're ready?"

"Why the hell not," muttered Dillon, elbowing his body into a sitting position, his head facing stiffly forward.

The doctor was kind enough to approach the bed from the right so Dillon could see him in his peripheral vision. He bent toward Dillon's face and tugged gently at the tape securing the padding. Dillon felt the tape give way and the gauze pad lift. As light hit the eye he squeezed it closed involuntarily.

"All right," said the doctor. "Open it slowly and tell me what you see."

After a few seconds Dillon did as he was told. The nausea returned. He knew before that something was wrong . . . depth perception, something. But now he was seeing clearly from one eye and that image was being combined with a hazy darkness. He closed both eyes again to regain a sense of normality.

"Come on, Captain," said the doctor, not unkindly. "I've heard the stories about you. Jesus, more than a couple in the past twenty-four hours. Who is that little piece of saddle leather who's been stalking the halls? Your top sergeant maybe?"

Dillon kept his eyes closed but nodded. "Rider. First Sergeant John Rider."

The doctor shook his head. "Is he always so rambunctious?"

"He's probably toning it down for you," said Dillon, a smile creasing the corners of his mouth despite his predicament.

"All right, if half of what he says about you is true, this won't be too bad. I want you to keep your right eye closed."

Dillon obeyed.

"Now open the left one, slowly."

The left eye didn't budge.

"Come on, Patrick," said the doctor. "What have you got to lose?"

"Half of my sight," muttered Dillon.

The colonel leaned into Dillon's face, close enough that he could identify Old Spice and cinnamon gum. "I'm not going to bullshit you, Pat. I'm the head ophthalmologist in country. I've seen cases like this before—flying glass, metal shavings from an industrial accident, you name it. If some type of foreign material has contacted the human eye, I've seen it. But all of the cases are different. You might never regain the sight in that eye. But guess what? A lot of men died that were on that aircraft. Worst case, you've got one eye and a full life. I'd consider myself fortunate, but you lie there and mope as long as you like." The doctor was silent for a few moments and then spoke in a quiet voice. "So what's it going to be?"

The more the man talked, the more he made sense, the angrier Dillon became. Who the hell was this rear-area asshole to judge how he should feel? He wasn't the one lying in this bed. Wasn't the one who'd seen his commander, his friend, blown to pieces. Nonetheless, he found himself slowly opening the left eye.

"Happy?" he asked in a low, guttural voice.

The doctor was already bending and looking into the eye. "Ecstatic. Describe what you see."

"Not a great deal."

"Could you be just a bit more specific?" said the doctor.

Dillon swallowed. "I can't see anything."

Dillon heard a click as the doctor turned a penlight on. "How about now?"

The black turned to gray with a slight pulsing in the center of what he assumed was his field of vision. "That's a little brighter, but I still can't see anything."

A click and the gray receded, replaced once more by darkness. "All right, Patrick, close your eyes and rest them. Nurse?"

A grim voice replied from outside the room. "Yes, Doctor?" The voice was next to his bed now.

"Could you bring me an eye patch, please?"

"Certainly." She hesitated a moment before leaving. "Good to see you awake, Captain Dillon. I assume you're responsible for that cretin outside. My nurses will never be the same."

"Oh, lighten up," said Dillon. He opened his right eye slightly, frowning as he saw the rank of a lieutenant colonel on the nurse's collar. Above the rank was a face he could only assume had just spit out a lemon. "Ma'am," he added, closing the eye again.

"I'm going to put some cream in your eye," said the colonel. "It's an antibiotic, but it will also make the eye feel a lot better. Keep it open . . . there. Now close your eye and work it around."

Dillon did as he was told. As he did so he felt a piece of gauze cover the eye. The doctor secured it with two pieces of tape. "You'll need to change that twice a day. I'm giving you two tubes of the ointment. Keep using it until it runs out."

"Wilco."

"And make sure you keep the eye covered, especially while you're still in the Middle East, where the sand tends to fly around. Not only would grit be uncomfortable but there always seems to be one parasite or another in the soil around here that just can't wait to infect the human body."

Dillon remembered a deployment to Kuwait in the late 1990s. He'd been in his battalion's S3 shop. His operations sergeant major had somehow gotten a small nick on the end of his nose. Two days later a bulbous growth had developed that was the size of a chili bean— a very angry-looking chili bean. No one knew what it was, what had caused it, or how to make it go away— which it did on its own a month later.

"I'll keep it covered," said Dillon with conviction.

"Thank you," said the doctor when the nurse returned. Dillon felt the nylon string going around his head and the slight pressure of the patch itself over his left eye. "All right, how's that?"

Dillon opened his eyes. "I'm a new man, Doc."

"Seriously."

Dillon straightened and turned his head toward the colonel. "It's much better than when I try to use both eyes at once."

"It will take a little while to get used to the limited field of vision, but not too long. I'll make a note for you to be reexamined in the States in a month."

"In the States? But I'm not going stateside, sir. I'm heading back to my company."

"You've been in a serious accident, Captain. You've seen a good friend die. You're in an area where a shooting war has already begun. And you have only one good eye."

"Your point?"

"Captain Dillon, I'm sure you think you're fine," said the colonel. "Do me a favor," he said, holding the penlight a foot from Dillon. "Grab this as quickly as you can."

Dillon reached out his hand. He missed the penlight by six inches.

"Just so we understand one another," said the colonel. "You can't function the way you could before the accident."

"The eye will heal. And I will adapt."

The doctor shrugged. "Maybe. Maybe not. I know that running around in the sand could aggravate the injury. I'm not saying it would . . . but it could. You might regain your normal vision, given time and the proper environment. I'm recommending you be placed on the next flight heading stateside. There are specialists in Colorado Springs. They might be able to help."

"Wait just a fucking minute, Doc," said Dillon, straightening. "I've got men out there—"

"Let me make one thing clear to you, *Captain*," said the doctor coldly. "I was a rifle platoon leader in Vietnam. You know what I figured out in the jungle? Your men are as good as you've trained them to be. If you've done your job and ensured they know how to fight, that's the best you can do. The world's not going to stop turning because you're not to their front. None of us is irreplaceable . . . except maybe to our families."

Patrick Dillon swallowed hard, the guilt pill going down none too easily. He'd fucked up with this guy, assumed him to be another white coat without a military bone in his body. He swallowed hard. "Sir, please . . ."

A sympathetic look crossed the colonel's face. "On the other hand, I also know how it feels to see my men heading into the shit and knowing nothing short of God himself could keep me from their side."

The doctor was thoughtful. Finally, he continued.

"Captain Dillon, I've told you what my recommendation will be, what it has to be. But I'll do this much for you. I'll leave it up to your commander. If he says you can stay, you stay. But it will be noted that it's against my better judgment."

"My commander?"

"Your *new* commander."

Dillon hadn't thought of that. Who the hell was his new commander?

The colonel was already on his way out. "He said he'd be by later in the day to check on your status," he called over his shoulder. As the doorway emptied, Dillon heard the doctor's voice one final time. "All right, Top, get in there."

Within seconds John Rider's short rangy form filled the doorway. As usual his voice sounded as if it was issued from a man three times his size. "By *God,* sir, good to see you!" he said, coming to the edge of the bed. Once there he hesitated. Finally he reached a hand out and grasped Dillon's shoulder. "Really good, sir."

"Thanks, Top," said Patrick Dillon, his throat tightening. There was the irony, he thought. As soldiers we live, fight, and die beside each other; build bonds that have a strength no one outside the military could ever understand, bonds forged in sweat and blood. But when confronted with the strength of their feelings for one another they tried to hide them beneath machismo. "It's really good to see your ugly face, too."

Rider rested on the edge of the bed. "I like the patch. You've got a whole Moshe Dayan thing goin' for you," said Rider.

Dillon raised an eyebrow. "Thanks."

"You heard about Colonel Estes, I guess?"

Dillon swallowed. "I was sitting in the seat next to him when 23mm rounds cut him down the middle," he said.

John Rider nodded. "Yeah," he said simply.

Both men sat in silence for a few moments.

"It wasn't just your aircraft," said Rider finally. "This ain't like our war against Iraq last year. Iraq didn't have a Navy or Air Force to speak of. The fuckin' Russians, on the other hand, are playing hell with our resupply efforts. We've had several aircraft with troops and equipment downed. And one of their subs got a RORO this morning."

ROROs, short for Roll-On Roll-Off, were huge ships built to carry an entire brigade's worth of tanks, infantry fighting vehicles, artillery, and all manner of supporting equipment. The loss of even one was staggering. Each M1 tank cost over two million dollars, each Bradley close to the same. Plus all of the other equipment. The loss was not only in dollar costs. It took a lot of seamen to man the ships.

"You a Tom Clancy fan, Top?"

Rider guffawed under his breath. "Sir, you know I don't have time for that shit."

"Well, I've read him a bit. And this is starting to sound more and more like *Red Storm Rising,* just in a different theater of operations."

"You met the new skipper yet?" asked Rider after a few moments.

"No," replied Dillon. "I don't even know who it is."

Rider couldn't keep the disgust from showing on his face. "Sutherland," he spat.

"You're shitting me," said Dillon.

Rider shook his head. "I shit you not, sir."

Dillon and Sutherland didn't know each other well, but that didn't change the fact that they shared a mutual distaste for each other.

A year earlier Sutherland had deployed from Fort Hood as part of a 4th Infantry Division group to Pinon Canyon, Colorado. His team had evaluated battalion-level training exercises for two weeks. During the capstone mission, Dillon's C Company was preparing to assault an enemy hilltop objective when they were told to hold and wait for air support; unfortunately for Cold Steel, they'd been within antitank missile range of the hilltop's defenders. After waiting fifteen minutes for the F-16s to make an appearance, Dillon was down to ten tanks. After sixteen minutes, he lost another tank. He'd already tried to back his company out of A.T. missile range, but another company and its associated evaluators in white-flag–festooned Hummers had taken up camp behind him. Rather than watch his unit suffer further losses waiting for the close air support—which it turned out had never shown up—he'd requested permission from Rob Estes to assault the objective. Estes agreed with Dillon's call and gave him the green light. Dillon took the objective, losing a single tank in the process, and all was well—until the After Action Review, the Army's formalized process that walked a unit through its mission from receipt, and then through planning and execution to gain lessons learned. According to Sutherland, Dillon and Cold Steel should have remained in place . . . didn't Dillon agree? Dillon's reply was that the Air Force had never shown up, he'd taken the objective, and sitting in place would have made him a dumbshit . . . didn't Sutherland agree? Things had gone downhill from there, not helped by Sutherland's appeal to Rob Estes—Estes had agreed with Dillon's decision, both on the ground and in the AAR.

"Fuck," breathed Dillon in a soft voice. "Fuck, fuck, fuck."

Rider grunted. "Yep. He is definitely *not* your biggest fan, sir."

Dillon looked at Rider straight-faced. "First Sergeant, have I told you what a comfort you are to me in my darker moments?"

Rider waved the comment off as though it were a backhanded compliment and then proceeded on with the conversation. "What I don't understand is how a man like that makes it as far as he has."

"Depends on who you talk to," said Dillon, sitting back on the bed and folding his arms across his chest. "Most people would tell you he's been riding his father's coattails."

It took a few seconds before the words sank into Rider's brain. "Don't tell me Iron John is his father?"

Dillon nodded. Major Iron John Sutherland had proven himself the best tactical commander of World War II. His exploits in France following Normandy were history and he'd ridden them to four stars. Rumor had it that the only reason the new main battle tank in development wouldn't be named after him was that the old bastard, now in his late nineties, just wouldn't die.

"That explains a lot," said Rider quietly.

Dillon nodded again. Unless he pulled his dick out and stomped all over it for the world to see, the Army wouldn't do anything to untrack Iron John's son's career.

Given the way the mood had plunged, Rider attempted to change the subject. "So when are you headin' back?"

Dillon, lost in thought, turned to Rider. "Sorry, Top. What was that?"

"When are they sending you home? You've gotta be lookin' forward to seein' Melissa and those girls of yours."

Dillon shrugged. "I've talked to the doc. Looks like I might not be going home."

John Rider's face reddened. "Sir, goddamn it, I *know* Melissa. I've sat down at her table more times than I can count. I also know your kids and can tell you every freckle on their little faces. By *God* I will not let you—"

Dillon turned a cold face to the NCO. "Steady, Top."

With an effort, the smaller man relaxed. "With all due respect, sir, *fuck you*. Over the past couple of years we've become more than commander and first sergeant. Or am I wrong?"

Dillon looked away and shook his head. "You know better than to even ask the question."

Rider wiped a hand across his face and sat on the edge of Dillon's bed. "I don't have a family, sir." He smiled warmly. "If I did, I couldn't ask for more than what you've got waiting for you in Colorado. They went through more hell last year, more not knowing than most families do in a lifetime. Don't make me be the one to have to explain to them how you had the chance to come back to them and didn't if something happens to you."

Dillon's features softened as he turned back to Rider. "Top, Melissa knows me as well as you do. Do you really think she would expect me to leave if I had anything to do with it?"

Rider shook his head slowly in resignation. "No, sir. I expect not."

"And it's not a done deal anyway. The doctor's leaving it up to Sutherland."

Rider laughed outright at the remark. "Let's see. Sutherland weighing your eyesight and future health against putting an unproven commander in command of Cold Steel as we head into combat ops—that's a toughie. Please, sir, spare me."

Dillon laughed quietly and leaned back into his pillow. "Now that you put it that way, I guess it is pretty much a done deal."

"Seriously, sir, you watch that man. I've seen a lot of different types of officers over the years. With you and Colonel Estes I always knew that as long as I was tryin' to do what was best for the men, you'd back me and take any heat that came from it." The senior Cold Steel NCO stared into space before continuing. "Sutherland's a different breed. He's out for himself and fuck anyone who gets in the way. He looks good if the unit looks good, which isn't a bad thing. But if it comes down to him or a subordinate I know the choice he'll make every time."

Dillon nodded somberly. "Noted. Now, how's the company looking?"

"Not bad. We drew equipment earlier today. The maintenance team is tweaking the tanks in the laager area as we speak. Lieutenant Wyatt, who was sitting next to your bed most of the night, is back with them now." A shadow flitted across the NCO's face. "I don't know if you've heard, but the Russians hit Doha last night, about fifteen minutes after we drove out the gate. Big air strike. Our battalion was clear, but some of the brigade's supporting units got banged up."

"But the company's intact?"

Rider nodded. "Yes, sir. So far you're our only casualty. And if it hadn't been for Boggs you would have been our first fatality."

Dillon frowned. "Boggs?"

John Rider laughed from deep in his belly. "You really don't remember much, do you? Your C-5 did a belly-skid into Kuwait International. Boggs drove me to the airport to pick you up. We were there and watching when the plane landed, for lack of a better term. Well, sir, when the C-5 finally stopped, there were military policemen and firemen everywhere. They wouldn't let anyone through. Boggs decided it was takin' too long and took off for the end of the runway, where your aircraft ended up." Rider laughed again. "Decked an MP en route. As personnel exited the aircraft he kept askin' questions, tryin' to figure out where you were. Finally ended up at your seat. He was the one that pulled you out and carried you to an ambulance." Rider shook his head, again serious. "And it wasn't none too soon. That aircraft burned pretty quick after that. Sir, I speak truth when I say you wouldn't be here if it weren't for that boy."

Dillon gave his NCO a smug look. "And you doubted my assessment of the young man."

"I don't think he was doin' it for you, sir. He said,

and I quote, 'I just wouldn't feel right, Fust Sergeant, if I had to explain to Missus Dillon how her husband died while I stood thayer watchin',' unquote.'' Rider guffawed. "Never seen a boy with such a puppy-dog crush."

Dillon smiled from his pillow, looking into space. "Melissa has that effect on men."

Rider nodded and smiled himself. "So I guess you won't mind speakin' to Sergeant First Class Stacy?"

Dillon's brow furrowed. "Who is Sergeant First Class Stacy?"

"The MP."

Dillon sat up. "The MP?"

"The military policeman Boggs slugged. He's pressin' charges."

The Steel commander settled back once more. "No worries, Top. I'll take care of it."

Rider stood. "Right-o, sir. I'm gonna get goin' and let you get some rest. If Colonel Sutherland decides to let you return to duty, I'll pick you up tomorrow."

Dillon closed his eyes as his first sergeant departed. "Sounds good, Top," he said, suddenly tired. His voice trailed off. "See you tomorrow."

It seemed only seconds later that a new voice was speaking to him. "So, how are we feeling, Dillon?"

Dillon opened his good eye. A tall, lean lieutenant colonel stood at the end of his bed, hands on hips. Dillon felt the man's cold blue eyes appraising him. Sutherland. "Fine, sir. I'll be back in the saddle tomorrow."

The visitor didn't reply. As Dillon watched the man watching him, he felt himself being dissected.

"I spoke to your doctor," said Sutherland finally.

"And?"

When it became clear after a few moments that Patrick Dillon wasn't going to add a "sir," Sutherland nodded, deciding that it was time for plain talk. "It's up to me."

What it was that was up to him didn't need to be spoken.

"And?" repeated Dillon.

Sutherland ignored the question. "We don't really know one another, Dillon, but I think we know where we stand. Correct?"

The captain remained silent.

"You didn't have the benefit of an Academy education," said Sutherland, referring to West Point.

Dillon looked at the large ring on Sutherland's hand and then back to the face of the man with his destiny in his hands. "No, sir. I did not."

The lieutenant colonel nodded. "Prior enlisted man, correct?"

Dillon felt himself getting angry. It was phrased more as an accusation than a question. "Yes, sir," he said tightly.

Myron Sutherland nodded. "Nonetheless, you seem to have done all right for yourself, Dillon. Cold Steel's a good company."

"I've been fortunate in the men assigned me, sir. They're what make Steel what it is."

Sutherland moved around the bed until he was standing directly next to Dillon. "If I let you retain command, Captain, you should know that things are going to change."

Dillon raised his one uncovered eyebrow. "How so?"

The Iron Tigers' new commander stood at the end of the bed, arms folded across his chest. Instead of answering directly, he cocked his head and peered at Dillon through cold blue eyes. "Rob Estes wasn't a bad man, Dillon. But he was weak."

Grabbing the railings of his bed, Dillon strained to a sitting position and sneered. "Excuse me, *sir,* but you wait a fucking minute . . . "

Sutherland smiled easily. "Easy, Captain. That's no way to get back to your men."

Dillon stared through hard eyes. "Colonel Estes was a fine officer. And a fine commander . . . you would do well to be half the man he was."

Sutherland waved a hand dismissively. "He was adequate at best, but he gave his commanders too much latitude."

"He had faith in his subordinates."

Sutherland nodded. "That's fine. But you will be on a tighter leash now, Captain."

"Sir?" said Dillon.

"I'm saying you fuck up in my battalion, it's your ass," replied the lieutenant colonel quietly. "Don't expect me to jump in front of any sabots for you. Am I clear?"

Dillon nodded. At least the man was honest. "Crystal."

Chapter 7

Dog Day Afternoon

Champions Sports Bar
Georgetown

The patron worked through the establishment's throng of customers. The crowd was diverse: frat boys; corporate types; lawyers; twenty- and thirty-somethings from the Hill. And everywhere one turned a television tuned in to a different sports event. The NBA was popular tonight. There was also soccer action from Europe. And a rugby match between Australia and New Zealand—the All Blacks currently leading in a close match.

The patron went around a dark corner and lifted the receiver from a pay phone, scanning the surrounding area. After depressing a series of numbers, the patron waited.

"Da?" came the electronic voice. Even if they hadn't known prior, the patron would have guessed that the voice was transatlantic by its tinny quality.

"You have a mole," said the patron simply.

The voice on the other end switched to English. "How do you know?"

"Trust me. Check your people. The president knew the offensive was beginning well ahead of time. That spells leak."

"Thank you."

The patron hung up and walked away from the phone, disappearing into the crowded bar.

1st Cavalry Division TAC
Southwestern Iraq

"SITREP," said Jack Jeffries.

"Sir, UAV feeds indicate that the Russians are coming in mass," said the division intel officer. "For the most part we're talking T-80s and BMP-3s. It looks like they have some T-90s holding back, waiting to exploit any breach in our lines."

"Range?"

"Lead units are within five kilometers."

Jeffries turned to the M. "All units . . . engage at will."

The 1st Cav commander knew that the Russians would hammer his team with artillery before they were within the T-80's main gun range of twenty-five hundred meters. His own M1A2-SEPs could kill out to almost twice the T-80's range, and Jeffries intended to make the most of that advantage before the Russian artillery struck.

The results of the fuel analyses had been conclusive. The Russians had sabotaged their fuel supplies with a type of biological agent. Unlike normal bio agents that were designed to infect the human body, these were designed to attack the anatomy of war machines: fuel lines disintegrated; engines seized; tanks and Bradleys dead in the water. Jeffries had diverted what precious fuel remained to his reconnaissance elements for the earlier fight, plus a little to top off his attack aviation as a backup.

The general heard MLRS rockets and artillery flying from positions behind him. The crack of American tanks joined the fray. The general watched the monitor that digitally displayed every vehicle in his command. He backed out of the display with a few keystrokes until only the company-sized units remained on the monitor—finer details would simply mean sensory overload. Every time a friendly tank or Bradley lased an enemy vehicle or an American UAV confirmed an enemy position red icons appeared on the display opposite his blue forces. While the blue were significantly outnumbered, the red forces were disappearing almost as fast as they came up on the screen.

"We're kicking some serious ass," said someone from the rear of the command track watching the electronic reproduction of the battle.

"Yes, we are," said Jeffries. Then he pointed to the red icons picked up by the UAVs that were outside of his forces' direct fire range. "But there's a whole lot more coming."

Slowly but inexorably the red icons closed. As they came in range of American combat systems many disappeared; enough remained. Those that did continued to the northeast, closing on the 1st Cavalry's positions.

Jeffries shook his head. "My God," he said. "We must have destroyed another two divisions, but they just keep coming."

Blue icons began winking out. The enemy was in main gun range of their tanks. The time ticked by as the battle raged on. Overhead artillery and rockets from both sides filled the skies. So far no chemical strikes. The Russians, confident in their numbers, had apparently felt the risks of using such extreme measures were not justified. After a half hour few of the blue company icons remained. Jeffries expanded the view on his display to include all of the 1st Cavalry's individual fighting systems. As a division commander he would normally see hundreds of icons—tanks, Bradleys, howitzers. He saw that his forces now numbered less than one hundred and that the numbers were falling. As good as his men and their machines were, the bottom line was that if they couldn't move they couldn't continue the fight.

He yanked off the headset he'd been using to monitor communications. "That's it. I won't throw away the lives of men who can't fight. Put the word out . . . all units, main guns elevated and to the rear. Cease firing."

"All units have reported, sir," said an aide after a few minutes. "They're adhering to your guidance and have gone into nonaggressive postures."

Jack Jeffries laughed to himself. "Nonaggressive postures." Well, it sounded a lot better than "surrender."

Kirk Shillings pointed at the screen. "Mother of God."

Jeffries grimaced. Blue lights continued to wink out. "The sons of bitches."

Despite the fact that the American forces facing them had surrendered, the lead Russian forces were continuing to destroy everything in their path. It was also clear that they were making a beeline path toward the 1st Cav's TAC. Grabbing his Kevlar, the general moved toward the exit. "Get my driver. By God, I will not stand by and watch this."

"Sir—" began Shillings.

"Just get the goddamned driver!" yelled Jeffries. He stopped at the exit and turned back to his maneuver assistant. "Please, Kirk. Just do it."

Shillings nodded. "Wilco, sir."

Jeffries, followed closely by the ever-faithful Phantom, departed.

After the general exited Shillings turned to a major. "You tell that driver to get the biggest piece of white fabric he can find and to hang it from the tallest antenna on that Humvee."

"Halt," called Colonel Sergei Sedov to his driver over the T-90's intercom system.

As the Russian tank came to a stop, Sedov raised his field glasses. His regiment was the lead unit in the exploitation—his dead countrymen to his rear in their older T-80s had paved the way to get Sedov and his men this deep. The T-90s had already passed through the forward American positions and were well into the rear now.

The Russian commander pulled his binoculars up to check out a large dust cloud coming straight toward him—it was a lone American all-terrain vehicle, a Humvee. Sedov smiled. "Message to all units, do not engage the crazy American."

The Russian pulled himself from the T-90's turret and stood on top of the tank. Smoothing his tunic, the colonel moved to the front of the turret and hopped down onto the hull. Another jump put him on the desert floor facing the rapidly approaching Hummer. It stopped in front of him in a hail of dust.

"Are you the ranking officer of this unit?" asked a large American as he leaped from the passenger seat of the vehicle. Behind him a small white dog with brown ears and spots bounded from the Humvee and followed in the large man's wake, hackles up.

Sedov looked at the dog with a smile and then looked to the American. He saluted. "General Jeffries, your fame precedes you."

Jeffries returned the salute. "And you are?"

"Colonel Sergei Sedov. And to answer your question, yes, I am in command of this regiment."

"And are you aware, sir, that the men of your regiment are blatantly violating provisions of the Geneva Convention by shooting American combat crews who are clearly in the act of surrendering?"

Sedov, ignoring the question, bent to pick up the small dog. "A Jack Russell, yes?"

"Yes," said Jeffries tightly. "Now would you answer my question? We realize you sabotaged our fuel supply. The fight is over, Colonel. I have surrendered my command and insist that your unit act in accordance with international agreements to which it is a signee." The pain in the American general's eyes was clearly visible. "There's no need for wholesale slaughter."

The Russian stroked the terrier's fur. Despite the attention the animal was restless, growling low in the back of its throat. "Wholesale slaughter?" asked Sedov, amused.

Jeffries stepped forward, looming over the Russian. "Let's not play games. You attacked across a border that is friendly to the United States. You got your ass waxed. Now the endgame is near, at least so far as my unit is concerned. But you continue to pump rounds into vehicles that cannot fight back. That, sir, is slaughter."

Sedov smiled as he reached for his sidearm with his free hand. "No, sir," he said, pulling the 9mm GSh-18 pistol smoothly from its holster. "*This* is slaughter."

Jack Jeffries's face had just enough time to display a look of shock before the 9x19mm round entered his cranial cavity through the center of his forehead. There was little blood as the general was dead before his heart could take another beat.

A movement from the direction of the Humvee caught Sedov's attention. He calmly watched as Jeffries's driver pulled an M16 rifle up and began to level it at him. The young American's body suddenly began dancing as if on invisible strings, struck by a three-second burst of 7.62mm machine-gun fire.

"*Spasibo,*" murmured the Russian colonel, glancing over his shoulder. *Thank you.* The tank's coaxial machine-gun barrel was still smoking. As ever his gunner had been itchy to get involved in whatever action presented itself.

The Russian squatted next to the body of Jack Jeffries. "Technology has made you and your army soft, General. You do well when your opponent is at long range, when you can use your satellites, unmanned aerial vehicles, and smart munitions with little threat of retaliation." Sedov spat in the face of the corpse, smiled sardonically, and stood. "Welcome to the world of real combat."

He scratched the back of the dog's neck and looked down to him. "And what of you, my furry friend?" The Jack Russell had become strangely silent since the shootings. Sedov placed the terrier on the tank's front slope and squatted to look him in the face. "How would you like to defect, my small friend, to become a mascot for Mother Russia, hmm?"

The dog stared into the Russian's eyes. The Reverend John Russell, the Englishman credited with breeding the terrier known today as the Jack Russell, did not have family pets in mind when he began experimenting with strains of fox terriers in the mid-1800s. Russell sought an animal that was small and compact enough to follow quarry into its underground burrows; with the patience to remain in a dark, subterranean world for days on end if necessary; and with the strength and ferocity to kill its prey in tight quarters and drag the carcass into the daylight. And the English minister bred a final characteristic into his dogs: loyalty to the death. Staring into the animal's face only inches from his own, Colonel Sergei Sedov was ignorant of these historical canine facts.

Without warning, without uttering a sound, Phantom leaped on the Russian. The terrier's small, sharp teeth bit deep into his enemy's nose, clamping down with the force of a mini bear trap. Sedov screamed. Arms flailing, the colonel fell over backward in a cloud of dust. The dog's efforts intensified as the Russian landed with a thud on his back. Phantom shook his head back and forth with sharp jerks of his small but powerful neck.

Sedov grabbed his attacker with both hands as he flailed on the ground, but when he tried to tear the animal from him the pain in his face blazed white-hot. The dog refused to relinquish its hold on his nose. More pain as Phantom's rear paws dug furiously into his neck, instinct telling the canine that his enemy's throat was a point of vulnerability to be exploited.

As he struggled with the dog on the ground, the Russian caught view of his gunner. The sergeant had come topside to investigate the noise. His bloodlust apparently unquenched, the NCO was pulling his pistol from its holster.

"*Nyet,* you fool!" screamed Sedov through clenched teeth.

The sergeant reluctantly lowered his weapon and jumped to the ground in two bounds. "Try to keep him still, Colonel," said the man.

As the gunner approached, Sedov grabbed Phantom's shoulders, holding the dog as steady as possible under the circumstances and trying not to scream as he felt canine teeth crunching into nose cartilage. The dog was so intent on the task at hand that he didn't notice the Russian NCO's approach. The sergeant bent over the struggling figures and delivered two sharp, powerful blows to the small animal's neck with the flat edge of his hand.

With a yelp Phantom released his hold and turned to meet the new challenge. The noncom's lips twisted into a leering semblance of a grin. The dog bit at rough leather boot. Kicking at the animal's head, the sergeant pulled his pistol once more from its holster, cursing at the white-and-brown dog as it went after his legs.

"*Nyet!*"

The NCO turned to his commander. Sedov was dragging himself from the desert floor. The colonel straightened his nose, a bloody piece of meat. In a voice almost too low to hear, a voice full of barely suppressed rage, he repeated the command. "No," he said. "That little bastard is mine."

Phantom turned his attention from the NCO to the colonel. He didn't understand human speech, but the speaker's tone had a threatening quality that penetrated to the part of the brain that identified and differentiated between threats. Keeping the sergeant in his peripheral vision, the dog focused his attention on Sedov. Baring his bloody fangs and squaring off, the animal growled deeply from his chest.

Once more the sergeant appealed to the colonel. "Sir, let me deal with him. You are in no condition to—"

"Yeb vas," growled Sedov. *Fuck off.* Pulling the GSh from its holster, the Russian officer raised the 9mm with a shaky arm, aiming toward the dog five meters away. Slowly, by sheer force of will, the colonel steadied his arm.

Phantom was a soldier's dog. He'd accompanied Jeffries everywhere and thus knew what the glaring black eye at the end of a steel barrel meant. With a final snarl he spun and sped into the desert. Sedov's bullet was a microsecond late, dust rising from its point of impact— the spot where the Jack Russell had stood only moments before. The dog rapidly receded into the desert haze.

"Machine gun! Now!" screamed Sedov. White spittle foamed at the corners of his mouth.

The sergeant didn't need to be told twice. In seconds he dropped into the T-90's turret and jumped into the gunner's station. He put his face to the sight piece. The tank's turret swung in the direction the dog had bounded as the Russian tried to locate the animal. Nothing.

"Switch to thermal sights, damn it!" yelled Sedov from outside the tank.

"Da, da . . . ," murmured the gunner, switching his sight from normal daylight view to thermal. After a few moments, the gunner yelled. "I have him, two hundred meters out!"

"Fire!"

Without acknowledging, the gunner engaged. The small hot spot, a white-green against a darker green background, veered right as 7.62mm machine-gun rounds erupted in front of him. Having fired his sensing burst and now with a feel for the engagement range, the sergeant fired another long burst. Just before the stream of lead impacted, the dog jinked to the left.

"That is not a dog, it is a devil," whispered the gunner. Putting his face back to the sight once more, he saw nothing but desert. Where the hell . . . ?

"Did you get him?" called Sedov, clambering back onto the tank.

The gunner took up a quick and careful box search pattern of the area he'd last seen the dog. Nothing.

Sedov reached into the turret and grabbed the first-aid kit. Pulling antiseptic and gauze from the box, he looked into the turret. "I said, did you kill that damned creature?"

The sergeant was still looking through the sight, and he still saw nothing. "*Da,* Colonel," he said after a few moments' consideration. He looked up through the turret hatch, sweat beading between his eyes as he stared at his commander. "I got him with the final burst."

The Russian officer nodded, satisfied. "Good. Now help me bandage my face. I do not want to pass out from loss of blood just as we are about to complete the greatest Russian military victory in a half century."

Hours later, miles from the site of his confrontation with the Russians, Phantom emerged from an opening in the desert floor, nothing more than a small slit in the ground barely large enough for him to squeeze his compact frame through. His short coat was smeared with dirt and fresh blood. Feeling cool night air gently blowing across his muzzle, the dog raised his snout. Sensing no threat, he relaxed for the first time in hours. He stood, his body stocky and solid, sniffing the night air. He knew his master, the tall human whom he'd accompanied all of his remembered life, was gone. Lowering his head, Phantom whined the pitiful and heart-wrenching mourning sound peculiar to canines. And then he made his way alone into the open desert.

Brigadier General Kirk Shillings was now the de facto 1st Cavalry Division commander. As night fell he continued the effort he'd begun hours earlier—to get all of his personnel possible aboard UH-60 helos and behind friendly lines.

He knew what had happened to Jeffries; not all of the details, but close enough. He and the rest of the staff had seen Pegasus 6's Hummer, in the form of a blue icon on their situation display, speeding to meet the lead Russian forces. The blue diamond had stopped directly in front of the leading red diamond. Within minutes, the red icons had continued pushing northeast. The blue icon representing his commander's vehicle had remained where it was, the red icons pushing past it one by one.

Shillings's face had taken on a steely resolve as he'd reached for the handset linking him to his brigade commanders. "*All First Team units, this is General Shillings. Pegasus Six is down and I've assumed command. The Russians are taking no prisoners . . . literally. I want those units capable of resisting to give those bastards everything you've got. Buy us some time to evacuate casualties and everyone else we can. Acknowledge.*"

One by one the subordinates had called in. Some reported that they'd already lost contact with entire companies. One brigade had lost all contact with one of its battalions, a unit of over seven hundred men.

The rest of the combat-effective 1st Cavalry units had opened up with everything they had. As their fighting vehicles had been rendered immobile, they were in effect fighting from steel pillboxes. The M1A2s pumped out 120mm sabot, HEAT, and TERM rounds. Bradleys fired every 25mm cannon round available, every TOW anti-tank missile they could find. They fought until the ammo ran out—or until they were destroyed. Many of the tankers and mech infantrymen then jumped to the ground, taking whatever cover they could find—and if none was available, they hunkered behind their tanks and Bradleys—to continue the fight with small arms. Infantry squads fired Javelin antitank round after Javelin antitank round from their foxholes with telling effect. Air defenders joined the fracas, lowering their weapons systems from the skies whenever possible and mowing down Russian armor and infantry with their cannons. Engineers continuously sacrificed themselves to enemy machine-gun fire, running into thick fires to rebuild minefields manually when their automated systems were depleted; dozens of their bodies hung like scarecrows in the concertina forward of the 1st Cav positions. The destruction these men wreaked on the Russians was huge, but ultimately the enemy force's numbers made the difference.

A captain walked to Shillings's side and stood quietly as the general watched his monitors. Both men watched with sad eyes as another American unit fell. One of the monitors displaying real-time UAV feeds showed several Russian T-90s at what had been the 1st Cavalry's last defending company position. A Russian tanker in black coveralls held the unit's tattered green-and-yellow guidon in one hand and a PP-90M1 submachine gun in the other. Four captured American soldiers stood by, hands in the air, in front of what had been the company command post. In the blink of an eye the enemy soldier raised the wicked-looking black submachine gun and sprayed the captured soldiers with 9mm fire. He stuffed the guidon into a cargo pocket and walked from the camera's view.

A tear slid down Shillings's cheek. This wasn't war. Becoming aware of the young officer standing next to him, Shillings turned to him. "Yeah, Bill?"

"Last chopper's ready to go, sir."

The general nodded and picked up a white phosphorous grenade that had been standing by. "Everybody loaded up?"

The captain looked uncomfortable. "Everybody that's going, sir."

"What's that supposed to mean?"

The younger officer shrugged. "The chopper can't hold everyone, sir. A couple of personnel are staying back. They will attempt to exfiltrate by land."

Shillings nodded knowingly. "You and who else?"

The captain, Shillings's aide of the past nine months, knew better than to try to figure out how his boss had known he was one of the volunteers. "Sergeant Jameson."

The two cav troopers fell into stride as they turned and walked from the command center. On reaching the exit Shillings pulled the pin on the white phosphorous grenade and threw it into a pile of combustible materials. As the first flames licked up he and the captain walked out. At least the bastards wouldn't be able to take any of the command center's high-tech gear to Moscow for reverse engineering. The WP grenade had a bursting radius of seventeen meters and would burn for roughly a minute at five thousand degrees. All that would be left was slag.

Shillings and the captain were halfway to the UH-60 Black Hawk that waited, rotors turning, when the command post detonated. White smoke billowed and flames shot out, illuminating the night for hundreds of meters in every direction. A short distance from the helicopter, far enough away that the dust being blown into a sandstorm around the chopper's turning rotors wouldn't flay the driver's skin to the bone as he waited, was Shillings's Hummer. The driver was clearly visible by the flames of the burning command post.

As Kirk Shillings approached, the driver saluted. "Sir, you need to get the hell on that chopper . . . ASAP or sooner." The sergeant pointed at his watch for emphasis. "There ain't a lot of time, General."

"Still trying to make sure I stay on schedule, Sergeant Jameson?"

"I'm tryin' to save your ass and get my own on the trail," said Jameson, jerking his thumb northeast toward friendly lines.

"Have you got enough fuel?"

The NCO nodded. "I drained out the bottom of all the generators. Took a while, but she's topped off and I've got a couple of spare five-gallon cans."

"Water and rats? Ammo? Night-vision equipment and batteries?"

The sergeant was getting impatient. "Yes, sir . . . now *go*."

Shillings reached out and pulled the stubby M4 carbine from Jameson's shoulder. "Get on the chopper, Sergeant."

"No way, sir."

Shillings gave the NCO a look that was taught only at Generals' School.

Jameson shifted uncomfortably. "Sir, I'm not going to let you do this."

"You don't have a choice. I'm giving you a direct order. Now go."

The crew chief of the Black Hawk ran over. He was out of breath and his aviator helmet bounced clumsily on his head. "Gentlemen, our window of opportunity is rapidly diminishing. The Russians are en route and we know they still have air defense systems left. We've got to lift off."

Kirk Shillings turned to his NCO one final time. "Sergeant Jameson . . . Jay . . . I'm single. I've got no wife, no children. Can you say the same?"

The sergeant didn't bother replying. They both knew he had a wife that worshipped him, a five-year-old son whose T-ball team Jameson coached, a six-month-old daughter with huge blue eyes.

Shillings walked around to the passenger side of the boxy all-terrain vehicle. "Get out of here, soldier."

Jameson gave a salute and a knowing nod. "Yes, sir."

Shillings turned until he heard the NCO call again. "Sir?"

"Yes?" said the general impatiently.

The sergeant's face was solemn. "Thanks, sir."

Kirk Shillings winked. "Get the fuck out of here, Jamie."

The NCO sprinted for the chopper as the captain got in the Hummer and started its engines.

Shillings entered the vehicle and was about to shut his door when the unmistakable sound of a 125mm tank cannon cracked over the noise of the helicopter's props spooling up to lift off. No friendly armor had a 125mm main gun; therefore the Russians were in the wire. This was confirmed moments later when the tank came into view, illuminated by the CP's flames. The captain jumped from the Hummer and ran to the back cargo hatch, lifting it as Shillings watched the tank preparing to take another shot at the unscathed Black Hawk. Nose down, the UH-60 was hugging the ground and moving east. But it wouldn't be a contest this time—the Russian tank's stabilized fire control system could easily track, engage, and destroy the slow-moving helicopter before it was out of range. The Russian gunner had fired his first round in a rush, just as surprised to see the large American helo as they had been to see him. He was taking his time now. Shillings saw the big Russian gun make its final lay—then a large whooshing sounded and a blast of light issued from behind the Hummer.

Shillings turned to see his aide with a Javelin antitank missile launcher at his shoulder. Turning back to the T-90, Shillings saw the Javelin's 8.4kg HEAT warhead as a blur coming down from the sky, impacting into the tank's turret. A catastrophic detonation followed close behind. The T-90's main gun sagged to the ground in mechanical surrender. No one made it out of the flaming tank.

The captain hopped back into the driver's seat in time to see the Black Hawk disappear into the eastern night sky, running lights blacked out. Throwing a set of PVS-7 night-vision goggles attached to a head harness to his face, the captain turned to Shillings. He looked insectile in the weak light. "Ready to roll, sir?"

"You have any more Javelins back there?"

"Nope."

"Then let's get the hell out of here."

The two men, the last living members of the 1st Cavalry division remaining in the field, disappeared into the desert's embracing darkness.

Chapter 8

Archangel

President Konstantin Khartukov sat behind his desk staring at nothing. "You are certain?"

His guest nodded and reached for the bottle of chilled vodka on a nearby sideboard. "Yes." He did not elaborate on the source of the information and Khartukov didn't ask him to.

Mikhail Lavrov directed the Foreign Intelligence Service, or SVR, the agency that had replaced the KGB in modern-day Russia as being responsible for foreign intelligence activities. Khartukov had known Lavrov for years and knew that the former KGB man rarely made mistakes. That was one reason he was selected for his current posting. If he had real doubts, he wouldn't have come forward.

Khartukov slammed a hand on his desk, angry. "A mole. I cannot believe it."

Lavrov seemed amused as he returned to an armchair with his glass. He sipped from it. "Why should yours be any different from any other political administration? It happens."

"But we screened our people so thoroughly. . . ."

"Yes, sir, I'm sure you did," he said. "Tell me this—how many people had knowledge of our forces' timetables?"

Konstantin Khartukov shrugged. "A handful—most of them military officers, for obvious reasons."

"Your personal staff?"

The Russian president shook his head. "No."

"None of them?"

"Isn't that what I said?" he snapped. The president then seemed to hesitate for a moment, but in the end he shook his head, dismissing the idea.

"What?"

"It is nothing," said Khartukov in an amused tone.

Lavrov leaned forward. "You never know. What did you remember?"

"My chef, he was fussing about over dinner and coffees when I spoke with the Saudi crown prince."

The SVR man's mouth smiled slightly. "Claude, isn't it?"

"Yes."

"Isn't he, how do I say this . . . a little light on his feet?"

"He's a fucking queer is what he is," snorted Khartukov. "I am having difficulty seeing him as the weapon of choice the United States would send into the lion's den."

Lavrov turned thoughtful. "That is true . . . very true. I think I shall speak with him."

"Claude? I truly cannot believe he is a cause for concern. A leak from the Saudi side perhaps?"

"I doubt that very much," said Lavrov with a quick shake of his head. "They have as much or more to lose from this than we do. Claude, on the other hand . . . it would be a masterstroke for a government to place an operative so clearly homosexual in place as a source."

Khartukov shook his head again. "My people were very thorough in checking his background before he became a member of my staff. They placed acoustic sensors in place to capture sounds from he and his—friend's—quarters."

"And?"

The Russian president laughed deep in his throat. "Trust me. He is the real thing."

"Still, I would like to speak with him," said the SVR director, rising. "Unless you prefer I do not? I realize this is a counterintelligence matter, but if I hand it over to the FSB . . . well, it may be in their purview, but I prefer not to get into a situation similar to the one the Americans find themselves in, that of having my asset compromised."

Khartukov waved a hand in the air. "By all means, you handle the matter. I'll take care of the FSB if they find out and get into a territorial dither over it." The Federal Security Service, or FSB, was the SVR's sister bureau, responsible for counterintelligence and suppression of groups attempting to attack Russia's constitutional system. "But do not stay long on this tangent. Satisfy your curiosity, but we need to find the true leak quickly."

Lavrov nodded. "Of course, Mr. President."

Thirty minutes later, a light knock sounded on Lavrov's door. "Come in," he called.

The knob turned and a tentative hand appeared around the edge of the door, followed very closely by a face. The rest of the man's body remained hidden, protected by the thick oak door. "Yes, sir, Mr. Director. The uh, the uh . . . President Khartukov phoned me at my quarters and said you would like to see me?"

The man phrased it as a question rather than a statement, the SVR director noted. He knew that no one was keen on being summoned to the SVR or FSB offices. While neither's reputation was something parents used as a tool to frighten their children, as the KGB's had been, both organizations remained frightening state apparatuses about which little was known to most Russians. Many said this was warranted, that the SVR and FSB were smoother in dealing with the outside world than their predecessors had been, but that there was little real difference in results. Citizens still disappeared at night into Lubyanka's environs, never to be seen again. The hulking pink-and-yellow neoclassical building, a fixture of Moscow tours, had already outlived one Soviet regime. And now it had become the home for the state security apparatus of a new government.

"Please," said Mikhail Lavrov, smiling disarmingly, "come in and sit down." He indicated a chair next to his desk. "Thank you for coming on such short notice, Claude."

The man's file described him quite accurately, Lavrov noted. Just under six feet tall; lean; striking blue eyes; dark complexion, almost Mediterranean; short black hair spiking out at every angle. And on his way to the president's quarters to begin preparing dinner, if his white cooking garb were any indication.

Claude folded himself into the chair and crossed his legs in the manner that a woman would, one leg lying along the other. "It is not a problem, Mr. Director, but I must be in the kitchen soon. If I do not begin sautéing the mushrooms . . ."

"Not to worry," Lavrov said and laughed. "And please, call me Mikhail. We culinary artists must stick together."

Observing his guest, the SVR agent thought he saw something—guardedness? wariness?—cross his face. If it had been there it was like a shadow, there and gone in half of a heartbeat.

"You cook, Mr. Dir . . . Mikhail?"

"I am not in the same league as you from what I have heard, Claude, but I dabble. Primarily in Oriental dishes."

Claude leaned forward. "Ohhhh, *mar*velous. Mandarin?"

"Vietnamese actually. I spent a great deal of time in Hanoi during my younger days."

The chef's eyes sparkled. "And your specialty?"

"Bun bao," responded Lavrov without hesitation. "It is—"

"Marinated beef flank," finished Claude with a laugh and a clap of his hands. "I find the most critical aspect of the preparation is—"

"Ensuring the peanuts are dry-roasted—not too much, not too little—or the dish is a ruin," Lavrov interrupted with a grin.

A giggle erupted from Claude. "You *do* know your Vietnamese cuisine, Mikhail."

Lavrov raised his hands in a self-deprecating fashion, but he was clearly pleased. "As I said, Claude, I dabble." The SVR man's smile cooled imperceptibly. "Claude, do you mind if I ask you a few questions?"

Finding himself thrust back upon unfamiliar ground, the chef answered hesitantly. "No, of course not."

"Are you married, Claude?"

"No . . ." He hesitated.

"Come now. A handsome fellow like yourself? No girlfriends?"

"I have a . . ." Claude hesitated, looked away. "A companion," he managed to finish.

"Ah, a *companion*. And her name?"

"Niki."

Mikhail Lavrov leaned forward, feigning an air of concern. "And *Niki* is short for what? Nicole? Is this woman a foreigner?"

Claude lowered his eyes. "Nikolai," the chef said in a low voice.

The agent's eyes twinkled and he nodded. "I understand now." Lavrov leaned over the desk. "Tell me,

Claude, have either you or—Niki—traveled abroad since your arrival in Russia?"

"Niki was in the Army. I believe he was stationed in East Germany in the late 1980s. . . ."

"Yes, I know of that." Lavrov smiled reassuringly. "What of yourself?"

"I . . . I returned to Paris for a year of culinary studies. It was approved by—"

Lavrov's hand made a dismissive gesture. "Yes, yes, I'm sure your studies were in order. But tell me, Claude, have you or Niki ever traveled to the United States?"

No hesitation. "No."

"Do you know any Americans?"

Now the chef hesitated. "I wouldn't say I *know* any. I have met a few here in Moscow while sampling the fare of the city's cafes and bistros. . . ."

Lavrov seized on this. "And do you know if any of them are associated with the American embassy? Have any of them asked you questions about the president or government affairs in general?"

"No," said Claude with a firm shake of his head. "I would remember that."

The director leaned forward. "You are certain?" The tone was accusatory.

Claude nodded. "I am certain."

Lavrov lit a cigarette as sweat glistened on his guest's brow. *This is like the old days in Lubyanka,* he thought with a smile, beginning to enjoy himself. He thumped ashes into an iron government ashtray without taking his eyes from Claude. "And were you ever offered money for this information?"

"No . . . I mean, as I said, I have never been asked such questions."

"And what of Nikolai?"

Claude squirmed. "What of him?"

A tendril of smoke slowly escaped from Lavrov's lips.

"Living so close to the West when East Germany was on the verge of collapse, perhaps someone approached him, encouraged him to put himself in a position to obtain state information; perhaps something along the lines of establishing a relationship with a deviant member of some influential minister's staff, eh? But the *president* . . . even better."

Tears sprang to Claude's eyes as he shook his head in denial. "That is not true. I knew Niki before I began working for President Khartukov. . . ."

Lavrov stood slowly and extended his hand. "That will be all, Claude. Thank you for dropping by. Perhaps we can do it again sometime?"

Uncertain, Claude stood. "Why . . . certainly, Mr. Director."

Lavrov grinned. "Perhaps we can exchange recipes, eh?"

"Yes. Certainly," said Claude, heading for the door.

Lavrov gave the chef time to depart the area then depressed a call button. "Tatiana, please send in Agent Gryzlov."

"Certainly, sir," came a mechanical response.

A few moments later, the door opened and Oleg Gryzlov stepped into the office.

"Hello, Oleg. Come in, come in."

Lavrov rose from his desk and waved the chief of Khartukov's protective detail to a seat.

"So, Mr. Director"—the burly agent winked—"to what do I owe this honor?" The men had known each other for over ten years and had shared many rounds of vodka.

Lavrov shook his head. "Nothing terribly important, I'm afraid. I wanted to pick your brain regarding one of the president's staff."

Oleg Gryzlov winked again. "Claude?"

"You saw him leaving the building, correct?" Lavrov smiled.

"Correct, Mikhail, correct," said the agent. "But do not worry, he did not see me."

"Very good. So . . . I assume you had him checked out thoroughly when he first insinuated himself with the president?"

Gryzlov laughed. "Mikhail, he is *harmless,* I promise you. A man could not ask for a better sister. And yes, he was checked out. But you knew that, yes?"

Lavrov nodded. "All right, all right, I did." The Russian shook his head, though obviously some vestige of concern was nagging him. "Still, there's something about him that I can't put my finger on."

"Rest easy, my friend," said Gryzlov with a grin. "Claude is harmless, trust me. Now, where's the vodka? I know you wouldn't invite an old comrade to your office and leave him thirsty."

The SVR director looked at his watch. Late afternoon . . . what the hell. He opened the door of a cabinet next to his desk and pulled out a bottle of Stolichnaya and two glasses. "I apologize," he said. "It is not properly chilled. Emergency rations, you might say."

"Because of our years of friendship, I forgive you," said Gryzlov as he accepted a glass and let Lavrov pour.

"To Mother Russia," said Lavrov, raising his glass, deciding that the two minutes of prose normally associated with a Russian toast were not necessary.

"Mother Russia," replied the security agent, raising his own.

Both men sipped for a few moments. Gryzlov broke the silence. "So, Mikhail, what bothers you so about our friend, eh? I know you well. Your inviting me here was perfunctory. I interact daily with someone you have questions about, so you want to speak to me about him as a matter of course." He raised his glass and pointed an index finger at Lavrov. "But now that you've met him, something bothers you other than his sexual orientation, yes?"

Lavrov nodded. "It was something in his eyes. When I attempted to put him at ease, told him to call me by my Christian name . . . for a moment I'd have sworn the eyes looking at me were scoffing, the eyes of a professional insulted by an amateurish technique."

Gryzlov sat forward. "Mikhail. I *know* Claude. It was your imagination."

Lavrov raised his glass. "You are likely correct, Oleg."

The Oval Office
Washington, D.C.

Chris Dodd paced in semicircles around the heavy blue rug, unconsciously avoiding the embroidered presidential seal.

The president sat to one side of the office, also thoughtful. He looked up at the CIA director. "Chris, sit down. You're wearing my nap out."

Dodd turned and collapsed into a heavy leather chair.

"You're sure they're onto your man?" asked Drake.

The younger man shook his head. "No, Mr. President, I'm not. But I am certain they're onto the fact that he exists." Dodd looked pointedly at his boss. "And I'm also certain someone with Archangel access has been talking to Moscow."

Drake grunted. "Son of a bitch," he muttered.

Archangel was the code name for both Dodd's source in the Kremlin and for information originating from him. Access to any aspect of Archangel was highly restricted. The handful of people with access were not only high-ranking, but had a defined need to know.

"Does anyone, other than you, know Angel's identity and position in the Kremlin?" asked Drake. He had made it a point that he himself did not need to know, guaranteeing no slip from his corner during midnight conferences when his mind was a blur.

"The DDCI," he said, referring to the deputy director

of Central Intelligence. "And my director of operations. That's it."

Both men were silent.

"And . . . ," Dodd began a moment later, thoughtful.

"And what?"

The DCI shook his head. "Nothing."

Two hours later Dodd's car pulled into the CIA's complex in Langley, Virginia. As it entered the grounds Dodd leaned forward from the backseat and patted his driver on the shoulder. "George, how about pulling in front of the old headquarters building? I'll walk from there."

The driver, a large black agent who'd commanded a U.S. Marine infantry company before moving on to the CIA, nodded. "Yes, sir. Any idea on your schedule for the rest of the day?"

Dodd shook his head as he opened his door. "No. Go grab a sandwich in the canteen. I'll give you a call if I need you."

As the car pulled away Dodd walked slowly to the lobby of the old headquarters building and opened the door. Turning right he stopped in front of a long sheet of marble: the Agency's Memorial Wall. Sculpted into stone were seventy-eight stars. Each star represented an officer who'd fallen in the line of duty. Of the seventy-eight operatives represented, only forty-three were identified in the Book of Honor that rested on a marble shelf below the five rows of stars. The other thirty-five names remained a national secret because their revelation could endanger other men and women in the field. Above the stars was a simple inscription: IN HONOR OF THOSE MEMBERS OF THE CENTRAL INTELLIGENCE AGENCY WHO GAVE THEIR LIVES IN THE SERVICE OF THEIR COUNTRY.

Dodd pulled a secure mobile phone from his pocket and dialed a number from memory. "Angela? Chris Dodd. I'm stuck at Langley all afternoon, but there are a couple of things I'd like to discuss with you. If you don't mind making the trip, I'll throw in a tour of the facility and dinner." Dodd nodded, listening. "Great. I'll see you at four."

Flipping the phone shut, Dodd continued to gaze at the wall. In times of crises it reminded him of what the Agency was really about—or at least what it was supposed to be about. He made a silent vow that Archangel would not become the latest anonymous star.

Angela Bennett wiped mayo from the corner of her mouth. "So, Mr. Big Spender, this is what you consider a dinner date?" she asked, arching an eyebrow.

Dodd smiled. "I would have taken you for a smoked turkey girl: whole wheat bread; lettuce and tomato; fat-free mayo; a couple of slices of bacon when you're feeling naughty."

The two civil servants sat at a side table in Dodd's office. The setting sun, visible through a nearby window, lent the room a pinkish cast.

Bennett returned the smile and shrugged. "What can I tell you? I'm a carnivore through and through," she said through a mouthful of corned beef.

"Grooowwwwllllll," said Dodd. "But that's our natural place in God's universe, isn't it? Despite what Californians would have us believe."

His dinner companion raised her wine. "I wouldn't have thought that you spend much time considering the higher universe and its natural order. You're just such a . . . *man*."

Dodd frowned. "I'll choose to take that as a compliment. And I'll have you know that I think about God and his creations a great deal. I have a particular fascination with angels."

"Do you really?" Bennett asked, looking around the room as though she might see something in the office that would lend validity to the statement.

"Oh, yes. Particularly the archangels."

"The archangels," said Angela. "And if I remember correctly, they are—"

"Angels created with a specific mission in mind by God," continued Dodd. "They engage upon these missions with absolute passion, perseverance, and devotion."

Angela Bennett put down her sandwich and clapped. "Very good. So Michael's mission was . . ."

"Protection."

"And Gabriel's . . ."

"Resurrection."

"You win," said Bennett. "My knowledge of the upper echelons of heavenly beings is now officially tapped."

"You mean you've never heard of the Archangel Luke?" he asked with a smile.

Bennett stopped, the sandwich halfway to her mouth. "The Archangel Luke? Was he related to the Archangel Ralph?"

"You know, Angela," said Dodd, "I think you know more about this particular angel than you're letting on. Why don't you share, hmmm?"

Angela Bennett sensed the conversation had taken a subtle but significant turn. Across the table, Chris Dodd was relaxed, too relaxed. Like a wolf that sees a rabbit caught in a hunter's trap relaxed; all the time in the world relaxed.

Dodd popped a fry into his mouth and reached for his beer, a Fat Tire Ale, available only within a couple of hundred miles of Fort Collins, Colorado. His smuggling network to keep the Fat Tire in stock was his way of living on the edge these days. Taking a pull, he looked at his dinner companion with eyes suddenly flat.

"Archangel," the CIA director repeated, sitting back. Reaching into a side drawer he pulled out a .45 caliber Colt Gold Cup Trophy and put the large pistol on the table next to him. The move had been nonchalant, but Angela Bennett couldn't miss the fact that the gun's gaping maw pointed directly at her.

Bennett took a deep breath and then spoke quietly. "Chris, I'm going to say this one time—I have absolutely no idea what you're talking about." She stood. "I'm leaving now. Thanks so much for a wonderful dinner."

As she turned toward the door the cocking sound of the big Colt was loud enough to stop her in her tracks.

"I'm afraid I can't let you do that, darling," said Dodd.

Bennett turned to face him. "Okay, Chris, I'll play. Who or what is Archangel?"

Dodd waved the big stainless steel automatic toward the recently vacated seat. "Sit."

Bennett moved back to her seat and sat down. Shoving her half-finished sandwich to the floor, she settled her forearms on the table. "One more time, Chris . . . what the hell do you want?"

Dodd grinned and shook the gun back and forth in front of her slowly. "You're very good, I'll give you that. It's going to be a shame when I call in the security detail stationed outside of the office," he said, nodding toward the door ten feet away, "to haul your lovely ass to a dark hole where you will rot for the remainder of your natural life."

Bennett stood again. "Okay, I get it—you're insane." She bent over the table and looked into his eyes. "Now hear this and hear it clearly. I'm leaving. If you want to shoot, then shoot. But that's the only way you're going to stop me." Turning on her heel, she took two steps before he spoke. The voice was no longer aggressive; the tone was that of a man with no hope.

"Archangel is my brother."

Bennett turned to him. "And . . ."

Chris Dodd put down the pistol and collapsed into his chair. In his time Dodd had been the best clandestine operative in the business. Unfortunately for him, his management and political skills were the equal of his street smarts and thus he now found himself in the heretofore unimaginable hell of being a bureaucrat. But his field instincts were still razor sharp and they were screaming at him now—Angela Bennett wasn't the leak.

He rubbed his eyes and then placed his hands flat on his thighs. He looked up wearily at Bennett. "Sit down."

Bennett stared at him from across the room.

"Please."

She walked back to the chair and sat. "Talk to me."

Dodd looked her over. Could he trust her? He thought so. God only knew he needed to trust someone.

"Archangel is my brother," he repeated. "My brother Luke to be exact."

"And Luke is in Moscow, correct?" asked Bennett.

Chris Dodd nodded. "As I told you, all of God's archangels have a single purpose, a single mission."

"And Luke's purpose . . ."

"To get close to Konstantin Khartukov and be prepared to take whatever action necessary should the insane son of a bitch ever come into power," said Chris Dodd.

"How close is he?" she asked.

Dodd smiled, but there was fear in his eyes. "Oh, you'd have a hard time getting much closer. And did I mention to you that we have a leak?"

Angela Dodd stood. "What's your driver's name?" she asked.

Dodd looked at her quizzically. "George. Why?"

"No questions," she said, holding out her hand. "Phone."

He pulled a small Motorola from his belt and placed it in Angela Bennett's outstretched hand. She studied the phone a few moments, just long enough to figure out its basic functionality, and then depressed the radio button. "Are you there, George?"

The surprised voice of the ex-Marine responded in seconds. "Yes, ma'am. Who is this? Where's the director?"

"He's here with me, George. Could you meet us with the car at the front entrance?"

The voice on the other end was all business. "Ma'am, you sound cute, but if I do not speak with the director in the next ten seconds . . ."

Dodd gave Bennett an impish grin and held out his hand. "George is worse than my mother about my mortal welfare. Better give me the phone or you're going to have six feet four inches of concerned bodyguard banging down the door."

Taking the phone, Dodd raised it to his lips. "It's all right, George. We'll meet you at the front."

As they walked to the door, Dodd turned to Bennett. "So where are you taking me?"

"My place."

Dodd raised one eyebrow. "Why, Ms. Bennett . . ."

Angela Bennett threw a well-aimed elbow into her escort's ribs. "Don't flatter yourself. We need to talk. And from the sound of it, it may take a while."

"Talk? What is there to talk about? If you're not the leak, I don't know who is. We're at a dead end."

"We'll worry about that later," she interrupted. "For the moment let's worry about keeping our angel's wings from getting clipped."

Chapter 9

_____

_____

Cyclops

The men of Patrick Dillon's tank crew stood outside of the C Company command tank, C-66. The other men of Cold Steel were methodically conducting last-minute precombat checks. The majority of the company's soldiers had been through a war together in the not-too-distant past and knew that attention to detail would ultimately save time and lives.

But these three stood waiting, watching as a blurry shape emerged from the band of desert haze on the horizon. Rider had radioed only minutes ago that he and Dillon were five minutes out and the crew wanted to be on hand to welcome the Old Man back. Not once over the past two days had the crew discussed the possibility that things had come close to working out very differently. The gunner, Sergeant Randy Bickel, and the driver, Specialist Donnie "Tommy" Thompson, had been members of Dillon's crew during the previous year's fighting. They knew Dillon and they trusted his judgment implicitly. Bo Boggs had only just joined the crew, but Dillon had shown faith in him for some unknown reason; plus there had been the C-5 crash in Kuwait City. The private felt he had a vested interest in Dillon's health.

"Sergeant Bickel?" said Thompson.

Bickel, like most tankers, was of average height and thick of chest. A natural gunner, he'd moved into the gunner's seat of an M1 tank earlier than most. Perpetual squint lines creased the corners of his eyes, signposts to the years he'd spent staring through gun sights. When the gunner looked at something you could almost see him estimating range, speed, and direction.

"Yeah, Tommy?" said Bickel.

The tank driver watched the distant speck take on the outline of a Humvee. "Do you think he's really all right?"

Bickel didn't answer for a moment. When he did it was with a confidence that he didn't feel. "If the C.O. didn't think he could fight this tank and company, he wouldn't have come back." Rider's driver, after speaking to one of the nurses at the field hospital, had already sent into the Cold Steel grapevine the story of how the doctor wanted their commander on the first plane back to the States.

Thompson looked uncertain.

The gunner glared. "The man knows his limitations."

Thompson nodded. "I hope you're right."

"I am," said Bickel, ending the conversation.

Two minutes later John Rider's Hummer slowed to a stop next to the command tank.

Patrick Dillon stepped from the vehicle dressed in olive drab Nomex coveralls, web gear, and Kevlar helmet. And of course wearing the eye patch. His men watched him intently.

Before anyone could exchange greetings, Top Rider returned from a trip to the back of the Hummer carrying a rucksack. "What with all of your shit getting toasted, I threw some TA-50 together for you; spare Nomex, a couple of pairs of BDUs, the regular kit." He held the olive drab bag out to Dillon.

With great deliberateness Patrick Dillon reached for the bag and grasped it. He didn't yet trust that his synapses were firing the correct target location data to his brain. The doctor had told him there was no way of knowing with any degree of certainty how long it would take his mind to compensate for losing half of his eyesight.

The men walked around to the opposite side of the vehicle. Dillon stuck out his hand. "Thanks, Top. For everything."

Rider took the proffered hand firmly in his own. "Sir, like I told you in Kuwait City, you've got no business being out here," he said in a voice low enough that Dillon's crew couldn't hear his words. Before Dillon could respond, the senior NCO squeezed Dillon's hand and continued. "But with the shit that's comin' at us, I'm damned happy you are." Rider grinned, remembering something. Reaching through a backseat window, he grabbed a plastic bag and tossed it to Dillon.

Dillon snatched it from the air without thinking. Only after he held the bag firmly in hand did it occur to him that his reflexes were much better if he didn't think so hard. "What's this?" He dug into the bag and pulled an object out, grinning. "Top, Melissa's going to kill you."

The first sergeant held up a hand in self-defense as Dillon shook one of two dozen cans of Copenhagen in his face.

"Sir, *she* gave me those, before I boarded the aircraft in Colorado."

Dillon was amazed. "She did? But why?"

"She said to give them to you only if I deemed it absolutely necessary. Emergency rations if you will."

The burly captain shook his head. "And what made you think it was necessary to give them to me now?"

Rider frowned. "The nurses told me you were asking for cigarettes after Sutherland left the room; that situation is only going to get worse. If you need nicotine, I figure Melissa would rather deal with a nasty habit she knows than a brand-new one."

Dillon was already running a fingernail beneath the lip of the snuff can's lid. "Have I told you lately that I love you, Top?"

With that Cold Steel's senior enlisted man turned on his heel and hopped into his vehicle. "I'm off to the combat trains, sir," he said with a wink and a wave. "I'll see ya on the high ground."

Dillon watched the Hummer recede to the north, thanking God that in John Rider he had more than just a great lead NCO. With an effort the captain turned to his tank and crew. The four soldiers regarded one another warily. Dillon was exactly where he wanted to be, where he desperately needed to be. Yet he was afraid that his injury might cause harm to these men, who were such an intimate part of his life, who would depend on him in the coming days even more than the rest of the company.

"So," said Dillon finally, "what the fuck are you dickweeds staring at?"

Boggs pointed at his face. "Captain Dillon, suh," the loader said in his heavy twang, "I would nevuh presume to speak for the rest of the crew, suh, but that eye patch . . ."

Unconsciously, Dillon reached toward the damaged eye. "What about it?"

Boggs ran a hand along his chin and cocked his head to one side. He turned to Randy Bickel. "Why, I think it looks rathuh *rakish*. Don't you, Sergeant?"

Bickel laughed, jumping down from the tank's front slope in a cloud of dust. He took Dillon's rucksack and threw it on top of the turret. "Boggs, you are so full of shit."

"Why, Sergeant Bickel," Boggs drawled, "you are surely not the fust to say so, by any means."

Tommy Thompson jerked a thumb at the gun tube. "What do you think, sir? Sort of a welcome home gift."

Dillon looked at the M1A1's long gun tube. At first, he didn't know what Thompson was talking about. Then he saw it. "I can see I'll get no sympathy here," he said dryly.

Tank crews name their own tanks. The basic rule is that the name begins with the company's assigned letter designation, in the case of Cold Steel, because it was C Company, the letter *C*. C-66 had been known as Cap'n Crunch throughout Dillon's tenure as commander of C Company. His crew, ever sensitive, had renamed it on hearing of Dillon's return. The tube now bore in large black letters the name *Cyclops*.

It's going to be all right, he thought. Mounting the front slope carefully, he pulled himself onto his sixty-eight-ton steel steed. "All right, let's get the fucking show on the road. Tommy, get your ass in the driver's hole and start her up."

"Yes, sir," said Thompson with a smile, jumping to the tank's front slope and nimbly clambering into his driver's hatch. He pulled on his CVC helmet and hit the start button. The fifteen-hundred-horsepower turbine engine whined into life. When hearing the sound for the first time, most people remarked that it sounded more like a helicopter spooling up than a tank starting.

As Dillon climbed from the front slope to the top of the turret he saw Boggs standing by the loader's hatch, grinning at him.

Dillon looked at him. "What?"

The young soldier stared, continuing to grin. "Suh, I realize I don't know you so well as Sergeant Bickel and Tommy, but . . . well, you had faith in me, suh, and I won't let you down. And I cannot imagine what Missus Dillon would have done if . . ." He came across the turret in two quick steps and wrapped Dillon in a bear hug. "I know I speak for the entire crew when I say it's good to have you back, suh. *Damned* good."

Dillon stood stock-still, twisting his head sideways after a couple of seconds to seek aid from Bickel. The gunner had already begun to clamber down the tank commander's cupola en route to his station in the forward part of the turret. He stopped.

Dillon raised an inquisitive eyebrow.

"Forgot to tell you, sir," said the NCO. "Boggs gets a little emotional from time to time. I think it's all that sensitivity crap they're spewing out in Basic Training these days. The Army will never be the same."

Dillon could only manage an acknowledging nod. Bickel disappeared, leaving Dillon and the loader standing alone atop the turret.

"Boggs," said the Steel commander.

"Yes, suh?"

"You've got to let go of me now," said Dillon.

The loader, as if suddenly aware of what he was doing, pulled back. "I'm sorry, suh. . . ."

Dillon held out a hand. "Did I tell you thanks for pulling my sorry ass off of that aircraft?"

"Suh, I assure you there's no need. As I said, I couldn't let anything happen to Missus Dillon's beloved."

"Thanks," said Dillon quietly.

Boggs smiled. "You're welcome, suh."

"And Boggs . . ."

"Yes, suh?"

"If your ass isn't in that tank and setting up the radios in two seconds, it *will* be mine."

As he looked at the empty swath of turret that his loader had occupied moments earlier, Dillon smiled and hopped into his cupola, half of his body remaining exposed as he stood on his commander's seat. Sliding his

Kevlar helmet off, he placed it into the sponson storage box to his right. Reaching forward, he removed his CVC helmet from its resting place atop his .50 caliber machine gun. A fresh coat of sand-colored paint had obviously been applied within the past day and his skull emblem on the helmet's front section freshened. Dillon settled the helmet on his head. Reaching into the turret the Steel commander grasped the end of his communications cord and plugged it into his CVC jack.

Reaching up, Dillon toggled the CVC's intercom switch. "All right, you jackasses, give me a crew report." He smiled. It was good to be home.

The two American infantrymen heard the Black Hawk before they saw it. Both dropped the entrenching tools they'd been using to improve their fighting position. Coming in from behind them it hovered on line and fifty meters to the south of their foxhole. Phase Line Doberman was the FLOT, or forward line of troops. Everything forward, or south and west of the FLOT, was Indian Country. The American troops in its vicinity kept a wary eye out at all times.

The Black Hawk, covered in antennas, hovered close to the ground. It rose slowly, keeping its position relative to the ground beneath it fixed. Whoever was on board wanted a look forward of the friendly positions.

"Antennas mean brass is on board," said one soldier to the other knowingly. "The more antennas, the higher the brass."

The other infantryman began counting antenna. "So who do you think it is?"

"Oh, I know who it is. Only the colonel has the balls to fly all the way to the FLOT in a Black Hawk and do a pop-up—"

Four streams of tracer rounds raced toward the Black Hawk. A ripping noise accompanied the streams of large-caliber fire. The UH-60's pilot, quick on the collective, threw his aircraft to one side and down. The aerial skid stopped twenty meters short of the earth.

The two soldiers on the ground missed the show. Both had dived into their fighting position as soon as the Russian air defense system had fired. Within moments one of them had thrown an M240 Squad Automatic Weapon, or SAW, over the lip of their position. The gunner extended the 7.62mm machine gun's bipod and was now glued behind the SAW's sight, scanning back and forth over his sector of fire. Nothing moved.

"It's clear," he said after a few seconds.

He and his partner looked to the helicopter. It had landed. They watched as a few soldiers hopped to the ground and spread out, securing the perimeter.

"Guess they don't figure landing in the middle of a company position is secure enough," remarked the gunner.

His partner snorted. "I'd be a little jumpy myself if I'd been in that chopper."

Once the security detail was set a large figure deplaned. He was immediately followed by another soldier just as tall but not nearly as thick through the chest and shoulders. Finally three other camouflage-clad men climbed from the chopper, one of them running a few feet away and falling to his knees a split second before projectile vomiting.

The gunner grinned. "How much of that do you think was goin' on inside the aircraft?"

The second soldier smiled and nodded. Both had spent plenty of time flying nap of the earth during training exercises to know that it's not wise to eat too close to flying. "That's gonna be one unhappy crew chief," he said. "Hopefully it wasn't Italian. Tomato-based puke is a bitch to clean."

The large soldier and his companion began walking toward the soldiers' position. As they approached, the pair in the hole could hear the thinner soldier. "Sir, I tried to tell you. But as usual, you don't listen. Noooooo, for you it's, 'Pilot, we've got to get a little higher or else this is just a wasted trip.' Just once I wish—"

"Goddamn it, O'Keefe, can you give it a rest?" He paused just long enough to snake a pack of cigarettes from a pocket. A silver Zippo flashed, there and gone. "You're as bad as my wife; no, come to think of it, you're worse. At least she gave up on me years ago."

"Oh, shit," said the gunner's partner. "That's the brigade commander."

The gunner nodded over his SAW. "The man, the myth—Jones."

As he did now, Jones had commanded the 3rd Brigade of the 4th Infantry Division (Mechanized), better known as the Striker Brigade, during the last Gulf War. The men under his command then knew that in large part Jones's tactical genius and sheer unmitigated cast-iron balls were responsible for them both winning the battles they had fought against overwhelming odds and for them still being alive.

Jones stopped short of the fighting position. They noted the man who'd been chewing Colonel Jones's ass was a staff sergeant.

Jones turned and looked southwest and then back to the men manning the fighting position. He took a deep draw on the cigarette and nodded toward the direction of the helo. "How'd you boys like the show?"

"Hot shit, sir," said the gunner. "But we'd kind of like to keep you around for a while."

The NCO behind Jones looked as if he was going to wade in on the issue and continue his haranguing. The colonel didn't even look back. He'd known it was coming and merely outstretched an empty hand with index finger extended toward the staff sergeant's face, cutting him off before he had a chance to start.

"Yeah, you're right, Corporal. Figured they had some

air defense forward, but I didn't know they'd be *that* close."

A high, whistling noise sounded.

"Incoming!" yelled the gunner. He and his partner dove to the bottom of their fighting position.

The artillery continued its flight, passing well over the FLOT. Seconds later a series of detonations was heard to the south and west.

"It's all right, gentlemen. That was friendly arty."

Two Kevlar helmets slowly rose above the edge of the fighting hole, followed by two sets of rapidly scanning eyes. Both heads stopped their ascent until they noticed Jones standing nonchalantly in the same spot he'd been in before their dive. He was cursing under his breath now, his cigarette already smoked down to a stub and an empty pack in hand.

The gunner fished his own pack out and held it up to his commander. "How'd you know, sir?"

"Thank you, son," said Jones, taking the pack. "But these things'll kill you. You should quit."

"Well, isn't that the pot telling the kettle he should change his colors," muttered O'Keefe, standing between Jones and the Russians to the south.

He might bitch, thought the corporal, but it was clear that any enemy soldier who decided to add a silver eagle to his collection was going to have to go through the NCO first. Then his memory clicked. The staff sergeant was O'Keefe, the colonel's Bradley gunner. Prior to the war, no one seriously thought a BFV's 25mm cannon was capable of taking out anything newer than circa 1950s tanks. During an exchange on the second day of the war O'Keefe had proven the critics wrong, using the new depleted-uranium version of the shells with telling effect on the Republican Guard's T-72Ms.

The colonel ignored the NCO's jibe. Handing the cigarettes back to the soldier he winked. "To answer your question, it was the acoustic signature," said Jones. "It would have been fifty to seventy-five decibels higher if the artillery were going to impact danger-close."

The men looked at one another and then back to Jones. "Sir?" said the gunner.

Jones laughed, rocking back on his heels. "Okay, you got me. I'm talking out of my ass, gentlemen. I knew it was friendly because I called for it. No more ZSU 23-4 to fuck with Mrs. Jones's little boy."

The soldiers assumed a wary upright position in the hole once more. "So what's the word, sir?" asked the gunner. As a corporal, he was the senior of the two men.

Striker 6 turned serious. "I'm not gonna lie to you, boys. It ain't good."

The corporal nodded to the southwest. "They're comin', ain't they, sir?"

Jones pulled on the fresh cigarette, exhaling slowly. "Yeah. They're comin', son. They're comin'."

The younger of the two men, a PFC, hesitated, then said, "Sir, how is everybody else doing?"

Extending an arm to the right, Jones pointed north. "Iraqis held up damned well in the northern desert," he said, referring to the terrain in the northern half of Iraq that bordered Saudi Arabia. "The terrain is rocky. Lots of wadis. A division of Russian tanks got the idea they could maneuver through it. Iraqi mech infantry taught them otherwise."

Most full colonels would have left it at that when speaking to their troops. Many of them would have merely given a perfunctory "they did a damned fine job," and left it at that. William Jebediah Jones was of a different breed. He believed his men functioned better when given the facts. He also knew the soldiers he spoke to would pass on the words from him as gospel from the mount, dispelling the rumors ever-present among the ranks.

"The Kuwaitis didn't fare so well," said Jones. "Their two forwardmost brigades held their ground for an hour or so."

"And . . . ," prompted the corporal.

A frown flicked across Jones's mouth. "Then the Russians ground them down with pure numbers. Of course, the bad guys had a surprise waiting for them at that point." The colonel smiled.

"What was that, sir?" asked the PFC, breathless and leaning forward over the lip of the foxhole. Information like this was hard to come by at the front. They were soaking it up.

"They ran into the U.S. Marines and a crazy leatherneck colonel by the name of Owen Hazzard. Those devil dogs de-boated and hauled ass across the desert faster than I'd have given any mechanized unit credit for. They punched Ivan in the nose and backed off before he had a chance to bring superior numbers to bear. Last I heard the Russians were regrouping down there." Jones smiled. "Seems no one told Hazzard he was outnumbered, outmanned, and underequipped for the task of going toe-to-toe with Ivan's armor, so he's gone on the attack."

"What about the first Cavalry, sir? They had to have done all right with all of those M1A2s and other fancy toys of theirs," said the corporal.

Jones looked away and thumped his cigarette to the ground. "They're gone," he said quietly, digging the butt into the sand with the heel of his boot. "The Russians threw several divisions at the cav's center. Most of the Ruskies died. I have no doubt that the cav would have stopped the bastards dead in their tracks if they'd been able to move. But as it was . . ."

The conversation came full circle. "And now they're comin'," said the PFC.

The colonel nodded. "Them and/or the Saudis. Either way, our lines have been breached, and it looks as though Third Brigade will have to step into that breach if the enemy is to be stopped."

The two young soldiers glanced apprehensively at one another. Understandable, Jones thought, considering what they were facing and the fact that neither was yet of legal drinking age. "Don't worry, boys, I've got a couple of ideas."

The soldiers smiled at one another. When Jones had an idea that meant bad news for the enemy.

He looked at the two men closely. "Were you two with me last year?"

Both men stood a bit straighter. "Yes, sir," said the corporal. "Both of us."

The Striker Brigade commander nodded. "Good enough."

And with that he walked away.

Chapter 10

Moscow Knights

The Kremlin
Moscow

"Will there be anything else, Mr. President? Perhaps a glass of brandy?"

"No, thank you, Claude."

The chef turned toward the young lady seated across the table and smiled with genuine warmth. "And for you, *chère*?"

Natasha Khartukov was in her late twenties. Tall and slender, she had her late mother's raven-black hair and eyes the color of sunlight reflecting off of Siberian snow. Her high cheekbones and slightly too-long nose lent her an aristocratic countenance ignored by few.

A graduate of Moscow State University with a degree in foreign languages, Natasha had taken advantage of her father's posting to the Russian embassy in Washington to attend Columbia University. While working on a master's of international affairs degree in Columbia's prestigious School of International and Public Affairs she'd taken on a part-time job translating at the United Nations. She'd fallen in love with both New York City and the U.N. On graduation from Columbia she'd continued her work at the United Nations, accepting a low-level posting with the Russian mission. Natasha had ex-

celled and was ultimately offered her current position—
assistant to the mission's Permanent Representative of
the Russian Federation to the United Nations.

Natasha returned the chef's smile, recalling their first
meeting. . . .

A year earlier Natasha had taken a leave of absence
from the Russian mission when her mother was diag-
nosed with breast cancer. She and her mother had always been close, more like sisters than mother and
daughter. After months of treatment and a radical mas-
tectomy, Inessa Khartukov had finally succumbed to the
ravages of her disease. At the funeral, despite the presence of her father, Natasha had felt more isolated than
at any time in her life. While Konstantin Khartukov was
stony-faced and dry-eyed, his daughter knew overwhelming grief lay hidden beneath the mask.

Always pushing for the upper levels of power—both
as a member of the Committee of State Security and
later in politics—Konstantin Khartukov was a ruthless
man. Natasha grew up hearing the whispers of other
children when they learned her father was a member of
the feared KGB. He never discussed this side of his life
at home, but Natasha knew that her mother had not
been happy about her husband's choice of professions.
Despite this Inessa Khartukov was true to the Russian
meaning of her name, *pure*. She'd loved her husband
with heart and soul. And he'd returned her love with
the same fervor. As she grew older Natasha often
thought her father's love for his wife was the lone golden
thread holding his soul together, the lone goodness that
kept him from turning into something dark. And then
she was gone.

Moscow's skies had been dark and overcast on the
day of the funeral. At the grave site her father had sat
next to her, silent and unmoving. They could have been
two strangers. Natasha had cried quietly, wishing the ser-

vice would end, allowing her to go home and deal with the grief threatening to overwhelm her. When at last it did she had walked forward and placed a single white rose on her mother's coffin. Natasha kissed her fingers and placed them gently next to the rose. *"Good-bye, Mamasha,"* she whispered.

She'd turned to her father. Retaining his seat, he'd continued staring at the coffin. "Papa, will you ride with me?"

His gaze had not moved from the grave. "No," he'd said in a flat voice. "You go along. I have a dinner later with some supporters. It is important."

Tears had spilled unbidden down Natasha's cheeks. "Can you not take *one day* from your precious mission to become Russia's next czar to grieve for your wife?"

Her father had turned his head then, looking her in the eyes. "I do not enjoy a sufficient advantage over my opponents to enjoy that luxury," he'd said quietly. "Your mother would have understood."

"What about me then, Papa? I'm still here. Can you not take a few hours from politics to comfort your only child at the loss of her mother?"

He'd faced back toward the casket. "I am sorry. No."

Natasha had turned then, shoulders slumped, and walked toward a waiting automobile at the opposite end of the cemetery. Blinded by tears, she stumbled and began to fall. A hand with a grip of iron had reached out to steady her.

"Careful, *chère,*" a quietly masculine voice had whispered in her ear.

Wiping her eyes with a handkerchief, Natasha had looked into the eyes of Claude Chapelle.

"It's all right," he continued in a soft voice. "I will walk with you, *non*?"

Natasha had nodded gratefully, taking the Frenchman's arm. Though they had not spoken, she recalled being introduced to Claude when she had arrived from America.

"*Bon*," said her savior. *Good*.

They'd walked slowly, paying no attention to the other mourners.

"The pain will pass, you know."

It had taken Natasha a few moments to assimilate the words. She'd glanced sideways at him and dabbed at her eyes with her fingertips. *Where the bloody hell had that handkerchief gone?* Without looking, Claude had passed his own to her.

As she put the proffered cloth to her face, Natasha had paused. The handkerchief had a subtle scent that reminded her of the sea, of wooden merchant ships plying the Caribbean with a cargo hold full of spices.

"Not to worry," he said with a wan smile. "It is . . ." He'd paused, seeming to search for the proper word. Then he'd smiled. "Unsullied."

They had continued walking, winding their way between tombstones.

"How do you know?" Natasha asked in a soft voice.

Claude had not asked her to explain the question. There was no need. "We all experience pain. Grief, it is part of the human journey, *chère*. If we will love, we must do so knowing that someday we will pay a price. For one way or another, we always lose the ones we love."

He had smiled at her once more, a knowing look in his eyes. "I for one am willing to pay the price. After all, what is life without love?"

When they'd reached the waiting black sedan Claude had opened the door and helped Natasha in, closing it behind her. She'd rolled down the window and looked at him then, clearly a question in her eyes.

"What is it?" Claude had asked. "Is something wrong, *chère*?"

"You . . ." Natasha had stopped, at a loss for words.

"I . . . ?"

She had frowned. "You do not seem . . ."

"Do not seem what, *chère*?" he had asked, a smile playing along the edges of his lips.

She had seen the realization reach his eyes. "I did not mean to pry . . . I mean, really it is none of my business."

Claude had wrinkled his nose at her and gave a flamboyant shooing gesture. "Do not worry yourself. You will have to work harder than that to offend me." He paused. "Love is love, *chère*. The fact that I am a homosexual makes the love no less real." He had tapped on the driver's window then and motioned for the man to move out. "Go home and get some rest, *chère*. I will bring you a cup of my hot chocolate later. It is simply *decadent*."

As the driver had pulled into the Moscow streets, Natasha had brought the handkerchief to her nose once more and smiled. She would have expected a more feminine scent.

Three days later she had returned to New York. But in those three days a friendship that had begun in a rainy Moscow cemetery had blossomed.

And now she was back in Moscow. And things had changed dramatically since her visit three months earlier. Her father had realized his dream. He was president of Russia—and she feared he was going to drive the country she loved into ruin. That was why she'd come back, to talk sense to him; to talk him out of this mad scheme. But it was too late. The United States and Russia were in a shooting war.

"*Chère?*"

Returning to the present, Natasha smiled. "No, thank you, Claude."

"Not even a cup of my cocoa?" he asked with a wiggle of black eyebrows.

For the first time in days Natasha Khartukov laughed. "No, thank you. But dinner was delicious. It is a good thing that I am returning to New York tomorrow," she added. "I would be as fat as a cow if I continued eating from your table much longer."

"What do you mean, returning to New York?" Khartukov interjected.

Natasha turned to him, surprised. "Why, to my job of course, Father."

The Russian leader's voice was flat. *"Nyet."*

Natasha turned eyes of arctic fire on her father. "What the hell do you mean, no? I am a grown woman. One well capable of making her own decisions."

"Not this time, Natasha. Have you not thought of what the American government would give to have my daughter in their hands?"

Natasha shook her head slowly. "Father, I am a representative of the Russian Federation to the United Nations. The American government would never—"

Khartukov did not give his daughter an opportunity to finish the sentence. He wiped his lips with a heavy linen napkin and pushed himself from the table. As he stood the napkin hit the tablecloth with a dull thud. "That is the end of the discussion, Natasha. They will never get the opportunity. At least for now you must remain in Moscow. Once this crisis works itself out we will discuss your return to the mission further."

"But, Father, I phoned Dr. Frolov last night and told him that I was returning. He has sent a private jet." She glanced at her watch. "It should be landing at Sheremetjevo-Two even as we speak," she said, referring to Sheremetjevo International Airport, twenty miles outside of Moscow.

Konstantin Khartukov grimaced and waved a well-manicured hand in the air. "Frolov is of no consequence. I am replacing him with a more suitable representative later this week."

Natasha slowly came to her feet. Father and daughter squared off against one another across the remains of duck à l'orange. "You mean someone more willing to look the other way as you stomp your people and the world beneath your jackboot! Ever since Mother died you have done nothing but—"

"Enough!" Khartukov was livid. "The servants have prepared a room. Your belongings will be fetched from your hotel later this evening."

"You can only push me so far, Father," Natasha said in a quiet voice. "I know you have the power to keep me from leaving Russia, but you most certainly do *not* have the power to keep me from walking out of this room and back to my hotel."

The Russian president's parental skills might be lacking, but reading people was one of his strong suits. He knew his daughter's threat was not an idle one. For now he'd settle for her remaining in Moscow. "Very well, my dear. But I insist that a security detail accompany you. There are subversive elements who might not understand that you and I do not share the same ideology."

Walking for the door, Natasha called over her shoulder. "No. Claude will be my escort. I do not want your storm troopers within a mile of me."

The chef looked to his employer.

Khartukov nodded. "Go, Claude. And for God's sake get her to the hotel as quickly and quietly as possible."

Claude nodded once and left. Khartukov sat down and bellowed through the door. "Oleg!"

Oleg Gryzlov entered silently. "Yes, Mr. President?" said the security man.

"You heard?"

Oleg nodded. Khartukov was well aware that every room in the house was bugged as Khartukov was the one who insisted on constant monitoring.

"Take two men and follow them. Be discreet and do not let Natasha see you, whatever you do."

The big Russian nodded and left.

Natasha bundled her heavy coat about her. The sky was clear but the temperature hovered just above freezing. "The *bastard,*" she said vehemently in a low voice.

Claude began to reply. Thinking better of it he kept his mouth shut.

Their footsteps echoed hollowly as they walked the five blocks to her hotel. Since the government had cracked down on the populace, Moscow's nightlife had declined. They were in their own cold world.

"Why can't more men be like you, Claude?" she said quietly, looking at him with a sad smile.

He returned the smile, reaching up to grasp the hand she'd placed through his arm. "Well," said the Frenchman, winking, "the male population would certainly have a better collective fashion sense if that were the case."

"That is true." Natasha laughed. Her eyes twinkled. "I'll miss you, Claude, if I ever leave. . . ."

A woman's scream interrupted Natasha as they passed a dark alleyway. It was followed by a broken cry. "Help me!"

Running around the corner, Claude and Natasha were ten feet into the alley when they saw her. Quiet now, the screamer leaned against a wall, her face illuminated by a burning cigarette. The woman smiled at them as though sharing a private joke.

"What is this?" asked Claude incredulously. "Why would you do that?"

"Good evening."

The voice was behind them. Turning to the alley's entrance they saw the dark shapes of four men detach themselves from the shadows. One, the speaker, stepped forward. He was a large man, well over six feet and broad through the arms and chest. An arm flicked out and the unmistakable sound of a blade snicking open was clear in the crisp night air. Weak streetlight silhouetted the figure and gleamed off the knife's long, narrow blade.

"What do you want?" asked Claude, unconsciously stepping between Natasha and the figure.

Without replying the man turned to the woman and tossed a roll of rubles. She snatched them from the air and walked away without further word or glance. The man turned and walked slowly toward his newly arrived victims, knife arm extended toward the ground.

"Do not come any closer," said Claude, voice rising.

The man continued his approach. "Or what?" he asked with a low laugh. "You sound like my sister. Are you going to stop me? Please."

Claude didn't reply, instead bracing himself in a parody of a fighting stance. This elicited laughter from the band of thugs.

Natasha stepped from behind Claude. "Leave him alone, you buffoon. I'll scream. The police would be here in minutes."

The ringleader caught a glimpse of Natasha's long legs and fine features before Claude stepped in front of her again. "Well, well," he breathed. "And to think all we wanted was your cash and jewelry. It looks as though we'll receive a bonus tonight. A tasty bonus, eh, lads?"

General shouts of agreement and catcalls sounded from the other three.

The big Russian smiled. "But I'm first," he said, taking a step forward. A bright light broke the night and shined on the man. He turned in surprise, forearm over his eyes to keep the light from completely blinding him.

"Stop where you are," called an authoritative voice. Natasha and Claude recognized it as Oleg's. As they watched, he and two other men from Khartukov's security force entered the alleyway at a run.

"Drop the knife." Oleg's pistol pointed at the group's

leader. It was clear that he hadn't yet seen the man's accomplices. "Now."

"Oleg," called Claude. "Behind you . . ."

Before the would-be rescuers could react to the warning, the leader's henchmen launched themselves from the shadows. Wielding homemade clubs, they quickly disposed of the two Russian security officers trailing Oleg. Oleg himself, a few feet farther away than his men, turned and fired. One man went down before the leader's knife sliced along Oleg's arm. Dropping the pistol, Oleg turned toward his attacker in time to catch a boot in the stomach. Sagging to his knees as he gasped for air, Oleg couldn't move in time to miss the second kick. It landed squarely across the bridge of his nose and the large Russian agent dropped like a stone.

Stepping to the now inert form, the lead thug slid the pistol a few feet from Oleg's hand. He then turned to Claude and Natasha. "Where were we?" He smiled. "After that buildup, I'm expecting quite a performance from you, young lady."

A look of resignation passed over Claude's face. "Put the knife down and leave," he said quietly.

A puzzled expression flitted across the face of their attacker. In some subtle way the situation had changed. The Frenchman, there was something different in his tone, in the way he held himself. There was no pretense of a fighting stance now, but rather a relaxed alertness; the voice was steady, not shrill; and his eyes were as cold as ice. But what really bothered the large man was that Claude no longer seemed frightened. Rather, he seemed—bored.

Natasha too had sensed the change in her friend. "Claude?"

"Stay back, Natasha. Everything will be fine."

"Fine? How can you say everything will be fine?"

The large man moved with a quickness surprising for

someone of his size. The knife flashed up toward Claude's stomach.

The man's last coherent memory of the evening would be the ghost of a smile that flicked across the Frenchman's face just before his hand snaked out, smashing into the bridge of the Russian's nose with the force of a jackhammer. Stopped dead in his tracks, the Russian collapsed slowly to his knees, and then onto his face.

Natasha stared, openmouthed. "Claude?" was all she could manage to say.

"Stay behind me," he said, walking toward the front of the alley and reaching back with a hand. Natasha took it and silently followed.

The fallen man's compatriots looked at the figure approaching them, felt him measuring them with his eyes . . . and finding them lacking. They looked to where their leader lay in a pool of cold, dirty water. By silent mutual consent they sprinted off into the street. Their echoing footfalls were the only sounds in the cold Moscow night.

"You just can't find good help these days," said Claude, pulling Natasha toward the street.

She pulled up short. "Are you going to explain how you did that?" she said, gesturing toward their attacker.

"No. I'm going to get you out of here." Claude jerked her forward again. "Now."

"I am afraid I have to agree with Ms. Khartukov, Claude. An explanation is in order."

They saw Oleg sitting with his back against the wall on one side of the alley. His pistol was in his hand.

Claude walked toward the Russian, a large smile on his face. "Oleg, I'm so happy you're all right."

"Stop," said the Russian agent brusquely. "Do not come any closer."

"Have you hurt your head, Oleg?" asked the Frenchman, a concerned look on his face. "It is me, Claude."

The security man struggled to his feet, back braced

against the rough brick wall behind him. The pistol stayed trained on Claude. "I know who you're *supposed* to be. But I also saw what you did to that man—and how easily you did it." With an effort he reached his feet. "I believe you have met a friend of mine. Director Lavrov. I think we will pay him a visit at SVR headquarters and see if we can get to the bottom of this mystery." He gestured toward the alley's exit with the pistol.

The security detail had brought a car along. The auto's driver had trailed two blocks behind Oleg and his men as they followed Claude and Natasha on foot. When they reached the street, the Russian agent stood under the nearest streetlamp, raised an arm and waved. A few seconds later the black sedan pulled next to the trio and stopped.

The passenger window rolled down with an electric hum and the driver leaned out. "Sir?"

"SVR headquarters," Oleg told him, opening the door. "The front seat," he said to the Frenchman. Claude did as he was told and the Russian closed the door. "Miss Khartukov?" he said, opening the rear door and gesturing for her to enter.

"This is silly, Oleg," she said, taking a step toward him and jabbing him in the chest with her index finger. "You *know* Claude. And you know how the SVR extracts 'the truth.' They do not care what the real truth is so long as their victims tell them what they want to hear."

The Russian, his gun hand now at his right side, took a step back as Natasha berated him.

Claude looked right and left and then closed his eyes slowly. He would have one chance, no more. He took a deep breath and exhaled it. His right and left arms flashed out simultaneously, the flat of his left hand smashing into the Adam's apple of the driver and the right grasping Oleg's right wrist in an iron grip. Before the Russian could react, Claude adjusted his grip on the wrist slightly and squeezed. The effect was instantaneous and the large Russian dropped to his knees, pistol clattering to the sidewalk. He looked at Claude incredulously.

Opening the door, Claude picked up the pistol. "There is a bundle of nerves in your wrist whose neural highways can make a man do anything—let us leave it at that. No way you could have known and not much you could have done about it if you had."

"What now?" asked the Russian. He saw the easy way Claude handled the large automatic. "Will you kill me?"

A faint smile played across the Frenchman's lips. "Tempting, but no. God knows why, but I have grown rather fond of you, Oleg." The pistol crashed into the back of the Russian's head at the base of the skull.

Claude stepped to the back of the car and opened the trunk. "Help me," he said to Natasha. "He's as big as a house."

"Who *are* you?" She stood on the sidewalk, unmoving, an incredulous expression on her face.

He smiled. "You know me. You know me better than anyone, *chère*."

"No. I thought I did. But Claude, *my Claude,* he could not do all of this," she said, gesturing first at Oleg's inert form and then to the driver and finally to the alley.

The chef grabbed Oleg beneath the armpits and pulled him to the rear of the car. "Do you mind if I work while we talk?"

Ignoring the question, she stood with arms across her chest. "Is your name really Claude? Are you really French? Are you really a chef?"

Throwing the Russian agent into the trunk, Claude left it open and walked around the driver's side of the automobile and opened the door. "No, no, and don't ever question my cooking abilities again," he said, pulling the driver from the seat and toward the rear of the car.

"Wha-what?"

Throwing the driver atop Oleg, Claude slammed the trunk closed and turned to Natasha. "No, my name is not Claude. No, I am not French—thank God. And you've tasted my cooking often enough that you should not have to ask if I am really a chef." He frowned. "That hurt."

"But . . . but . . ."

He walked around the sedan and stopped in front of her. She looked as though she were in a mild state of shock. Standing directly in front of her, he placed his hands on her cheeks and looked into her eyes. "You know me, *chère,*" he said in a husky whisper. Bending his head toward her he placed his lips on hers. The kiss was gentle and long.

Natasha's eyes fluttered and then fixed on him. "You're not gay either, are you?" she asked quietly.

A low laugh escaped him. "No."

"And . . . and what is your real name?"

"Luke."

"Luke," she said, rolling it off of her tongue, testing the sound of it. "The only men I have met named Luke were . . ."

His hands remained cupped around her face. He nodded once slowly. "I am an American. And we're both in big trouble if we don't get out of here fast."

"But where will we go?" she asked, climbing into the sedan's passenger seat.

Luke climbed behind the steering wheel of the already running vehicle. Quickly checking the rearview mirror, he made a U-turn. "I'm taking you back to your father. That's the only way to keep you distanced from—"

"No," she said firmly.

Luke took a deep breath. "Natasha, I am on the run. I've got to get out of Russia tonight or I'm as good as dead."

She turned to him and raised an inquisitive eyebrow.

"Why are you in Russia? Who are you working for that would require a commitment of so much of your life?"

He looked at her quickly, gave her a ghost of a smile, and then returned his attention to the road. "I really can't say."

She nodded. "All right." She sat silently, obviously waiting for more.

Still only blocks from the Kremlin, Luke nonetheless pulled the car onto a side street and stopped. "I have a relative that is rather high in the organization for which I work."

"Your father?"

He shook his head. "No, my brother."

For the next few minutes Luke explained how he'd become Archangel. He'd followed his brother's footsteps in all things . . . sports, university honors, government service. "I'd been working in the field for a few years. I'd done well, but had nothing major in my clandestine resume," he said. "Then we identified what we call an up-and-comer. These are people who we think may play a major role in their respective countries in the future."

"My father," she said quietly.

Luke nodded. "Yes. Konstantin Khartukov appeared to be a man on the rise," he said. "We knew he had a taste for the good life, particularly good food . . . especially French cuisine."

"But how did you become so adept in speaking French and in cooking . . . so very fast?"

"My mother's family is from Baton Rouge," Luke said. "Her people are Cajuns, so we grew up learning French. Insofar as the cooking goes . . ." He paused, blushing. "I've enjoyed preparing food since I was a child—that's really the difference between my brother and me; he can barely make a peanut butter and jelly sandwich. Tell me you're sending me to the Cordon Bleu as part of my training for an assignment and it's not going to break my heart."

"All of this to get close to my father? But why? Was he so important?"

"He wasn't then, no," said Luke, shaking his head. "But Russia wasn't doing well. The political winds were blowing your country toward a takeover by the old guard. And if that happened . . ."

"My father would be one of the men likely to come to power."

Luke nodded.

"And me?" she asked, looking deep into his eyes. "Was I a part of your assignment?"

He shook his head. "Never. You were the one good part of these past years."

"What do you mean?" she asked, eyes suddenly glistening.

He looked at her earnestly. "Do you know what it's like, being someone other than yourself twenty-four hours a day, seven days a week? Knowing there's no one you can trust? When your mother fell ill, when you came to stay by her side . . . well, I admired you, admired your love and devotion to her. Once I got a chance to know you, it was like you were the only real thing in my life." He took her hand. "I cherished your friendship, looked forward to nothing more than seeing you, speaking with you, taking care of you however I could."

Tears spilled down her cheeks as she laughed quickly. "You were very good at your role. I truly thought you were gay." She paused. "I even thought of bringing home some friends from New York to meet you. Men friends, I mean."

He looked at her and raised an eyebrow. "And . . ."

"And I couldn't." She looked away, then slowly back at him once more. "I wanted you to myself, no matter what form that relationship took, no matter how idiotic and ridiculous it may have seemed."

Luke laughed to himself bitterly. "Easy. That almost sounds like love."

"It is . . . I do."

"Oh, God," he muttered. They hadn't covered this one at the Farm. He turned to her. "Natasha, you'll never know how much I care for you. Never. But you have to go home. Now."

She straightened, wiping her eyes. "No."

He beat the steering wheel with his hands. "Why, for God's sake? You'll be back at the U.N. in no time. But if you stay with me . . ."

"Luke, I love you. I've loved you since the first day I met you. And you love me, too."

"That's ridiculous. . . ."

"Luke," she said in a quiet voice hoarse with emotion, eyes pleading. "Look at me and tell me you do not."

He turned to her angrily. "You became part of the assignment. That's all. Now get out. . . ."

"Luke," she whispered quietly, eyes full of tears.

"Oh, crap," he whispered. Leaning across the seat, he put his arms around Natasha Khartukov. With his lips next to her ear, he whispered, "All right, Natasha, I do love you, from the bottom of my heart, from the bottom of my very soul. And I have for so long. That's why I can't take you with me."

A thumping noise sounded from the trunk.

"I think we better be going," Natasha said, wiping her eyes. "Oleg and his friend are going to draw a crowd if we do not."

Luke hesitated, unsure of what to do.

"Luke," Natasha said quietly, "we cannot stay here. Neither of us."

The thumping from the trunk increased in tempo and volume.

"Luke, we must go. I have a plane waiting to take me to New York. Drive . . . *now*."

"Right," said Luke, pulling another U-turn and merging with the Moscow night's traffic. "But I don't like it."

Two hours later Luke and Natasha lay hidden in the woods adjoining the south end of the airport. Slowly pushing aside low-hanging pine limbs, Luke stared at the aircraft under the lights two hundred yards from their position. The only thing separating them from it was a chain-link fence.

"Does Dr. Frolov have a crush on you?" Luke asked.

"*No*. He's a seventy-year-old man, for goodness' sake," replied Natasha.

"Be that as it may . . . and I'd still be a bit randy for you at seventy," he replied with a wink, "he hasn't just sent a private jet for you. That," he said, indicating the aircraft under the runway lights with a nod of his head, "is a Gulfstream V-SP. Nautical range of sixty-seven hundred miles. All the luxury of a five-star hotel while flying at Mach 0.8."

She frowned. "That's not like Dr. Frolov. He's conscientious about not abusing the mission's small budget. Russia isn't exactly rolling in cash these days."

"Maybe that's not the right aircraft? Could he have canceled your plane for some reason?"

She shook her head. "No, he would not do that. He was very concerned about me traveling to Russia because of the political turbulence here, so I know he is anxious to get me back. And this is where he said it would be waiting."

Luke shrugged. "Stay here. I'm going to check it out. If everything is all right, I'll give you three flashes," he said, holding up a large flashlight. "Then you hustle over."

Natasha Khartukov shook her head. "I'm not staying

here by myself. We've come this far together; we'll go the rest of the way together.''

"Natash—"

She rolled over onto her right side and kissed him.

When she broke contact he rolled his eyes. "God but I'm a pushover. All right, come on."

Reaching into the tool bag by his side, Luke pulled out a large pair of wire cutters. "I have to say your father's security detail leaves nothing to chance."

"I only hope poor Oleg is all right," Natasha said with a shake of her head. "Two clouts to the head in one night; it hurts just to think about it."

Luke laughed. "He's got a skull like an ox. And remember that I asked him nicely—twice—to give me the tool bag and not make trouble."

Once at the fence line it was but two minutes' work to cut through the wire. After they'd both climbed through, Luke turned and rearranged the fencing. It would do until daylight, by which time they would be long gone.

The pair had watched the Gulfstream being refueled earlier from their hiding place in the woods. It should be ready to go. Hand in hand, they proceeded across the tarmac to the jet.

No one was outside, but the aircraft's steps were down. They climbed them, eased the door open and emerged into the central cabin.

"It looks abandoned," murmured Natasha as they walked through the compartment. Her eyes widened as she viewed the plane's opulence. The main cabin looked like a high-tech entertainment room, complete with overstuffed leather seating, a large-screen digital television, and satellite television system.

"Cockpit," said Luke, moving forward.

When they reached the front of the plane they saw the captain sitting in his seat going over his logbooks, his back to the door. Walking lightly, Luke stopped directly

behind him. Reaching into the waistband at the small of
his back, the American pulled the big auto. The sound
of the slide retracting to chamber a round was thunderous in the small space. Placing it against the back of the
pilot's head, he said softly, "This may sound like a cli-
ché," he said in Russian, "but I do not want to hurt you.
Turn around slowly and keep your hands where I can
see them."

The pilot turned his head, a frown on his face. The
frown turned to a smile when he saw his hijacker. Luke
lowered the pistol, a look of relief on his face. "Thank
God. I didn't know if you'd make it or not."

Natasha looked confused. "Luke? Who is this man?
And how do you know him?"

The pilot's face turned serious. "Later, ma'am. Right
now you two need to strap in so we can shag ass out
of this berg." He activated the intercom. "Ladies and
gentlemen, this is your captain speaking. We are about
to go wheels up and make for the Ukrainian border as
fast as this little rocket will carry us. Please keep your
seats in their upright position, ensure your trays are
stowed and locked, and above all—keep your seatbelts
fastened."

The Kremlin
Moscow

"Where is Oleg?" said Konstantin Khartukov in a barely
controlled rage. "He should have returned hours ago, as
should Claude."

The assistant head of the presidential security detail
shook his head in frustration. "I have tried reaching him,
sir. He isn't answering his mobile."

A figure burst into the room. Despite the rumpled suit
and mud stains, Khartukov recognized him as one of
Oleg's men. "Where is Oleg? More important, where is
my daughter?"

In a few brief sentences the man outlined what had happened.

"So they were all gone when you awoke, Natasha, Claude, and Oleg?"

"Yes, sir." He looked up suddenly. "And the driver. The car was also gone."

Khartukov struck the man a stinging backhand blow across the face. "Why didn't you say so, idiot?" He turned to the other security man. "Do we not have tracking devices built into our vehicles?"

The man had already spun toward the door. "Yes, Mr. President. I am on it," he yelled over his shoulder.

Two minutes later the agent returned. "The car is somewhere in the vicinity of Sheremetjevo International."

"Get a team there *now*." Khartukov's looked turned thoughtful. "And check the status of a Russian Federation aircraft chartered to return to New York in the morning. I do not want it leaving the ground until we have a look in it and question the passengers and crew."

Konstantin Khartukov turned to the window and stared into the night. "Where are you, Natasha?" he whispered. "Where *are* you?"

"Sir . . ." came a timid voice from the door.

The Russian president turned. "What is it? You should have enough to keep you busy," he said to the agent who'd only just left.

"It is the United Nations aircraft, sir. It took off without permission two minutes ago."

Sheremetjevo-2 Airport (Sheremetjevo International) Twenty-nine Kilometers Northwest of Moscow

The pilot ignored Luke and turned to Natasha after leveling the Gulfstream and turning the controls over to his copilot. "Miss Khartukov, please excuse my friend's poor manners. My name is Ted Moran, pilot extraordinaire. If it has wings, I can fly it." The man grinned an infectious smile. "And if it doesn't have wings, it doesn't have my interest."

Natasha did not smile. "At least I know your name now, Mr. Moran. But again, how do you know Luke?"

"Captain Moran, actually, ma'am; but, please, call me Ted."

"Very well. Ted. Now again . . ."

Moran looked to Luke Dodd. "What have you told her?"

Dodd shrugged. "Only the high points necessary to get her attention."

"Will you two *stop it*," said Natasha. "What the hell is going on? And who in blazes are they?" she asked, jerking a thumb at a small group—three men and two women—garbed in black tactical spandex and body armor. They'd appeared in the cockpit doorway like wraiths.

Luke smiled. "Is that you, Fuller?"

A large man with a handlebar mustache winked and nodded. "Hey, Luke."

"And you, Vanderjack?"

A woman smiled and raised her 9mm Beretta in salute. "Losing your touch, Luke. You never knew we were here."

Ted Moran took Luke by the elbow and led him into the salon. After directing the security detail to keep watch outside and turning over the aircraft controls to one of his teammates, he sat with Luke and Natasha.

Picking up a remote control, Ted indicated the Sony stereo system built into the wall next to the galley. "What'll it be?"

"Buffett," replied Luke. "I'm ready for some changes in latitude."

Ted Moran depressed one of the buttons on the remote and the first strains of "Pirate Looks at Forty" played quietly in the background. "I had a feeling," he said, easing back in his seat. He then turned toward Natasha, his smile gone. "Has our boy told you who he really works for?"

She shook her head. "Not in so many words, but I'm guessing it's not the Cultural Affairs division of the State Department."

Moran looked to Luke, who nodded. "Luke and I were in the Marines together. He was Force Recon; me, I was a chopper pilot—and a damned fine one, I might add." His grin returned for a moment. "After Desert Storm, things slowed down. That's when young Captain Dodd decided to follow his brother to the CIA."

Natasha's eyes widened. "The CIA?"

Luke nodded, watching her work through the implications of what that small piece of data meant.

"Captain Dodd," she whispered, "and your brother is a high-ranking official in your organization." Her eyes widened. "You are *Christopher Dodd's* brother? The *director of Central Intelligence* Christopher Dodd?"

"He prefers Chris to Christopher, but yes."

"Oh my God," she breathed. "And you were right under my father's nose. He would be humiliated."

Luke smiled. "That's what Chris said."

Moran interrupted. "Okay, you two, shut your pieholes for a minute. I'm betting we don't have much time." He leaned forward and stared at Luke. "You were right, Luke. There's a leak in the White House. We don't know how much Khartukov knows, but they *do* know Archangel exists."

Dodd nodded, thinking back to his interview with the SVR director at Lubyanka. A leak had been the only explanation for that conversation. He'd known then that it was time for him to take flight. Luke Dodd didn't mind risking his life for his country, but he was also smart enough not to buck a stacked deck. The potential payoff of extending his time on the Russian president's personal staff was far outweighed by the likelihood that he'd have been found floating facedown in a Moscow sewer within the week. One scrambled, high-burst message later and assets were assembled to get him out. And then tonight's festivities had forced him into moving early.

"Did they figure out that it was you? Is that what this late-night excursion was all about?" Moran's face turned angry for a moment. "You almost blew the whole op by accelerating the timeline and forcing us to take off into enemy airspace without permission."

Dodd shook his head. "No, that's just bad luck." He briefly explained the night's events. "Suddenly I had to get to the aircraft ahead of schedule," he said, looking briefly at Natasha. "So I improvised."

Natasha had sat listening to the exchange in silence. "Improvised? Luke, what are you saying?"

Luke Dodd forced himself to look into the Russian beauty's eyes. "I'm sorry, Natasha. It was nothing personal."

"It was lies," she said hollowly. "All lies?"

He didn't answer.

"All I was to you was a ride, something to be used." Wiping tears from her face with the back of a hand, Natasha straightened her back and smiled a bitter smile. "Congratulations, Claude, or Luke . . . whatever your name is. You are very good at your job. Very good indeed."

Luke Dodd shrugged at Ted Moran's inquiring glance as Natasha moved away from them toward the aft section of the aircraft.

**The Kremlin
Moscow**

President Konstantin Khartukov slammed down the phone after speaking to Oleg. Claude? *But how*? And now the U.N. aircraft was in the air.

He turned to his air defense officer. "Have you managed to pick them up, General?"

The Russian officer shook his head. "We have sporadic contact, sir. The jet is a fast one, and the pilot is outstanding. He's kept his craft on the deck. . . ."

"Enough," Khartukov said, turning to an Air Force officer. "And you, General?"

"We are in the process of scrambling MiGs for an interception now, sir. They will be in missile range before the Gulfstream reaches the border."

The Russian leader nodded. "Get me a phone patched into the Gulfstream's frequency."

Russia
Two Hundred Miles West of Moscow

What the hell have you managed to do, Dodd? Luke thought. He'd been torn regarding using Natasha the way he had, but he'd had no choice. He stared out the jet's dark windscreen from the position he'd taken up behind Ted Moran, who'd once more taken over the piloting duties.

Moran looked to Luke and tapped his headset. "It's for you."

Frowning, the agent placed a headset on. "Yes?"

"Claude, or whatever your name is," said the unmistakable voice of Konstantin Khartukov, "you will turn your aircraft around and bring my daughter back. Immediately. And I promise you, if she has been harmed . . ."

"She's fine," said Luke. "But I'm afraid the aircraft won't be turning around."

"Claude—I'm sorry, what should I call you?"

"Archangel will do," said Luke Dodd.

"How melodramatic. Good versus Evil overtones and all of that. All right, *Archangel,* a pair of MiG fighters carrying the latest in Russian air-to-air missile technology are trailing you," said Khartukov coldly. "Turn around now or your wings will be clipped."

"Aren't you forgetting something, sir? What about your daughter?"

Silence greeted Dodd's inquiry.

Luke shook his head, speaking low and harsh into the headset's boom mike. "You're a bigger bastard than I thought—something I considered impossible until this moment."

"Who is it, Luke?"

Luke turned to see Natasha Khartukov standing behind him. "Your father."

She frowned and then gestured for the headset. "Father?"

"Natasha, are you all right?"

"I am fine," she said quietly.

The voice was angry and switched to Russian. "Do you realize that our Claude is a foreign agent? That he has been spying for the American government for years?"

She nodded, though he couldn't see. "Yes, I know. And if the information he gained can stop this mad war you've begun, I am glad for whatever small role I could play."

Luke Dodd stared at her in surprise. This wasn't the way scorned women were supposed to act.

"Natasha, tell him I will have the jet shot down," said Khartukov in a low voice. "Tell him he has one minute."

"Good-bye, Papa," whispered Natasha. "I am sorry things could not be different between us."

Natasha Khartukov took off the headset. She looked through the windscreen at the night sky's endless blackness. "He says if we do not turn around in one minute we will be shot down."

Moran and Dodd exchanged looks. Moran shook his head—no, they would not make the Ukraine border in sixty seconds, and no, they probably couldn't avoid radar-guided missiles.

The Kremlin
Moscow

"Our aircraft have lock, sir, and are requesting permission to engage," said the Air Force general.

Konstantin Khartukov stood motionless, staring at a photograph of himself, his wife, and Natasha. *My God but we were happy once,* he thought, looking at the smiling family. So long ago. So very long ago.

"Sir?"

"Wave them off," said Khartukov softly, staring at the image of a little girl who had grown into a remarkable woman. It struck him that he rather *liked* the person she'd grown into, despite the headaches she caused him.

"But, sir . . ."

"Wave them off, *now,* General, or it will be your balls," snapped the Russian president. "And stand down the air defense batteries tracking them as well. Am I being clear, General?"

The officer nodded. Fifteen minutes later he turned to Khartukov. "The Gulfstream has entered Ukrainian airspace, Mr. President."

Konstantin Khartukov simply nodded, his mind years away.

Chapter 11

_____

_____

_____

From the Halls of Lejeune . . .

**42nd Guards Motorized Rifle Division Forward
   Headquarters
Vicinity Ash-Shaqayah, Kuwait**

General Georgy Suvorin, commander of the 42nd Guards Division, turned from the hastily constructed situation map. His driver had emplaced it outside of his command-and-control vehicle, a modified BTR-70 armored personnel carrier festooned with antennas, only minutes earlier.

Spitting a gob that was more dust than spittle to one side, he looked to his chief of staff. "Have the Nineteenth Regiment moving toward Al-Jahra within twenty minutes."

Exhausted from the forced night march across two hundred kilometers of desert, the colonel merely nodded and stepped off toward a set of radios in the armored vehicle's rear compartment.

"And tell the Thirty-eighth to pick up their pace!" the general yelled at the retreating figure in order to be heard over the rumble of dozens of idling vehicles. "I want them here and drawing fuel within five minutes of our departure!"

The colonel waved an arm in acknowledgment and kept moving.

The 19th Motorized Rifle Regiment, the unit with whom General Suvorin was traveling, was the lead element of the 42nd Guards Division. The 42nd Guards, who now spearheaded the Russians' second echelon exploitation forces, had stopped only minutes earlier in order to carry out required maintenance and fueling. The divisions that had preceded his own were still in a shambles following a brief but violent encounter with U.S. Marine ground forces a day earlier. The general slapped a dusty glove in his palm. He wasn't to have taken the lead until the Russo-Saudi forces were well into Kuwait. Instead the 42nd Guards had been forced into the lead less than ten kilometers across the border. *Well,* he reflected not for the first time in his life, *plans are a basis for change, not written in stone.*

"Sir!" the colonel yelled. "The Nineteenth is still fueling!"

Suvorin didn't turn but instead began walking toward the head of the column. "Tell them to fuel faster!"

The general's goal was simple: to drive as deep into Kuwait in the shortest time possible. If the gods of war were with him the 42nd Guards would make it to the Kuwaiti coast and its port facilities. Suvorin shook his head in the dawn light. Despite the efforts of Russian naval forces, American men and equipment continued arriving in the theater of operations, more with every passing hour. For each ship his countrymen sank, a dozen more made it safely through the Gulf to disgorge military cargo that would be aimed at Russian sons.

The 42nd Guards commander scanned the horizon to the east. The sun, barely above the horizon, was a translucent pink. Beneath it, as far as the eye could see, the 42nd's T-80 tanks, BMP-3 infantry fighting vehicles, and other combat systems spread across the sand. Half were lined in orderly columns waiting their turn to draw fuel from large diesel tankers. The rest, having completed fueling, had pulled forward along the east-west piece of asphalt passing itself off as a highway awaiting word to continue the march.

While he couldn't see them, Suvorin knew his reconnaissance teams were several kilometers to the east, ensuring their fellow soldiers did not run into an enemy force without warning. Since taking the lead the 42nd had thus far moved unopposed; because of this they were making good time toward the coast. The general saw little reason to anticipate a change to the situation. Once the vaunted American 1st Cavalry Division and its high-tech weaponry fell, all that was left between the attacking Russian forces and the coast were the Kuwaitis and a U.S. Marine force of indeterminate size.

The Kuwaitis were no longer an issue. Their M1A2 tanks had damaged the divisions preceding the 42nd Guards. No question the American-built tanks were fearful offensive weapons. Unfortunately for the Kuwaiti forces manning them, the export version of the M1A2 did not include the classified armor that made the American variant near indestructible against conventional rounds. Of course even the American armor could not withstand the depleted-uranium rounds being thrown at them by the Russian and Saudi armored forces; still, it was better than nothing, which was what the Kuwaiti M1A2s had.

Nothing further had been heard of the U.S. Marines since their hit-and-run assault the day prior. This was because American and Russian military scientists had now become prime players in the unfolding war. While the scientists had taken differing approaches, the end results were the same: for all intents and purposes the two groups had negated each other's satellite reconnaissance capabilities.

Rumors had surfaced at the tail end of the Second Gulf War that the United States had blinded French satellites beaming imagery to Iraq, frying their circuitry with electronic pulses fired by sniper satellites. The whispers were being lent credence now as the Russians were experiencing similar satellite failures at the moment.

The Americans had problems of their own. Someone had hacked into the major defense agency computer networks and released a virus. Teams of computer specialists were working around the clock to isolate the cause and repair the damage, but for now they had no control over their birds.

Where were they? Suvorin wondered again of the Marines. The general shook his head, pulled a pack of cigarettes from his tunic pocket and lit one. The cheap Russian tobacco smelled—and tasted—like a haystack set afire. Suvorin squinted against the harsh smoke as a desert breeze wafted it into his eyes. He missed American cigarettes. He smiled then. When his armor reached the Persian Gulf and took the American camp at Doha he would have all of the Winstons and Marlboros he could smoke.

"Sir!"

General Suvorin turned to see the portly chief of staff running toward him. With Russian soldiers constantly complaining of lack of adequate food, how the hell did the man manage to get fat?

"Yes, Colonel?"

"Our short-range air defense units report radar contact from the northeast!"

The general turned and walked quickly back toward his command-and-control vehicle. "Range?"

As if on cue a jet aircraft roared directly overhead, 25mm cannon rounds spewing like dragon's breath from a centerline gun. The Russian officer classified the aircraft automatically: AV-8B Harrier. The jet was barely off the deck, explaining why his longer-range air defense radar systems had not picked up the aircraft sooner. Suvorin was close enough to the Harrier to see the bulldog painted on the fuselage. He couldn't help noting that one of the dog's arms was lifted, the paw's center claw extended in the air. Though these were not the ground forces he had been contemplating earlier, the Russian now knew where *some* of the U.S. Marine Corps were located.

A booming explosion signaled that one of his precious fuelers was now useless to him. Fuel was the lifeblood of a mechanized force. Without it, like a man without water in the desert, his steel beasts would roll to a stop and die. The criticality of maintaining the fuel carriers was magnified exponentially when on the attack.

Another fuel truck blew as the Harrier continued its run.

A roar to the east made the Russian turn in time to see a second Marine jet fast on the heels of the first. As Suvorin watched he saw the lone pilot's head jerk as he made a slight course correction; he was now aligned directly down the highway. Despite the man's intentions, Suvorin found himself admiring the pilot's nerve. Russian combat vehicles sprayed 12.7mm, 30mm, and 7.62mm across his path, but the man would not be denied. The Marine kept his craft centered on the road as he released a string of CBU-99 antiarmor cluster bombs on the armored vehicles that moments earlier had been idling along the side of the road. Three T-80 tanks and five BMP-3s blossomed fire as Mk 118 bomblets penetrated their thin top armor. The aviator jinked hard to throw off the Russian gunners and to align himself for another pass.

Suvorin sprinted for his BTR-70, the colonel huffing close behind. Scant feet from the comparative safety of the armored personnel carrier a line of sand kicked up as 25mm shells walked toward the vehicle.

"Get down!" the general yelled to his chief of staff as he threw himself to the ground, ramming his face into the sand. Suvorin grabbed his helmet and pulled it firmly against his head. The concussion he had known was coming lifted him several inches off the desert floor. The

Russian officer dropped back onto the hard sand like a bag of potatoes, the breath knocked out of him. Flames from the BTR's ruptured fuel tanks roiled inches over his back, then withdrew with a whoosh.

Suvorin sensed a thud next to him. The colonel, body blackened and smoking, was on his knees two feet away. The chief of staff's hands were at his sides and he stared sightlessly up at the sky as if in search of the party responsible for his sad current state of affairs. The corpse toppled forward, ending facedown in the sand.

Another series of detonations sounded from the rear of the column. Looking in that direction General Suvorin grimaced. Two more pairs of Harriers. Having regained the ability to breathe, the general turned from his ruined vehicle and began low-crawling toward a BMP twenty meters away. The journey took several minutes. Twice during the short but arduous trek he had to play dead as strafing U.S. jets flew low over him, cannons blazing. He arrived at the side of the armored vehicle physically and mentally exhausted. The general threw his back against the BMP, his chest heaving for air.

The sound of the jet engines receded to the east. Suvorin looked around. *"Mother of God,"* he muttered, surveying what had once been a regiment of over one hundred combat vehicles. He buried his hands in his face.

"Sir, are you all right?" called a voice from above.

Looking up, General Suvorin saw the BMP's commander looking down at him, concern etched on his face.

The general gave the sergeant a quick nod and forced himself unsteadily to his feet. It was time to lead. The 19th wasn't completely disseminated. Roughly a third of his combat vehicles appeared to be intact. Enough for a decent reserve at any rate.

"Sergeant, call the Thirty-eighth Regiment's headquarters and get a situation report on their estimated time of arrival here." Suvorin looked at the carnage surrounding him. "And tell them to ensure their air defense systems are alert."

The NCO nodded and began to drop into his vehicle to make the call. The sergeant pulled up short as he and the general heard the unmistakable sound of approaching diesel engines.

The general began to smile. "Never mind, Sergeant. It appears the Thirty-eighth is already . . ."

The near-smile faded quickly from Suvorin's face. A large red, white, and blue flag fluttered from the antenna of the lead armored vehicle.

Phase Line Husky
Southwestern Iraq

Though it was early morning the two Americans already felt the heat building. The larger of the two soldiers stood at the rear of their Hummer. He reached into the rear of the reconnaissance vehicle, grabbed a large cardboard container of MREs and threw it backward. A cloud of dust billowed around the second man as the case of rations landed with a thud at his feet.

"Thanks much, Sergeant Krieger," said Muddy Waters with dry sarcasm as he looked toward the cardboard box at his feet. He beat his hands against his sand-colored Desert Camouflage Utility, or DCU, uniform. The action had little effect other than to move around the dust that had already accumulated on his clothes over the past two days.

Krieger moved next to his platoon leader, looked at him speculatively and then shook his head. He could not be sure, but he thought he might have detected a note of sarcasm in the officer's voice.

"You are welcome, sir." The tall blond squatted next to the cardboard box and unclipped a matte black knife from his pistol belt. Flipping the three-and-a-half-inch blade out, it seemed that Krieger had barely touched the box's thick plastic restraining strip when it sprang open, neatly sliced.

Waters whistled. "What the *fuck* is that?"

The big NCO looked up from his squatting position, flipped the knife deftly in his hand and handed it to the lieutenant hilt-first. "It's a Columbia River Carson; an M16 Special Forces edition, to be more exact."

Muddy Waters admired the knife's craftsmanship: a black dual-grind Tanto-style blade, light of weight, with a locking system that in effect turned the folding knife into a fixed-blade weapon. Krieger smiled as, predictably, the lieutenant touched his thumb lightly to the blade's edge. A line of blood appeared immediately.

"Holy *shit* but that mother's sharp," muttered Waters.

Rolf Krieger reached over and took the knife, wiping the blood from the blade on the leg of his utility trousers. "I am rather fond of her."

"Her?"

"A quality knife is like a good woman, it must be appreciated." Krieger held the M16 up. "This particular blade was designed by a good friend of mine who resides outside of Fort Knox, a retired cavalryman named Kit Carson."

Waters laughed. "A scout named Kit Carson? You're shitting me."

Krieger frowned. "I shit you not, Lieutenant. Kit is a craftsman second to none. He designed this particular knife for the Special Forces when they needed something lightweight yet durable enough for field missions."

Krieger cut the last strap and held the Carson up. "It is . . . how would you put it? *Old school*. Not sexy like the twelve-inch pieces of chrome crap a lot of the men strap to their legs; instead it is sturdy and very, *very* dependable when you need it."

"Much like you?" said Waters with a straight face.

Rolf Krieger stood. "That is correct, sir. I am both sturdy and dependable."

The lieutenant rolled his eyes. Talk about taking things literally. His quick wit and natural charm were a total waste of time with Rolf Krieger. The guy was competent as hell, but his interpersonal skills and sense of humor could use some polishing.

"I should also add," said the big German American as he looked down at Waters, "I have been told I'm *extremely* sexy."

Waters stood and looked at Krieger through squinted eyes. "Why, Sergeant First Class Krieger, was that a joke?"

Krieger's mouth twitched for a split second, threatening to split into a smile. He punched his lieutenant on the arm lightly with a massive paw. Waters collapsed to a sitting position.

"So what will it be, Lieutenant? Pasta or beef stew?"

Waters rubbed his arm. "Pasta, please."

Krieger threw a prepackaged meal at him. "Wrong answer, sir. The pasta is a vegetarian meal. You need protein. We will both have the stew."

"Roger. I meant beef stew; no idea what I was thinking." Waters knew better than to argue. He'd only receive a lecture for his efforts. After spending the previous night preparing their position along the recon phase line and running back and forth between observation posts checking the positioning of their scout teams, he was too tired to listen to Big Rolf preach that wise battlefield nutrition equaled superior battlefield performance.

Both men tore into their meals, laying aside the thick plastic outer bags for later burial. By late morning the sun would have warmed the MREs to the point where the entrees did not need heating. The solid feel and coolness of the foil packaging told the soldiers this wasn't yet the case. Waters pulled out a Flameless Ration Heater, or FRH, to warm his meal. Rolf Krieger watched, amused, as the lieutenant went through the

cumbersome process: open the FRH bag, slide the pack
of beef stew into the bag next to the playing-card-sized
heater tab, add water. The lieutenant leaned the results
of his efforts at an angle against a large rock and waited.
He saw the bemused expression on his platoon sergeant's face.

"What?"

Krieger said nothing but reached into his rucksack and
pulled out a small can of Sterno and a small collapsible
wire stand. Extending the stand, he placed it on the
ground. He then pulled a package of waterproof matches
from a cargo pocket, lit the gelatinous Sterno, slid the
can under the stand, and placed his foil pack of beef
stew on the wire platform. In less than five minutes he
was digging in with gusto.

Waters munched on a tasteless MRE saltine cracker
as he contemplated the steam just now beginning to seep
from the top of his own meal.

Krieger burped in satisfaction as he finished the last
of his stew. "If it is any consolation, Lieutenant, the
FRHs are excellent for heating your meal while forward
and maintaining light discipline."

Waters scowled.

22nd Marine Expeditionary Unit (MEU)
Vicinity Ash-Shaqayah, Kuwait

The two Marines hopped from the eight-wheeled Light
Armored Vehicle, or LAV.

"You sure that's the Russian division commander's
vehicle, sir?" asked a rangy Marine, nodding at a ruined
BTR-70. The gunnery sergeant, like the Marine officer
he spoke to, wore the standard Marine desert combat
utility uniform. Unique to the Marine Corps, rather than
being composed of large blotches of differing colors, the
uniform was made up of thousands of computer-
generated squares that enabled the wearer to blend with

any terrain. "I know it's got a lot of antennas, but it could belong to anyone, sir," the NCO continued.

The other Marine wore black eagles on his collar. Surveying the area he saw an intact BMP-3 twenty meters from the burning BTR. The vehicle commander stood in the cupola, but the man with the eagles dismissed him, focusing instead on the figure standing next to the BMP. "Yeah, Gunny, I'm sure."

As the two Marines walked toward the BMP more LAVs moved in and spread out, approximately a company's worth. A platoon of tanks took up station on the flanks. They all used the LAV-C2 vehicle with the fluttering American flag as a point of reference. TOW antitank missile systems and 25mm cannons bristled, aimed at any Russian vehicle that wasn't smoking. The M1A1 turrets rotated slowly, the 120mm gun tubes scanning the area, their only sound a hiss of hydraulics.

A squad of Marines fanned out from the nearest LAV and sprinted forward, providing a protective perimeter around the two men as they advanced.

The officer was in his mid-forties, tall and straight. He stopped in front of the Russian next to the BMP and saluted. "Good morning, General. I am Colonel Owen Hazzard, commander of the Twenty-second Marine Expeditionary Unit, United States Marine Corps," he said in a well-modulated Oklahoma accent.

Despite the circumstances, the Russian could not help but smile. "General Georgy Suvorin, Colonel. Commander of the Forty-second Guard Motorized Rifle Division. I take it you are the reason my unit has been thrust forward as the main effort so soon?"

Hazzard's teeth flashed whitely in contrast to his black skin. "That very well may be, sir. I did run across a few of your friends west of here yesterday."

Suvorin nodded. "Colonel, you would not happen to have a cigarette, would you?"

Owen Hazzard shook his head. "Never touch the

things," he said. Reaching into a side pocket of his trousers, he withdrew a stainless steel flask with a leather cover. "This'll have to do."

Suvorin took the proffered flask and unscrewed the cap. He hesitated and looked at Hazzard questioningly.

"Jack Daniel's sour mash whiskey; brewed in Lynchburg, Tennessee, population three hundred sixty-one."

"Spasibo," said Suvorin, tilting the flask toward the American colonel.

"You're welcome, sir. And might I ask if you will issue the order for your men to disarm?"

The Russian general, the flask still to his lips, choked on the liquor. He handed the flask back to Hazzard. "Colonel, despite your grand entrance and the damage caused by your air wing, I still outnumber you. . . ." He paused, surveying the area. "Approximately three to one."

Owen Hazzard turned in a circle, slowly surveying the scene. The remaining Russian T-80 tanks and armored infantry vehicles—thirty to forty of them—had their weapons systems locked on the smaller American force. "I take it that is a no, sir?"

Suvorin's eyes twinkled. Despite himself, he liked the American. Much better, in fact, than he liked his Saudi allies. "Colonel, I assure you, you and your men will be well treated. Lay down your arms."

Hazzard's face was stony, betraying no emotion.

The Russian leader's eyes hardened as he handed the flask back to the American officer. "Colonel, I do not have much time. I have a forced march ahead of me to the Persian Gulf. If you do not—"

A drone filled the air. Suvorin turned. Two platoons of AH-1W Super Cobra helos—eight total gunships—had appeared from nowhere. While the attention of the remaining crews of the 19th MRR had been focused on the Marine ground contingent the Cobras had slipped in behind them. Each of the small agile helos hovered like an evil bird of prey, antitank missiles and 20mm cannons focused on the Russians.

The general reached out a hand and took the flask again. "I believe you have the advantage of me, sir. Shall we discuss terms?"

Hazzard looked at his watch, a stainless steel Seiko 200m automatic. "General, I like you. In another life you would've made a good Marine. As it is, you have two minutes to have your men dismount their vehicles."

"Two minutes . . . ?"

Hazzard nodded toward the nearest gunship. A 2.75-inch rocket rippled off its pylon and impacted into a burning vehicle. The vehicle, already abandoned by its crew, ceased to exist. "That was the small stuff, General. The next one will be a TOW antitank missile on a live crew."

Looking up, Suvorin said something to the BMP commander in Russian. The NCO disappeared into his vehicle for a moment and then reappeared with a hand mike in his hand. He tossed it to the division commander. The general spoke a few phrases into the handset and then returned it to the sergeant atop the BMP.

Owen Hazzard looked to his own NCO. The gunnery sergeant nodded.

"You speak Russian, Sergeant?" asked Suvorin.

"Just a little, General," said the NCO. "My grandmother was from Minsk."

Suvorin looked from the black colonel to the Russian-American noncommissioned officer. "You truly are a mixed lot, aren't you, Colonel Hazzard?"

Hazzard smiled. "Negative, sir. We're all United States Marines."

Five minutes later all of the ambulatory Russian soldiers were disarmed and herded together several hundred meters off of the road. The injured were moved to a separate area where they were being treated by their own medical personnel.

In order to save missiles the Cobras didn't participate in the destruction of the remaining Russian combat vehicles and fuelers. Instead the four M1A1s opened up. The tank crews had determined their targets prior to trigger squeeze; 120mm gun tubes spat depleted-uranium sabot and HEAT rounds at regular intervals. In less than two minutes, the 19th MRR was no more.

Suvorin looked on woodenly.

"It could be worse, General," said Owen Hazzard.

"The men," said the Russian.

Hazzard nodded. "You lost your equipment, but your men, they are the heart of this regiment. Quite a few of them remain."

The Russian nodded. "Well said, Colonel."

Neither spoke for a few moments.

"You heard what happened in Iraq, with your First Cavalry Division?" asked the Russian.

Hazzard didn't speak for a moment, not trusting his voice. Then he nodded. "I knew some of those men. Attended the armor schools at Fort Knox, Kentucky, with them."

Suvorin stared at his men. The Americans, preparing to depart, were passing out cases of rations and bottled water to them. "We are not all like that animal Sedov."

Hazzard turned. "Sedov—was that his name? You know him?"

The general nodded. "Sergei Sedov. I know *of* him; a wild dog. He lets nothing—not the enemy, not his leadership, not even his own men—stand between him and his goals."

Hazzard nodded. "Unfortunately we all have our pariahs. But I gave you the benefit of the doubt."

"How so?" asked the Russian, puzzled.

"I gave you the opportunity, when you thought you

outgunned my forces, to do the same as Sedov. Instead you were willing to let us surrender peaceably."

"And if I had indicated otherwise?"

The American's smile was dark. "Those Cobras had been on station and monitoring for quite some time."

Suvorin shuddered, thinking of the attack helicopters with him and his men in their sights. They'd had no idea. He turned to Owen Hazzard once more. "Was it tempting nonetheless to loose your war dogs, Colonel, considering Colonel Sedov's actions?"

The Marine grimaced as though he had a bad taste in his mouth. "God help me, but yes . . . yes, it was." Then he smiled. "But that bastard will get his. He's on the karmic train to hell and doesn't even know it."

Chapter 12

Phantoms in the Night

Phase Line Husky
Southwestern Iraq

First Lieutenant Waters and Sergeant First Class Krieger sat in a foxhole staring at the open expanse of desert to their front. There was some undulation to southwestern Iraq's desert, but for the most part it was flat and barren. Waters had a set of binoculars to his eyes, scanning the expected enemy avenue of approach. If their intel was correct they would see the Saudis soon.

In the early years of the twenty-first century the Saudis had seen the writing on the wall. Relations with the United States had been on the decline, particularly after so many of the September 11th hijackers were found to be natives of the kingdom. They stopped importing American arms other than spare parts for their M1A2 tanks, M2A2 Bradley Fighting Vehicles, AH-64 Apache attack helicopters, and other combat systems they'd already purchased from the United States. Though they had a new arms deal with Russia, much of the equipment purchased in the past year—particularly the LeClerc tank—were of French manufacture.

While the French appeared to be sitting this one

out—other than for a few calls in French papers to boycott McDonald's—the Saudis' role in the current war was becoming more and more active. Instead of merely allowing Russian forces to use their soil for staging purposes, the Saudis had now rolled across the border and into Iraq.

"What do you see?" asked Rolf Krieger.

Waters laid the binoculars on the edge of the fighting position and turned to Krieger. He was too tired for another lesson. "You have binos, Sergeant Krieger. Use them."

Krieger continued, nonplussed. "Not a good idea. You have only a limited field of vision when using the binoculars. Therefore it makes sense—"

"For one of us to scan using the old M1-series eyeball so he can see the whole front, not just a small piece of it," finished Waters. He shook his head and rubbed his tired eyes. "Sorry."

The platoon sergeant shrugged. "Why don't you get the night-vision equipment ready while I call higher? It will be dark soon."

Indeed, the sun was rapidly setting to their front. Middle Eastern sunsets were quick and dramatic. One moment the sun hung in full view over the western horizon, and then it was gone. As the lieutenant began unpacking the night-vision case, he reflected that he would much prefer watching the sunset over drinks with a female companion. Unbidden, Shelly Simitis came into his mind. The sun was setting to her back as she sat on the balcony of a five-star hotel overlooking the Persian Gulf. Waters did not know where they were, but he could smell clean salt air and the alkaline scents of the desert night. Behind Shelly a full moon had risen, its double reflected on the dark gulf waters.

"What are you thinking about?"

Rolf Krieger's voice had startled Waters. "Nothing."

Krieger's mouth twitched with what Waters was coming to know as the man's smile. "You're a bad liar, sir."

The lieutenant sighed. "What do you know about Shelly Simitis, Sergeant Krieger?"

"You mean Captain Simitis?" asked Krieger tightly.

"Shit . . . she's a captain?"

Krieger nodded. "Military Intelligence; she's on the brigade staff."

Waters cocked his head, remembering the brief exchange between Krieger and Simitis at the gym. "Have you two had a run-in somewhere in the past?"

The burly NCO didn't respond initially, instead busying himself checking the night-vision equipment's batteries. Finally he turned to his lieutenant. "Sir, if you're interested in the captain, that's fine. But I am tired of this conversation." With that he picked up the radio handset. *"Knight Six, this is Lighthorse Seven, negative contact. Continuing to observe, over."*

A few seconds later the radio's speaker crackled quietly. By SOP the volume was set to the lowest level at which it could be heard. At the point of the spear, insofar as combat operations went, scouts had to be able to blend in with the surrounding terrain as enemy troops moved around them, continuously reporting to their headquarters what they were observing; noise and light discipline were critical.

"This is Knight Six, roger. Keep me informed, out."

Knight 6 was Captain Mike Stuart, the Bravo Company, or Team Black Knight, company commander. Stuart's ten M1A1 Abrams tanks and four M2A2 Bradleys were the counter-reconnaissance team for Task Force 2-77 Armor, the Iron Tigers. As the counter-recon team, Stuart and his men had operational control of the scout platoon during the current phase of operations. At the moment they were five kilometers to the scout platoon's rear, or east. The scouts passed back any activity forward of Phase Line Husky to Team Knight, keeping out of sight and trusting Stuart's men to handle the enemy forces once they passed the scouts' positions. Knight itself was positioned several kilometers forward of the Iron Tigers' main battle area, its mission to take out any enemy reconnaissance elements identified by the scout platoon before those enemy forces had an opportunity to observe the location and disposition of the Iron Tigers' battle positions and report them to their headquarters.

Krieger put the binoculars down on a sandbag, ensuring no glass faced west; reflected light carried for miles in the desert. For the same reason, soldiers did not wear goggles on top of their helmets.

Krieger looked to his new charge. "You have done well, Lieutenant. I will be honest—I had my doubts. Taking over an organization such as our platoon on the eve of war is not something most men could handle."

At last a compliment from the man. "Ah, shucks, Sarge; you're making me blush."

Krieger pointed a finger. "This does not mean that you know it all. Your fieldcraft is excellent, primarily because it is intuitive to you. Still . . ."

"Still what?"

Krieger sat up and looked west over the position's sandbags, ensured himself the tactical situation was unchanged, and then leaned back. "I will give you an example. Yesterday, as we moved forward, there was a slight elevation along our route . . ."

Waters held up a hand. "Okay, I know where you're going. I didn't have one of the scouts dismount and go forward to check out what lay ahead. That's because while there was an increase of elevation of a few feet, it occurred over the course of a mile or so. How far did you want the guy to walk?"

Krieger stared. "Better tired than dead."

Waters couldn't fault the logic, so he said nothing.

Both men froze as they heard a noise to their front. They peered over the lip of their position. The lieutenant looked right, the sergeant left.

"There," whispered Waters, pointing slightly to the right and ten meters out. Dust was settling from a minor disturbance. "Saudi recon?"

"No," said the NCO with disdain. "A man could never get that close to me without my knowing."

Waters smirked. "All that and modest, too?"

Krieger shrugged, continuing to look at the point of interest.

A small head, white with brown ears, rose slowly as they stared.

"A dog?" asked Waters incredulously.

"So it would seem." Krieger gave a short whistle.

A body rose beneath the head.

"Not very big, is it?" said Waters. The dog appeared to be just over a foot in height.

"No, but he has a large heart," replied Krieger quietly.

"How the hell would you know that?"

The German American looked to his platoon leader. "That is not a wild dog. It is a Jack Russell terrier. My mother had one for many years—tenacious animals."

"So?"

"How many Jack Russells have you seen in the middle of the Iraqi desert, Lieutenant?"

"None."

"Precisely. He came from somewhere—obviously nowhere nearby—and yet he lives."

Krieger whistled again. It was clear as the animal took a few tentative steps toward the observation post that he was on his last legs. His tongue lolled and his short white coat was covered in what looked like dirt mixed with dried blood. The dog stopped, staring at the pair of soldiers. The men could see the Jack's fighting spirit remained as they looked into his eyes. The dog sniffed the air as though through his olfactory senses he could tell friend from foe. Maybe he could. Apparently he liked whatever he smelled, for with a couple of bounds he was in Rolf Krieger's lap.

The big NCO stroked the dog's neck and back gently, murmuring reassurances. "So where did you come from, eh, my small friend?"

Waters watched, amazed. This was more emotion than he'd seen Krieger display the entire time he'd known the man. "Dog lover?"

Krieger snapped his response. "Watch the front."

Waters picked up his binos once more and scanned the desert to the west: nothing. He picked up the radio handset. He, his other scouts, and Stuart were all working off of a common frequency in order to ensure any enemy sightings were disseminated to all of the Iron Tigers forward at the same time.

"All Lighthorse elements, Lighthorse Six, SITREP, over," said Waters, indicating he wanted a situation report from each of his teams.

"Lighthorse One, negative contact."

"Two . . . nada."

"Lighthorse Three, nothing."

"Four . . . it's quiet, L.T. I got nothin'."

"Lighthorse Six, roger, out."

As Waters replaced the handset he heard a jingle behind him.

"Well, well," murmured Rolf Krieger. "You have been traveling."

"What do you have?" asked Waters, turning to the NCO.

Krieger was reading a dog tag attached to the animal's collar. "His name is Phantom."

"Yeah, but how the hell did he get here?"

Krieger turned the tag so his lieutenant could see the name, then flipped it over, exposing a triangular emblem with a vertical slash and a horse's head.

"That's the First Cavalry's insignia."

The NCO stroked the dog's head. "Yes, you have made a great journey indeed. What a brave dog you are."

Beneath him Phantom breathed a heavy sigh and settled in more snuggly, at last content.

"I do believe you're the proud owner of a Jack Russell."

Krieger pulled out his canteen. "You are supposed to be keeping an eye out for the enemy."

"I just got negative reports from all of our OPs—"

All at once the Jack was up, a growl in the back of his throat.

Waters looked at the dog. "What the . . . ?"

"Shhhh," whispered Krieger, staring at the animal. The dog faced southwest; the fur on his neck and back was rigid.

Phantom turned to his new friend. He and Krieger locked eyes for an instant and then the dog's head swiveled back to the southwest.

"*Scheisse,*" Krieger growled, and grabbed his map. He looked in the direction Phantom faced: nothing. Looking back to the map he saw that it was to the direct front of Staff Sergeant Morales's position. *"Lighthorse Two, Lighthorse Seven. You have something in your sector and it is close. Go to ground. Now."*

Unlike Waters, the men of the scout platoon had worked with Rolf Krieger long enough that they would not even consider questioning the NCO's uncanny field sense. Morales and the corporal manning the position with him pulled a sand-patterned camouflage net over their hole and ceased all movement.

Taking notes from Morales, the other members of the scout platoon went to ground as well. Within seconds Phase Line Husky appeared just another barren stretch of desert.

A small dust cloud swirled from behind the scout's screen line and moved west into the setting sun. As it passed over what had been an empty expanse of ground five hundred meters to their front a figure materialized through the fine curtain of sand. It was a soldier, definitely Arab, not Russian—and therefore a Saudi.

Krieger grimaced. The Russians would know whom they faced. Colonel William "Wild Bill" Jones's 3rd Brigade Strikers were a combat-hardened force, one of the few in country—and the Russians did not want to waste their own soldiers probing for the Strikers. That was why they were leading with the Saudis. And unless Krieger missed his guess that was an infantryman, which meant they had not bothered sending a reconnaissance force forward. In the late 1990s Krieger had participated in exercises with the Saudis and knew that while there was the occasional "soldier's soldier" in their ranks, for the most part they were a lazy lot. No reconnaissance indeed—that would cost them.

The enemy soldier stood still, scanning the ground to his front. Satisfied, he motioned over his shoulder. An American-built M2A2 Bradley—the same fighting vehicle used by 3rd Brigade troops—eased out of a wadi. With the wind blowing in the direction of the enemy vehicle, the sound of its diesel engine hadn't reached the scouts. But thanks to the dog they'd had a warning.

Phantom growled again. Krieger felt the terrier's body go taut as it prepared to spring forward. The NCO didn't say a word, but laid a reassuring hand on the dog. Phantom relaxed but continued to snarl silently, his lips curled and teeth bared.

"They will not be alone," Krieger whispered to Waters. "Call Stuart."

The lieutenant nodded. "That's some dog."

Krieger gave Phantom's flank a pat but said nothing.

"Knight Six, Lighthorse Six . . ." As Waters began his transmission more Bradleys followed the first. *"Multiple enemy M2A2s, Avenue of Approach One. So far I count four, but more are coming, over."*

"Knight Six, roger. Keep me informed. Out."

As a good company commander was wont to do, Stuart hadn't peppered his scout platoon leader with a barrage of questions but had instead trusted Waters to tell him what he needed to know. Waters also knew that Mike Stuart and his Team Knight were getting busy themselves. The M1A1s and M2A2s the team had drawn in Kuwait would be scanning west, on the lookout for the enemy mechanized infantry located by Waters's scouts. Having been a company commander he knew Stuart would start moving his tanks and Brads into the best position to intercept the enemy formation. Counter-recon was a high-adventure mission. You were on your own, and your battalion and brigade, busily preparing a welcome party for the enemy to your rear, trusted you not to let any guests arrive early. Throughout the centuries, one point had proven itself over and over from the mountains of Europe to the plains of America: lose the recon battle and you will die. The Saudis were about to become history's next example.

Chapter 13

_____

_____

Night Moves

"Give me a range, Sergeant Slate."

The M1A1 gunner pressed his face tightly to his sights. "I'm trying, sir! The son of a bitch keeps driving into dips every time I try to laze his ass. . . ." The NCO paused as the enemy vehicle moved out of the low ground it had been moving through. "Ohhhh, you're *my* bitch now," whispered the gunner. "Who's your daddy, Abdul? I am, aren't I. . . ."

Using supple wrist movements to center the Saudi-manned Bradley in his thermal imaging system display, the gunner tracked the vehicle for a few seconds. Satisfied with his picture he depressed the laser range-finder button with his right thumb. In milliseconds the tank's onboard fire control computer processed the distance between the M1A1 and the Bradley. Taking into consideration lead angle, wind velocity, and cant, the computer spit out a digital display of 1-5-0-0 as the fire control solution successfully processed.

"Range one five hundred meters," reported the gunner. "Want me to pop his ass, sir?"

Captain Mike Stuart shook his head. "Negative. Not yet."

Stuart reached to the three-position switch on the left ear cup of his CVC helmet. Flicking it forward he called to his left-flank tank platoon. *"Red One, Knight Six. What have you got?"*

In the seconds before the platoon leader reported in Stuart examined the map folded on his lap and shook his head regretfully. He and his Bravo Company had begun transitioning to the state-of-the-art M1A2-SEP tanks only three weeks earlier. If he and his team had the SEPs now, Stuart would be able to look at a digital display that showed him where he and his other thirteen tanks and Bradleys were as well as the locations of all known enemy elements. Position updates would be virtually real-time.

But when Task Force Iron Tigers and the rest of 3rd Brigade had reached Kuwait, they'd been issued Old Reliable: the M1A1. Instead of a digital display giving him an electronic view of everything within several kilometers of his position, Stuart could only see what the TIS sight extension showed him.

In order for him to visualize the battlefield the Knight commander depended on the detailed planning he'd conducted before moving west in front of the rest of the Iron Tigers. He'd broken the counter-reconnaissance sector into alphanumeric grids on his map and labeled the identifiable enemy avenues of approach. He'd gone forward to conduct a recon, selecting the best positions for his ten tanks and four Bradleys to overwatch the identified avenues. Because of their ability to reach out and touch a target quickly, Stuart had placed his two tank platoons forward in the security zone: 1st Platoon on the left, 2nd Platoon on the right. He stationed his own tank, B-66, in the center between the two tank platoons for command and control. His mech infantry platoon and his XO's tank backstopped the tank platoons, two kilometers to the east.

Two ground surveillance radars, or GSRs, were also

attached to Stuart's team. Most maneuver units placed the GSRs forward with the scout teams because of their ability to detect moving vehicles at a distance of ten kilometers and a man walking out to six kilometers. Instead, because he had full faith in his scouts to detect the enemy, Stuart placed the radar teams on the flanks of his security zone a few hundred meters behind his tanks but forward of his XO and the mech platoon, facing inward rather than west toward the enemy. The GSRs were a trip wire. If a stealthy enemy recon team penetrated both his scout screen line and his tank platoons without being seen—a near-impossible task—the GSR teams would pick them up in time for the Brads to take them out.

Before sending the scouts forward Stuart had issued them strict guidance: do not fire unless fired upon. While the recon boys knew this basic tenet, you couldn't tell an aggressive bunch like the scout platoon often enough. They were too valuable of an asset to lose, thus their primary weapon was a radio. Krieger and Waters's men had done their job well; the team knew the Saudis were coming. The ball was now in Stuart's hands; he listened as his tank platoons reported in.

"Knight Six, Red One," called his 1st Platoon platoon leader. *"We have eight Mike-Twos; I say again eight Mike-Twos, Avenues of Approach One and One-Alpha, vicinity TRP Four. They are continuing west, over."*

"Roger, prepare to engage on my order."

Looking at his map, Stuart assessed the situation. Target Reference Point 4, or TRP 4, sat fourteen hundred meters forward of 1st Platoon. Eight M2 Bradleys . . . two platoons. The scouts had reported a company, which meant there were roughly six more Saudi vehicles somewhere in the night. His gunner had one in sight. Where were the others?

"Sir," reported his gunner, "I got two more Brads, one hundred meters behind my boy."

Thirteen. That *could* mean the Saudi infantry company had experienced a maintenance problem with one of their tracks and were thus a vehicle short at the moment. Then again, it could mean one Bradley was out there unseen by his men. They couldn't allow any of the Saudis to escape. If they told their higher headquarters—and thus the Russians—where the American security zone began, the bad guys would do the battlefield math and calculate the location of the main battle area; Stuart couldn't allow that to happen. Even if the crew's map-reading skills were for shit and they had no global positioning system receivers, they could still lead enemy forces back.

"Roger, Red One. White, any contact?"

The voice of 2nd Platoon's platoon sergeant was clear. *"This is White Four. Negative, Knight Six. We're clear. Continuing to observe."*

"Roger. Have your southern section keep an eye on the center of sector, TRP Five to TRP Six. We're missing one bad guy, break . . . Knight Five, Knight Six."

"Knight Five," replied Stuart's executive officer, First Lieutenant Frank Sawyer.

"Knight Five, radio higher. Let them know we've got approximately a company of enemy infantry in the zone and are preparing to engage, over."

"Knight Five, wilco. Going higher."

Mike Stuart leaned into his commander's sight extension to view the thermal picture his gunner was looking at. "All right, Sergeant Slate. Get ready."

In the gunner's station, Slate's smile broadened. He fine-tuned the image of the Bradley, already trying to decide which M2 would be his next target.

Stuart turned to the left and looked at his loader, raising an eyebrow in silent inquiry. The dim blue interior lighting lent a ghoulish cast to the corporal. The young NCO gave his commander a thumbs-up. Stuart smiled at the kid and returned the gesture.

"Red One, Knight Six. You're cleared to engage. Send me a SITREP when you can, over."

"Red One, roger." The lieutenant was relatively new. To Stuart's relief, he could hear tension—very understandable under the circumstances—but not panic in the young officer's voice.

Stuart gave the sight picture a final once-over. Slate was on. "Gunner, sabot, PC."

The sergeant's voice was cool as ice. "Identified."

"Up!" yelled the loader as he armed the gun and threw himself flat against the side of the turret, well clear of the breech.

"Fire, fire HEAT," said Stuart. Stuart's voice was as calm as his gunner's. He and his crew had been through the drill before and knew what to expect. Per unit SOP, Team Knight battle-carried a sabot round in the breech. But sabot was overkill for anything short of a tank. As the next two targets were also Bradleys, Stuart's command told the loader to load high-explosive HEAT rounds for the subsequent targets and the gunner to switch his index from sabot to HEAT after he fired the sabot round currently in the gun tube.

The sixty-eight-ton M1A1 rocked backward as its 120mm gun threw the depleted-uranium-tipped sabot round into the surrounding darkness; the smell of cordite filled the turret.

As Stuart and Slate attempted to see through the dust and smoke filling their thermal optics, the loader hit the ammo compartment knee switch. The ammunition door that was part of the turret's rear wall whooshed open with a hiss of hydraulics and he pulled out a HEAT round. In one smooth motion the corporal flipped the large round over and slammed it into the gaping maw of the big gun's breech, slamming it home with the heel of his hand. Throwing the arming handle back he yelled to be heard by the commander and gunner. "Up!"

"Get on the Bradley behind him! I'll sense the first

one." Stuart popped out of his hatch and threw his PVS-7 night-vision goggles to his face. The biggest threat to B-66 at the moment wasn't the Bradley they'd fired at; they'd likely destroyed it, but if they hadn't, the crew was not very happy and would be too busy trying to find cover to engage the American tank. But one of the other two Bradleys could even now be stopping to fire a TOW antitank missile at Stuart and friends. The Knight commander caught bright flashes in his peripheral vision to his left—1st Platoon's position five hundred meters away. Glancing in that direction he saw fiery red sabot tracers streaking west. Several thunderous concussions followed moments behind.

Quickly returning his attention to his own tank's targets, Stuart barely registered that Slate scored a catastrophic hit on the first Bradley when he saw the other two enemy machines. The big Abrams shook beneath the crew as it fired again, banging the tank commander around his cupola like a pinball.

"Target on first engagement!" he yelled into his CVC's boom mike. "Traverse left!"

Prior to Slate firing, Stuart had noted that the third M2 was still moving, looking for some cover. He had also noted its 25mm cannon was aimed in their direction. While the Saudi gunner wouldn't score a kill with the chain gun, it could screw up the Abrams's optics or cause other minor damage. If the Saudi crew was given time to stop and raise its TOW launcher, B-66 could be in trouble.

Loud dull thumps sounded at what seemed to be the ten o'clock position from their tank. Too much smoke from the second engagement surrounded him for Stuart to see the enemy Bradley, but he had served with mechanized forces long enough to know a 25mm cannon when he heard it.

Beneath Stuart the M1's turret began quickly rotating left in the direction of the chain gun—Slate was looking for their attacker. The Knight commander estimated the gun tube was aimed roughly in the direction of the firing cannon now. "On!"

Sparks flew in Stuart's face as a 25mm round scoured across the top of the turret six inches in front of his .50 caliber machine gun. Shit. The captain dropped back into the protection of the turret interior.

"I've got him! His TOW launcher is coming up!" yelled Slate. "Give me a HEAT, loader!"

"Up!"

"On the way!"

B-66 rocked again. Stuart and Slate stared into their optics, straining to see if they'd scored a hit.

"Driver, move to your alternate position," said Stuart into the boom mike.

"Moving!"

Rather than wait for the smoke to clear, Stuart was knocking out two birds with one stone: get out of the smoke so they could see and move from the position that any possible enemy gunners were now taking a bead on. They'd already pushed their luck far enough in the old position.

"I count three smokin' turds, sir. They ain't movin'," said Slate.

Stuart continued to monitor the area. "Concur; crew, report."

"Gunner's up, still have HEAT indexed," reported Slate through the intercom.

"Loader's up, HEAT loaded."

"Driver's up. All gauges in the green."

Quickly looking over his system's indicators, Stuart reported. "Roger, TC is up."

Stuart threw his CVC transmit switch forward as he stood in the turret once more. Things had been quiet for almost a minute and he hadn't heard from 1st Platoon. *"Red, Knight Six. SITREP, over."*

Silence.

"Red? Report, over."

"This is Red 4," called the Red element's platoon sergeant. *"Engaged and destroyed eight enemy PCs. No further contact . . . slant three, over."* The man's voice had a dead quality.

The words hit like a hammer: slant three. That meant three of 1st Platoon's four tanks were operational. If the other tank had been damaged, Red 4 would have called it in as "bent."

Stuart left it up to his platoon leaders and platoon sergeants to decide for themselves who would monitor the company net and pass information between it and the platoon and who would run the platoon's command frequency. Red 1 always talked to Stuart on the company command net—always.

Buying himself some emotional time, Stuart called his XO. *"Knight Five, Knight Six. Did you monitor?"*

"Roger," he said. *"Sending a report to the TOC now."*

As Knight 5's transmission ended the radio spooled down into silence. Normally chatter filled the counter-reconnaissance network, particularly with enemy in sector: Stuart, the scouts, and the "killers" passing intelligence and instructions back and forth. Now a post-midnight silence reigned over the airwaves.

Stuart slowly moved his hand to the CVC transmit switch. *"What happened?"*

The platoon sergeant didn't identify himself and no one asked for clarification. They knew who Stuart was calling and what he was asking. *"Red One. He only identified one M2 in his sector. They took it out pretty quick . . ."*

Every member of the counter-recon team heard the old NCO's voice catch. When a new lieutenant and his platoon sergeant bonded, something of a father-son relationship often ensued. Such had been the case with Red 1 and Red 4. They'd been together for over a year and had formed a seasoned team.

"He then shifted fire to support Red Two. One of the Saudis had gone to ground, had time to get his launcher up and light off one TOW. We took him out . . . but not quick enough."

Thoughts of First Lieutenant Bryan Palmer, his gunner, Sergeant Schmidt, the B-11 driver, Specialist Moon, and the loader . . . God, the kid was so new to the unit he couldn't even remember his name: big kid; red hair; lots of freckles. And Palmer had just married last month. Schmidt . . . twin girls and a wife that kept him on a short but loving string. Moon . . . the company's card shark, always cleaning out the pockets of the unwary on payday. All gone.

Chapter 14

_____

_____

Beneath a Hunter's Moon

Phase Line Husky
Southwestern Iraq

In the darkness Krieger shook his head. "He must maintain control. This is not the time to grieve."

Waters looked at the shadow representing Rolf Krieger. "Palmer had been in the Black Knights a long time. So had most of his crew."

"I know," said the other voice from the darkness.

"He's human."

Krieger's voice sounded cold. "He's the commander."

"Four of his men are *dead*," said Waters.

"Many more might become so if he does not take charge of this team."

A movement next to Krieger reminded the men of their new companion as Phantom stood. Once the Saudi company had moved past the scouts and continued east into Team Knight's trap, the dog had eaten two MRE ham slices, drank half a canteen of water, and then settled down in a ball next to Krieger. Since then he'd been in a near-comatose sleep—until now.

Phantom's small head cocked to one side as though he couldn't decide what had awoken him. Suddenly the dog threw himself toward the rear of the position and in one quick movement bounded from the hole and onto the desert floor. He stood silently looking east toward Team Knight.

"What's his problem?" asked Waters.

Krieger shrugged. "I don't know, but after this afternoon I trust his instincts."

"True."

The dog took a half step forward, growling, one front paw off the ground.

"Phantom . . . *sitzen*."

Waters chuckled. "You think he understands German?"

The Jack Russell looked back defiantly in Krieger's direction once, then sat on his haunches.

"He is a dog of superior intellect," said the NCO. "And I have noticed he does not overly care for you."

From the darkness a low rumble sounded; it was a diesel engine, barely discernible. And it was coming their way.

"Man. I'm going to write an article for *Armor Magazine* recommending the addition of a K-9 section to each scout platoon," said Waters.

The terrier looked over his shoulder toward the lieutenant. His lips curled from his teeth in what appeared to be disdain as he barely raised a leg from his sitting position and squirted a short stream of urine in the direction of the lieutenant's gear.

"And I'll suggest they use Labrador retrievers," said Waters, pulling his rucksack closer to him with the toe of his boot.

Krieger reached for the radio handset. *"Knight Six, Lighthorse Seven. Are any of your elements moving west, over?"*

Krieger waited patiently for fifteen seconds. "Come on, man," he said. His voice was quiet and urging.

Ten seconds later, the radio remained silent.

Krieger raised the hand mike slowly to his lips. *"Captain Stuart. Pick up the hand mike, sir."*

A few seconds later, the radio silently hummed. *"Last calling station, Knight Six. Say again."*

The two scouts blew a collective sigh of relief.

"Knight Six, this is Lighthorse Seven. We have a vehicle moving from east to west toward our position. Can you identify it, over?"

"Negative. Stand by," said Knight 6 quickly. *"Knight Five, Knight Six. Confirm with higher that no friendlies have wandered into the counter-recon zone, break . . ."*

Krieger nodded toward Waters. He could tell by the commander's voice that he'd fought his way out of the dejection he'd sunken into after his men's deaths.

"Lighthorse Seven, Knight Six. There is a possibility that one Saudi Mike-Two is unaccounted for. Attempt to get eyes on the approaching vehicle, over."

Waters stared east through his PVS-7s. The engine noise was growing louder. "That's not going to be a problem," said the lieutenant. "It sounds as if he's coming right at us."

"This is Lighthorse Seven, wilco." Krieger knew he needn't bother passing the instructions to his other scouts; they'd already be pointing night-vision devices toward the east whether they'd yet heard the Bradley or not. Desert winds could be perverse; the team closest might be the last to hear the engine noise.

The radio crackled to life. *"All Knight and Lighthorse elements, Knight Five . . . all Iron Tiger elements accounted for. None reported forward of Husky."*

"This is Lighthorse Two," came a new voice. *"I've got eyes on. It's a bad guy; Mike-Two; five hundred meters east of Lighthorse Seven's position in the low ground and moving west. He's creepin' and tryin' to be stealthy."*

Despite the situation, Krieger and Waters chuckled. At over ten feet high and with a rumbling diesel engine, the Bradley was many things, but stealthy wasn't one of them.

Lighthorse 2's voice continued. *"They're stopped.*

Looks like they're takin' a quick recon before continuing on to higher ground. They just dismounted two men."

"Lighthorse, Knight Six. Can you stop him? Quietly?"

Krieger fingered the Javelin lying next to him in the position; effective, but not very quiet.

"Sergeant Krieger," said Waters quietly. "We've got more company."

Krieger turned west in the direction Waters faced. Bringing up his PVS-7s he could just make out more armor, a lot more armor.

Turning to the lieutenant, the NCO handed him the hand mike. "All right, sir. They are yours. Tell the commander I'll handle the Bradley."

Waters knew better than to argue. Besides, there really was no other option. He nodded in the darkness.

Krieger turned to Phantom. Seeing his new friend preparing to depart, the dog had risen.

"Stay."

The dog whined low in his throat.

"Take care of the lieutenant."

Phantom whined once more, jumped into the position, and lay down.

"Good dog," said Krieger, ruffling the fur on the back of the Jack's neck. Without another word Krieger disappeared into the surrounding darkness.

Waters leaned against the front of the OP position. He held the night-vision goggles to his face with his left hand and the hand mike was in his right. He began to transmit a situation report and request for indirect fires on the approaching Saudis when he heard Phantom.

The dog lay in the bottom of the position, miserable. He stared at Waters.

Waters chewed on his lower lip. "Don't look at me like that."

Another soft moan passed from the dog's throat.

Muddy Waters shook his head and cursed silently. He would surely catch hell for what he was about to do.

And the funny thing was, he couldn't say exactly why he was going to do it.

He looked down at the terrier and pointed in the direction Krieger had disappeared a few moments earlier. *"Go."*

The dog leaped from the position and was gone without a sound.

Waters picked up the hand mike again. Yes, he was surely going to catch hell.

Krieger paused three hundred meters east of the OP. The moon had risen a few minutes earlier. It was full and the details of the desert landscape stood out clearly. As the NCO cocked his head, listening, a watcher would have said he appeared the embodiment of his German family name: Krieger; *Warrior.*

His face was camouflaged not in a tiger-striped pattern as popularized by Hollywood, but the way professionals were taught in their earliest field training. Krieger had applied dark loam-colored camo cream to his forehead, cheekbones, and other areas that tended to reflect light. The eyes, throat, and other hollow areas received a lighter sand-colored shade to offset shadow. Other exposed skin was also covered with random patterns. Krieger had then wrapped an olive drab handkerchief around his head in gypsy fashion to conceal his blond hair.

In order to travel light he had elected not to carry his M-16A2 rifle. A 9mm Beretta pistol rested in an old, well-oiled shoulder holster and his Carson knife swung on his right hip. Other than a couple of fragmentation grenades, these were his only weapons.

Because of the bright moonlight the sergeant allowed his PVS-7s to dangle from his neck rather than strapping them to his head. For the moment, it was his ears he depended upon. Listening to the engine noise he modified his course slightly and continued east.

The rattling diesel sound was louder now; he was close. Pausing, Krieger raised the night-vision goggles. He smiled; poor light discipline. While the Bradley itself was faint in the NVGs—a slightly darker shade of green than the surrounding desert—the light emitting from the turret hatch atop the vehicle pierced the night as clearly as a homing beacon. It was likely only a small bulb, but the state-of-the-art PVS-7s magnified the dim light so that it appeared a spotlight reached into the night sky.

Hearing movement to his right, Krieger froze. A lone soldier marched toward him, slowly scanning the surrounding terrain as he went. The American scout went slowly to one knee; at night it was movement that betrayed you. As the soldier moved closer, Krieger adjusted his position in order to intercept him, at the same time wondering where the second enemy soldier was. Reaching to his hip Krieger pulled the Carson M16 knife loose and silently flicked it open. The moonlight that touched the wicked black blade cast no reflection, instead seemingly being absorbed by the metal.

The Saudi infantryman walked within a half step of Krieger. He saw a shadow in his peripheral vision at the last moment. Before the soldier had time to react the big scout rose, stepped behind him, and locked his left arm around the man's head, twisting it roughly to one side. The Arab barely had time to register the cool sensation on his throat before the Carson sliced across it.

Moving his arm down and across the infantryman's mouth to keep him from calling out, Krieger forced the enemy soldier to the ground. He held the Saudi tightly, feeling the man's warm blood pump out onto his arm as his life ebbed away. The soldier struggled, not willing to acknowledge that his time on earth was over. His thrashing slowed. A few moments later, after a final shudder, the body went still and the eyes glazed over.

Krieger pushed the body aside and lay unmoving a few more moments, listening to the night. The enemy

Bradley had not moved. Before standing he rammed the knife into the sand to cleanse it. After wiping it on the dead Saudi's uniform Krieger released the Carson's safety, folded the blade to its stowed position and returned the knife to his pistol belt.

Feeling more than a little regret, Krieger glanced down at the dead man before moving off. He had never killed. Instinct and training had taken over from the time the encounter began until the man's death rattle echoed in his arms. *Did he feel guilt?* Krieger reflected on the question, finally shaking his head. No, he admitted to himself, he did not. *Should he?* They'd both chosen the warrior's path as their profession. No, it was fate who'd taken a hand this night and decided their paths would cross. While he had not wanted to kill the soldier, he'd had no choice. Turning, he moved off.

Bending at the waist as he moved toward the Saudi vehicle, Krieger pulled a combination earpiece and wire boom mike from his load-bearing equipment and put it on. After plugging the assembly into the squad light radio on his equipment belt the NCO turned the radio on.

"Lighthorse Six, Lighthorse Seven," he whispered.

A faint voice hissed back into his ear after only a short delay. *"Lighthorse Six. Good to hear from you."*

"I'm approaching the objective. How are things on your end, over?"

Both soldiers were well aware that their communications were unsecured. Their messages were thus both brief and cryptic.

"Continuing to monitor approach of earlier identified element and setting up a welcome committee, over."

Krieger understood Waters perfectly. The lieutenant was tracking the incoming Saudi mechanized force and preparing to fire artillery. *"Roger. Continuing mission, out."*

The big scout pulled the headset off and stowed it

once more. Fifty meters from the Bradley he stopped, knelt, and pulled a fragmentation grenade from his LBE. He walked quickly and silently to the front of the Bradley. Good, the driver's hatch was closed. Hopping onto the front slope, he was halfway to the top of the vehicle when he pulled the M67 fragmentation grenade's pin.

"*Giff,*" came a voice from the ground in Arabic. *Stop.*

Krieger froze. Turning slowly, he looked to the side of the Bradley opposite from which he'd approached. The soldier held a rifle and was raising it to his shoulder. The American briefly considered tossing the grenade at the soldier and just as quickly rejected the idea. The Arab would have plenty of time to shoot him and move around the armored vehicle to a safe position before the grenade cooked off. And the approaching enemy forces would be alerted by either the grenade or by the crew of the Bradley.

Before he could consider further options a white blur separated itself from the curtain of the night. Phantom hit the soldier from a running leap, striking him in the chest. The soldier staggered as the force of the terrier's fifteen pounds hit him. Phantom clamped his jaws tightly on the soldier's uniform collar, growling fiercely and thrashing his head back and forth, his hind legs at the same time digging into the man's abdomen.

Krieger released the grenade's spoon, activating it. In two strides he was on top of the Bradley. No sooner had he landed on top than the vehicle commander's torso popped out of his hatch, a shocked look on his face as he saw the fiendish apparition coming toward him.

The American never broke stride. He dove toward the Bradley commander with the same speed and power he'd used years earlier when filling holes in the defensive line to stop opposing running backs in their tracks. Keeping a tight grip on the grenade with his right hand, Krieger extended his body in flight and threw a vicious forearm to the Arab's face. The enemy soldier dropped back into the turret as though struck by a poleax. Krieger opened his hand, releasing the frag grenade into the now empty hatch and rolled backward off of the front slope.

Landing on his feet, he turned toward the struggling pair at the front of the vehicle as a muffled woof sounded from the Bradley's interior. Designed to have a killing radius of five feet, the grenade's effects were devastating as it exploded in the cramped metal confines of the infantry fighting vehicle.

"Phantom . . . *Off!*"

Without further struggle the small white figure detached itself from the Saudi and dropped to the ground. The soldier reached toward the rifle he'd dropped to the ground while struggling with the dog. In a single fluid motion Krieger pulled the Carson from his hip, flicked it open and sent it flying in an underhand throw. The knife's momentum buried it in the throat of the Arab. Before the soldier had time to fall Krieger moved forward, jerked the jet-black blade from the soldier's neck and sprinted in the direction of the OP position. The terrier fell in at his heels and they moved away from the Bradley as a huge fireball blossomed into the night sky.

"*Scheisse,*" whispered Krieger, furious with himself. He was supposed to dispose of the vehicle quietly. He hadn't thought the grenade would detonate the onboard ammunition. Apparently he'd been wrong. Picking up his pace, he hustled toward Waters's position.

"Almost there, almost there," whispered Waters, silently urging the vehicles on as he watched them through his night-vision goggles. At least two battalions of Saudi armor and mech infantry along with various support vehicles were moving toward Phase Line Husky and his scouts: over one hundred tanks, Bradleys, and APCs. In a few seconds the bulk of the force would be where he wanted them: dead center in the middle of two artillery

group targets. As the Saudis had not shot any preparatory fires of their own, it was clear they didn't know
where the American lines were. "A little more . . . a
little more . . ."

A huge explosion sounded behind Waters. The lieutenant whipped around in time to see the mini–
mushroom cloud of the fireballing Saudi Bradley. *Shit!*
he thought. He spun around and looked through his
NVGs at the approaching enemy formation. The vehicles
had begun moving tactically and seeking cover in whatever low ground was available, now aware a threat
loomed in the night. *Shit, shit, shit!*

He jerked the hand mike to his mouth. *"Knight Six,
this is Lighthorse Six. Have Lightning fire group targets
Alpha-Two-X-ray-Seven and Alpha-Two-X-ray-Eight,
time now, over."*

Stuart replied immediately. *"This is Knight Six, roger.
Stand by to spot. Going higher."*

As Waters waited for Stuart to contact the Iron Tigers' fire support officer, call sign Lightning, he shook
his head and continued looking west through the PVS-
7s, ready to adjust the indirect fires that were about to
fall. *What the hell had happened?*

Dirt spilled into the position as Krieger's large body
jumped in, followed closely by Phantom.

"Welcome home, honey," said Waters, continuing to
watch the Saudis. They'd begun moving forward again,
but by sections and platoons in a cautious manner.

"Lighthorse Six, Knight Six . . . shot, over."

"This is Lighthorse Six . . . shot, out," said Waters
into the hand mike.

Krieger elbowed up to the front of the position and
pulled up his own night-vision goggles. "You could not
even keep a dog under control?" he asked.

"It wasn't my fault," said the lieutenant. "He started
yappin' and cryin' and—hey, hold on." The scout platoon leader turned to his senior NCO. "Instead of asking

me questions, why don't you tell me what the big boom behind me was that nearly tipped off our new friends too early?''

Krieger continued watching the Saudis. "Our direct support artillerymen are getting a bit slow," he said.

Waters shook his head. "Uh-uh. Answer the question."

The big NCO put down the PVS-7s and turned to his lieutenant. "I made a mistake," he said quietly, hanging his head.

"Say again," said Waters, holding a hand to his ear. "I couldn't quite hear you. It sounded like you said you fucked up. Not the great Rolf Krieger?"

"It will not happen again," said Krieger.

"Loosen up, Arnold," said Waters.

Krieger leaned toward the young officer. "What have I told you about . . . ?"

"At ease, Sergeant," said Waters sharply.

Krieger automatically obeyed the authoritative tone and sat back.

Waters took another glance west. "Come on . . ."

After a moment he glanced at Krieger. The NCO sat dejectedly in the corner of their position. "Rolf, listen to me. We all fuck up. Hell, man, I do it all the time. You're human," he said in a not unkind voice. "So learn to live with it."

Phantom walked over and curled next to Krieger's leg. The NCO stroked his white coat.

"Lighthorse Six, Knight Six . . . splash, over."

Both men now watched the approaching formation.

"This is Lighthorse . . . splash, out."

A whistling overhead sounded the entrance note for the long-awaited 155mm artillery. Dozens of fiery explosions blossomed in the night directly on top of the Saudi formations. The air around the scout positions, only one kilometer from the targets, sizzled. The men dropped to the bottom of the position, Krieger pulling Phantom beneath him.

Waters grabbed the hand mike. *"This is Lighthorse. Tell Lightning he's dead-on. Repeat, I say again, repeat!"*

As the ground rumbled beneath them Krieger reached out an arm and shook Waters's shoulder. He said something Waters could not make out above the roaring artillery.

"What?" yelled the lieutenant.

Krieger looked his platoon leader in the eye and bent to his ear. "I said thank you, sir."

"For what?"

Krieger merely shook his head, smiling despite the din surrounding them. "I have chosen well, I think. Your training is over. I'm . . . I'm proud to follow you, Lieutenant."

Waters, for the first time in as long as he could remember, was at a loss for words.

Chapter 15

The Worm Turns

White House Situation Room
Washington, D.C.

The president looked at the briefer. "General, I hope the import of what you have to say merits your request to meet at this point in time."

The briefer was an Army major general and the head of the Army's Program Executive Office–Ground Combat Systems, the office responsible for managing the development, acquisition, testing, systems integration, product improvement, and fielding of the Army's various ground combat systems; among the systems he was responsible for were the M1 series tank and the M2/M3 Bradley. And he was clearly uncomfortable. Standing at the briefing table, the general felt the eyes of the chairman of the Joint Chiefs, the national security advisor, other key staff, and last but not least, his commander in chief, boring into him.

"Sir," the officer began, "information came to me this morning that impacts directly on the war effort."

Jonathan Drake nodded.

The two-star hesitated. Finally, he stood. Over a dozen plasma displays on the surrounding walls showed the real-time data of both their own troops in Iraq and Kuwait and the corresponding locations of known enemy forces. Every thirty seconds or so the icons flashed as updates occurred. His eyes moved to those identified as Saudi icons. *Fuck it,* he thought, *just tell them.*

"Mr. President, I received a call yesterday from Ron Carter, the head of General Dynamics Land Systems Division. You may recall, sir, that he is a retired three-star general."

The president nodded over steepled fingers. "Yes, and he was your predecessor as I recall. I've heard nothing but good things about General Carter."

The general nodded. "That's my opinion as well, sir. General Carter has never wished to do anything but serve the United States honorably, sheltering her from her enemies, whether he was in or out of uniform. Please remember that, sir, as I relate the details of my meeting with him."

The president nodded his head in silent assent.

The general continued. "Ron asked me to meet him and a group of others at his Sterling Heights, Michigan, facility. I agreed to the meeting, despite the fact that it was no notice, as he said it involved national security interests. It turned out the other attendees included his counterparts from a number of other defense industry contractors: Lockheed Martin, Boeing, the Carlyle Group, and Raytheon among others."

"Jesus," said General Tom Werner. "How did he get all of those competing firms into the same room without all hell breaking loose? Whenever one of them is awarded a contract, it's money out of the others' pockets."

The general hesitated. "True, sir. But those corporations, like General Dynamics, have a history of employing retired military personnel—personnel that understand the full spectrum of what it means to develop military weaponry. Personnel with full knowledge of, shall we say, what makes the systems tick?"

"Okay . . . ," said Werner.

"And like General Carter, the men and women involved are patriots."

President Drake closed his eyes and massaged the bridge of his nose with thumb and forefinger. "General, while this is all very interesting, what does it have to do with the war we are fighting in the Middle East?"

"Sir," continued the PEO-GCS, "something else these people have in common are misgivings regarding many of the foreign military hardware sales we've made over the past few years—despite the fact that the sales meant desperately needed cash during a time when their industry was in the midst of a downturn. It scared the hell out of them that they were selling state-of-the-art military hardware to 'allies' that might one day point the U.S.-made weapons at our own boys."

"Like the M1A2s and Bradleys we sold to the Saudis?" asked the president.

The general's eyes twinkled. "Exactly, sir."

"You have my undivided attention, General," said Drake.

"Mr. President, these corporate patriots decided on a plan. . . ."

Phase Line Doberman
Cold Steel Battle Position
Southwestern Iraq

Dillon squeezed his good right eye tight as he concentrated on the reports coming in from the task force command net. Mike Stuart was his best friend—and Mike was in the shit. The Saudis now knew someone was in front of them. Unsure exactly where Stuart's forces were located, they'd nonetheless conducted massive artillery strikes of their own. Most of the rounds had impacted a few kilometers behind Team Knight. The unobserved fires had had no effect on the team's tanks and Bradleys, but several of the vehicles in Knight's combat trains had received damage. The worst was the M113 medic track. A 155mm high-explosive round had impacted within five meters of the APC and it was a total loss. The Knight support elements located in the combat trains were scrambling to evacuate casualties using every vehicle available.

Dillon listened as Stuart sent the task force commander a SITREP. He hoped that Estes would give Stuart and his counter-recon team the word to move back to the reserve position. Leaving them forward at this point in the battle would be a dangerous proposition—foolhardy really. The counter-recon force was designed to take out an enemy commander's eyes—his reconnaissance elements. If they stayed in place too long, waiting to engage their adversary's main body, there was a better than even chance they wouldn't make it back. In this case pulling them back also meant more tracks on which to evacuate the wounded men.

It struck Dillon like a blow to the stomach when he realized it wasn't Lieutenant Colonel Rob Estes on the receiving end of the report. Old habits died hard. Still, whether he liked the man or not, he would give Myron Sutherland the benefit of the doubt until he proved otherwise.

". . . *scouts report that the Saudi main bodies are on the move,"* continued Stuart. *"Request permission to begin withdrawal of my team, over."*

There was no hesitation from Myron Sutherland. *"Negative, Knight Six. I need you to remain in place. The other company/teams have not completed preparations in the main battle area. Buy me some time, Knight."*

An electronic silence hummed across the Iron Tigers command frequency. Dillon knew Mike Stuart. The Black Knight commander would not make the request a second time no matter how badly he wanted to. Stuart knew his team needed to pull stakes, but he wouldn't want to leave the task force hanging. Dillon also knew that Stuart had no idea what the situation was in the main battle area. While not one hundred percent complete in its preparation—a defensive position never was—the task force was very close. Sutherland was playing it safe; but in doing so he was risking an entire company of men. Dillon shook his head. The son of a bitch would rather risk the lives of over a hundred soldiers than take a chance on defending a battle position that was not dress-right-dressed to his standards.

Screw this, thought Dillon. *"Tiger Six, Steel Six. My tanks are dug in and I have a dozen men on the ground helping the engineers complete the final obstacle belt; ETA on completion is one-zero minutes. The other companies are near-complete with their battle positions as well. Recommend Knight withdraw while he still has time, over."*

"Steel . . . ," replied a cold voice, *"I didn't ask for your opinion. Tiger Six, out."*

Dillon paused. Sitting in the dim light of C-66's turret, he flipped up his eye patch and rubbed the back of a grimy hand across his left eye. *Don't get your Irish up, Dillon,* thought the Cold Steel commander. *You know your mouth gets you in trouble. Do you really want to test your seven-year-old accounting degree in today's job market? You've got a family to think of. What would Melissa tell you to do?* Patrick Dillon smiled. Flipping the eye patch back into place, he reached for the CVC's transmit switch. He knew exactly what Melissa Dillon would tell him to do.

"Tiger Six, Steel Six. You've got a unit's shit hanging in the wind. That unit has casualties and no way to evacuate them. Request you reconsider . . . sir."

The reply was immediate. *"Steel Six, get off the net. Discussion over."*

Dillon's temper rose. *"There was a discussion? I must have missed it."* The captain took a deep breath and then continued. *"I'm directly behind Knight's position. At least let us assist with his casualty evacuation."*

"Denied."

Dillon flipped the CVC's transmit switch back and forth several times, speaking as he did so. *"Sor . . . , Ti . . . Six . . . you're break . . . up. Please . . . confirm that was . . . affirmati . . . sponse, over."*

"Negative, negative . . ." replied Sutherland. *"You will not . . . !"*

"Rog . . . sending assist . . . forward now. Will advise when ba . . . in position. Steel Six, out," replied Dillon. He switched radios from task force command to company command. *"Steel Seven, Steel Six, over."*

Rider's gravelly voice replied immediately. *"This is Seven. Monitored higher and am en route with the medic track and my 113, over."*

"This is Steel Six, roger. Contact Knight Se . . . on their internal frequency and let him know you're en route," said Dillon. *"And shag ass, old man. I want you back here before the fireworks start."*

"Wilco," Rider said and laughed. *"And glad to see you're off to such a good start with the new old man. Your interpersonal skills just keep getting better and better."*

Beginning to cool off, Dillon sighed and shook his head. *"Roger that, Top. Keep me informed. And stop reading* Cosmopolitan. *Out."*

Dillon heard Sutherland's voice bellowing from the task force command radio's speaker. He looked across the turret to Boggs. "How about turning that shit off for a few minutes, Bo?"

The loader's smile stretched from ear to ear. "Yes, suh," he drawled.

Dillon returned the smile. "And Boggs . . ."

The private turned from the radio, eyebrows raised in question. "Yes, suh, Captain?"

"You ever try that shit on me when you're a tank commander and I'll have your balls for breakfast."

The smile disappeared. "Understood, *suh*."

Phase Line Doberman
Iron Tiger Tactical Command Post (TAC)
Southwestern Iraq

The loader of Myron Sutherland's HQ-66 tank was terrified. He faced aft, PVS-7s to his eyes. Another M1A1 raced toward them and he didn't see any way that it could stop prior to a collision. Grasping the lip of his hatch with one hand, he flipped his CVC switch to the intercom position.

"Brace yourselves!"

Tiger 6 rose from the tank to a standing position in the cupola in time to see the tank approaching his own skid to a stop mere inches behind HQ-66. A huge cloud of dust obscured the moonlight.

The tank hadn't rocked to a stop before the tank's commander jumped from the cupola. He quickly crossed his turret, jumped from his own front deck to the rear deck of Sutherland's and then climbed atop HQ-66's turret.

As the dust settled the figure took off his CVC. Sutherland saw the carefully cultivated mustaches, the tips tightly rolled and waxed; wire-framed Giorgio Armani glasses; a yellow cavalry ascot tucked carefully into the Nomex tanker coveralls was the man's pièce de résistance.

"What are you doing here, Barnett?" asked Sutherland coolly. "And what the devil is the idea driving into this position like a maniac?"

Major Dave Barnett was the Iron Tigers' operations officer, or S3. Many had mistaken his somewhat dandified appearance as being incongruous with the responsibility of planning and integrating the combat forces of a tank battalion. He'd proven otherwise under fire, with the Elephant firmly in his sights. And Dave Barnett didn't look happy.

"I need to speak with you, sir. Now."

Myron Sutherland stepped out of the cupola and stood on the turret facing his S3. "Major, if you have something to say, say it. Combat operations are imminent and my task force *will* be ready."

Barnett looked to the loader and nodded. The soldier disappeared down his hatchway and pulled the cover closed. Looking back to Sutherland, Barnett stuck a finger in the man's chest. "You need to pull Knight *right fucking now*."

Sutherland looked down at the finger and then up and into Barnett's eyes. He said nothing, but an amused expression crossed his face.

When Barnett removed the finger the lieutenant colonel smiled. "That's better. Now let me tell you something, *Major*: Watch yourself. I do not care how much you have ingratiated yourself with the brigade commander. Question my authority and you will find yourself in the same hot water as Dillon. As soon as the tactical situation permits I am going to deal with his insubordination, and harshly."

A sneer crossed Barnett's handsome features. "Dillon's the best commander you've got and you know it—you can't afford to do jack shit to him right now." The major stepped closer. "And don't threaten me, *Colonel*. I'm here to do one thing—my job. Our teams are ready; I told you that a half hour ago. Bring Knight in."

Sutherland flicked up an index finger. "The obstacles are not complete." The middle finger came up. "Anvil Company is still in the process of digging in two tanks. Shall I go on?"

Barnett's index finger came up. "The obstacles will be complete before Knight makes it back." The middle finger came up. "Those two tanks in Anvil have hull-down positions dug and good alternate positions identified. Shall *I* go on? This task force is ready to defend. Bring Knight back."

The amused expression on Sutherland's face disappeared, replaced by a cold mask. "I believe we're finished here, Major—and Knight stays forward where I need them. And if you ever question my orders again, I will ensure that you never command a battalion of your own. Am I being clear?"

Barnett smiled but it didn't reach his eyes. Taking off his glasses, he slid them into one of his Nomex breast pockets. "I truly hoped I wouldn't have to sully myself," he said sadly as he stepped toward Myron Sutherland.

White House Situation Room
Washington, D.C.

The general wrapped up his bombshell and sat down. No one spoke for a full minute. President Jonathan Drake broke the room's collective trance. "Holy shit," he said in a low voice.

General Werner nodded. "Unbelievable," he muttered and then turned to the briefer. "General, you're telling me that no one, not you nor any of your program offices within Ground Combat Systems, had any idea that this, this . . . contractor cabal . . . had decided to take such a unilateral action on their own? Do they have any idea what would have happened if the purchasers of their hardware had gotten wind of it? And rightly so, might I add?"

The general nodded. "They knew. And they knew it would be their private careers as well—or worse. Within their own organizations they kept the information close-hold to the point that even their CEOs were ignorant of the plan."

"I never knew what a fine line it was between being a criminal and being a hero," said Jonathan Drake quietly.

"General, get Central Command on the horn and bring them up to date."

As Werner stood and walked to the communications suite in the corner of the room, the president turned to the GCS executive. "Sir, please pass on the thanks of a grateful nation to General Carter and his associates."

United States Central Command (USCENTCOM) Forward Headquarters
Doha, Qatar

The Cisco IP phone connected into the top secret computer network rang only once before a colonel picked it up. As he did so the officer continued watching the plasma display to his front. Fewer red icons marched east than had fifteen minutes earlier when the American artillery barrage had hammered the Saudi lead elements, but the enemy vehicles were built to the American military specifications to withstand virtually anything but a direct hit. The lead brigade had sustained damage, but at least half of its combat power was on the move once more. Behind it two additional brigades followed, prepared to maneuver on the American forces based on the lead brigade's contact. That brigade had already moved past the 3rd Brigade, 4th Infantry's recon troop. Now it was advancing past the battalion scouts' positions on Phase Line Husky. It looked like Task Force 2-77 Armor's counter-recon would make contact within minutes. The colonel, an ex–tank battalion commander, shook his head in bewilderment as he looked at the counter-recon team sitting in the enemy's path. *What the hell were they still doing forward?*

"Operations, Barker speaking," the colonel finally replied into the mouthpiece. He listened to the speaker identify himself and his jaw dropped. Looking to the phone's display he received confirmation of the caller's location: W.H. Situation Room.

"What can I do for you, sir?" said Colonel Barker.
Barker listened. "You can't be serious, sir."

The caller went on for another minute.

"Holy shit," Barker muttered into the phone.

"That's exactly what the president said, Colonel," replied Werner. "It's your ball now. Make the most of it."

"Roger that, sir," replied Barker, hanging up on the nation's highest-ranking military officer and sprinting out of his shelter to notify the USCENTCOM commander.

Phase Line Akita
Southwestern Iraq

"Knight Six, White Four," called the 2nd Platoon platoon sergeant. *"Contact, tanks, west; Avenue of Approach Three-Bravo . . . range four-five-hundred meters, over."*

The captain nodded from his position in the cupola of B-66. *"Roger, keep me informed. Out."*

Here they come, thought Stuart. He flicked his transmit switch. *"Knight Seven, Knight Six . . . SITREP on your move, over."*

"This is Knight Seven. The last of the casualties are uploaded and being evacuated now, over."

Stuart smiled grimly; that was one less worry at any rate. *"Roger. Pass on my thanks to Steel . . . break . . . Green One, Knight Six,"* he said, calling his Mech Platoon platoon leader. *"Are you in position, over?"*

"This is Green One, roger."

In order to bring more combat systems to bear as quickly as possible, Stuart had moved his Mech Platoon forward from their positions farther east and constructed a hasty engagement area in which he intended to hit the advancing Saudi forces.

"We've got one, sir," said Sergeant Slate from the gunner's station.

Stuart looked into the sight extension in time to see

the range pop up in the display: an M1A2 forty-two hundred meters. This would be the first time American troops faced enemy Abrams tanks and his boys were definitely *not* looking forward to the experience. "Roger, I see him," he said into his boom mike.

"Knight elements, Knight Six. Wait until at least two companies are in the engagement area. We'll try to gain a little surprise, break . . . Redleg," he said, talking to his fire support officer. *"When we hit the lead force I want smoke and H.E. on the units trailing them; give us some time to deal with those in the kill sack."*

"Wilco," replied the lieutenant. *"I've already worked the targets."*

"All right. Check your systems one last time and settle in. On my command, open fire . . ."

Phase Line Doberman
Southwestern Iraq

Barnett had only taken a half step forward when the loader's hatch banged open with a loud clang. "Sir, the brigade TOC is calling you."

The two officers stared at each other, neither moving. "Sir? The brigade TOC . . ."

"Give me the hand mike," said Sutherland, extending a hand. His eyes remained locked on Barnett's.

The soldier disappeared for a moment and then reappeared with the hand mike.

Squatting next to the loader's hatch Sutherland threw Barnett one last glare before taking the hand mike. *"Striker TOC, Tiger Six, over."*

He listened, a frown creasing his face. *"This is Tiger Six, say again."*

"Roger, out," he said, handing the mike back to the loader. "Get me the battalion net. Quickly."

"What's going on?" asked Barnett.

Sutherland shook his head, his anger at his subordinate forgotten for the moment. "You wouldn't believe me if I told you."

Phase Line Akita
Southwestern Iraq

"That's it," whispered Stuart as he watched over thirty Saudi combat systems roll into the Black Knight engagement area. *"All Knight elements, Knight Six . . ."*

The task force radio squelched. *"Knight Six, Tiger Six, hold fire. I say again, hold fire!"*

What the fuck, thought Stuart. *"Tiger Six, I've got almost a battalion in my E.A. . . ."*

"I said hold fire, Knight! Acknowledge, over."

Stuart watched more and more armored vehicles rolling toward his small force. If they didn't engage now he and his men were as good as dead.

The captain turned to his loader. "Turn off the battalion radio."

Seven hundred miles above the earth's surface a constellation of low-earth-orbit satellites came to life. Owned by an anonymous group of U.S. investors, the Central Intelligence Agency would be hard-pressed to discover the identities of those responsible for the constellation's launch and operation—they'd already tried twice and failed miserably.

After reading their initial broadcast instructions the majority of the satellites winked into standby mode again. Those over the Middle East, however, continued to whir with activity. Ten seconds later these satellites rotated into position to carry out their directives. One by one they locked onto the coordinates they'd received and maintained their positions relative to earth. Once all were in place, a final high-frequency burst sent them into action. The satellites beamed their signals into every corner of Iraq. Mission complete, the orbiting hardware went into standby mode like their brothers, waiting for the day they might be needed again.

What the fuck, thought Stuart for the second time in thirty seconds. The armored vehicles in front of the Black Knights had ground to a halt. Not a shot fired against them, no obstacles . . . and yet they weren't moving.

"Knights, Knight Six. Hold fire, I say again, hold fire! Continue to monitor your sectors. I'm going higher."

Thirteen sets of thermal sights remained locked on Saudi targets; thirteen gunners' fingers twitched, ready to send hot steel into their intended prey. But they held fire for now, watching what could have been a ghost formation.

**Phase Line Doberman
Southwestern Iraq**

Sutherland and Barnett stood in front of the HQ-66 tank, their confrontation forgotten in light of the past hour's events.

"How do you think they did it?" asked Barnett.

Sutherland shook his head. "Someone—government or industry—must have installed electronic surprise packages deep in the hearts of those systems. No harm, no foul so long as relations were stable. But if those systems were ever to be used against us . . . "

"Indeed," muttered Barnett. Pulling a briar pipe from his pocket he thoughtfully tapped it against the tank's front slope before filling it with Ashton Celebrated Sovereign. "This isn't going to go over well with friendly countries we sold the same systems."

"My guess is we'll spin it. Claim the Saudis lost their nerve at the last minute." He looked at Barnett.

"Not unheard of for Arabs," said Barnett slowly. "And the Saudis haven't been to war for years. It might fly. Of course the fact that they'd simply abandon the equipment without a shot being fired, that will look a little strange."

"The artillery will have done some damage before it was lifted, but it wouldn't destroy many of the tanks and Brads unless they scored a direct hit." Sutherland sat thoughtfully a few moments. "When you go forward, tell Dillon and Stuart to destroy one or two vehicles per company with direct fire."

Barnett nodded as he pulled a pipe lighter from one of his many Nomex pockets and drew the bowl of tobacco to life. "That would lend some truth to the lie; on the other hand, that's a lot of combat systems our side could use."

"I'll clear it with higher first and recommend the other task forces do the same," Sutherland said.

"Right. Steel should be ready, so I'm off," Barnett said. "And for the record, sir . . ."

"You still disagree with my earlier tactical assessment regarding Stuart and his team," finished the Iron Tigers commander. He looked at his ops officer. "And you'd like a piece of my ass."

Barnett's lips curved into a slight smile around the pipe's stem. He turned and made for his tank, a brief nod his only reply.

Sutherland watched his operations officer clamber aboard his tank and begin preparations to move forward. "Yes, I believe we understand one another, Major," he said to himself. "And your day, too, shall come."

Phase Line Akita
Southwestern Iraq

The Saudi battalion commander stood in the turret of his M1A2. *For the love of Allah.* The colonel paused and tapped his knuckles across his heart several times, looking into the night sky and silently asking forgiveness for this slight blasphemy against the Prophet. But what had happened? One moment he and his battalion of tanks and Bradleys were trailing the lead elements of the attacking Saudi division, then there'd been artillery—targeted against the units forward of his own, *Allah is truly good*—and then two things had happened simultaneously: the artillery fires had stopped; and so had his tanks and Bradleys. Engines had spooled into silence; fire control systems were rendered useless; all electronics . . . dead.

It was not only his tanks and infantry fighting vehicles. Their newer howitzers had also stopped dead in their tracks, along with their Hummers. And they had not even seen the enemy.

As if in answer to his last thought bright red machine-gun tracers flew over his head, blinding him. Before the Saudi commander could recover, a thundering voice rolled over him.

"Dismount your vehicles now. Do not attempt to take any weapons with . . ."

One hundred meters to his left the tank commander of the adjacent M1A2 opened fire in the direction of the voice with his .50 caliber machine gun. The man, a lieutenant eager to prove his mettle, had barely begun the burst when a red streak blurred in from the east. The big Abrams lurched once, tilted sideways and fireballed. Flames licked the night sky and the vehicle's onboard ammunition began cooking off.

"Dismount your vehicles now. Do not attempt to take any weapons with you. Begin walking west. You may take one bottle of water per man, nothing more. Dismount your vehicles now . . ."

Suddenly the entire area lit up as if it were noonday. Dozens of enemy vehicles had crept up on him and the rest of the division while they were busy troubleshooting their stalled fighting systems. In the harsh white light the colonel saw dozens of Arab crews leaping from their vehicles, hands in the air. They moved west, the first steps in a long journey home.

The battalion commander shook his head, unbelieving. *En Shallah,* he finally said to himself and climbed off of the tank.

Patrick Dillon's command tank, Cyclops, pulled to a stop next to Mike Stuart's M1A1. Dillon climbed from the turret and hopped onto the Knight tank. For the past hour the two commanders had overseen the security of the abandoned Arab vehicles to their front. Mech infantrymen had dismounted to check each one. Only two die-hard Saudi crews had had visions of glory; Cold Steel and Black Knight crews punched each of the vehicles a one-way ticket to Paradise.

"Nice eye patch," said Stuart as his friend clambered over the top of the turret to the commander's hatch. "A bit Rooster Cogburnish for my taste, but nice."

"Yeah, sexy, ain't it?" replied Dillon, grinning.

"Does it slow you down much?"

Dillon shook his head. "Taking a little while to get the eye-hand coordination thing going again, but I'm catching on. Since the commander's station sights are monocular, no real difference once the shit is on."

"What about when you're outside the hatch and using your binos?"

Dillon grimaced. "That one's a little awkward."

Stuart reached into the bustle rack at the rear of the tank and pulled out a dusty package. It was wrapped with a month-old copy of the *Khaleej Times.* Handing the package to Dillon, he smiled wickedly. "Open it."

"What's this?"

"Just open it."

Dillon unwrapped the newspaper and then opened the cardboard box that was hidden beneath it. Reaching inside he pulled out a brass tube. Holding it up, he grinned. "It's a telescope. A real honest-to-God pirate's telescope." Grasping it and extending the telescopic body, he put the three-foot piece to his eye. "Can't see much. It's kinda dark."

"Yeah, but you look good with it," said Stuart, throwing the newspaper into the box and stuffing the garbage back into the bustle rack. "Saw a peddler outside Doha before we trucked out here. I couldn't resist. And it's not just for looks; that baby's twenty-power."

Dillon collapsed the telescope. "Sweet. Thanks, Mike. This is much better than the case of Pabst Blue Ribbon you gave me for my birthday."

"But I like Pabst," said Stuart. He then turned serious. "Besides, I owe you anyway for tonight."

Dillon shrugged. "The hell you do."

Stuart shook his head. "Look, I caught the chatter between you and Sutherland. While I appreciate what you did—and I do—you know Sutherland is going to be gunning for you now." He laughed. "The malfunctioning radio performance wasn't exactly Academy Award material: 'Ti . . . Six . . . is . . . eel-Six . . . you . . . brea . . . up.'" The Knight commander slapped a knee, causing a cloud of dust to surround him, and laughed. "Very bad, Patrick."

A grunt of disgust escaped Dillon but he said nothing. Reaching into a pocket, he pulled out a tin of Copenhagen and placed a dip of the snuff in his mouth.

"I thought you quit."

Dillon repocketed the can and shrugged. "I did," he replied, leaving it at that.

"Seriously, Pat, from what I've heard from friends at Hood, the bastard will—"

"Fuck him," spat Dillon. He stalked back and forth across the turret. "If there's one thing I learned from the last war it's that you gotta prioritize. I know he's the commander. I know he made a decision. I know I'm supposed to back him up. But it was the *wrong freakin' decision.* So fuck him, fuck his 'my way or it's your ass' reputation, fuck—"

Stuart threw up his hands. "Okay, I get it."

Dillon squatted next to the .50 cal and exhaled deeply. "I'm fucked," he said in a low voice, running his hands through his close-cropped silver hair.

"If it makes you feel any better, I'd have done the same for you," said Stuart. "Of course, my malfunctioning radio would have been a little more believable."

Dillon smiled despite his foul mood. "Asshole."

From behind them they heard the rush of rotor blades.

Dillon checked the time on his Zodiac Super SeaWolf. Designed for use in waters over three thousand feet deep, the big dive watch's hands glowed brightly. The buzz-saw bezel and almost one-pound weight gave it the added capability of doubling as a weapon if he ran out of ammunition or as an opener if rations were low and he needed to bust into a coconut.

He yelled in order to be heard over the noise of the descending chopper. "Right on time!"

As the UH-60 Black Hawk flared for landing they saw the 1st Cavalry's distinctive yellow-and-black insignia on its fuselage.

A lone figure jumped from the helicopter before the engines completely spooled down. Seeing the two tanks nearby the man jogged in their direction. Dillon and Stuart hopped down from B-66 and waited in the lights of the M1A1.

"Are these my vehicles, boys?"

As the man reached them the two Iron Tiger commanders made out the single black star sewn to the wearer's Kevlar helmet cover.

"General Shillings?" asked Dillon.

The senior officer walked up, hand outstretched. "Roger that, Captain."

Dillon took the proffered hand. "Sorry to hear about

your losses, sir. And yes," he said, indicating the abandoned combat systems littering the battlefield. "They're all yours."

"Have they been checked out?" asked Shillings.

"We've had teams go through them, sir. They're not booby-trapped if that's what you're asking," said Stuart.

Shillings nodded. "Good. We don't have much time. A report came down a couple of minutes ago; the Russians know what happened and are preparing to move forward to take over the fight."

"How the hell are we supposed to get all of these vehicles behind friendly lines, sir?" asked Patrick Dillon. "We don't have enough men to move them all. And as of now they'll have to be towed—that's a lot of Mike-88s," he said, referring to the big armored recovery vehicles. Each company had only one and there were only a handful of the workhorse maintenance vehicles in the entire task force.

Kirk Shillings's eyes twinkled. "The same satellite network that brought the systems down is about to reactivate them. They'll be as good as new. And so far as manpower goes . . ."

More Black Hawks flew in, throwing sand in the air as they settled. AH-64 Longbow Apache gunships roared past the armored vehicles low to the ground and took up guard positions to the west. The yellow and black of the 1st Cav marked all of the helos.

Kirk Shillings's smile broadened as he watched armored crewmen disgorge from the troopships and run toward the empty armored vehicles. "Gentlemen, the First Team is back."

Chapter 16

_____

_____

Beauty and the Beast

3rd Brigade, 4th Infantry Division (Strikers) TOC
Southwestern Iraq

The scout Hummer pulled to a stop inside the 3rd Brigade TOC compound. Waters and Krieger grabbed their LBE and helmets and dismounted from the vehicle. Several days of dust covered the men and their uniforms, lending them a uniformly tan color from head to foot. As they watched soldiers in clean utilities moving about the compound they subconsciously patted themselves down in an attempt to be more presentable.

"The task force S2 will be on hand for the brigade order," said Krieger as they walked toward the collection of armored M577A3 command post carriers, antennas and tents marking the brigade TOC location. "I do not see why they are requiring us to be present for it as well."

Waters laughed. "You don't enjoy the rear much, do you?"

Krieger grunted.

"Look, enjoy it. Grab a shower and some hot chow."

"We have better things to do," replied Krieger. "When the Russians attack . . ."

"Estimates are we have forty-eight hours," pointed

out Waters. "They're still building up their combat power to take over the fight."

Krieger scowled. "I would not count on that luxury. Would *you* give your enemy forty-eight hours to consolidate his position?"

Before Waters could reply a loud voice interrupted. "How are they collectively hangin', gentlemen?"

The scouts turned to find Colonel Bill Jones approaching. Both men came to a relaxed position of attention but did not salute. Jones had a strict no-salute policy in the field.

"Great, sir," replied Waters. "Just came back for the order."

Jones nodded. "Sorry to pull you from the line but I want to ensure all of my task force scout platoons are tied into the plan with the brigade recon troop. It's going to be a team effort and I believe in face-to-face coordination when the stakes are this high."

The scouts nodded.

"Now who is going to introduce me to the little fella?" the colonel asked, gesturing behind Krieger.

Rolf Krieger rolled his eyes. *"Scheisse,"* he muttered. He patted his chest with his right hand twice. "Phantom, come."

The dog, trailing unnoticed a few steps behind the pair, sprinted the intervening distance and jumped into Krieger's arms. The big German American caught him and ran a rough hand affectionately over the animal's head. "You were to remain with the vehicle, my small friend."

Jones pulled a pack of cigarettes out, followed closely by his old battered Zippo lighter. "Bouncy little bastard, ain't he?" The colonel squinted through a haze of smoke. "Did you say Phantom?"

Krieger nodded. "Yes, sir. He wandered up to our position on the screen line yesterday."

"And he's adopted Sergeant Krieger," added Waters. "Good thing, too . . ." The lieutenant related the events of the previous evening.

"That," said Jones after hearing the tale, "is a hell of a dog. Guess the general raised him right."

"The general?" asked Krieger.

Jones nodded. "This dog," he said, scratching behind Phantom's ears, "was General Jack Jeffries's prize pooch. Damned mutt went everywhere with him." He smiled kindly. "Glad to see he's found a home."

Krieger shook his head worriedly. "I like the animal well enough . . ."

"Oh, please," interjected Waters. "You *love* that dog."

The NCO's face turned crimson and he gave his lieutenant a sharp look. "As I was saying, sir . . . I like the dog well enough, but obviously he cannot stay with us."

Jones gave Krieger a kind look. He was a dog man himself. "We'll work something out, Sergeant Krieger, don't you worry. Now," he said, putting an arm around Krieger's shoulders and leading him toward the TOC. "Why don't you tell me more about this doctoral work of yours; it sounds like something I should have been read into a long time ago. . . ."

Three hours later Waters and Krieger walked through the flap of the TOC as the Arabian sun set in the west, a large fiery orange-red ball that yielded slowly to the darkness. Phantom trailed after them as they moved toward the Hummer.

"Hey, soldier boys, don't I know you?" called a voice.

They turned to see a female Military Intelligence captain approaching. Despite the full field gear and protective mask she was clearly a beautiful woman. It took Waters a moment to realize who it was.

"Hello . . . ma'am," he said. "Good to see you again."

"How are you?" she said with a smile. "You look a

little better without the barbells crushing your chest," she said.

Krieger remained stone-faced.

"Sorry," stammered Waters. "I'm being rude. Captain Simitis, I think you know my platoon sergeant, Sergeant First Class Krieger . . . though listening to him, I'm not sure how or how well."

Simitis held out a hand. "Yes, Sergeant Krieger and I have met. I'm afraid I upset him a little."

"Yes," replied Krieger. "I gave you and some other S2 officers a briefing last year—"

"On the Russian threat," finished Simitis with a smile. But then the smile faded. "I wasn't very nice to you, was I?"

"You were cordial enough, Captain," Krieger replied. But his disposition toward her said otherwise.

"If I remember correctly," she continued, "I told you that you were fixated on the Cold War and needed to move on with your life."

"Something to that effect."

A grin spread across her face. "Guess I look pretty silly now."

Krieger's lips twitched in the reaction Waters had learned to know so well, but he gave no other indication that he indeed found the remark humorous.

A Klaxon mounted near the TOC screamed to life, startling the trio of soldiers: two long electronic wharps, a pause, then two more. The pattern then repeated itself.

The scouts looked at Simitis questioningly. Depending on the unit, various Klaxon patterns indicated different threats—an incoming SCUD, a chemical warning, and so on.

"That's the signal for a ground attack in progress; but we've got security out and would know—"

A major broke out of the TOC before she could finish the sentence. "Listen up, people! We've received a report that a Russian prop-driven aircraft came in under the radar a few minutes ago. It's probably nothing, but get to your security—"

A short sustained burst of automatic fire cut the officer's sentence off in a gurgle of blood and he collapsed lifelessly into the sand.

"Spetsnaz," sneered Krieger.

Spetsnaz, the Russian Special Forces, were trained to operate deep behind enemy lines. They were tough, seasoned, and most had combat experience from years of fighting in Chechnya. Normally they parachuted into the enemy's territory to perform special missions, anything from a deep reconnaissance to disruption of the enemy's command, control, and communication nodes . . . the latter included headquarters facilities such as the 3rd Brigade's TOC.

Looking in the direction of the automatic weapons fire Krieger identified the shooter and pulled his 9mm Beretta. Flipping off the pistol's safety he extended one leg and swiveled into a modified Weaver stance and rapid-fired three shots. All of the shots hit their mark, throwing the Russian backward into the sand.

"Come on," yelled Krieger. He grabbed Simitis by the shoulder and spun her in the direction of the Hummer. If he remembered correctly an M113 armored personnel carrier had been parked a few meters away.

Green tracer fire from the Russian commandos flashed throughout the compound as they sprinted over the hard-packed sand in the direction of the APC, Phantom fast on their heels. Red tracers from M-16 rifles interspersed with the Russian fire as American troops reacted to the threat.

"There!" yelled Krieger. "Get behind the APC!"

A long burst walked along behind them as they approached the M113, getting closer the nearer they came to their target. A geyser of sand walked past them as they threw themselves behind the APC.

"Fuck me," said Waters, gasping for air. "That was too close."

A whooshing explosion sounded and the night sky blossomed fire from the direction of the TOC.

"What the hell was that? A grenade?" Simitis asked, sticking her head around the corner of the Stryker.

A split second after Krieger yanked her back behind the APC a 7.62mm round ricocheted off the vehicle's armor directly opposite her head's previous location.

"No," he said, crouching low and firing off the remaining twelve rounds in his Beretta as he identified the attackers by their muzzle flashes. "Too loud for a grenade," he said, ducking behind the Stryker again. "More like a satchel charge or rocket-propelled grenade."

"Oh my God," breathed Shelly Simitis. Brigade TOCs were the nexus for planning and control of over four thousand soldiers. Dozens of people manned them at any given minute, day or night.

"Any great ideas, Sergeant Krieger?" asked Waters.

"Yes," he replied. "I'll reload. You pull out your own weapon and begin engaging the enemy."

"Fine," Waters said sarcastically. "What about him?"

Krieger turned to his lieutenant and saw the officer was barely containing an armful of struggling Jack Russell.

"Your killer dog tried to take off after the Russians," said the lieutenant.

"The animal is a good judge of character," Krieger said through a tight smile. "Put him down, Lieutenant. He will be fine."

No sooner had Waters released the dog than Phantom growled low in his throat and bunched his muscles in preparation for an attack on the man-things who smelled like his first old friend's killers.

"Phantom," hissed Krieger. "Come."

The dog hesitated and then moved to Krieger's side.

"Stay," said the NCO. Without another glance at the dog he turned again to check his sector.

"That's some dog," said Simitis, taking up a kneeling position beneath Krieger, 9mm extended.

"That's the consensus," said Waters dryly before heading to the opposite end of the APC and taking up a security position of his own. Peering around the corner of the vehicle he extended his arms, lining the Beretta's muzzle with a figure running directly at him and lifting a rifle. The running man—unrecognizable in the dimming light—fired first. The lieutenant jerked his head instinctively as the man's round zipped past his head. Hearing a dull thud and an almost inaudible intake of breath behind him, Waters turned. A dead Spetsnaz trooper fell unmoving to the ground ten feet from his position.

Colonel Bill Jones completed his run and ducked behind the Stryker. "I'm getting too old for this shit," he wheezed, doubling over.

Waters suppressed the double chill running down his spine from having almost shot his brigade commander and almost getting himself shot. "Where the hell did you come from, sir?"

There was a pause before Jones replied. "I was at the . . . ah hell, no need to lie; the bastards caught me on the shitter."

Waters struggled to keep a straight face as he searched the local area for more targets, but the mental picture of Jones trying to pull his pants up and charge from the latrine was too much. Two short snorts escaped him.

Jones nodded sagely as he ejected the empty ammunition clip and exchanged it for a full one. "Laugh it up, Muddy," he said. "But I'm still your senior rater, dickweed. And I meant to tell you—nice rear security." The colonel nudged the dead Russian soldier with the tip of a boot.

"Ouch," muttered Waters, dropping a Spetsnaz trooper sprinting across his field of view.

Russian Special Forces raids like this one were designed to be quick-in, quick-out. Their primary mission accomplished, the remaining attackers now began exfiltrating toward their extraction point. Unfortunately their route sent them directly toward the M113 the Americans were using as cover.

"This could be a near thing," muttered Jones, squinting through his sights at over a dozen Russians sprinting in their direction. The increasing fire from the opposite end of the APC told him that Krieger and Simitis were also heavily engaged.

Krieger stood leaning around the edge of the armored vehicle, pistol extended in a two-hand grip, as he fired the remainder of his fifteen-round clip at the right edge of the group moving toward their position. Shelly Simitis kneeled on one knee beneath his extended arms. The two formed an effective team, unconsciously working together with telling effect on the Russian ranks.

Rolf Krieger thumbed the Beretta's magazine release and the metal clip dropped to the ground. "I'm out!" he yelled, reaching to one of the ammunition pouches on his pistol belt.

Simitis, working her way from left to center, automatically reassessed the group target as a whole. One of the enemy soldiers on the right had cocked his arm back. The captain swiveled in that direction from her crouch and aligned the Russian in her sights. She squeezed the trigger three times; too late. Even as he fell the soldier's arm completed its forward arc. In slow motion she watched the globular object headed directly for her and Krieger.

"Grenade!" she yelled, unconsciously slipping in front of Krieger and rising to shield her still-reloading partner.

The grenade bounced to a stop thirty feet from the edge of the 113. The vehicle blocked the brunt of the explosion but the concussive force threw Simitis into the side of the armored vehicle. Her head hit its edge hard and she fell forward into the open, unmoving.

Krieger, reloaded and recovered, took the situation in at a glance and threw himself forward on the prostrate Simitis. Feeling a lump he recognized beneath him, the big NCO continued engaging the Spetsnaz with 9mm fire using his right hand while he fumbled with Simitis's' web gear, finally pulling free the fragmentation grenade he'd felt beneath him.

Krieger ignored the fiery tug he felt burn across his shoulder. Dropping the pistol he pulled the pin free and tossed the grenade in front of the charging figures. He realized that both he and Simitis would be in the outer edge of the grenade's danger radius, but there had been no choice. Lying flat on his companion, Krieger covered her body with his own as best he could and waited.

The blast took his breath away and he felt shrapnel pull at his exposed skin. At that point conscious thought left him and he sank into oblivion.

A diesel rumble sounded behind the M113. An M2A2 Bradley skidded to a halt beside the APC and threw on its headlights. The bright lights stopped the Spetsnaz in their tracks, their night-vision goggles magnifying the source to the point of pain. Before they could recover the American vehicle opened up with its 7.62mm coax machine gun. Sand flew as the Bradley gunner fired a z pattern without letting up on the triggers. Ten seconds later nothing moved in the kill zone.

Shelly Simitis's eyes fluttered open. In the darkness the only feeling she had was one of a crushing weight on her. Struggling to move she realized the weight was

Rolf Krieger. Seeing the distance from the Bradley and reviewing the sequence of events, she realized what had happened. She struggled from beneath the big man and sat, rolling his head into her lap. "Sergeant Krieger," she said, softly but urgently. Grasping him by a shoulder, she gave the scout a gentle shake. "Sergeant Krieger, can you hear me? Are you all right?"

From the depths of his unconsciousness, Rolf Krieger rose. From somewhere a soft but gentle voice was calling to him . . .

He opened his eyes. The Bradley a few meters away backlit a figure above him. He thought it was an angel.

"You're alive," breathed Shelly Simitis. The relief in her voice was clear.

Krieger attempted to sit up.

"No," said Simitis, gently holding the big scout by his shoulders. "Just lie still a minute until we figure out how badly you're injured."

The NCO took stock of himself, wiggling toes, moving legs, turning his head back and forth. His arms were sore, but overall he seemed all right.

"I'm fine," he said.

"I'll be the judge of that," she said, pulling a flashlight from her LBE suspenders. Sliding from beneath him she gently laid his head on the ground and began a quick but efficient check of his condition. After a few moments she kneeled next to him. "Looks like a round grazed your shoulder—it's not bad, but you might need some stitches. Other than some cuts on your hands and arms, that's about it." She smiled. "You'll live."

Krieger felt some small portion of his inner iron core soften at the smile. "Thank you . . . for what you did. You should not have jumped in front of me like that, but . . . thank you."

Holding out a hand and standing, Simitis helped Krieger to his feet. "And exactly how did I end up beneath you?"

The NCO blushed in the cast-off light of the Bradley. "I . . ."

She reached up on tiptoes and gave him a quick but soft kiss on his dirty cheek. "Thank you."

Rolf Krieger opened his mouth, but no matter how hard he tried, he found he had no voice.

The Bradley's rear door clanged open and an NCO jumped out. "Sir!"

The vehicle's lights captured the pain in Jones's face as he turned to Waters. "Oh Lord. Brace yourself, Muddy."

"Sir . . . where the hell have you been? Do you know how long I've been trying to find—"

Jones held up a hand. Knowing the ritual and knowing that it would do no good to argue, the man ceased his badgering. For his part, Jones patted down his DCU shirt until he found cigarettes and lighter. Mission complete, he took a deep draw on the cigarette and waved for the Bradley commander to continue.

"Damn it, sir, you can't just run off and not tell anyone."

"O'Keefe . . ."

The NCO held up his own hand this time and shook his head resolutely. "No, sir. You'll let me finish . . ."

"I was taking a shit. The forces of nature cannot be argued with."

The NCO opened his mouth to reply. Realizing what Jones had said, he closed it abruptly. He had no reply.

Jones smiled his joy at finally having found *something* that could shut up his gunner and self-appointed bodyguard's henpecking after so many months. "Staff Sergeant O'Keefe, you know Lieutenant Waters."

O'Keefe nodded. "Good to see you again, Lieutenant. And pulling your company from you was bullshit in my opinion, for what it's worth, sir."

"Thanks for stopping by," said Waters with a chuckle.

He looked to Jones. "I'm going to check on Sergeant Krieger and Captain Simitis, sir."

As Waters approached Simitis and Krieger's position he saw no sign of them. His heart hammered. In his mind Krieger had become some indestructible fighting machine; it simply wasn't possible that he was dead. And Simitis . . . she'd been in his thoughts more and more of late.

Turning the corner of the APC Waters stopped short. Despite feeling like a cad, he watched as Simitis and Krieger spoke together quietly. There was something intimate about the scene. When he saw Shelly kiss the other man he felt a sinking sensation. So much for his first true love.

It wasn't as bad as it could have been at the TOC—two dead, five wounded. But one of the deaths hit Jones's team hard. The explosion had been a satchel charge and it had landed in the center of the operations center. Major Tom Proctor, the brigade S3, had been running for the exit to help coordinate a defense when it hit. Making an instant decision the major had thrown himself on the explosive device as its fuse ran down. While the explosion that followed caused damage in the area, Proctor's body and the flak vest he was wearing had taken the brunt of the blast.

Jones stood in the rotor wash of the helo taking the last of the casualties away, among them a body-bagged Tom Proctor. Images of Proctor's family throwing their arms around the major on his return from the last war flashed through Jones's mind. The old warrior had experienced this type of loss too many times over the years. He felt the accumulated grief weighing on him, threatening to make him scream "Enough!" and walk away.

"Sir." The voice at his elbow was quiet, just loud enough to gain Jones's attention.

Bill Jones did not turn at first, instead continuing to

watch the Black Hawk until it disappeared to the east
with its cargo of broken dreams. Closing his eyes, he
took a deep and cleansing breath; then he turned to his
executive officer.

"Talk to me, Max."

"You're going to have to appoint a new S3, sir," said
the lieutenant colonel. "And he's not going to have
much of a break-in period."

Jones nodded. "Recommendations?"

"You'll need someone with field savvy, preferably
combat experience. I could run a few names by you, but
I'll cut to the chase: Barnett."

Bill Jones grunted a laugh and tapped out a cigarette.
The Iron Tigers' S3 made him laugh and cry. The neck-
erchiefs, the totally unauthorized semi-handlebar mustache, his superior attitude.

The Striker Brigade commander's face glowed orange
as he pulled from the cigarette and turned to his XO.
"Perfect."

Shelly Simitis escorted Waters and Krieger to their
Hummer. They were greeted by the vehicle's driver, a
young scout in a jumpy disposition.

"You all right, Owens?" asked Waters.

The corporal nodded. He began to speak, and then
stopped.

"What?" asked the lieutenant.

The scout looked like he was about to explode.
"Where the *fuck* were you guys, sir? I had to shoot a
couple of people and I didn't even know what the *fuck*
was going on."

"We'll fill you in later," said Waters with a chuckle.

The corporal looked doubtful but nodded nonetheless.

Shelly Simitis stopped at the front bumper. "You guys
be careful." She smiled. "I hear it can be dangerous
where you're going."

The smile Waters returned to her had a sad twist. "Yes, ma'am. You, too."

Simitis saw the sadness in his eyes. "Is everything all right, Bob?" she asked, the concern in her voice evident.

Waters nodded. "I'm fine; it's just been a long day. You take care, ma'am." With that the lieutenant threw his LBE into the vehicle and climbed into one of the rear seats.

Simitis took hold of Rolf Krieger's arm as he began to climb into the front passenger seat. "I, uh . . ." She flushed. "I just wanted to remind you to change those bandages twice daily," she said, indicating his swathed forearms and shoulder. "Otherwise you're sure to get an infection."

"I will, Captain," he said formally.

Simitis's face showed her frustration. "Don't you ever loosen up?"

The big NCO shrugged, taking the question at face value. "No."

Simitis's expression softened. "Well, we'll work on that. Just be careful, okay?"

Krieger again felt something strange within him as he looked at her, the same as he had when he awoke with his head in her lap after the firefight. He had never felt its like. Something about the woman moved him. Was it her eyes, deep brown with faint golden flecks in the iris? Or the curve of her jaw and high cheekbones? Her intelligence? Her bravery? He inwardly shrugged. Rolf Krieger was an intelligent man; though he had never felt love, he recognized the feelings for what they were despite the lack of practical experience. But it did not matter. She was a captain, an officer; and he was an enlisted man. Two separate worlds, forbidden to meet in the way his heart wished they could.

"I will. And"—he hesitated—"and you do the same, Captain."

Krieger was about to turn away, his wish to say more to this woman battling with the realization that there was nothing more to say. Looking toward his feet it occurred to him there was one more thing that he could say to this woman. "Captain, may I ask a favor of you?"

Shelly Simitis watched the Hummer rumble toward the forward edge of the battle area. Her heart grew heavy, knowing as she did that the action that had occurred in the TOC compound a few hours earlier was light contact compared to what the scouts would see when the Russians moved east.

In her arms Phantom also watched the Hummer disappear into the night. From deep within the small animal came a low but heartbreaking whine.

Wiping an eye, Shelly Simitis hugged the dog close to her chest and whispered into his ear, "I know, boy. I miss him already, too."

Chapter 17

_____

_____

Does This Tank Make My Hips Look Big?

Phase Line Doberman
Cold Steel Battle Position
Southwestern Iraq

Dillon stood on a .50 cal ammo box at the end of Cyclops's big gun tube. A long cord ran from his CVC helmet, over the top of the tank, and into his hatch; it connected into his commander's weapon station communications box, giving him the ability to communicate with his gunner via the M1A1's intercom system.

The captain had placed the boresight device—a ten-power telescope with a right-angle viewing window—into the end of the big 120mm gun tube a few minutes earlier and was now talking Sergeant Bickel onto his "target," a rectangular panel placed on the rear end of another Steel tank twelve hundred meters away. In the early dawn light the other C Company crews carried out the same task. The reason behind regular boresighting was simple: to ensure that what the gunner thought was dead center was what the fire control system considered dead center. The team would repeat the procedure again just before dark. Life as a U.S. Army tanker had its more predictable aspects and boresighting at first and last light was one of them. The big guns were of little use to anyone if they couldn't hit their targets.

Through the boresight device's view window Dillon saw the panel on the back of the other tank. The window itself was bisected horizontally and vertically by a set of black crosshairs. Dillon's goal was to place the crosshairs directly on the upper right corner of the panel.

"Bring it right," he said into his boom mike. "Steady . . . a little more."

The crosshairs moved a trifle past the mark. "Shit. Bring it back . . . stop. Left, left. A little more . . ."

A vehicle roared past and a dust cloud enveloped Cyclops. Dillon raised his head from the boresight device and hopped off of the ammo box, irate. "It's ass-munching time," he muttered.

Twenty feet away two Hummers rolled to a halt. One was the classic Army command-and-control version, an M998 festooned with antennas: Myron Sutherland. The other was a white civilian model H2.

Dillon wiped the dust from his good eye and pulled the boom mike to his lips. "Bick, send Bo out here to finish up." He started to disconnect the comms cord connecting his CVC to the tank but stopped. "And tell him to make damned sure he uses the manual."

Pulling the cord loose he walked to the Hummers. Sutherland stood in front of the H2 talking to one of the passengers. The man looked to be in his early thirties. Slightly over six feet, he was thin with an athletic build; longish brown hair, but not too long; khaki trousers fashionably long so that a couple of inches fell over his leather hiking boots; a military flak vest over an olive drab T-shirt. The latest in field chic.

Dillon knew what he was looking at—the Pentagon's latest pet project, embedded reporters. America was receiving a firsthand view of the war from the tactical level. A few of the journalists had been assigned to the

1st Cav. One of them was responsible for getting out evidence of Russian atrocities via video phone; he was still missing. *But why would Sutherland bring him here?* wondered Patrick Dillon. And then he answered the question himself. *Oh shit.*

The captain stopped next to his two visitors and removed his CVC.

"Patrick," Sutherland said and smiled.

If Dillon hadn't known he was in trouble before, he did now. Sutherland had never called him by his Christian name; Dillon or Captain, yes, Patrick . . . definitely not.

"Sir," he replied.

The smile never left the colonel's face. "Patrick, I'd like you to meet Nate Ryan. Nate's a reporter for *Fox News.*"

Dillon nodded and held out a hand. "Nice meeting you, Nate. I wish you luck with your reporting. Keep your head down and your film dry." He looked down at the big Super SeaWolf on his wrist. "Unfortunately we're a little busy, so I'm going to have to say goodbye."

The smile grew and threatened to break Sutherland's face. "You don't quite understand, Patrick. I'm embedding Nate in C Company. It shouldn't be any bother, just go about your normal routine."

Dillon forced a smile of his own. "Sir, can I speak with you? Privately?"

Expansive now, Sutherland clapped a hand on Dillon's shoulder. "Why of course, son. Why don't you walk me back to my vehicle?"

When they reached HQ-6 Sutherland climbed in and closed the door. The smile disappeared as he leaned one arm on the window frame and turned his head to Dillon. "This one's nonnegotiable, Dillon. You've pissed me off. I can't afford to give up a combat-seasoned commander at the moment, but that doesn't keep me from giving you every shit detail that comes along; case in point, babysitting a news crew."

Dillon grabbed the large side mirror mounted to the vehicle's door and took a deep breath. "Sir, I understand that you've got a case of the ass, but—"

"Grow up, Captain," said Sutherland. "I didn't ask for the reporter, but we got him. And now he's yours."

Patrick Dillon wasn't finished. "Sir, put him with the combat trains. Put him at the TOC. Put him anywhere but up here. I don't have time for this shit." He paused a moment before continuing. "And if he gets killed, that wouldn't look so good for you, would it?"

The Iron Tigers commander hesitated as he ran that one through his mind and then put a forefinger to the tip of his nose and smiled knowingly. "Nice try, Dillon. Nice try. But you bring up a good point—if something happens to that news crew, it's going to look bad for someone . . . and that someone is you, Captain." The lieutenant colonel laughed. "Enjoy the exposure." He turned to his driver. The specialist was diplomatically observing the boresighting operation being conducted by a tank crew fifty meters from his side of the Hummer. "Let's go, driver."

Dillon stood in the dust of the Hummer as it pulled away. Turning back to the H2 he saw Nate Ryan leaning with his back against the front bumper, arms across his chest. He'd been watching the exchange.

Walking slowly, Dillon returned to the reporter.

"Nice patch," said Ryan with a wry smile. "Bet there's a great story behind it."

Dillon shook his head once, frowning. "Not one you'll ever hear," he said quietly, thinking of Rob Estes.

Realizing he'd hit a raw nerve Ryan held out his hand. "What do you say we start over? Nate Ryan."

Dillon's frown disappeared, replaced by a reluctant smile. "Patrick Dillon. Call me Pat."

Ryan nodded in the direction of the departing Hummer, nothing but a sand cloud in the distance now. "He doesn't like you much, does he, Pat?"

Dillon raised an eyebrow. "Oh, you're *good*."

Ryan chuckled. "Is he as big an asshole as he seems?"

The Steel commander nodded. "Nate, you have no idea."

"I know this gig is new to you," said Ryan. "Why don't I lay down the ground rules?"

Dillon pulled out his Copenhagen and nodded. "All right."

"Okay," said Ryan. "Here you go: first, information relating to ongoing engagements will not be released unless authorized by you."

Dillon nodded again. "Fair enough."

"The date, time, locations, and details of previous engagements are only releasable if couched in general terms."

"Okay."

For the next ten minutes, Ryan filled Dillon in on the Pentagon's rules of engagement, or ROE, for the media community. "Any questions?"

Dillon shook his head. "Nate, I like you. And call it a gift of my Celtic blood, but my first impressions are generally proven out over time."

"What did you think of Sutherland when you met him?"

"Dick with ears."

Ryan nodded.

"Here's my bottom line," continued Dillon. "Do not do anything to put my men in jeopardy."

"Got it."

"If you do"—and Dillon smiled—"the world will see me embedding your microphone so far up your ass that you'll be singing soprano for the rest of your natural life."

Ryan examined the Steel commander's face long enough to decide he was serious. "I'm clear."

"Great," said Dillon. "As long as we understand each other. What say we grab some breakfast?"

First Sergeant John Rider's vehicle stopped next to Dillon as Ryan got his crew together. The Steel commander motioned his senior NCO to the side and informed him of the new addition to the Cold Steel team.

"Fuck a duck," muttered Rider in a low voice.

"Concur," said Dillon conciliatorily.

Dillon looked again at the H2 as the crew approached them. The white vehicle stuck out like a sore thumb. He leaned to Rider and spoke a few words in a low voice. Rider nodded.

"Nate," said Dillon when the reporter, his cameraman, and his driver arrived. "This is my first sergeant, John Rider. Best topkick in the Army."

The men exchanged greetings.

"You guys hungry? Top Rider just brought in chow," said Dillon.

"Sounds great," said Ryan. "We haven't had anything but Slim Jims and bottled water since lunch yesterday," said Ryan.

"Then you're in for a treat," said Dillon, leading the group away. "The Army breakfast is legendary."

A half hour later, breakfast finished, Dillon walked Ryan back to the H2.

"Thanks, Pat," said the reporter. "That surely hit the—" Ryan stopped twenty feet from the H2. "What the hell?"

The Hummer had been purchased brand-new from a Kuwait City showroom floor with all of the options, including a GPS system. "That vehicle cost my network over sixty thousand dollars American," he breathed.

Dillon walked over and clapped a hand on Ryan's shoulder. The formerly white H2 was now a mottled sand and brown. And the paint job was anything but professional. Paintbrush strokes were visible throughout and the windows were spattered. "You have to admit, Nate, it's a hell of a lot more tactical. Welcome to Steel."

The reporter sputtered a couple of times and then his shoulders sagged as he thought of the woman in the network's accounting department to whom he would have to answer. "Oh, that bitch is going to have my balls," he muttered to himself.

CIA Headquarters
Langley, Virginia

A large grandfather clock stood in the corner, the tick of its brass pendulum swinging back and forth in a slow arc as it marked time the room's only sound. The men sat low in large dark brown chairs of Italian leather.

"So exactly what do you think you did wrong, little brother," said Chris Dodd finally.

His brother Luke didn't bother looking at Chris Dodd, but instead chose to stare out the window. "I could have stayed in place longer, been of more use."

"Your cover was blown," said the CIA chief patiently.

"The Russians knew there was someone on the inside; they didn't know it was me." Luke's head swiveled to stare into his brother's eyes. "I could have handled it. I made the pullout call too early."

"It's a moot point now," said the elder Dodd. "But my take: It's clear from your debrief that Oleg Gryzlov was on to you after your altercation with the muggers. You were finished in Moscow, Luke. I was getting ready to pull you out myself if you hadn't made the call."

Luke sat forward. "The hell you say. That's one thing you and I have always agreed on in our professional relations—I make the call when it's my balls on the line."

Chris Dodd grunted, shrugging. "So shoot me. You're

my brother and I love you. I'd have done it and then we could have argued over it once you were safe."

Silence.

"And you'd do the same if the shoe were on the other foot," finished Chris Dodd.

It was Luke's turn to grunt. "Touché," he muttered.

They sat in silence for another minute.

"Why don't you tell me about Khartukov's daughter?" said Chris.

A wan smile lit Luke's face at the mention of Natasha. "What about her?"

"According to Ted, you two seemed kind of . . . chummy."

Luke Dodd shrugged. "You read my reports. I knew after her mother's funeral that she was a potential—albeit unknowing—ally and source within the Kremlin walls. It would have been unprofessional of me not to cultivate a relationship with Khartukov's only child, given the opportunity."

Chris Dodd gave him an elder brother smirk. "Yes, I noted at one point that you used the term 'close.' But how close was it? Like good friends close? Like sisters close—remembering for the time being that you were a nancy boy in Russia? What exactly does 'close' mean?"

Luke shifted. "We became friends. Good friends. It was clear that . . ." Luke Dodd hesitated. A field operative's professional reputation took years to build. Admitting mistakes didn't come easy. "Our relationship evolved. Particularly that last night in Moscow. All the masks came off and all that was left were raw feelings." He looked at the floor. "I probably could have handled it better."

Chris Dodd leaned forward, elbows on his knees. "Is this serious, little brother? Or the result of a lot of hormonal juices flowing after your Moscow adventure?"

"I used her feelings for me to expedite my way onto the aircraft. It made things simpler."

"You could have left her behind, along with Khartukov's thugs, and made your way to the airport," his brother pointed out quietly. "Why take the extra risk?"

"She *needed* to get out, all right? You don't know what a son of a bitch her father is," said Luke hotly.

Chris Dodd sat back and folded his arms. "So you used her, did you? All part of the assignment?"

Luke shrugged. "Yeah, I used her. All right?"

His brother nodded. "Okay, man. Good enough for me."

By silent consent the men changed topics, knowing they'd never come to closure on Luke's best course of action today. There were simply too many unknowns.

"So what's the Agency's plan for me now? Instructor at The Farm?" asked Luke, shuddering.

Chris Dodd smiled. Having been an operations officer himself for so many years, he knew that thoughts of returning to a REMF—short for rear echelon motherfucker—job gave active field operatives nightmares. "We'll talk about that later." He stood. "Right now, you have an appointment. Someone wants to meet you."

Luke stood and took a beaten and stained oversized suede jacket with sheepskin collar from the back of his chair. "So who is it? If it's Emeril making a last-ditch effort for me to divulge the secret of my raspberry dressing now that he knows I'm back in town . . ."

"It's the president."

Luke Dodd stopped in his tracks. He looked over the jacket he'd shrugged into and then down at his faded jeans and hiking boots.

"What?" said Chris Dodd.

"I'm feeling a little underdressed for the Oval Office, bro," said Luke. "Mind if I run by my place and change?"

Chris Dodd took his brother's arm and led him down the hallway. "Come on, cowboy, you're fine." He laughed. The brothers had been raised in Alpine, Wyoming, just south of Jackson Hole. Their parents still operated a thousand-acre ranch, though these days the operation focused more on the horse-breeding end than when the Dodd brothers had filled in as free labor. During those years their dad, Big Red Dodd, had run cattle, and lots of them. And he'd taught his boys to love the land.

"No time," said Chris Dodd. "Besides, the boss isn't big on formalities." He shook a clear rectangular dispenser filled with orange pellets at Luke. "Tic Tac?"

"No," replied Luke, thinking of meeting the nation's chief executive face-to-face. "But a few dozen Rolaids would be nice."

Chris Dodd laughed. "You'll be fine." He noted the direction of his brother's gaze as he stood in the doorway. Following it his eyes lighted on the walnut hat tree in the corner of the office. Rolling his eyes, he said, "Go ahead."

Walking quickly to the corner Luke pulled a dark brown Stetson with a worn leather band from one of the tree's arms. He shrugged. "I feel kind of naked without it."

The White House
Washington, D.C.

"Would you gentlemen like some coffee while you wait?" asked the president's personal assistant.

Luke Dodd shifted nervously in his seat and smiled. "No, thank you."

Chris Dodd made a dismissive gesture and smiled. "Don't listen to him, Betty. We'll both take a cup."

Luke looked at his brother questioningly.

"Never turn down White House coffee. It's the best you'll ever taste," said Christopher Dodd with a wink.

A Navy steward arrived within thirty seconds and poured for both men.

Sipping from a thick white mug emblazoned with a simple yet elegant gold presidential seal, Luke raised his eyebrows. "This is fantastic. Guatemalan?"

Chris Dodd frowned. "I don't know. The sons of bitches keep it a secret. It's blended especially for the president."

"You're the director of the Central Intelligence Agency for Christ's sake," said Luke. "You can't find out where the president gets his coffee? That's sad, my brother."

"How many times the president of China has been treated for the clap during the past year, that I can tell you. Number and names of gay congressmen—easy. The secret of the presidential coffee . . ." Chris snorted. "No. Embarrassing, I'll admit. It comes in five-pound plain paper bags once a week through diplomatic channels."

"Your chiefs of station are of no help?" asked Dodd, referring to the lead CIA operatives in each U.S. embassy around the globe.

Chris Dodd shook his head, shamed. "Useless bastards."

As the men warmed to their coffee a woman walked in. The first word that sprang into Luke's mind was "stunning"—an angular and intelligent face; corn-silk-blond hair cut just above the shoulders, pulled back at the moment; dark blue, almost navy, eyes; dressed for success in a Ralph Lauren jacket of Italian stretched wool with matching slacks, a slim TAG Heuer titanium timepiece her sole ornamentation. The lady's look announced to the world that she had arrived but that she didn't need to flaunt it.

"Angela," Chris Dodd said, rising, "this is my little brother, Luke. Luke, Dr. Angela Bennett."

Luke rose and took Bennett's hand. "The national security advisor, of course. Nice to meet you, Dr. Bennett."

Angela Bennett gave him a sparkling smile and

squeezed his hand. "I've heard a great deal about you, Luke. And I'm glad you made it home safely." She gave Luke's attire a once-over and then looked to Chris Dodd questioningly.

"We were in a bit of a hurry," he said. "Got caught up in family issues and lost track of the time."

Bennett smiled disarmingly. "And I assume the old Jeep outside is yours?"

"Yes, ma'am," said Luke sheepishly, shifting his booted feet. "I'd have felt out of place in Chris's M3 dressed like this."

"Director Dodd," interrupted the president's assistant quietly. "The President would like to see you alone first, sir."

"Of course. Thank you, Betty." Dodd turned to Angela Bennett and Luke. "See you two in a few minutes."

"Coffee, Dr. Bennett?" asked Betty.

"Yes, please."

The two sat quietly for a few minutes, each lost in their own thoughts. Luke nervously twirled his Stetson in circles with his hands.

"*God,* this is good stuff," murmured Angela Bennett, taking another sip.

Luke Dodd just smiled.

"Luke," Angela Bennett said, putting down her cup, "I'm glad we've got a few minutes. I need to speak with you."

"Dr. Bennett, if this is mission-related, you really need to speak to my brother."

"It's not."

Luke Dodd leaned back. "All right, now I'm intrigued."

"It's about Natasha Khartukov. We're not sure exactly how to handle her. Considering the amount of time you two have spent together, your input would be helpful."

"Just let her go back to work at the U.N. She's got no part—nor interest—in her father's plans."

"It's not that simple, Luke," said Angela Bennett quietly.

Cold fire burned in the operations officer's eyes. "The hell it ain't, lady. You're the fucking national security advisor. Make it happen."

It was Bennett's turn to sit back. A look of understanding dawned on her face. "Why do you care?"

Luke looked away. "I don't care, Dr. Bennett. I'm giving you the facts as I know them—my professional observation after working inside her father's office for two-plus years. She's of no use to you."

"She was more to you than part of an assignment, wasn't she? She got to you."

"Bullshit, lady. I've been in deeper shit than a Roto-Rooter man on his worst day and come out smelling like a rose. If you think—"

"I've spoken with the lady," said Bennett. "I don't think it's that simple. Either that or you are a more overbearing ass than your brother ever thought of being."

Dodd sat forward and began playing with his hat again. "Just let her go. Trust me on this one."

"I'll see what I can do, all right?" said Angela Bennett, not unkindly.

Luke Dodd merely nodded, ending the topic. A moment later he began speaking again, as much to himself as Angela Bennett. "I'm tired of this job."

Bennett looked at him, surprised. "Why?"

He spun the Stetson in his hands, eyes focused on it. "Why can't we do the right things by God and country without hurting innocents, without giving up some piece of ourselves?"

"I don't know, Luke," said Bennett quietly. "All we can do is the best we can. You had a mission to accomplish. A mission very few people in this world could have pulled off, much less pulled off and survived. But you did it. That should be worth something to you."

"Then why do I feel like shit?"

Angela Bennett frowned. "I don't know, Luke. That's a question you'll have to answer yourself."

"So what's going on between you and my brother, anyway?"

The change in topic surprised Bennett. She flushed and sat up straighter. "I have no idea what you're talking about."

Luke smiled slowly, continuing to look at the spinning hat. "The sexual tension between you two was so tight that I could have cut it with a knife."

Bennett opened her mouth to protest, but was interrupted by the president's assistant. "The President is ready for you."

Luke stood and placed the Stetson on his vacated seat. "Oh boy," he said beneath his breath as he moved toward the door.

The first thing Luke Dodd noted on entering the Oval Office was the large blue rug with the presidential seal. His brother, standing next to Jonathan Drake, had already drilled it into him not to step on the seal—major faux pas, stepping on the eagle.

"Hello, Luke."

The speaker had been sitting out of his line of sight, but he knew the voice well. Luke slowly turned toward the voice. "Natasha," he said, nodding.

Natasha Khartukov walked toward him slowly, a shadow of sadness visible in her smile. "How are you?"

Luke Dodd glanced toward his brother and the President of the United States. "I'm fine. And you?"

"I am being treated well. Hopefully I can return to New York soon."

An awkward silence ensued.

"I take it you two need no introductions," said President Jonathan Drake dryly.

When Luke began to explain the president stopped

him with an outstretched hand. "I'm kidding, Officer Dodd. Mrs. Drake—that's my wife, not my mother—says my sense of humor is a little off-kilter." He walked to Luke Dodd and held out a hand. "I want you to know that your nation is grateful for the services you've performed at such great personal risk." He nodded to Natasha. "Miss Khartukov was kind enough to add further details to your exploits above and beyond those briefed to me by your brother." Jonathan Drake grasped Luke's hand firmly in both of his own as he looked Luke Dodd in the eye. "I am in your debt, sir."

Luke could find no words. He simply nodded.

The president looked over Luke's western attire, but not in a critical way. He smiled. "Your brother told me about your family's spread out west. You know I have a ranch myself down in Florida."

"In Florida, Mr. President?"

"Lots of horses and cows in Florida, Luke. Mine is a little over three hundred acres; mostly pasture with oak hammocks. Running about nine hundred head of cattle. Of course it's nowhere near as large as your father's place, but not too shabby. You'll have to come visit sometime, tell me what you think of it."

"Come for a visit?"

Jonathan Drake nodded. "We'll take the scenic tour, by horseback."

"By horseback?" *Note to self,* thought Luke Dodd. *Stop repeating the president.* "I'd enjoy that. Thank you, sir."

Jonathan Drake caught Angela Bennett's eye, clearly ready to settle down to matters at hand. "And now, Angela, I believe you have business with Miss Khartukov?" The words were phrased as a question, but Bennett knew it for the dismissal it was.

As she left the room Natasha looked toward Luke Dodd. He refused to meet her stare, instead staring at his booted feet. And then she was gone.

Drake walked to his desk. Built from pieces of the HMS *Resolute*, it had been given to Rutherford B. Hayes in 1880 as a gift by the Queen of England. Going to the bottom drawer the president pulled out a pack of cigarettes and a lighter.

"Mr. President," said Chris Dodd in an accusatory tone, but smiling.

"Shut up, Chris," Drake said.

Dodd nodded. "Yes, sir."

The president guided his guests to the seating area. "Make yourselves comfortable, gentlemen," said Drake, taking a seat in the great chair next to the fireplace. A knock sounded and another man entered without waiting. "Sorry I'm running behind, Mr. President, but I think we've got everything we need now. The op should be a go within twenty-four hours."

"Luke, I don't believe you've met Marc Sterling, director of the FBI?" said Drake, making introductions.

"Director Sterling," said Luke, standing and shaking the beefy man's hand.

"How do you do, son," said Sterling. "And I believe I owe you an apology."

"How's that, sir?" asked Luke, frowning.

"Well, if I was doing my job right, our Moscow leak would have been plugged a long time ago. As it is, I hear you barely made it out of there with your skin intact."

Luke looked to his brother. He didn't know how much the FBI knew about the Agency's ongoing activities abroad and was well aware of the rivalry and territoriality of both organizations. Chris Dodd sent a small nod his brother's way. The FBI chief had been briefed.

"How about I make it up to you?" said Sterling. "Would you like a hand in taking down our mole?"

Luke Dodd didn't hesitate. "Shit yes. . . ."

Chris Dodd put a hand over his eyes and shook his head. "Sorry, sir," he said to Drake. "You can take the boy out of Wyoming, but . . ."

Jonathan Drake smiled benignly but didn't reply. It was good having muddy boots in the Oval Office for a change.

Forty-five minutes later the sting's details were complete. Marc Sterling stood. "Luke, it was a pleasure to meet you. If you ever want honest work, the FBI will be here."

"Kind of hard breaking away from the family business, but I appreciate it, Mr. Director," said Luke, standing and taking Sterling's extended hand.

Once the FBI chief was gone, Chris Dodd turned to the president. "Sir, we have another item to discuss if you've got a few minutes to spare."

Drake glanced at his watch. "Go, but make it quick. I've got a Girl Scouts award to present at the top of the hour in the Rose Garden. If I miss it, the First Lady is going to raise hell."

The two CIA men stared at Drake.

"Don't give me that 'we're at war' look, boys. It's five minutes of my life and a shitload of goodwill. Now press."

Dodd nodded. "As you know, Angela—Dr. Bennett—and I have been discussing the quickest way to end the conflict. That's by getting Russia to the peace table—all agree that the Saudis are a nonplayer once Ivan's out of the equation. To that end, we have an idea, sir."

Drake nodded. "Go on."

"It would involve great personal risk to one man. We send him into Moscow after Konstantin Khartukov."

The president thought about that for a moment in silence. "Tell me more," he said finally.

"Sir, indications in the country are that the people are not behind the new government. Their first taste of democracy may have stung them a bit, but they were free too long. Russia—Moscow in particular—is a powder keg. Without the iron will of Khartukov at the reins,

they'll sue for peace. We already have indications from
the field that the military leadership is unhappy, and they
were his chief endorsers."

The three sat, thinking about Dodd's words and what
they meant. The difficulty involved in pulling off the
operation. The snapping of a log in the fireplace was the
only sound in an otherwise silent Oval Office.

"It's got to be me," said Luke quietly.

"No," said Chris Dodd.

"I have to agree with your brother, Luke," said Jonathan Drake. "You've done enough. You were under-
cover in Russia for over two years. They know you."
A paternal tone entered the president's voice. "You've
earned a rest, son, and you'll have it."

"No other way, sir," said the young operations officer.
"Not on short notice."

"No," said Chris Dodd again. "We've got an excellent
man selected for the mission. I'll want you to give him
the lowdown on the physical area, Khartukov's activities,
the personalities involved, and so on. That's it for you."
And the CIA director's face reiterated the fact that he
would brook no further discussion over the matter.

Luke Dodd sat back and shook his head. "There's not
enough time. You'd be condemning the man to a slow
and certain death in Lubyanka."

Jonathan Drake looked first at Christopher Dodd,
then to his younger brother, and finally to the elder
Dodd again. "I have to agree with Luke, Chris. If this
operation is to have any chance of success, then it needs
to happen now. And I, *like you,* know that there's no
one else that has a chance of succeeding."

"The last time I looked the Central Intelligence
Agency was my organization to run as I see fit," said
Dodd coldly.

"Chris," said Jonathan Drake. He spoke the single
word slowly but with authority.

Dodd looked at the floor. "Sorry, Mr. President. That was out of line."

"You're too close to this one, Chris."

"But, sir . . ."

"Remember, Mr. Director, you run the CIA—but you run it for me. If Luke is willing to go, it will be him."

Christopher Dodd didn't like it, but he reluctantly nodded. "Do you want to give guidance on the mission's parameters, sir?"

It took Drake a moment to realize what his chief clandestine operator meant. "You mean . . ."

The CIA director nodded. "Yes, sir."

Jonathan Drake thought the question over. "Is there a better chance of success if Khartukov lives?"

"Neither Angela nor myself believe there is, sir. So long as Khartukov is out, one way or the other, we will be able to deal with the Russians."

The president wrapped the mantle of commander in chief around himself and said stonily, "Luke, I want you in and out of Russia as quickly as possible. Take Khartukov out and get the hell out of there. Clear?"

Luke Dodd's thoughts briefly turned to Natasha Khartukov. *Shit on a stick.* "Crystal, sir," he replied.

Chapter 18

Takin' Care of (Unfinished) Business

3rd Brigade, 4th Infantry Division (Strikers) TOC
Southwestern Iraq

"How're you doing, Dave?" asked Bill Jones, a smile playing across his craggy features.

Major Dave Barnett sat on the proffered camp stool. The look on his face answered the question in no uncertain terms. "Fine, sir," he said tonelessly. "Damned happy to be here."

"You're a bad liar, Dave, but that's all right. The brigade staff will grow on you."

"I'm sure it will, sir," returned Barnett. "Mine is but to serve."

Jones stood up and smacked his new S3 across the back. "Ohhhh, we're going to get along great! Now let's draft a FRAGO."

Despite his glumness regarding moving from a fighting unit to the brigade staff, Barnett was intrigued. "What kind of FRAGO, sir? You just issued the mission order last night."

Jones pulled out his smokes and knocked one into a massive paw. Putting it in his mouth, he lit up and squinted into the rising sun. "Yeah, but I've been thinking. . . ."

Two hours later both men hunched over a large map laid out on a field table. Red and blue marker strokes outlined the mission changes they envisioned.

"Does that work for you, sir?" asked Barnett.

Jones took a deep drag off his cigarette and exhaled through his nostrils and then nodded. "Yep. What do you think of it, Dave?"

Barnett grunted. "Are you familiar with the British Special Air Service motto, sir?"

"Yeah . . . *Who Dares Wins*."

The Striker S3 nodded. "That about sums it up."

"This is as much your plan as mine," said Jones. "If it doesn't work, you've gotta shave off the 'stache."

Barnett reached up, rolling one of the mustache tips between his fingers, the whole time continuing to examine the areas where red and blue symbols intersected. "If this doesn't work, I'm not going to be worrying about the mustache or anything else."

Iron Tigers TOC
Southwestern Iraq

Two hours later Myron Sutherland looked over his plan and smiled. The plan devised by Jones and Barnett called for one of the Iron Tigers companies to be out on a limb—a very thin limb. For the past week he'd seen nothing but disrespect from Captain Patrick Dillon. The Iron Tigers commander's smile broadened. Selecting which company was to take a fall wasn't a difficult decision.

Sutherland's face turned serious for a moment. An entire company was going to suffer because of his personal feelings regarding one subordinate. How did he feel about that? The colonel shrugged it off. Maybe he wasn't the soldier his father was and maybe he never would be, but young Myron had learned one thing if nothing else from his old man—sacrifices had to be made for the greater good.

Myron Sutherland's smile returned. No, he'd learned one other thing from his father—how to recognize men who could make up for his own shortfalls. Dillon would get the job done; and then the man would be out of his hair for good. And the Tigers—and thus he himself—would come out smelling like a rose.

Phase Line Doberman
Cold Steel Battle Position
Southwestern Iraq

". . . that's all. More to follow when I have it. Steel Six, out."

Dillon stretched his back, having just passed on the warning order issued by the Iron Tigers TOC. As if things weren't hectic enough. They'd completed the preparation of their battle positions less than three hours earlier and now they were told there was a change of mission coming. The most he could do was give his platoons a warning order to ensure they were prepared to move on little or no notice. He flipped his eye patch up and scratched around the left eye. There was hardly any pain now, but the itching was driving him nuts.

The tank's radio squawked. *"Steel Six, Tiger Six, go to your alternate push, over."*

Myron? thought Dillon as he listened to the familiar voice. *Why was Sutherland calling him on his company frequency? And why does he want me on the alternate frequency? Something he doesn't want anyone else to hear?* A bad feeling descended on the Steel commander.

"Steel Six, wilco," replied Dillon simply.

Looking to his left Dillon saw Bo Boggs was at him.

Having monitored the transmission the private was standing by to execute the change in frequency. Dillon half smiled. Despite the fact that Boggs had been in the Army only a few months and assigned to an active-duty unit for mere days prior to this deployment, he was rapidly becoming a valued crew member. Dillon nodded.

Boggs turned to the radio for a few seconds, looked back to Dillon and pointed an index finger at him—he was on the new frequency.

Dillon threw the young loader a thumbs-up and keyed his CVC switch. *"Striker Three, Steel Six, over."*

"Roger, Steel Six . . . your new orders follow," began Sutherland.

Five minutes later Dillon was staring up through the open turret at a blue sky. *Why me, God?* he thought. *"This is Steel Six, roger."*

"This is Tiger Six, out," signed off Sutherland.

Dillon looked to Boggs and nodded for him to go back to the primary company push. He thought about the best way to pass on the new information, finally pulling a notebook from his pocket and scribbling for a couple of minutes. If he called Muddy, even on the Knight counter-recon push, someone at the TOC was sure to be monitoring. Finishing his note, Patrick Dillon keyed his CVC switch.

"Steel Five, Steel Six, meet me at my fix, over."

Two minutes later Dillon was leaning against Cyclops's front slope when Bluto Wyatt walked up to him.

"What's shakin', sir?" asked the big XO with his perpetual good-natured smile plastered to his face.

Not for a minute did Dillon doubt that most of his company leadership, hearing Sutherland's call, had switched to the alternate frequency as quick as or quicker than he himself had. The captain smiled—it was the same thing he would have done as a lieutenant. And judging by Bluto's scowl, the lieutenant knew that something fishy was going on.

"You heard." It was a statement, not a question.
Wyatt nodded.

"Take my Hummer. I already called Almo. . . ."

Even as Dillon spoke the voice of Toby Keith floated across the desert toward him. Looking east Dillon saw his Hummer, Charlie-66, approaching in a cloud of dust. His driver and training NCO, Sergeant Almo, had listened to nothing but Garth Brooks since 1991 on the custom sound system he'd installed in the vehicle. After September 11th things had changed for Almo, musically speaking. He'd discovered Keith, the Angry American. Not coincidentally that was the name of the song blaring through the dry Iraqi heat.

Dillon looked to Wyatt. "We don't have much time, Bluto, and we've got a lot to do if we're going to pull this off. Here's what I need you to do. . . ."

The Hummer screamed to an abrupt halt ten feet from the two Armor officers just as Dillon was wrapping up his instructions. *". . . man, we lit up your world like the Fourth of July . . ."*

The big lieutenant shoved his notebook into a breast pocket. "Not a problem, sir," Wyatt yelled over his shoulder, hopping into the Hummer.

The Hummer pulled away in a cloud of dust. *". . . we'll put a boot in your ass, it's the American way . . ."*

Looking west, Dillon cursed under his breath. This shit was hard enough without the Myron Sutherlands of the world wading in.

Chapter 19

_____

_____

Smoke, Mirrors & the Depleted-Uranium Sandwich

"What have I missed?" asked Patrick Dillon. He stood in front of a sand table, roughly twenty feet by sixty feet, hewn from the desert floor in the middle of the C Company position. It was illuminated by a dying Middle Eastern sun that sat precariously on the western horizon. Built by one of his NCOs with an eye for terrain, the model depicted in accurate detail the major terrain features Steel would potentially be operating in for the next forty-eight hours. Twine stretched east to west depicting the current operations order's phase lines. The names of the phase lines were printed on three-by-five cards mounted to wooden stakes; more labeled stakes marked the company's target reference points. A large loop of black yarn designated C Company's battle position. Within the loop the company's three tank platoon positions were marked by smaller loops of yarn in the color of their respective platoons—red for 1st Platoon, white for 2nd, blue for 3rd. Fourteen metal miniature M1A1 tanks sat on the terrain board where their actual sixty-eight-ton Abrams counterparts would operate during the mission.

Dillon's officers and senior NCOs continued to stare at the sand table. Unlike many of his contemporaries, who included only platoon leaders and their executive officers at their orders, Dillon found it useful whenever time permitted to have each of his thirteen tank commanders present for the order. In this way the men executing the plan received his intent directly from him rather than secondhand. While the Steel commander trusted his lieutenants, it was too easy, especially when everyone was near the point of mental and physical exhaustion, for something to get lost in the translation.

The model looked like any one of a hundred they'd been briefed over by the captain. But this one was different. This time they looked at the steel miniatures representing their tanks and knew the sabot rounds and AT missiles being briefed were real; that the red sandbags representing artillery preps—which Dillon casually dropped on the yarn ovals—would do more than raise a small puff of dust when they fell.

Bluto Wyatt raised a hand.

"XO," said Dillon, leaning on the end of a whip antenna that he'd been using as a pointer during the order.

A small dust cloud swept through the group and obscured everything, from miniature tanks to real-life soldiers. Wyatt waited until it passed before continuing. "What's the Russians' not-earlier-than attack time?"

"Zero-five-hundred hours," said Dillon. "Sunrise is shortly after six." The men knew that while sunrise might occur at six o'clock in the morning, there was a period preceding it known as Beginning Morning Nautical Twilight, or BMNT. During these minutes before the sun rose, the light conditions approached those of daylight. The same was true at night, as there was a time period following sunset—Early Evening Nautical Twilight—in which unaided visual recognition was also possible.

"The intel gurus at division believe the Russians, knowing their night capabilities are inferior to our own, will wait until close to daylight to attack in order to somewhat even the scales.

"And keep in mind, gentlemen," Dillon added, "these assholes field the same tank ammunition that the Iraqis used last year . . . it *will* penetrate an Abrams, particularly at ranges short of two thousand meters. Fire once, twice max, then back down and move to your alternate positions."

He continued. "Bottom line: there will be a helluva lot more Ivans on the field tomorrow than Cold Steel troopers. I'm going to need all of you. Fight hard, but fight smart. Clear?"

A chorus of "hooahs" answered his question.

Leaning on his staff Patrick Dillon surveyed his leaders. His back faced west and to most of them he was but a black gargoyled silhouette in the gathering darkness, but his voice rang out low and strong. "Most of you have been here with me before, and by 'here' I mean on the eve of battle. The most I can ask of you is to take care of your crews and take care of your wingman. If a leader tank goes down, pick up the ball—get on the radio and talk to me." He kicked sand at the terrain model. "I know this looks like a bear," he said. "And it is. A big Russian bear. But you men are a band of eagles, prepared to scream down on the enemy in a way they've never encountered. You're not Chechnyan rebels firing rocket-propelled grenades from a building, you're American M1A1 crewmen. God pity them for the destruction you will wreak upon them tomorrow, for I know you will have none."

A spontaneous roar arose from the thirteen. Not a celebration, but a call to war. Highland clansmen rallying to meet English invaders and Viking berserkers preparing to beach their vessels on rocky shores would have recognized the cries for what they were—a fierce need to join the battle. The preparations were over. It was time for war.

Two hours later Boggs roused Dillon from the hasty nap he'd forced on himself. "Suh, there's a Humvee approachin'."

The loader's metallic southern twang came to Dillon through his CVC. He was semi-sleeping in a sitting position, his face cushioned against his gunner's sight extension. Standing, he flipped his eye patch up and rubbed both eyes with the backs of his fists before flipping the patch down again. Pulling his PVS-7s from his chest he pulled the night-vision goggles up to his good eye and turned the power switch on. A green desert came to life, revealing the approaching vehicle. Yep, a Hummer.

The vehicle stopped next to Cyclops. Through the PVS-7s Dillon recognized Mike Stuart. Looking to his left he saw Boggs glued to the loader's M240 machine gun, prepared to send 7.62mm rounds blazing. Dillon smiled. It was becoming easier and easier to forget that only six months earlier his loader was a fresh-faced high school graduate. "It's all right, Bo. Stuart's one of the good guys."

Dillon met his visitor in front of the tank, hitting the ground as Mike Stuart reached C-66. "What the hell are you doing here?" he asked. "With the night you've got ahead of you, you should already be moving out with your team."

Mike Stuart stood in the darkness a few moments before answering. "This is bullshit, Pat."

"What?"

"Don't give me that, you know damned well what I'm talking about," snapped the Knight commander. "Leaving you guys here to cover the entire task force position."

Though his friend couldn't see him, Dillon shrugged. "We all follow orders—and before you say it, I know what you're thinking. Sutherland is hanging me, and my guys along with me, out to dry. But it wasn't his plan. It was the colonel's."

When either of the men made reference to "the colonel," it went without saying that they were talking about Colonel Bill Jones.

Stuart leaned his elbows against the Abrams's front slope. "Yeah, but don't tell me the son of a bitch wasn't shitting himself for joy when he saw an opportunity to stick it to you. And I'll damned well bet that the brigade order said to leave 'a force in place,' not 'a company.' Sutherland conveniently interpreted the order the way he wanted to interpret it," he said bitterly.

"Despite our mutual concerns regarding the current battalion leadership and his interpretation of the order," said Dillon quietly, "it's a damned good plan."

Stuart grunted. "Yeah, that's what sucks about it."

The friends stood in silence a few moments longer before Dillon clapped a hand to Stuart's shoulder. "You need to move, Mike."

Stuart ran his hand along a beard-stubbled jawline, the slowness of the gesture indicative of how tired he was. He and his men had been on the move back to friendly lines for over two hours. They'd pulled out slowly, a vehicle or two at a time, in an attempt to keep the Russians a few kilometers west of them from noting the withdrawal; like the Americans, their enemy would have reconnaissance out in force attempting to capture information on their adversary. The less they knew the better.

Once clear of the counter-reconnaissance line there had been the usual tension involved with approaching the main battle area from the enemy side; the fear that some gunner wouldn't have gotten the word that friend-lies were moving back, or that some young troop would be so on edge that he wouldn't recognize the sharp, distinctive lines of the M1A1s or the tall silhouettes of the Bradleys, confusing them with Russian vehicles and sending a sabot or TOW missile into the night en route to a fratricide. They'd made the move without a hitch; unfortunately, they were far from finished for the night.

"The son of a bitch could have at least given you priority of fires," muttered Stuart. With priority of fires, normally bestowed on the current operational phase's main effort, a company could very quickly bring 155mm artillery and 120mm mortars into play, a significant combat multiplier.

Dillon barked a laugh. "On that count I couldn't agree with you more."

"My supply sergeant dropped off the equipment you requested," Stuart said dryly. "I'm assuming you asked for the other companies' as well?"

"Yep. Under the circumstances, I figured I need them more."

Stuart nodded. "Cagey. Does Sutherland know what you're planning?"

"He has no idea and I don't think he really gives a shit about the details of how I carry out my Little Big Horn. But what could he say anyway? It's no skin off his ballsack."

"True," said Stuart, pushing himself away from the tank with an effort. He held out a hand. "Gotta go."

Dillon took the hand firmly in his own. He and Stuart were more than friends, more than brothers. They'd been through combat together and shared the responsibilities that only combat commanders can know. "See you on the high ground, Mikey."

"See you on the high ground." Stuart smiled, moving toward his waiting Hummer.

Dillon watched the departing vehicle blend into the night and jumped stiffly onto his tank's front slope.

Climbing into his turret the Steel commander pulled on his CVC. *"Knight Five, Knight Six, over."*

"Five," came back Bluto Wyatt.

"How's the collection effort coming, over?"

"I've got everyone's but Anvil's. En route there now with the supply truck."

Dillon nodded. Good news. *"ETA for completing installation?"*

Through the radio's silence Dillon could picture Wyatt doing the labor calculations. *"Can you gimme four hours?"*

Dillon looked at the still-dark eastern horizon and then to the Zodiac's green glow on his wrist. *"Affirmative, but no more. You've got to be in position by zero-five-hundred."*

"Roger, boss."

Dillon knew he'd better make himself clear. *"Bluto, if it looks like you're not going to make it back, cut the mission short and head for your tank. Acknowledge."*

"Not a problem, Steel Six. I'll have that ever-lovin' hunk of steel wrapped around me in plenty of time."

Patrick Dillon smiled. He hadn't heard the term "ever-lovin' " used in over two decades, not since his childhood when he'd read the adventures of Captain America and Daredevil at home in bed following his weekly comic-book runs. But then again, Wyatt did remind him a little of Ben Grimm. It wouldn't have surprised the Steel commander at all to hear his XO scream *"It's clobberin' time!"* over the company net when the Russians hit the wire.

Dillon relaxed his knees and allowed himself to settle back into his commander's seat in the turret. With a slight smile he placed his face once more on the cushioned gunner's sight extension to catch a short nap. The smile didn't last long.

"Suh, we certainly are populuh t'night. Another vehicle is approachin'."

Dillon was sorely tempted to tell Boggs to spray down the new arrivals with 7.62mm machine-gun fire. Instead he sat up and stood in the turret.

"I believe it's our friends from Fox, suh," said Boggs. He could see the green night-vision camera filming. As it was pointed in his direction, the loader leaned with easy grace over his M240, for all the world a born killer. "The gals back home will be all over themselves in tryin' to win my interest."

"Just keep an eye out, Casanova," said Dillon, grasping the edge of his hatch and popping his feet out onto the turret. A minute later he was on the ground with Nate Ryan.

"Nate," Dillon said sarcastically, "great to see you."

"Pat, have you got a minute?"

Dillon ran through the mantra Melissa had taught him—*Pat, don't be an asshole; Pat, don't be an asshole; Pat, don't be an asshole* . . . He showed a sparkling smile that was clear in the moonlight. "For you, Nate, always."

"I was present for your operations order this evening."

"I know. The camera crew filming it was a dead giveaway." A small feminine voice rang in his mind—*You're being an asshole*. Dillon dismissed it.

Ryan, however, ignored the sarcasm. "Off the record . . . is our Colonel Sutherland setting you up for a fall?"

Dillon's face lost all traces of humor. "If you're asking me if my commanding officer is sending my men and me out on a mission that can't be won, I would say no. If you're asking me if I think it would particularly bother him if I failed . . ." The Steel commander left the sentence unfinished. "And Nate, I would highly suggest that you and your crew get yourselves back a few kilometers."

The reporter shrugged—he'd found a hole next to Dillon's own in which he intended to sit the H2. He and his people knew the score when they'd volunteered for this gig. "So what are you going to do?"

"Win."

Nate Ryan's face clouded, confused. *"But how?"*

The Cold Steel commander looked about himself in the dark. "Nate, you can't see my men in the darkness, but they're out there: thirteen tank crews, each with four of the U.S.'s finest. Behind us we have medics waiting to rush forward to evacuate these crewmen if they fall, no matter how many bullets are flying or how close the Russians are; there are engineers just over that rise, prepared to go forward to replace obstacles if it becomes necessary—to go forward with nothing but a blanket of smoke as protection. There are more. I've trained these men, Nate. I've led them in battle, bled with them, laughed with them, cried with them. And I love every damned one of them." Dillon was silent a few moments, turning his head as if inspecting his troops in the night. "Myron Sutherland be damned. I can't afford to lose, because that means a lot of these men die—and that's not an option." Patrick Dillon shrugged. "So we win."

Nate Ryan nodded. "But how?"

"I've got a plan," said Patrick Dillon simply.

Ryan smiled. "Dillon, you are either very good or totally full of shit."

Patrick Dillon's smile flashed in the moonlight as he leaned against Cyclops. "It should be interesting seeing which, eh?"

Four hours later Fred Wyatt sat in the dark passenger seat of the C Company supply truck, his mission for the night complete. Looking to the G-Shock on his left wrist, Wyatt depressed the illumination button and checked the time; they'd never make it back to his tank by the appointed hour and the truck was not very well protected to stop anything larger than a small-caliber bullet. "Stop. Let me out here," he told the driver.

The young supply specialist braked automatically on his XO's command, but that didn't stop him from questioning the officer. Both men wore night-vision goggles mounted to their Kevlar helmets.

"Huh," Wyatt said with a laugh. "You look like a freakin' insect, Specialist Rios."

"I ain't lettin' you out here, sir," answered the specialist, ignoring the XO's joke. "We're still over a klick from your tank; that's over a half mile."

Wyatt opened the door of the big truck. "You ain't got a choice, Specialist. Now get this truck and your ass back to the combat trains."

"But, sir . . ."

Wyatt hopped to the ground and then turned to the open passenger door. "Rios, listen to me. I'm a big guy, but I can flat-out run. Once I get to my tank I ain't worried about no artillery." He looked at the driver pointedly through the PVS-7 monocular. "Can you say the same about this rig?"

The driver briefly looked about him at the unarmored cargo vehicle. Despite his obvious fear, the young soldier shook his head. "Sir, get your ass back in here."

Wyatt smiled. "Let me make this easy for you, Specialist Rios . . . get back to the combat trains; *that's an order*. And if you don't move in the next five seconds, I'm going to climb back in that cab and pound you until you agree. Am I making myself clear?"

Specialist Cesar Rios looked over the six-feet-two, two-hundred-fifty-pound lieutenant. "I ain't sayin' I'm scared of you, sir, but all right."

Wyatt's smile was genuine now. "Move out, soldier."

Rios didn't reply, but he threw Wyatt a salute so sincere that his arm shook from the tension.

Wyatt returned the salute, feeling his throat tighten with emotion. "Now get out of here." With that the big man placed his left arm around his protective mask to keep it from bouncing against his body and started sprinting toward C-55's position.

Reports began trickling in of the advancing Russian force. The scout platoons' LRAS3 surveillance systems were paying dividends tonight, picking up the enemy formations over ten kilometers out. The LRAS's additional bennie of providing target locations through its integrated laser ranger finder were also being well utilized. Already Muddy Waters heard MLRS rockets streaking overhead to meet the approaching hoard.

"Steel Six, Lighthorse Six, over."

Dillon gave his neck a quick twist in the turret of Cyclops. Time to put the game face on. *"How you doin', Muddy?"*

"Freakin' great, sir," said the lieutenant. *"And how are you doin' . . . considering this call is to let you know that over a division of Russians are coming your way, with nothing between you and them but me and my little group of great Americans."*

"You guys just keep your heads down, clear?"

Waters sounded exasperated. *"I know, I know, observe and report only."* The scout's voice turned serious. *"Sir, there's a lot of shit headed your way. My estimate is that they'll be hitting your position in approximately forty-five minutes. I'd expect the arty party to start anytime."*

When massed armor was in the attack the attacking unit normally fires artillery on their objective for fifteen to thirty minutes prior to its attack. This forces the defenders to keep their heads down. Once the attackers get close enough to the objective to make a rush, they shift the fires off of the poor bastards on the receiving end to other targets, such as reserve or supply positions. Best case for the attacker—by the time the men on the objective are over their shell shock, he's on top of them.

In this case Dillon hoped it didn't work out that way as he and his men were the attackees, not the attackers.

"Roger, thanks for the update. Steel Six, out."

Dillon keyed the CVC again. *"Steel Five, Steel Six, over."*

Nothing. A glance at the SeaWolf's luminescent hands told Dillon that this could be trouble.

"Steel Five . . ."

"This is Steel Five-Golf," replied Wyatt's gunner from aboard C-55.

"Roger Five-Golf . . . has Five-Actual made it back yet?"

"Negative."

Fuck, fuck, fuck, thought Dillon. *Bluto, you son of a bitch . . .* He calmed himself. Fred Wyatt was a big boy. He knew the score and would be acting accordingly. *"Roger, Five-Golf, let me know when he arrives."*

Dillon could hear the jitters in the young sergeant's voice. *"Roger, Steel Six."*

"All Steel elements, Steel Six . . . if you're not in open-protected, go there now; repeat, go to open-protected now."

The three platoons called in acknowledging the order. No tank commander enjoyed being in the "open-protected" position. In this mode, the tank commander's hatch was pulled down just short of fully closed. He could still squat and see the outside world—albeit not much, but a little was better than nothing. On the plus side, enemy machine gunners, snipers, and artillerymen had a much more difficult time puncturing the tank commander's hide with sharp and pointy projectiles.

Dillon knew that with the almost certain proposition that enemy artillery was about to rain down, it was a good time to get everyone under cover and to batten down the hatches. Before another coherent thought could cross the Steel commander's mind, Cyclops rocked beneath him as the first waves of Russian artillery slammed home.

"And you're on in three, two . . ." The cameraman's arm flashed to Nate Ryan, index finger extended. The night-vision camera whirled to life.

"This is Nate Ryan reporting to you live from my position with the men of Cold Steel—C Company, Second Battalion, Seventy-seventh Armor—somewhere in southwest Iraq."

Despite his flak vest, Kevlar helmet, and location within a ten-foot-deep position dug for an M1A1 tank, Ryan nonetheless flinched when the first round of the expected artillery slammed to ground a kilometer from his position.

"Nate, do you want to cut it and pick this up later?" asked Mack in a shaky voice. She was a six-foot blonde who looked like she could hold her own with any Russian dismounts who made it to their position. But Ryan heard the fear in Mack's voice as surely as he felt it in his own bones. But this story was close to Ryan.

Ryan had not told Patrick Dillon that for eight years he'd been in the U.S. Army. Assigned to the 2nd Armored Cavalry Regiment as a tank commander during the first Gulf War, he knew the score and what the stakes were from the battle of 73 Easting—the only serious armor-on-armor fight between the Americans and Republican Guard during Desert Storm. And he wanted to ensure that whether he and his crew made it out or not, the story of this company would be told.

The camera's light still shone. Nate Ryan pulled his shoulders back and shook his head. "Keep rolling, Mack."

Thousands of viewers watched as Ryan, eerily green in the camera's night-vision light, reported to them from Iraq. Overhead it looked like the Fourth of July as the skies filled with fire. The ground shook beneath them as artillery struck again, closer this time. Mack stumbled as the earth heaved beneath her, but then she steadied the camera. "We're still hot," she said in a voice as calm as she could muster.

Ryan nodded. "As you can see we've just come under attack from the Russian forces to our west. These artillery fires are not unexpected . . ." Ryan paused as another explosion hit a few hundred meters away. "Captain Patrick Dillon, fifty yards from my position in his M1A1 tank, briefed his men late this evening that prior to the Russian ground attack, we would be 'prepped.' "

The Fox anchor in New York came through Ryan's earpiece after a few seconds' delay. "Nate, are you and your crew in danger?"

A near miss, or near hit depending on one's perspective, lit the scene with enough light that the picture went blank for a few moments. When Ryan again appeared to viewers, he forced a smile. "John, I have been assured that the Russians are not targeting journalists."

The anchor nodded seriously, entirely missing the sarcasm in the response. "Please explain to our viewers, Nate, what you mean by 'prepped.' "

For two minutes Ryan went into detail about the expected flow of the coming battle as briefed by Patrick Dillon—the bombardment of the American positions by artillery, the shifting of artillery to allow for the Russian ground attack, and the formations and types of equipment the friendlies expected to encounter.

"In case our viewers don't realize it, Nate, I have to tell them that you're a seasoned veteran of Desert Storm. From your perspective, what's the morale of Cold Steel?"

Ryan nodded. "John, these soldiers are ready. I would pass on to their families and friends that I've never met a finer bunch of men, or a unit better prepared."

After a few more minutes of questions and answers Nate Ryan signed off. He signaled to the cameraman. "Keep rolling, Mack. I want the rest of this piece shot for posterity. We'll beam it as soon as the battle is over."

That both knew Ryan wanted to film it now in case they weren't around to film it later was left unsaid.

Mack pointed. "Go."

"This is Nate Ryan reporting from southwestern Iraq with Cold Steel. I would like everyone to understand that this broadcast has been delayed so that we do not undermine operational security or threaten the success of the mission. This, ladies and gentlemen, is a record of what C Company faces tonight—and why they're facing it alone."

Bluto Wyatt ran. Beneath him the ground trembled. In his short twenty-four years of life on this earth, never had the big man moved so fast. Through the night-vision goggles the lieutenant saw his tank. He estimated it to be two hundred meters out. At his current pace he should reach it in short order . . .

Wyatt pulled himself from the ground. Looking at his watch he saw that over a minute had passed. His mind groggy, the Steel XO tried to figure out what had happened. The explosive force of a Russian high-explosive artillery round impacting one hundred fifty meters to his right gave him a good clue. Though his legs were stiff and his body felt as though he'd just finished twelve rounds with Apollo Creed, Bluto Wyatt forced himself forward one halting step at a time. In his mind, unbidden, came a picture of his wife. His stride lengthened, boots digging deep into the desert floor. Another barrage almost sent him to his knees, but he managed to stay on his feet. *Focus,* he thought. *Focus, Wyatt.* His wife's face was replaced by that of his newborn child's, a daughter he'd hardly begun to know. Wyatt picked up his pace, legs loosening the farther he made it.

Beneath his breath the big man muttered one sentence. "No, *fuck you*, Ivan." The artillery barrage continued. Bluto Wyatt ignored it, focusing on his objective.

"Talk to me Lighthorse," said Dillon into his boom mike. His voice was calm, belying his nerves. He'd always thought that once he was a combat veteran situations like this would be old hat . . . wrong. *"What have I got?"*

Normally the scouts spoke in nothing but whispers. It was clear from Muddy Waters's voice that he had no concerns regarding being overheard.

"You're not going to like it, sir," screamed Waters in an attempt to be heard over the din in the background. *"I'm sitting in a little spider hole, I've got sand pouring down my ears, and from the sound of it the entire Russian army is moving toward you."*

Dillon swallowed hard. Looking around the turret he saw his gunner and loader observing him in the dim blue lighting. *Steady, Dillon,* he thought, *you don't want to alarm the boys.* "Could you be a little more specific?" he asked, forcing serenity into his voice where none was felt.

"Hold on!" yelled Waters into his hand mike. *"John Wayne Krieger has decided to stick his godforsaken bigassed torso up from our hide position to get a better view . . . stand by."*

Patrick Dillon waited patiently for news that he knew couldn't be good.

"Steel Six, Lighthorse Seven, over."

Dillon laughed to himself. He was attempting to sound calm; hell, he was handling himself damned fine considering his position. Rolf Krieger, on the other hand, *was* calm. *"Go ahead, Lighthorse Seven."*

The radio crackled as silence filled it for a few seconds. *"Steel Six, this is Lighthorse Seven. I cannot give you an accurate count of what's approaching. There are simply too many vehicles. I was only up for a few seconds, but the horizon is packed with tanks and infantry fighting vehicles; it looked like a company of rats rolling over the ground. My estimate is that the better part of a motorized rifle regiment is in our sector, maybe more. They appear to be T-80s and BMP-3s, and they're packed tightly."*

Dillon keyed his CVD transmit switch. *"Roger, understand. And thanks, Lighthorse. Now you and your boys hunker down. Steel Six, out."*

Patrick Dillon sat back hard against his tank commander's chair. *Fuck me,* he thought. They're packed together because they're throwing mongo shit against the 4th Division's front to achieve a massive breakthrough, the breach through the American lines that the Russian follow-on forces needed desperately if they were to control Iraq. And of course the force opposing him was trying to achieve a three-to-one advantage against the Iron Tigers; only in this case, it wasn't against the four-company task force they expected to see, but rather against only Cold Steel—which meant something in the magnitude of twelve-to-one odds in their favor; the only silver lining was the Russians didn't know they had those kinds of odds in their favor.

Patrick Dillon shook his head. The breach will not happen here, he promised. Looking to the turret roof he threw a silent scream of defiance at the gods of war. *Not here, do you hear me! Not here!* And then he and the other Cyclops crew members began their final preparations for battle.

Chapter 20

Viva Las Vegas

The White House
Washington, D.C.

"You're becoming a regular customer, Mr. Dodd." Betty Pollard smiled as Luke Dodd appeared for his appointment with the president. In her mid-forties, the assistant was a vibrant, attractive, and—most importantly to her at the moment—*single* woman. She had to fight off the advances of most male visitors to the Oval Office, be they kings or carpenters. The cowboy spy intrigued her.

Though Luke Dodd had traded in his western attire for a navy Brooks Brothers pinstripe of good cut, one that hung off his slim and muscular frame rather well, she noted, he still chose to wear boots; in this case highly polished cowboy boots of soft, hand-tooled leather. She sighed and unconsciously extended her arms and fingers like a cat stretching, knowing it was about to be scratched.

Luke Dodd's eyes twinkled. "Betty, you know that I would only come to the White House for two reasons."

She twisted her mouth in a mischievous smile and raised an eyebrow. "Black, right?" she said, handing him a cup of coffee.

Luke nodded. He took the cup from her, brushing her hand a little too long in the process, and sipped from it.

"Ahhh. Sure you can't tell me where the big guy gets this stuff?"

"National secret," she said coquettishly. "But tell me, Agent Dodd . . ."

"Luke, please."

"All right, Luke . . . what's the second reason you come to the White House."

Dodd gave her a crooked grin. "Betty, do you really need to ask?"

The assistant slapped him lightly on the arm. "Why, Mr. Dodd! You are a bad boy, aren't you?"

Luke's smile grew. "Yes, ma'am."

President Jonathan Drake and Chris Dodd sat in the Oval Office, both silent and waiting. The phone on the table next to the president's armchair—the only phone other than a red phone that ran through no operator of any kind—rang once. "Yes," he said simply.

Drake listened for several seconds. "Very well."

He slowly and deliberately placed the handset back in its cradle. "The Bureau is in position . . . and they've confirmed everything."

The nation's chief executive shook his head sadly. Looking at Drake sympathetically, Chris Dodd thought the man had aged ten years in the past twenty-four hours. "You ready, sir?"

Drake nodded but didn't move. Dodd waited with him, deciding the president of the United States deserved whatever time he needed to come to terms with this betrayal.

"I don't know what could be taking them so long," apologized Betty. "Normally the president is very punctual about his appointments."

Luke Dodd yawned and stretched from his seat next to Betty's desk. "That's all right. Hey, I've got an idea for passing the time."

Betty raised an inquisitive eyebrow. "Agent Dodd, I'm many things. Easy isn't one of them."

Luke blushed. "That's not what I meant," he said. "Not yet anyway," he added with a wink.

It was Betty's turn to blush, but she didn't attempt to dissuade him from the suggestion.

Reaching into a pocket, Luke pulled out a pack of playing cards. "I'm heading to Atlantic City this weekend. Interested?"

As he shuffled the cards Luke watched the assistant. Her eyes seemed mesmerized by his hand actions.

"Perhaps," she said.

"I've got reservations at the Trump Taj Mahal. One of the Rajah suites, fourteen hundred square feet . . . and two bedrooms."

Betty continued to stare at the cards as Luke shuffled. "That might not be necessary," she said softly.

"Are you kidding?" Luke laughed. "At this time of year, if you don't have a reservation . . ."

She stared into his eyes. "Not the reservation; the second bedroom."

Luke smiled and quickly dealt out two cards to each of them, one faceup, the other facedown. "Quick hand of blackjack?"

"Why not?" she replied with a predatory smile.

"What are the stakes?"

"I wouldn't worry about it, cowboy." She looked him directly in the eyes. "Either way, you win."

With practiced grace Betty picked up her hand and examined it. "Hit me."

Luke bit his lower lip lightly. "Owww."

Into the spirit of the game and the promise of the coming weekend, Betty Pollard smiled and almost purred as Luke Dodd laid a card on the table faceup. She studied the hand carefully and looked into Luke's eyes, fully engaged in the game. "Hit me again."

Luke sipped his coffee, returning her stare. He threw another card faceup.

Betty looked at the card and then jumped as the office's main door burst open. Men in medium-priced dark suits spread out through the room. No firearms were apparent, but by the men's stances and the placement of their hands it was clear that they could be . . . and very quickly.

"Betty Pollard?" asked one of the intruders as he approached the desk. He held out a billfold identification for her inspection.

"Yes," she murmured, comparing the man's picture on his credentials with his actual face.

"Special Agent Graham, FBI," he said as he snapped the I.D. closed. "You are under arrest for—"

"There must be some mistake," she said.

"No, ma'am," replied the agent solemnly.

She stood, angry now. "I work for the president of the United States. He's just on the other side of that door," she said, pointing. "And when I have to interrupt his schedule for what is obviously a mistake of major proportions on your part, he is not going to be happy. And I daresay that *you* will not be very happy then, Special Agent Graham."

The door Betty had indicated opened. Jonathan Drake and Chris Dodd walked out, neither smiling, neither surprised.

Betty looked at Luke Dodd in confusion, and then dawning understanding.

Still sitting, Luke Dodd shifted his eyes to the hand of cards she'd dropped on the desk. The queen of spades stared at him, cold and indifferent. He looked up and met Betty Pollard's eyes. "Busted," he said icily.

Jonathan Drake stared as the last agents departed from the Oval Office, Betty Pollard in tow. "How in the hell did this happen?" he wondered out loud. "The background screenings to become part of the presidential staff are intensive, to say the least."

Chris Dodd shrugged. "Gambling is a disease, Mr. President, every bit as real as alcoholism. Ms. Pollard owed money—lots of money—and to the wrong types of people. That kind of debt doesn't turn up during a background check, no matter how thorough the investigator. She was ripe to be plucked by someone who could use her debt as leverage, someone who could get her back in the black and bankroll a few years at the tables."

"I liked Betty," reflected Drake quietly, almost to himself. "I wish . . . I don't know. If I had known, maybe I could have helped her."

Dodd's voice turned cold. "Sir, she almost got my brother killed. No, she didn't know him, but she knew what she was doing."

The president nodded silently and turned away. Betty Pollard was just one more casualty in this mad war.

Eight hours later Luke Dodd popped the lid off a bottle of Fat Tire Ale, one from a case he'd stolen from his brother's place on arriving back in Washington. Walking through a sliding glass door off the kitchen, he stepped outside onto a wraparound deck and selected one of a half dozen rockers strewn haphazardly about the porch. The chair he selected faced the inlet that opened up behind his house. Luke relaxed, sipped his beer, and watched a sailboat as it made its way slowly toward Chesapeake Bay, water glistening off its hull.

A familiar thud sounded next to his chair. Looking down languidly through hooded eyes, he noted his chocolate Lab had decided to join him. "Hey, Trooper," he muttered, reaching down and scratching the top of a large brown head. Heavy panting and a doggy smile were the animal's only replies.

Dave Matthews Band played in the background as Luke Dodd contemplated his life. He liked listening to

Dave when troubled, because it was difficult to listen to Dave and stay in a bad mood. Today it wasn't working. Luke looked at the mobile phone he held in his hand. *Might as well get it over with, Dodd,* he thought. *You're not going to be able to get anything done until you do, and you need the closure.*

Placing his flip-flop-covered feet on the deck railing, Luke leaned back, took a deep breath, and dialed from memory the number his brother had given him.

"Yes," answered a noncommittal voice. Luke could almost see the clean-cut face, nice haircut, cheap suit, and sunglasses.

"This is Blockbuster Video at the corner of Ash and Main," Luke Dodd said, trying to keep a straight face as he went through the prearranged challenge and password routine. "I'm calling to remind you that the copy of *Naughty Nancy the Nanny* you rented is two days overdue."

Luke knew there would be a few seconds of silence as the agent on the other end checked his response against the safe house's daily operating instructions. And another couple of seconds' delay while the man pondered Luke's choice of films. "Stand by," the voice on the other end of the phone said.

"Hello?" said a feminine voice a minute later. The woman was clearly not expecting callers.

"Hello, Natasha," he said quietly.

"Luke." It was a statement, not a greeting, not a question.

Luke Dodd took a quick swallow of beer to wet his suddenly dry mouth and throat. "It was real. I just wanted you to know it was real."

"What was real, Luke? What are you trying to tell me?"

"The friendship we shared," he said, letting out a deep sigh. "It was very real."

"I see."

Luke waited for Natasha to say more, but she didn't. "Anyway, that's about it. Take care, Natasha. Have a happy life."

"Wait." Her voice had lost the aloof tone it had held moments earlier. "Luke, was that all I was? A friend? When I poured out my heart to you in Moscow that night, were you responding as a man or . . . or was I merely part of your assignment, a pawn to be used and cast aside?"

Luke Dodd rubbed his eyes. This was a no-win situation. "Good-bye, Natasha. I have a flight in a couple of hours and I've still got to pack."

"Will you call me later?"

Luke shook his head, though Natasha Khartukov couldn't see it. "That won't be possible. I'm going to be out of the country for a while; I have no idea how long."

Her voice was a plea. "I *need* answers, Luke. I need to know the direction my life is going. And there are so many questions that only you can provide the answers for."

"I don't have any of the answers, Natasha," he said. "I'm sorry."

"But . . ."

He tilted his head back and closed his eyes. "Move on with your life, Natasha."

Silence for a few moments. Luke thought she'd hung up when she said quietly, "It's my father, isn't it, Luke? You are going after him."

Luke Dodd ended the call, put the phone down, and took another long pull of Fat Tire.

Chapter 21

And the Beat Goes On

**Cold Steel Battle Position
Southwestern Iraq**

"Steel elements, Steel Six," said Dillon over the company radio net. *"Stay down. They see jack shit. And anything they do see is* not *you, so don't react to their fire."*

The Russian artillery had lifted five minutes earlier. Since that time enemy tank fire had peppered all along the Iron Tigers' battle position—a battle position built for over fifty defending tanks and Bradleys. Currently it was occupied only by Dillon's fourteen M1A1s. The men manning the Abramses could feel their tanks shaking beneath them. But now it wasn't from artillery bombardments, but rather from the sheer weight of the approaching Russian formation. It was all they could do to sit silently in their fighting positions, the earth trembling beneath them as though a herd of stampeding buffalo was about to overrun them.

Hidden below the earth's surface they had thus far given their attackers no clue as to their actual positions. But while Dillon's troops sat silently in their holes, other nearby systems engaged the oncoming Russian formations.

* * *

"There are tanks everywhere, Captain!" screamed the lieutenant over his company radio network.

"Continue to engage," said the Russian captain calmly as he looked at the large American position in front of him. From the heat signatures and flashes he knew it was the battalion–task force forecast to be in their line of march. And with that many enemy vehicles to his front, his flanks had to be secure; the Americans simply did not have enough vehicles to concentrate so much firepower in the positions to his front and to conduct a flank attack. *"All elements, concentrate your fires to the east . . . I repeat, the Americans are concentrated to our front. Attack!"*

"Yes, sir!" yelled the lieutenant.

The captain put his face back to his optics after notifying his higher headquarters of the Americans' confirmed location. He smiled as his unit continued its attack without the loss of one of his combat systems. Which made him stop and think.

Despite the number of American vehicles arrayed before them, the rapidly decreasing distance between the two forces, and the number of rounds fired by the defenders, not one of his tanks or BMPs had been hit. *Why?* It was things on the battlefield that didn't make sense that caused him concern. And this did not make sense.

One of the key figures of World War II was a magician by the name of Jasper Maskelyne. Though not as well known as George Patton or Audie Murphy, Maskelyne's contributions in many ways were as great.

In 1942 Field Marshal Erwin Rommel knew a British counterattack was coming at El Alamein. At the northern end of the German line, Maskelyne disguised a thousand British tanks as trucks. At the southern end of the line he built two thousand dummy tanks complete with false explosives. But Maskelyne didn't stop there. His crew constructed a fake railroad line, broadcast false radio reports, and used sound effects to mimic construction work. The cherry on top of the effort that finally convinced the Germans that the counterattack would come from the south? Maskelyne's team built a decoy water supply line at the southern end of the German line that was easily visible to German aircraft. Rommel, knowing that the water line was critical to the success of the British attack and seeing that it couldn't possibly be completed earlier than November 1942, decided to go on leave. The British attack on the morning of October 23, 1942, took the Germans by complete surprise. In ten days Rommel's Afrika Corps lost twenty thousand men and were forced into a retreat. And the British were poised to take the North African theater, all thanks to a magician who would later be recognized by Winston Churchill as one of the heroes of World War II.

Two holes away from Cyclops sat a mock-up M1 series tank. Composed of fiberglass, the model was fabricated to the exact dimensions of its real-life counterpart—same width, same height, same dimension gun tube. A thermal blanket powered by a generator twenty meters behind it heated the model to roughly the same temperature as an idling M1. Simulated charges mounted to its gun tube were electronically detonated by a nearby observer, in this case Private Boggs.

To the Russian forces it looked as though an M1A1 tank in a hull-down position had engaged them. Seconds later two Russian sabots destroyed the mock-up. But there were over three dozen of its brethren spread throughout the Iron Tigers' battle position. As they moved closer the Russians continued to batter the "defenders," whittling them away one tank at a time.

* * *

"Give me a range, Bick," said Dillon.

"Twenty-one hundred meters," replied the gunner, face glued to his optics.

"Get ready, boys," Dillon breathed over the intercom. *"Steel, Steel Six . . . two rounds sabot at my command."* Patrick Dillon paused for two seconds, giving his tank commanders an opportunity to relay the order to their crews. "Boggs, just keep the sabots coming," he told the gunner, glancing left across the turret.

The private gave him a sickly smile and a thumbs-up.

"Top hat, top hat, top hat," said Dillon, issuing the command that brought all fourteen of the Cold Steel Abrams tanks from their hidden positions for the first time. The banshee scream of Cyclops's fifteen-hundred-horsepower turbine could be heard throughout the tank as Tommy gunned the throttles and pulled forward.

"Identify a shitload of tanks!" yelled Bickel as his gun tube cleared.

Boggs armed the main gun and jumped back. "Up!"

Silently Dillon forced himself to give the other crews two seconds, just long enough to pull forward and identify targets. *"Fire!"*

Cyclops rocked. Smoke filled the thermal picture. "Fire and adjust."

"You got it, sir!" yelled the gunner. "Give me a sabot, Boggs!"

Dillon glanced left in time to see the loader shoving another sabot round into the breech. Arming the gun, the loader moved clear of the breech's recoil path. "Up!"

"On the way!" The big Abrams reared again, throwing the crew hard against their guards. All along the Iron Tigers' position the tanks of Steel sent red sabots of depleted uranium streaking toward the approaching Russian forces. Each tank fired two rounds per Dillon's fire command and then backed down, moving along concealed routes prepared by their engineers to alternate firing positions not yet identified by the enemy forces. Each tank in the battalion had prepared two positions; as the Steel tanks were the only occupying force, there were over a hundred holes to choose from. Each C Company tank had identified three to four positions earlier in the afternoon and rehearsed moving to them until they could find them blindfolded in the dark.

"All right, Tommy, get us out of here!" yelled Dillon. "Take the position to the left."

"Roger," replied the loader. "Moving."

As their tank backed down and maneuvered to its new position, Dillon keyed his radio. *"All right platoon leaders, it's your fight. Make sure your crews don't stay in one position too long. We've got the element of surprise. Use it. Steel Six, out."*

Patrick Dillon keyed the Battalion net. *"Tiger Six, Steel Six, request fires at group targets . . ."*

"Steel Six, Tiger Six, I'm afraid the guns are unavailable. I'll get you some support as soon as possible, over."

Dillon could almost see the smile on Sutherland's face.

"Tiger Six, the guns should be in position by now. If they're not, give me some mortars . . . anything. We're killing everything in the engagement area, but there's a ton behind them. I need some separation, over."

Dillon's engagement area was filled with over one hundred Russian combat systems. What he was looking for was something to occupy the massed vehicles behind those so he could provide the one hundred his undivided attention.

"I'll see what I can do for you, Steel. And you and your men are doing a great job, by the way."

Patrick Dillon grunted. *"Fuck the pep talk, I need fires, over."*

Sutherland's voice was flat. *"Tiger Six, out."*

"You fucking prick," muttered Dillon.

*   *   *

Fifteen hundred meters to the west the Russian captain watched another of his tanks explode. *"Lieutenant . . . Lieutenant! Give me a situation report!"*

"Sir . . . I've lost both of my wing tanks. I am trying to get a handle on exactly what is happening but . . ."

Static filled the airwaves. Around him the ten T-90s of his company, at least what was left of it, continued to engage.

"I have a tank, sir! Range twelve hundred meters!" yelled the captain's gunner.

"Fire!"

As Cyclops pulled up for what seemed the hundredth time a fireball erupted to his right. *Shit,* Dillon thought. That was C-33, the 3rd Platoon tank adjacent to their position. "Nail that fucker, Bick," he said coldly.

The Abrams rocked.

"Done," said the gunner quietly.

"Roger," said Dillon. "Fire and adjust."

The Russian company commander saw flames leap one hundred feet into the air as the American tank exploded. "Excellent shooting, Sergeant!" he cried . . . just as he saw another of the predatory-looking Abrams tanks, this one with its gun tube aimed squarely at him.

"Driver, back up . . ."

Flames leaped skyward in the darkness. And nothing further was heard from the captain.

Dillon took a deep breath. *"Tiger Six, Steel Six, request fires . . ."*

Sutherland sounded exasperated now. *"Steel, when I've got guns available I'll let you know. Until then . . . handle it."*

"Steel Six, Striker Six, over," said a calm voice.

Dillon and Bickel exchanged quick glances. *Jones?*

"Steel Six, over."

"Steel, Striker. I've got some of them MLRS rocketeers with nothing to do. If your FSO can give them some targets, it'll get 'em off of my ass, over."

Dillon knew that Jake Dumphy was monitoring. *"Jake, shag your ass to the fire support net."*

"I'm gone," came back Dumphy. Dillon could almost see the glee on the young field artillery officer's face. Instead of the 155mm artillery he'd been begging for they were getting multiple launch rockets; it was Christmas in Iraq for the artilleryman.

"Tiger Six, Striker Six. I'll be curious to hear what the problem is with artie. I've been talking to the cannon cocker battalion commander and he says they've been standing by awaiting targets for a while . . . over."

A pregnant pause ensued before Sutherland replied. *"This is Tiger Six. Roger, Striker; it must have been a miscommunication between my artillery officer and the guns. I'll straighten it out, over."*

Bill Jones's voice was cold. *"See that you do. Striker out."*

"The son of a bitch," muttered Jones.

Dave Barnett said nothing. He'd been monitoring the Iron Tiger frequency because he was afraid something like this might happen. He'd hoped to be wrong.

"The son of a *bitch*," repeated Jones. "I'll have his balls."

Shaking his head, the Striker commander looked to Barnett. "How are we looking, Dave?"

Barnett tweaked the finely manicured tip of one mustache unconsciously. "Very well, sir. Very well indeed."

To the front of C Company a firestorm brewed. MLRS rockets dropped across the width of the battlefield. But the rockets didn't come close enough to Steel to hit the doomed regiment in the engagement area; they were slowly but surely being picked off by Dillon's gunners. The only problem was seeing through the dust and dirt created by the rockets—at the time the Russians were hard to see through the brownout.

"Target!" yelled Bickel.

"Move, Tommy!" said Dillon.

"Roger!" said the loader.

Three kilometers to the north Mike Stuart watched the firefight occurring to his front. He swallowed hard. All of that fire was being directed against Pat Dillon and Steel. Stuart made the sign of the cross and looked to the sky. *Dear God, be with my brother,* he prayed silently.

Stuart turned his attention back to the mission. If his tank was a racehorse it would now be in the starting gate. And the gate was about to open.

"All Tiger elements, Tiger Six," came the voice at long last. *"Attack!"*

Other than Cold Steel, every combat system that the Tigers owned was now positioned on the flanks of the attacking Russian forces. The enemy ground reconnaissance had been taken out early on and there was still no satellite coverage. The Russians were coming in blind; that was a good thing so long as English was your native language.

Stuart checked his weapons systems and then glanced at his loader. "You got a target down there?!" he yelled to his gunner.

The sergeant laughed as he stared at multiple T-90 flank shots. "Oh yeah."

"Fire!"

"Steel, Steel Six, give me slants," said Dillon.

"This is Red One, slant four, over."

"White Four, slant four, over, over."

"Blue Four, slant three, over."

Son of a bitch, thought Dillon. *After this shit storm—*

not over yet by any means but well on its way—we've only lost a single tank? But wait—three platoons times four tanks each was twelve; plus his own tank made thirteen . . . Wyatt. *"Steel Five, Steel Six, come in, over."*

"This is Steel Five, we're good," said the ever-pleasant voice of Bluto Wyatt.

Dillon slumped in relief and looked to the turret roof. *Thank you, God. "Roger, Steel Five. From here out, keep your ass on the net and let me know what the hell is going on . . . or it's your balls, mister."*

Wyatt barely kept the chuckle from his voice. *"Steel Five, wilco."* Bluto Wyatt tapped his chest with his ham of a fist three times. "And I love you, too, sir," he said quietly with a smile.

"What have you got, Bick?" said Dillon.

Bickel, tired beyond comprehension from the past hour's work, looked through his sight. "I've got nothing, sir."

Dillon looked forward into the commander's sight extension. *Son of a bitch,* he thought. *We did it.* "Continue to observe. If it moves . . ."

Cyclops reared back, a 120mm sabot shooting from her gun tube.

". . . shoot it," Dillon finished.

"Roger," said the gunner dryly.

Meagan Dillon ran into her mother's bedroom. "Mom, turn on the television! It's the reporter who's with Daddy!"

Melissa reached to the nightstand and grabbed the remote, aiming it at the television with a trembling hand to turn up the volume. Suddenly she was surrounded by all four of her pajama-clad daughters. Where had they come from?

The last few hours Melissa Dillon had run the emotional gauntlet. Thanks to the reporter with her husband's team she knew Pat was alive. On the other hand, she'd also seen that Cold Steel was about to be attacked. And now she'd find out what happened. A cold hand gripped her heart as Ryan's now-familiar face appeared on the screen. . . .

Nate Ryan took a few deep breaths and looked into the camera. He was positioned in front of the fighting position in which he and his two crew members had spent the fighting. The camo'd H2 was clearly visible behind him.

"Hello, America. I'm happy to report the night is over and that Cold Steel has held their position, turning back the Russians aimed against them in the most furious fighting I have seen since the first Gulf War in 1991. Exactly why this company was cast out alone against such tremendous odds can be judged by another court somewhere in the future—more to follow in a tape-delayed report on that subject later—but the results of the Steel fight cannot be challenged. We have faced the enemy and we have won." Every watcher couldn't help but note the pride in Ryan's voice when he said "we."

"During this battle C Company, a unit comprised of just fourteen tanks, faced over one hundred enemy combat systems." Ryan paused. "We know that during the course of the fighting one tank was lost, but we have no word yet on casualties. The Russian losses, on the other hand . . . well, I'll let you see for yourselves."

The reporter walked forward, followed by Mack. The two climbed up the front of their hide position to its forward edge, camera panning over the battlefield. The Middle Eastern sky looked like noontime in Riyadh . . . albeit green. Tanks burned across the horizon. Russian crews spilled out, arms in the air, attempting to surrender to an enemy they could not see.

"One company did this, America . . . C Company,

Two-seven-seven Armor. The men of Cold Steel." Ryan turned and gestured to someone off-camera.

A stocky figure clad in tanker's Nomex coveralls walked into the picture. In Colorado Melissa Dillon looked closely at the man. Muscular, 9mm Beretta pistol in an old-fashioned leather shoulder holster designed for a big .45 caliber piece, crew-cut . . . and wearing the leather eye patch she'd sent him in a care package to replace the one issued by the hospital. Her heart leaped and she pulled her girls close, tears of joy streaming down her face. She'd felt as if she were playing Russian roulette when she'd heard that a crew had been lost, praying that it wasn't Pat, then feeling guilty because that would mean that some other son or father wouldn't come home . . . but she'd continued praying the prayer nonetheless. She could live with the guilt; she didn't know if she could live without Patrick Dillon by her side.

"And this is Captain Patrick Dillon, the commander of Cold Steel. Any words for America, Pat?"

A cold shiver ran through Melissa as Patrick Dillon looked into the camera and grinned crookedly. "That's his Snoopy grin," she said and laughed through her tears.

"Not for America, but for the ladies in my life back home in Colorado." The grin softened. "Hi, Melissa. I love you." The words seemed to catch in his throat. "*God* but do I love you. And to my girls . . . I love you all and miss you so much. But Daddy will be home soon. I promise."

"I love you, too," Melissa Dillon whispered.

Carson, all of three years old, leaned her blond head forward intently toward the screen. She smiled Pat's crooked grin. "Mommy, Daddy looks like a pirate!"

Melissa held the child tightly to her. "He sure does, honey," she said through tears of relief. "He sure does."

Ryan took Patrick Dillon's elbow and turned him toward the burning Russian tanks. "Any comments on tonight's fight, Captain?"

Dillon shrugged wearily. "They came. We did what we train to do." He looked at the multitude of burning vehicles, at the countless deaths caused by him and his men. "We did what we had to do," he concluded, this time with a note of sadness in his voice.

"Get back!" yelled the Russian division commander to his brigades. *"Get back now! There are American forces on the right. Move back!"*

"Yes, sir," replied his lead brigade commander. *"I see them. My battalions are moving back to checkpoint . . ."*

The communication died.

The general bowed his head in exasperation. *"Colonel, please complete your situation report."* He waited fifteen seconds and repeated the message.

The general knew his division had been hit in the flank by an entire brigade and that the two trailing divisions were receiving serious rocket fire, but that was all he knew. Turning to his radio operator, he gave instructions for the sergeant to get the corps commander on the radio.

"Fire!" yelled Mike Stuart. A T-90 disappeared in a shower of sparks and flame. All the Knight commander could think of was Pat Dillon as he watched the enemy tank burn. Stuart had listened as artillery rained on his friend and then as the Russian main body had closed on Cold Steel's position. Now it was time for some payback.

"Target!" yelled Stuart, observing the Russian tank's onboard ammunition fireball dozens of feet into the early-morning sky. His M1A1 was on the move and it felt *good*. Normally he'd pick the most dangerous target and assign it to his gunner. As it was there were so many targets to choose from, all focused on C Company to their front, it was like shooting fish in a barrel.

Screw it, he thought, *let the gunner figure it out.* "Fire and adjust!"

The gunner laughed. "Roger that, sir. Identify tank . . . *on the way!*"

Chapter 22

The Greatest Mother of Them All

White House Situation Room
Washington, D.C.

Tom Werner looked at his president. "It's a wash, sir."

Jonathan Drake gave his ranking military officer a blank stare. "Please elaborate, General."

The four-star shrugged. "Sir, without satellite imagery this is one big guessing game, but our intel says the Russians have thrown everything they have at us. Our boys held. They have western Iraq, but the rest of Iraq and Kuwait are ours. Odds are that given a week we'll pump their asses all the way out of Iraq, but if we continue with purely conventional fighting, we'll lose a lot of troops, sir."

Jonathan Drake nodded and looked to his CIA director. "Chris?"

"They'll continue to attack until their leadership tells them otherwise," said Chris Dodd softly.

Drake nodded once more and looked to Werner. "You have permission to use the MOABs, General. Give CENTCOM the green light."

"Yes, sir," replied Werner. "I'll call General Pavlovski now."

The president turned now to Chris Dodd. "You work on the Russian leadership piece."

Dodd nodded grimly. "Already being worked, sir."

Southwestern Iraq

From the east American warplanes screamed, their targets Russian air defense batteries scattered across the battlefield. The aircraft flights were so thick that from a distance they looked like a huge swarm of insects—Air Force F-15E Eagles and A-10 Warthogs, Navy and Marine F-18 Hornets, F-16 Falcons. They came from Turkey, from Kuwait, from aircraft carriers, some from as far as Europe. Above them other American fighters patrolled, providing air-to-air protection against scrambling Russian jets rushing to meet the oncoming air armada.

Puffs of smoke from the desert floor marked the launches of Russian surface-to-air missiles, or SAMs. The American pilots' and aviators' skills combined, backed by their crafts' state-of-the-art onboard defensive systems, were enough to make most of the missiles miss—most, but not all. Smoke and flame dotted several spots in the desert, marking the last resting places for crumpled piles of hardware that in their not-too-long-ago former lives had been multimillion-dollar twenty-first century aircraft. Parachutes fluttering to earth indicated that many of the pilots would live to fight another day; already Air Force and Army Special Operations units sped low over the desert sands in dark helicopters, the grim-faced warriors within intent on bringing out their comrades regardless of the personal risks they faced to do so.

But all of this was a prelude to the grand show. Behind the fighters lumbered the craft that would bring the Russian forces to their knees: four-engine, prop-driven, C-130 cargo aircraft. The C-130s carried very special payloads— MOABs. MOAB officially stood for Massive Ordnance

Air Blast. Unofficially the military called them the Mother of All Bombs. The MOAB's thirty-foot length and massive twenty-one-thousand-pound weight—eighteen thousand pounds of which was explosives—made it the king of the battlefield.

Several of the large cargo craft were shot down by Russian air defense systems that had managed to stay hidden. Others went down to brave Russian fighter crews running the gauntlet of American warplanes in order to get a missile shot or guns on the lumbering craft. But despite the efforts of Russian sons, the C-130s continued to drone west. And now cargo bays were opening. . . .

"Continue the attack, I tell you!" screamed the corps commander. He and his sister corps to the east were the primary Russian maneuver forces left in Iraq. Mounted in Russia's newest tanks and infantry fighting vehicles and supported by the most modern artillery and rocket systems, he knew that this attack must not stall. American forces continued pouring into Iraq and Kuwait by air and sea. For now the American 4th Infantry Division was the only armored force facing his men, though he'd heard rumors of their 1st Cavalry reconstituting to some extent—for the most part he ignored this latter information as he knew the devastation the forces of Russia had wreaked on the Texas-based division. His country had overwhelming power in position to push to the Gulf and their window of opportunity was closing; he did not intend to see his nation fail. He'd trained all of his adult life to fight the Americans and win. Now he would see the thing done.

Overhead he heard the aircraft. Not the scream of jet fighters but a dull buzz like a flight of locusts. And then he saw parachutes. . . .

Too large to be dropped through conventional bomb bays, the C-130 crews pushed the MOABs on wheeled pallets to the rear of the aircraft and out of the cargo doors. Parachutes pulled them into the slipstream behind the planes. As they fell to earth the bombs released from the pallets. Guided by global positioning satellites, the MOABs cruised to their directed positions.

The Russian commander watched the large object plummeting to earth to the east—the area where his lead division was. Just as it was about to strike the ground the object detonated. *Dear God,* he breathed. It was unlike any bomb he'd ever seen. Flames as if from hell itself spread across the horizon and a mushroom cloud reached into the sky like the fist of God Himself.

The American plan became clear to the general as he watched dozens of the parachutes fill the sky at regular intervals. The enemy was painting the ground with fire and none of his forces would go untouched. And then he saw the chute above him. The general slowly closed his eyes, picturing in his mind's eye his family's farm outside of Minsk, the farm where his wife and son waited for him.

The MOABs continued to drop for a half hour, each detonating six feet from the ground. The weapon's air-burst design meant that its payload of eighteen thousand pounds of tritonal—a composition 80 percent TNT and 20 percent aluminum—blew along the ground and spread.

Russian vehicles burned. Those soldiers on the outskirts of the blast radiuses ran, uniforms bellowing fire. Those closer to the center ceased to exist.

The Striker commander turned from the situation display in the back of his Bradley. "What are you hearing, Dave?"

The Striker S3 gave a weak smile. "Sir, this area of operations just became a lot friendlier."

"Shit," said Jones, lighting a Camel. "I hate to add to their already too-large egos, but I gotta throw the fly-boys a bone this time." He took a deep pull on the cigarette, burning a third of its length to ash. "That was some Class-A good shit."

Both men sobered as they thought of the Russian troops being hit by the MOABs. They'd seen the briefings on the ungodly bombs. While they'd been the means of gaining the tactical—perhaps even the strategic—advantage in the war, it was not the way warriors wished to dispose of the enemy. Eye-to-eye or gun-tube-to-gun-tube, but not in a cloud of fire that didn't understand courage, loyalty, and training.

Barnett returned to the map and jammed a finger at the Iron Tigers' engagement area. "Sir, Steel has destroyed everything in there . . . over a hundred vehicles. The brigade's attack into the Russian flank has also wreaked havoc. I don't have numbers for you yet, but trust me . . . you'll be happy."

Jones smiled. "I trust you, Dave. Not with one of my daughters; other than that, I trust you."

The single Barnett had seen Jones's three daughters—beautiful young ladies, all in their early to mid-twenties. "Good call," he said beneath his breath with a smile.

Jones frowned. "Did you say something, Dave?"

"Negative, sir. Not a thing."

The anchor leaned forward in his seat from New York. "And this is *Fox News,* your twenty-four-hour source for world news. Before returning to Nate Ryan's embedded reports from the Fourth Infantry's Striker Brigade, we have a tape made last night." The anchor's face darkened—he'd obviously seen the tape and wasn't happy with its message. "It will cast more light on last night's battle. Some of you will have questions following this report. I know I do."

America watched as Ryan's message went out.

Melissa Dillon sat in Colorado Springs, mesmerized. She'd never met Myron Sutherland, but she now felt she knew him well. "Why that son of a bitch . . ." she breathed.

"So far so good, sir," said General Tom Werner in a tired voice.

Jonathan Drake watched the news reports flow in. "The MOABs worked rather well, didn't they, General?"

Werner nodded darkly. Yes, they'd been effective . . . gruesomely so.

The president motioned toward one of the monitors set to a cable news channel. "Have you been watching the reports from the Fourth ID?"

"Nate Ryan?" asked Werner. The old warhorse nodded, frowning. "Yes, sir."

"Find out why that tank company was left out on burning string, Tom. *Now.*"

General Colonel Nikolay Kornukov, the equivalent of a U.S. three-star general, was the ranking Russian officer remaining in Iraq. At least he figured as much when he heard the other corps commander's radio transmission end abruptly in mid-sentence.

He turned to his meteorological officer. "What did you say, Colonel?"

"Sandstorm, sir," replied the staffer as he looked at the printout in his hand. "A big one. They're predicting force twelve winds." The meteorologist continued looking over the paper. "It looks like it may be only twelve to twenty-four hours in duration, but . . ." The officer looked to the general to emphasize what he was telling him. "Winds that strong, sir, we could see a leading edge—a sheer wall of sand—a thousand meters high."

Even combined with what was left of the other corps, Mother Russia didn't have many forces remaining in

Iraq. The storm would halt all movement, both ground and air. If he consolidated now before the storm hit they could move south as soon as it lifted. Saudi Arabia, and its army, was less than one hundred kilometers distant. He smiled. This storm might just be the break he was looking for.

Turning to his chief of staff, he issued the orders. The man nodded and began to move away, then paused. "Sir, Colonel Sedov has arrived per your orders."

Kornukov smiled. The general was a hard-liner who'd cut his teeth staring at American cavalry across the East German border. This Sedov seemed to be somewhat of a butcher. Though the general didn't have a problem—in spirit—with the younger officer killing every U.S. soldier he was afforded the opportunity, the colonel's cold-blooded killing of surrendering 1st Cavalry Division troops had gotten attention as far away as the General Staff in Moscow.

"Send him in," said Kornukov.

Thirty seconds later the colonel came to stiff attention in front of the general. "Colonel Sedov reports, sir!"

General Kornukov looked over the officer. He'd obviously taken a few minutes to dust off his field uniform. The blond hair and blue eyes harkened back to the old European Russia, perhaps even to the Romanovs. But the nose—well, perhaps it had once been aristocratic, but now it was a mess. "What happened to you, Colonel?"

Sergei Sedov briefly described the problems he'd encountered with General Jack Jeffries's dog.

"I hope you at least killed the little bastard."

Sedov assured him this was the case.

"Colonel, how are you and your men logistically."

The colonel never moved from his stiff position of attention. "Sir, we are fully armed and fueled, awaiting our next mission. I request—"

"Your requests do not matter to me in the least, Colonel," replied the general. He walked in front of Sedov and examined him at some length. "You have caused our superiors a great deal of discomfort through your actions."

Sedov jerked his head to face the general. "What? For showing an enemy no mercy? Did you see what they did to our regiments and divisions before we were even within range to fire?"

Kornukov nodded sympathetically and patted the junior officer's shoulder. "Colonel, I fully understand—and condone—your actions. Unfortunately, I have to be able to tell Moscow I am taking action."

"But sir . . ."

"Colonel, what have you heard about me?" asked the general blandly.

That you are a cold-blooded bastard, thought Sergei Sedov. "That you are a fine leader who holds high our past glories, sir."

"I will not, how would our American friends put it— hang you out to dry," said the general.

Sedov stared blankly.

"Colonel, you do what I tell you—follow my orders to the letter—and I will see that the matter of your, shall we say 'indiscretions,' is taken care of."

"And what are your orders, sir?"

Nikolay Kornukov smiled. "You have a regiment of tanks?"

Sedov nodded. "T-90s, sir."

"Excellent. And I need a praetorian guard."

"Dave," called Bill Jones. "Get your sorry ass in here."

Dave Barnett ducked into the Bradley command-and-control vehicle. "Sir?"

"We need to talk."

Barnett raised an eyebrow. "About what, sir?"

Jones looked at him seriously. "Your replacement."

The eyebrow went up farther. "I haven't even been your S3 long enough to have fucked up that badly, sir. What gives?"

Jones guffawed and pulled out a cigarette.

"Not in the vehicle, sir," called a voice from the turret.

Cigarette dangling from his lips, Jones turned and saw Matt O'Keefe glaring at him. Looking to Barnett, he gave a shrug and nodded toward the troop door. Once outside he flipped his Zippo open and lit up.

"Dave, it's time to take care of the mess in Two-seven-seven Armor."

Despite the fact that the Iron Tigers had just won a battle of historic proportions, Barnett knew what Jones meant. "Can you survive the political fallout of relieving an American legend's son, sir?"

Jones laughed. "Dave, I have two replies. Knowing me as you do, the first one won't surprise you . . . fuck the politics. That son of a bitch put a lot of good men at risk." He took a deep draw on the Camel, reveling in the smoke's filterless pungency. "Second, I just got the 'no worries' from Washington. Everyone from the president on down watched Ryan's news report on Sutherland's little play." The big officer barked a laugh. "Bet Myron's regretting sticking that news team with Steel now."

"But what does this have to do with me, sir? Are you sending me back down as the Iron Tigers exec or S3?" asked Barnett.

"You're taking over the Iron Tigers, Dave," said Jones flatly. "I want someone down there that I trust and that can pull that team back together. I've been talking to my senior enlisteds since Sutherland took over, taking the pulse of morale. It ain't been good— and it's worse since C Company was left manning the battalion position with no support."

Dave Barnett shook his head in disbelief. "Sir, I . . . I honestly don't know if I'm ready for this."

"The hell you aren't," barked Jones. "You've been ready. You know that as well as I do, you poor-mouthing son of a bitch."

Barnett's natural alphaness once more asserted itself. "Yeah, you're right. I can handle it."

"You'll need to pick your new S3 too," Jones said.

Barnett played with his mustache abstractedly. "Anyone I want?"

"Yep."

Barnett stuck out a dusty hand. "Done."

Cold Steel Tactical Assembly Area (TAA)
Southwest Iraq

Dillon looked over the circle of men around him that included Rider, Wyatt, the FSO, platoon leaders, and platoon sergeants. Cyclops's big 120mm gun was pointed over one side of the tank. A tarpaulin had been stretched over it and staked down to provide a modicum of shade. Beneath it the Cold Steel leadership each sat on their own version of the proper field stool. Some were canvas, some metal, all collapsible and easy to stow quickly in a bustle rack. The canvas of Dillon's chair had been repaired so many times with O.D. green duct tape that many of his troops questioned whether there was any of the original fabric beneath the hundreds of strands of green adhesive.

"All right then, if there are no questions, get your men some sack time—that is, once you've completed rearming, refueling, and performing maintenance on your vehicles. Keep one tank in each platoon on security at all times. Lieutenant Wyatt and I will alternate monitoring comms with higher. Until we hear from the TOC, we'll . . ." Dillon paused, seeing Sutherland's Hummer pulling into the middle of the assembly area. *Speak of the devil,* he thought. The Iron Tigers commander didn't stop until he was abreast of Dillon's tank. Dust enveloped the Cold Steel leadership and curses rang out.

"Gentlemen," said Sutherland, stepping out. "Fine work last night. Fine work indeed." He stood in the harsh afternoon sun, hands clasped to his pistol belt. The dozen or so officers and senior NCOs stared at him, no comments forthcoming.

"Well," said Sutherland uncertainly. "All right then. Carry on." He gestured to Patrick Dillon. "A word, Captain?"

Dillon stepped from beneath the shade of the canvas and followed Myron Sutherland toward his Hummer a few feet away. "What about your Kevlar, Dillon? You're not setting much of an example for those men."

The Steel commander stopped, rubbing a hand over his dirty scalp. The frustrations that had been building with Sutherland bubbled to the surface. "Fuck the Kevlar, sir."

Dillon, why did you have to say that? the Steel commander thought.

"Pardon me?"

Because, Patrick, the man is an overbearing asshole who had no qualms about seeing you and everyone else in C Company dead, the Steel commander answered. *And besides, you know he's going to screw you anyway.*

Dillon bent close to Myron Sutherland and spoke slower. "Fuck . . . the . . . Kevlar."

Sutherland sneered. "Fine. Dig your own grave, Dillon. Which brings me to the point at hand. Your insubordination last night is all I needed to get rid of you for good."

Dillon's look of puzzlement was genuine. "What insubordination? We followed orders."

"I'm talking about your grandstanding for a national

audience," roared the lieutenant colonel. "Trying to make it look like I was out to get you. . . ."

"What kind of freaky-assed fantasy world do you live in?" returned Dillon hotly. "I have no idea what you're talking about."

"The hell you don't!"

"Colonel, it was your idea to stick the news crew with me—not mine. But if you're insinuating that I had anything to do with some report . . ."

"That's exactly what I'm saying, Dillon. Now get in the vehicle," he said, jerking his thumb toward the Hummer. "You're relieved."

Dillon sneered but kept his mouth shut.

But the colonel had a grudge to settle and wouldn't let it go. "You want a piece of me, Dillon?" He smiled.

Dillon's men crowded forward. Money began changing hands as bets circulated regarding how many punches it would take the Old Man to knock Sutherland out. Then another Humvee pulled into the position. Dave Barnett stepped out.

"What do you want, Barnett?" said Sutherland, upset that Dillon had been about to make a major career mistake when the man had decided to interrupt the change-of-command party.

"I could ask you the same thing," said Barnett, stepping next to Dillon.

"What the hell does that mean? Your days in this battalion are over, Barnett. Get out of here."

Barnett smiled. "That's where you're wrong, Sutherland," he said. "My days here are just starting."

Sutherland noticed for the first time that Barnett's subdued major's rank on his helmet and collar, brown oak leaves, had been replaced by the black oak leaves of a lieutenant colonel.

"I've had enough of this," said Myron Sutherland. "If you don't move out of my battalion area now . . ."

Barnett held up one hand calmly and walked to his Hummer. "Give me a minute, Myron." Picking up the hand mike, he turned to face his audience. "Sir?"

The tinny speaker whirred to life. *"Sutherland? You recognize my voice?"*

Sutherland walked over and took the mike. *"Yes, Colonel Jones, I do. But I'm a bit confused exactly what it is Major Barnett is trying to tell me, sir."*

"What Lieutenant Colonel *Barnett is trying to tell you, Sutherland, is that you're fired."*

Myron Sutherland was dumbstruck and stood silently staring at the radio. Finally the words struck home. And Myron Sutherland was pissed. Turning on Barnett, he raised a fist.

"Don't make things worse for yourself," said Jones in a calm voice.

Sutherland dropped the arm, defeated.

Dillon and Barnett looked around for some sign of Jones's presence; nothing. The man was fucking magic, their exchanged glances said.

Three kilometers to the east, Jones popped out of his Bradley's commander's hatch. Laughing, he pulled out his cigarettes.

"Sir . . ."

"Shut up, O'Keefe."

Matt O'Keefe sighed. *Why do I even bother trying*? he wondered. "So I take it you're finished with my TOW sight?"

Barnett turned to Patrick Dillon. "You need to get packed up, Pat."

Dillon stared at him. "Sir, you're now the *second* field grade I've prepared to throw down on in the past hour. Don't fuck with me, please."

Barnett laughed and pulled out his pipe. "I'm not fucking with you. You've got a new job."

"New job?"

"I need an S3," replied Barnett simply. "Per Colonel Jones, I can have my pick." He flipped open his lighter and pulled deeply on the pipe until the tobacco lit a glowing red. He flipped the lighter closed and it disappeared into his pocket. "I want you."

"Jones won't let a captain take the job," said Dillon.

Barnett grinned. "He's already signed off . . . but it's nonissue. As of today it's *Major* Dillon—orders to follow, of course. Congratulations."

Dillon was silent as thoughts flew through his mind. If he had to have any job in the Army other than a command, the S3 of a tank battalion or cavalry squadron would top his list; and he'd worked for Barnett in the past—no one better to have as a boss. But doubts remained.

"Sir," he said quietly. "Who would take over Steel?"

"A combat-proven leader. I think you'll approve of the choice."

Dillon thought about it for a few moments. "Waters?"

Barnett nodded. "Muddy. He proved himself last year; plus the training Lieutenant Krieger's given him over the past month should prove invaluable."

This was all too fast. "*Lieutenant* Krieger?"

Dave Barnett grinned as smoke swirled about his head and shoulders. "Our new scout platoon leader."

"Let me guess . . . you got Muddy his captain bars back as well?"

"You bet."

Dillon shook his head. "You've been a busy boy, haven't you, sir?"

Barnett's grin broadened around the pipe stem as he nodded. "War sucks, Pat; but it does allow for one to get rid of some of the red tape."

Chapter 23

_____

_____

_____

Check

Somewhere over Russia

"You're going to have a ten-second window," Ted Moran said quietly into his boom mike. "Once I give you 'go,' you've got to be moving. I may be in a near-invisible stealth aircraft at high altitude, but once that cargo door opens, I'm going to light up Russian air defense radars like the Fourth of July." Moran paused. "You reading me, Luke?"

"Yeah, yeah," said Luke Dodd into his oxygen mask, beginning to feel the first adrenaline rush of the night. Even at supersonic speeds the flight from Scotland had seemed to take forever. But now it was go time. He felt his heart rate move from its standard fifty-five beats per minute to sixty. *Calm down,* he told himself, closing his eyes, *you're getting jumpy.*

"Get ready," called Moran. "Five, four, three, two, one, GO!"

Luke Dodd stood in total darkness, alone in the rear of the aircraft but for the jumpmaster standing silently by his side. He heard a roar of air as the aircraft's cargo door opened and felt a blistering sting of freezing pain high on his cheek where his balaclava and mask failed to overlap properly. A patch of gray appeared in the wall of black to his right front. The jumpmaster gave

Luke a gentlemanly touch that couldn't really be described as a shove, but the CIA operative was already halfway out the door and tucking himself into position for a high-altitude, low-opening, or HALO, jump into the Russian night. The goal of the HALO jump was to get the stealthy black bomber—tonight being used instead as a one-man troop carrier—into and out of enemy territory without being seen.

Free-falling from thirty thousand feet, the air around Luke was fifty degrees below zero and he was moving toward the ground at a speed of over one hundred twenty miles per hour. He concentrated on nothing, instead settling back for what he knew would be a two-and-a-half-minute free fall prior to his chute opening, followed by another two to three minutes under his blackened canopy before touchdown in an unmarked field northwest of Moscow.

Overhead the black-project bird piloted by Ted Moran kicked in afterburners and moved swiftly toward friendlier climes.

Random Checkpoint
Ten Miles Northwest of Moscow

Two uniformed soldiers stopped the priest as he came out of Customs. "Papers," said the senior soldier in Russian, extending a gloved hand.

The cleric, gray-haired and bearded in the tradition of the Greek Orthodox Church, reached into his breast pocket and pulled out his passport. He handed it wordlessly to his inquisitor.

The soldier, a senior sergeant, looked at the passport photo, at the priest, and back to the passport. "Yuly Berezovsky?" he said in a flat voice.

"Father Berezovsky," said the priest simply, adding a small nod toward the floor.

"Your Russian is very good," said the sergeant, his tone suspicious.

The priest's face remained straight, but his voice was dry. "It should be. I am Russian."

The sergeant ignored the remark. "I see here that you have been abroad for some time. In the United States." He placed an ever-so-slight emphasis on the name of the country Russia was currently at war with. "Why would a Russian priest be in America for over two years?"

The priest's stance remained relaxed. "I was a visiting professor at Holy Cross Greek Orthodox Theological Seminary."

The sergeant stared at him.

"It is in Massachusetts," the priest added, nonplussed, knowing the man in front of him had no idea what or where Massachusetts was.

For the moment satisfied, the sergeant closed the passport and held it, clearly in no hurry to return it to its owner. He was a senior NCO enjoying the winds of change in Russia. Once more a man in uniform had power over the common rabble. He also enjoyed being able to again put "believers" in their place. "So why return now . . . *Father*?" he asked with a conspiratorial wink at his companion.

"Because my country—and its flock—are in jeopardy." The look he gave the sergeant could not be considered challenging, but it fell far short of being cowed by the soldier's authority.

"Really? I had no idea," said the noncommissioned officer belligerently. "And your plans?"

"I am returning home, Sergeant."

The soldier tapped the passport in his hands. "That is where?"

"Suzdal," said the priest, referring to a small town north of Moscow.

"Of course," said the sergeant with a laugh. Suzdal was a poor, primarily agricultural area ringed by a number of Orthodox churches and monasteries. "Are your parents cucumber millionaires then?" he asked with a sneer of derision. The other soldier laughed at the nickname for the local inhabitants, who toiled away at the soil for little or no profit.

"They are farmers, yes."

The sergeant handed the passport back. "Things have changed, priest. Watch yourself . . . for we will certainly be doing the same."

Luke Dodd took the passport wordlessly, returned it to his jacket pocket, and headed for the transportation area.

Cold Steel Tactical Assembly Area
Southwestern Iraq

Muddy Waters sat back after completing the operations order for Steel's upcoming mission. As the NCOs and platoon leaders walked away he exhaled deeply. His head was still spinning from the changes initiated over the past twenty-four hours and already he'd received and briefed an order that would be brutal for an experienced commander.

He turned his head when he realized he wasn't alone. Bluto Wyatt hadn't moved from his position to the right of Waters after everyone else left. The big man only now folded his notebook and placed it into the breast pocket of his Nomex coveralls. While he and Wyatt had always gotten along well, it suddenly occurred to Waters that the big man might resent not having been named Dillon's successor—a resentment Waters could understand.

Wyatt grinned and shook his head. "Don't even worry about it," he said as though reading Waters's mind. He stood and walked over to his new commander, hand outstretched. "I just wanted to tell you that you can count on my full support, sir."

Waters mentally exhaled and took the massive paw. "Thanks, Bluto."

Wyatt nodded to the graphics board leaning against the side of Waters's tank. The upcoming mission's graphics were displayed on the board and Waters had used it to brief the order. "She's shaping up to be a bitch, ain't she?"

The wind picked up and sand sprayed into both men's faces, a prelude of the coming storm.

"That she is, XO. That she is."

1st Cavalry Division TAC
Southwestern Iraq

Newly promoted Major General Kirk Shillings looked up as a familiar head poked into the door of his command center. "Well I'll be . . . Wild Bill Jones!" he exclaimed, walking quickly to his visitor and grabbing him in a bear hug. "How are you, you old ugly son of a bitch?"

Jones laughed. He had served under Shillings in the 24th Mechanized Infantry during Desert Storm and knew the man well. "Good, sir. I was glad, but not surprised, to see you make it out of that first fight."

Shillings's expression darkened as he recalled that night and the subsequent flight across the desert. "Thanks, Bill. And thanks for the extra armor for this mission—I appreciate you going to bat for us with your division commander, especially considering you boys have a hell of a mission getting ready to kick off yourselves."

Jones pulled out a pack of cigarettes and lifted an inquiring eyebrow at the general.

Shillings shook his head. "I gave them up a couple of years ago, but you go ahead."

Jones nodded and lit up. "Helluva mission is right. But you definitely needed some extra muscle, especially considering your troops are mounted in Saudi equipment without the additional armor protection the American-built stuff has built in."

"Yeah, don't I know it," said Shillings. "But the fire control systems are the same as our M1A2s and Bradleys, and we're using our own ammunition. We should be all right." The general paused, looking at Bill Jones seriously. "And I know the real purpose behind the visit, Billy. You don't have to ask—I'll take care of your boys."

Jones nodded. "I know you will, General. But it makes me feel better to hear you say it. The Iron Tigers and I have grown kinda close over the past year."

"I met the new commander tonight. Seems to be a fine man. He was your Three, right?"

"For a short while, yes, sir. And he'll do you proud."

Shillings's eyes twinkled. "That's a hell of a mustache he's sporting," the general said with not a little admiration.

Jones laughed. "Yeah. Took me a while to get used to that fur piece."

Kirk Shillings pointed to the map posted on the side of the shelter. "So what do you think, Bill? You were always my sharpest tactician."

Having been briefed by Dave Barnett a few hours earlier, Jones was intimately familiar with the upcoming 1st Cavalry operation. "Risky, sir. Very risky."

"And?"

Jones pointed to the area south of Rutba in which the two remaining Russian corps were bedding down to weather out the approaching storm. "If you can get in there before the storm lifts, take out the command and control, it's possible." What Jones left unsaid was that if they didn't make major headway quickly, the Russian forces that outnumbered the 1st Cav's understrength ground force by greater than six to one would make mincemeat of them.

"And?" prompted the general once more.

Bill Jones looked from the map. "I like it, but . . ."

"But you're worried about your men."

The Striker Brigade commander nodded. "Sir, you know as well as I do that the Iron Tigers are mounted on old M1A1s and M2A2s from the Kuwait storage site. They're not even digitized. If they become separated in that sandstorm . . ." Jones trailed off.

Shillings put a brotherly arm around the colonel. "Bill, you've got my word, old friend—I *will* take care of your Tigers."

Jones nodded. "Good enough." He held out a hand. "See you on the high ground, sir."

Shillings smiled. "On the high ground it is."

President's Quarters, the Kremlin
Moscow

Konstantin Khartukov sat in his study before a roaring fire, staring at a photo of himself with his wife and daughter taken in happier times. First one of them had left him, now the other. He'd had time to rethink many things since his daughter's hasty departure, not the least of which were his failings as a father. Without taking his eyes from the photo, he picked up a chilled glass of vodka from the table next to him and took a long drink.

"Life is tough," said a quiet voice from the shadows. "It's tougher when you're an asshole."

The heavy glass thumped off of the carpet as Khartukov jerked around in his seat. "Who is there?"

A figure separated itself from the shadows in the darkest corner of the room.

"Claude! Where . . . how did you get in here?"

The Russian president's former chef shook his head over the barrel of a silenced 9mm Sig Sauer pistol. "Please don't call me Claude. I never did like that name."

"Who *are* you?" asked the Russian president, still shocked that an intruder could reach him in the inner sanctums of the Kremlin.

"It doesn't matter," the man said in a conversational tone. "What matters is that you've turned the entire planet on its ear for nothing more than your own egotistical ends." He looked hard into Khartukov's eyes. "Tonight it ends."

The Russian leader looked dejectedly at the floor. "It doesn't matter. . . ." He stopped speaking and swung his eyes to the door as it opened abruptly. Oleg.

"I thought I heard you talking to someone, Mr. President," said the security chief, looking about the room.

Too stunned to speak, Khartukov shifted his gaze back to the corner where Luke had stood moments earlier. He was gone. But where?

Khartukov looked once more to the door as it clicked shut and Oleg collapsed to the floor.

"What have you done to him?" shouted the Russian president, for the first time showing any emotion.

Luke Dodd raised an eyebrow. "Don't worry about Oleg, Mr. President. Just a little tap to the head. He'll wake up—tied and gagged of course—in a little while."

"And me?" asked the president.

Khartukov saw a shadow that could almost pass for sadness cross Dodd's face.

1st Cavalry TOC
Southwestern Iraq

The impromptu meeting quieted when Kirk Shillings entered the tent—a normal occurrence when subordinates saw their commander would be watching their planning.

Shillings looked to his intelligence officer, or G2. The lieutenant colonel shook his head. "We're still working on it, sir."

Shillings looked around at the assembled officers' faces—things didn't look promising.

"Sir, I've got every brigade's recon troop commander here plus my staff. For the past two hours we've been working on how to get eyes on the Russian maneuver units before we stumble into them. The problem is the weather guys are telling us our thermals may do us little good." As if to emphasize the officer's point, the wind picked up outside. The tent supports began jumping up and down as the shelter's fabric took a beating. A fine dust cloud filled the air, lending it the feel of an opium den minus the narcotics.

Shillings raised an eyebrow and looked at the roof, wondering if the shelter would make it through the next five minutes, much less the rest of the night's planning session.

"Gentlemen, an old subordinate of mine came to see me tonight. He seems to think one of his men—currently attached to us, by the way—may be able to help."

Looks of hope sprang up among the group. Shillings stepped aside and a giant form separated itself from the doorway's shadow. "This is Lieutenant Rolf Krieger."

Most of the men, all captains or higher, rolled their eyes in disgust.

"What?" asked Kirk Shillings. "You haven't come up with anything, have you?"

"Sir," said a captain, one of the brigade recon troop commanders, "I'm sure he eats steel and craps full metal jackets, but how much good is a lieutenant with less than two years in the Army going to do us?"

Another captain stepped behind the speaker and whispered urgently in his ear.

The recon troop commander paled and turned to his counterpart, whispering. "Why didn't you tell me he was *that* Krieger?!" the captain hissed.

Word quickly spread from man to man as Krieger was recognized by the more experienced troopers. The "green lieutenant" was in reality one of the most experienced scouts in the U.S. Army. He'd instructed many of the officers in the room at the Fort Knox Scout Leader's Course—three arduous weeks most of them would rather forget.

The captain turned to Rolf Krieger. "Lieutenant, whatever tactical insights you have would be welcome."

"Sir," said Krieger to the intel officer. "May I take a look at the latest reconnaissance photos?"

The G2 pointed at the wall. "These are from a Global Hawk pass two hours ago. Because of the deteriorating weather, they're likely the last hard locations we'll get from our air assets before sand obscures all observation."

Krieger nodded but didn't look at the officer.

"Can you get us close to them? Close enough for the tanks to engage?" asked the G2 as Krieger studied the UAV shots.

"Gentlemen, I can do better than that."

Only those who did not know Rolf Krieger doubted the veracity of the claim.

Axis of Attack SABER
Southwestern Iraq

"Sir, I can't see shit!" yelled Tommy over the intercom.

Forced to button up and observe only what his gunner was looking at as he scanned back and forth in the night, Dillon understood his driver's nerves. He thanked God that no one had had a problem with him taking his own crew with him to the task force headquarters—the middle of a war was no time to break in a new team. But they had to trade tanks out; no way around that one. They'd been given Barnett's old tank. Dillon and the crew had then given HQ-63, rechristened Cyclops II, a shakedown cruise earlier in the afternoon. All hands had pronounced her landworthy.

"Just pick up the speed a little, Tommy," the Iron Tigers' new S3 replied calmly. "Knight is directly in front of us. You should be able to see the lights mounted to the rear of their bustle racks in no time."

"Roger," came Tommy's electronic voice in a subdued tone. Dillon couldn't see his driver, but he could picture him hugged up against his night-vision periscope.

Bickel, as always, was alert and manning his weapons systems, hands on the cadillacs and face to his sight.

Boggs, with no mission at the moment, had opened his ammunition door and was arranging his sabot and HEAT rounds where he wanted them. All the loader could see was the rear end of the aft caps, but he'd used a marker and written an *S* or an *H* in large block letters on each.

A relieved voice from the front—"Sir, I've got them," said Specialist Thompson.

"I had faith," replied Dillon. "You doing okay, Bick?"

The gunner gave his commander a thumbs-up without turning around.

Dillon sat back in his seat to relax for a few moments. In the dim interior lighting he saw the picture of Melissa and the girls he'd Scotch-taped at eye level. How he missed them. As nervous as he was he knew it was nothing compared to the uncertainty they were experiencing.

He looked to the turret. "Be with my girls, God, that's all I ask. Keep them safe and help them not to worry too much." Patrick Dillon didn't add "especially if something happens to me." Whether it was the God, Father, Holy Ghost and saints of his Roman Catholic childhood looking over him or Mars himself, for the past year Patrick Dillon knew one fact for certain: he would not die in war. The lack of a functioning left eye, though, made him wonder how intact his body would be after the next engagement. He laughed quietly, wondering if all soldiers felt the same sureness regarding their mortality going into battle, if it was something a fighting man had to tell himself in order to not face the realities of what war could do to him on a personal level . . . and if dead heroes had felt the same invincibility prior to meeting the sabot round with their name on it.

And Cyclops II moved east, deeper into the night and sand-shrouded Iraqi desert.

The wind howled as the Scout Hummer proceeded slowly toward the Russian bivouac area. The constant dings of sand blasting the vehicle's glass and body kept the crew on edge. The driver stared intently at the thermal enhancer in front of him; although advertised as allowing an operator to see clearly on a "dirty" battlefield through dust, smoke, and other obscurants, at best it left him something other than totally blind. The two scouts in the rear seats sat silently, weapons ready. In the vehicle's passenger seat Rolf Krieger bent over his GPS receiver.

"Stop," said Krieger.

The Hummer moved from crawl mode to a full stop with little effort. Krieger picked up the radio's hand mike and reported higher that they were in position. For miles around the armored vehicles of the 1st Cavalry Division and Task Force Tiger stopped in place.

As he put the hand mike down, one of the scouts in the rear of the Hummer asked the question: "What now, sir?"

Krieger frowned for an instant before remembering he was now a lieutenant. He turned to the scout. "Time to dismount."

To Krieger's left and right teams of scouts and engineers climbed from their comparatively comfortable vehicles and into a dark maelstrom. All of the soldiers were wrapped tightly head to foot so that no skin was exposed to the blasting sands. Behind them their support

teams fired up LRASs to guide them to their targets: the
Russian tanks and fighting vehicles ringed in defensive
positions to wait out the storm. Past these vehicles lay
the generals in charge of the Russian invasion. These
men had looked to breach the American lines in Iraq;
now the Americans were looking to create a breach of
their own.

Krieger stopped next to a T-90 tank and looked to
the scout behind him. "Give me a mine!" he said, yelling
to be heard through his face wrap over the wind. This
was their fifth stop and they had two more to go.

The scout handed the lieutenant an M21 antitank
mine. Krieger took the seventeen-pound weapon and
placed it in front of the Russian tank. He ensured that
it was centered on the tank before inserting the mine's
twenty-one-inch tilt rod and arming it. When the tank
pulled forward more than six inches it would take only
a small amount of pressure on the tilt rod to send the
mine's eleven pounds of high explosives straight into the
hull and crew. But Rolf Krieger wasn't one to take
chances; he looked to the end of the big 125mm gun
tube. He could barely make out the engineers who were
busily packing down the big gun with hastily filled sandbags or whatever else was handy—just in case the Russian tank crew decided to back out of their position and
thus miss the A.T. mine. The tank could move, but it
would receive a hell of a surprise if it tried to engage
an American vehicle.

Two minutes later the scouts and engineers disappeared once more into the storm.

"Sergeant," said the sleepy T-90 gunner to his tank
commander. "Did you hear something?"

The NCO wiped the sleep from his eyes. Other than
the fact that there was no easy way to relieve oneself
with the storm raging outside it hadn't been bad the past

few hours. His crew hadn't had a full night's sleep in days and had desperately needed the rest. "What? No, I heard nothing."

A dull roar reverberated throughout the Russian combat vehicle strongly enough to make the metal machine shake. An explosion somewhere in the distance?

"Are you picking up anything on your thermal systems?" he asked the gunner.

"I just turned it on a few minutes ago when I heard the first noise . . . wait, it should be warmed up now." The gunner put his face to his site and pulled it immediately back. "Sergeant! American tanks!"

All thoughts of sleep and rest fled. "Driver!" screamed the sergeant. "Get us to another location! Quickly!"

The driver, now fully awake and the dreams of full-breasted Moscow university girls dispelled, rammed the tank into reverse. Outside, the M21 antitank mine tilt rod vibrated as the T-90 moved away from it, but not sufficiently to detonate the explosive charge.

"M1-series tank, five hundred meters to the front!" yelled the gunner.

"Engage!"

The young gunner aligned his reticle on the American tank. "I have him!"

"Fire!"

Despite the threat of the moment, the gunner felt a tug of guilt. *I've never taken a life,* he thought. Did it make it all right simply because someone of superior rank told him to do so? Then again he'd likely die quickly himself if he didn't take action, he reflected.

The gunner squeezed off his trigger, releasing the 125mm sabot round inserted into the breech by the tank's automatic loader. The penetrator separated from its casing and screamed down the tube. Instead of exiting the gun tube for its short but lethal voyage through sand and wind to its intended target, however, the round met

a tightly filled sandbag. The contained force first blew
the gun tube to pieces, the result looking like a trick
cigar that had exploded in the smoker's face, its tip
shredded. But the damage didn't stop there. The force
blew backward into the Russian tank. The fireball blew
into the crew compartment so fast that the gunner didn't
have time to note that he'd go to his grave with a
clear conscience.

Fuck this. Patrick Dillon threw open his hatch. After
six-plus hours stuck inside an already claustrophobic vehicle like the M1A1 he was going nuts. The order had
come down from higher—the 1st Cav and Iron Tigers
were going into the attack. Immediately upon raising his
head from the hatch Dillon was aware of an explosion
to his right. Looking to the source he saw a burning
T-90. The turret was twisted back like it had been un-
rolled and the tank was a flaming hell. *Krieger,* Dillon
thought. The S3 said a silent prayer of thanks that the
big German American was on his side.

Though it was still dark, the glow of the Super Sea-
Wolf told Dillon that the sun should already be coming
up. As if racing to beat its rays to their enemies, the
American tanks poured through the erupting gaps in the
Russian lines like a wave of steel.

Chapter 24

And the Cradle Will Rock

**Office of the Russian General Staff
The Kremlin, Moscow**

The harried analyst rushed headlong into the general's outer office with a fistful of papers. An unsuspecting secretary about to enter the hallway barely avoided spilling coffee down the front of the man's cheap suit before sidestepping out of the way. Seeing the intruder's target—her superior's office—the woman attempted to stop him. But it was already too late. Winded, the man stopped in front of the room's only desk and bent over, hands on knees, trying to catch his breath.

The secretary ran in behind him and began to protest to the officer sitting behind the desk. He waved her off. Exiting, she closed the door behind her after a final angry glare at the wheezing man.

The general, a senior member of the intelligence staff, leaned forward toward the intruder and spoke with obvious annoyance. "Who are you and what do you want?"

The best the analyst could do was an unintelligible series of gasps—he'd sprinted up four flights of stairs and down a very long hallway to get to the general.

"Speak, you imbecile, before I summon security!"

The man shook the papers in his hand in front of the general.

"What are they?"

"Im . . . imagery. Iraq," the man managed after a few moments.

The general's eyebrows shot up. Finally! With no satellite imagery assets left in space, the Russians had fired off their latest spy satellite from the Baikonur Cosmodrome in Kazakhstan only thirty-six hours earlier, hoping upon hope that it would remain in orbit long enough for them to get a picture of the latest developments in western Iraq.

The officer grabbed the photos and quickly sorted through them. From the time stamp he saw that they were less than an hour old. Though the sandstorm was dying down it was clear that it maintained enough power to render most of the shots useless. And then he saw the final photo.

"I assume this ring of vehicles is the remainder of our combat maneuver forces in Iraq?" he said, pointing to what from space looked like a large circle consisting of hundreds of dark dots.

The analyst nodded emphatically.

The general looked closely at the southwest corner of the circle. Something there, something that looked like a huge dark arrowhead, had penetrated the circle.

"What are these?! Tell me they're not . . ."

"Americans," finished the civil servant.

"Where is the satellite now?"

"Well to the east of that location and continuing in its programmed orbit." He looked at his watch. "It should be moving over the Gulf in the next five minutes."

"Turn it around! Now!"

"But, sir, that will expend much of the satellite's—"

The officer shot to his feet and slammed the desk with his fists for emphasis. "Turn it around or I will have you shot!"

The civilian ran. An hour of feverish activity later the

Russian ground support team breathed a collective sigh of relief. The satellite's maneuver had been completed. The smiles faded as the series of coded signals used to communicate with the satellite stopped. The team chief rushed to a keyboard and tapped feverish instructions into a computer. Nothing. He hunched over his keyboard and typed in an override command. Finally he sat back, removed his glasses, and ran a hand through his thinning hair. "It is gone."

In space an American hunter satellite went from active to standby mode, returned its laser cannon to its stowage position, and winked once more into sleep.

Axis SABER
Eighty Kilometers South of Rutba, Iraq

The sun was up and the sandstorm, while still alive, looked nothing like the monster weather system of the day before. The sand made it difficult for either side to see with the naked eye beyond a few meters, but their combat vehicles' thermal imaging systems were now usable.

Kirk Shillings switched from his command track to his Hummer—despite his staff's protests—for the greater mobility the big four-by-four provided. He would have liked to be overhead in his chopper in order to gain the best perspective on how the battle was shaping up. Unfortunately his helicopter, like all air assets, was still grounded. However this war ended, it would do so on the terms of the ground warriors.

Shillings called instructions to his brigade commanders, talking them through their parts of the coming battle one final time as a coach would, positioning them as best he could for success. His artillery commanders fired at the deeper Russian units, separating them from their comrades who were at the point of the American attack. Like a chef wielding a wicked knife the American maneuver units peeled back the Russians as they attacked from the rear and flanks.

The sun tried to burn through the dust. The effect was an otherworldly landscape with a bloodred sky. Beneath it hundreds of armored vehicles manned by the two strongest armies in earth's history were about to lock in mortal combat.

"All Tiger elements, Tiger Six . . . move for Objective Waterloo, time now. Acknowledge, over."

Dillon pulled behind Team Knight as Mike Stuart's company moved into the lead of the task force wedge per unit SOP. He hoped that, per the colorful planners' intentions, the Waterloo reference applied to the Russian forces and not their own.

Within minutes the command radio frequencies of both forces lit up as the battle proper was joined. American and Russian armor fought against one another with an intensity and rage as red as the sky above them. As the 1st Cavalry reaped cold-eyed retribution on the outer ring of guard forces, the Iron Tigers broke loose and went for the heart.

Patrick Dillon's Cyclops II took a position behind Team Knight's thirteen-vehicle wedge formation. Sand sprayed dozens of feet in the air behind the big Knight tanks and Brads as they sped across the desert.

The Russian plan had been to remain stationary only long enough to ride out the sandstorm and to then head west to consolidate with the Saudi forces across the border. What they had not planned on was an American attack through the storm—and their lack of defensive preparations showed it.

The sounds of armor clashing slowly died away as the Iron Tigers moved further into the Russian perimeter. The last intelligence they'd received showed a large group of armored vehicles and tents at the center that was purported to be the enemy corps headquarters. It was toward this target they moved.

General Colonel Nikolay Kornukov stood in his headquarters tent listening to reports from his subordinate commands telling him that a contingent of American armor was en route to his location.

The general grabbed his aide's arm savagely. "Get Colonel Sedov on the radio and tell him to stop the approaching Americans at all costs."

When the colonel moved out to deliver the order Kornukov smiled. Sedov's crack band of killers were now his personal bodyguards and they had only one standing order—to protect his headquarters as the Russians withdrew from Iraq.

The general yelled after the fleeing staff officer. "Tell him if he fails he will lose more than a nose!"

Sergei Sedov stood in the turret of his T-90 and watched the dust cloud build on the horizon. Formerly looked on by the ladies as a handsome man, what was left of his nose was covered by a steel prosthetic wrapped tightly around the back of his head by an elastic band. Despite medical attention, one or more of the numberless forms of bacteria prevalent throughout the Middle East had seized on the colonel's wound as a food source and wreaked havoc. He held slim hopes that Moscow plastic surgeons could make him look remotely like his old self. The injury had done nothing to alter his normal, decidedly non-sunny disposition. As the dust cloud moved closer his whole being hungered for the slaughter to begin.

"Range!" he yelled to his gunner.

"Four thousand meters!"

When the war began Sedov's regiment had consisted of three T-90 tank battalions—each with thirty-one tanks—and one motorized rifle battalion of over thirty

BMP-3s and their accompanying infantry troops. The 1st Cavalry had trimmed out half of the regiment's fire-power; still, it was a force to be reckoned with.

"Engage with AT-11s!"

The T-90s' 125mm gun tubes were designed to fire not only tank main gun rounds but also the AT-11 antitank guided missile, code-named Sniper. Close to fifty of Russia's most modern tanks belched flame as missiles flew south.

As they'd become accustomed to, the Iron Tigers faced heavy odds. In the attack against a hastily em-placed enemy position doctrine dictated they needed two-to-one odds in their favor to have a fifty-fifty chance of success. Instead they faced a force almost 50 percent larger than their own. Dave Barnett thought about this fact. In the words of the immortal George Patton, he had a two-word reply: *Fuck it.* At least in Barnett's mind that is what the great American general would have said under the same circumstances.

Barnett and the other Iron Tigers saw the missiles headed their way. "Evasive maneuvers, company commanders! Have some Bradleys go to ground and throw some TOWs for cover. Keep moving and close to main gun range!"

No replies were expected and none were forthcoming. Every combat vehicle in the American task force juked and jived to throw off the aim of the Russian gunners. Most M1s upon seeing a puff of smoke signifying a Russian ATGM launch sent a sabot round in that direction—the fire didn't have to be accurate to divert a nervous Russian gunner's attention enough to send his missile off the mark.

Seven American vehicles were halted in their tracks as Sniper missiles found their marks. The rest continued on their deadly course north.

"Range!?" yelled Barnett from a standing position in the turret.

"Thirty-one hundred meters!" replied his gunner.

"Fire!"

The Iron Tiger commander's gun tube belched flame and a T-90 erupted in a shower of sparks. At the same instant a Russian missile found its mark on HQ-66 and Barnett's right track leaped from its sprockets. The sixty-eight-ton vehicle skidded right as the left track continued its forward momentum. Finally the vehicle shuddered to a stop in a shower of sand.

"Out! Now!" yelled Dave Barnett to his crew over the intercom system.

Rather than reply, Barnett's loader and gunner pushed past him and out through the loader's hatch. "Get behind the tank where you've got some cover!" he yelled to his crew. He began to unclip his own CVC from its communication cord to dismount, then paused. *"Tiger Three, Tiger Six, over."*

"This is Three," replied Dillon.

"You've got the ball, Pat. We're hit."

Dillon felt as though he'd been slammed in the stomach with a sledgehammer. He'd gone from command of a fourteen-tank company to a forty-four-vehicle battalion in less than twenty-four hours. But his response was instinctive. *"Roger. I've got it."*

Dave Barnett jumped off his M1A1 seconds before it fireballed into the morning sky.

Patrick Dillon pulled the brass telescope Mike Stuart had given him and extended it to its full length. Russian vehicles with gun tubes pointed in his direction jumped to life as he lifted it to his eye and focused. Approximately fifty systems, the majority of them T-90 tanks, in a classic firing line oriented directly across the Iron Tigers' path. Not much imagination, he reflected, the maneuver snob in him raising its ugly head.

His own force was rapidly closing the distance to the Russians with Knight in the lead, Anvil on the left, and

Cold Steel on the right. He saw a piece of slightly undulating terrain directly to his front in their line of march, reviewed several options, and made his decision.

"Mike! Go to ground and occupy a support by fire position at your twelve o'clock!"

"Roger," replied Stuart.

"Anvil and Steel . . . find some good terrain ASAP and hold in place."

Both of the flank companies acknowledged.

"Thunder, give me smoke across our front," he called to his mortar platoon. Dillon's mortars were his most responsive indirect fire trigger pullers, each of the four tracks able to go to ground quickly and pump out up to sixteen 120mm shells in their first minute of firing—and they could reach out and touch a bad guy over seven thousand meters distant.

"Wilco," called the mortar platoon leader.

"Lightning . . ."

"I'm on it," called the fire support officer. *"One-five-five HE en route shortly. I've got a good fix on them."*

Dillon nodded to himself and moved on. *"Roger, break. All Tiger elements, Tiger Three . . . don't stay in one place too long. Guaranteed we aren't the only ones calling for indirect fires . . ."*

As if on cue a barrage of 152mm high-explosive rounds sailed five hundred meters over Anvil; it wouldn't take the enemy gunners long to make the necessary adjustment, at which point dozens of rounds would saturate A Company's current position. Knowing this the Anvil commander was already moving his vehicles, shifting to a different location a few hundred meters away—far enough away to throw off the Russians' corrections, not so far he couldn't react to Dillon's orders once he gave them.

Dull thumps—the mortar platoon firing—sounded behind Dillon as he watched Knight's mech infantry platoon send a volley of TOW II missiles downrange. As

the wire-guided missiles struck their intended targets—
all tanks—Dillon thanked God that the mech company
commander who owned the platoon took his gunnery
training seriously. He had just enough time to see the
T-90s' secondary explosions begin before a rapidly building wall of smoke obscured the Russians from his sight—
and him and his men from theirs.

Dillon dropped into the turret and looked through his
sight extension . . . good; Bickel had monitored the call
for smoke and had already switched to thermal mode.
Their day sight would be useless for the time being. He
stood in the turret again and keyed the task force net.

*"Steel . . . hold in place. Anvil, I want you to swing
behind Knight and take up a position to Steel's right.
Move now. Acknowledge."*

"Steel, roger," called Muddy Waters.

"Anvil, we're moving."

Dillon almost laughed at the relief in Anvil 6's voice.
No tanker worth his salt would rather have his horses
sitting, not with the M1's speed and fire-on-the-move
capability.

"Tommy," Dillon called over the intercom. "Move to
a position on Steel's right. I want us positioned between
them and Anvil."

Dillon felt Cyclops II surge beneath him even as the
driver acknowledged the order.

"I'm on trigger hold until we get there," yelled Bickel
from the gunner's compartment, placing the main gun
on safe to ensure an accidental bump didn't send a sabot
round up one of the Knight's iron asses—an uncomfortable proposition in anyone's book.

As they pulled into position next to Steel's far-right
tank Dillon turned his head hard to check Anvil's
progress—it was a pain in the ass having only one good
eye, he thought, not for the first time. He could see the
company's dust rising in the air. The Russians wouldn't
be able to see the maneuver through the smoke unless

their thermal systems were better than Dillon had been briefed. The Iron Tiger S3 doubted that was the case. In fact, he was betting their collective asses on it.

Huge booms sounded to the south and Dillon thought he could see the flight of 155mm artillery overhead moving toward the Russian line, though that was likely a trick of his eye. The ground trembled seconds later as high-explosive rounds peppered the Russian front.

"You're on, Lightning . . . repeat, then shift to the center and western positions." Dillon's intent was to pound the Russians for several minutes and then to shift the fires to the middle and left of the enemy line as Anvil and Steel attacked into the right flank; Knight would provide direct fire support from their support by fire position. *"Thunder, once the artillery shifts I want smoke between the far right of the Russian line and the central and western forces."*

The fire supporters acknowledged. As Dillon watched more fires pouring onto the Russian position he saw Stuart's M1A1s and Bradleys were enjoying some success through the smoke. Contrary to the beliefs of some people, particularly their manufacturers, thermal sights couldn't cut through smoke as if it weren't there; but they were definitely better than nothing. Dillon estimated that the Russians had thus far lost at least five or six vehicles to his unit's direct and indirect fires.

"Fires shifting!" came the FSO's call.

"Roger, Lightning," said Dillon. *"Anvil, Steel, commence your attacks. Keep it online as we sweep the position."* He switched to intercom. "Tommy . . . move!"

Now the M1A1's gift of speed and firepower would be exploited to best effect. Anvil still had twelve tanks, Steel thirteen; add his own tank and the Iron Tigers had an assault force of twenty-six Abramses sprinting across the desert. Gun tubes blazed as the smoke shifted and the ten vehicles on the Russian right flank came into view. They were oriented on Stuart's company and never saw what hit them. After ten seconds all were piles of smoking slag and Dillon's team continued its assault without letup.

"Shift the smoke and fires!"

Thunder and Lightning were ready for the call. The artillery danced from the center to the far left and the smoke followed, obscuring the view of those farthest from the Iron Tigers' line of assault.

Some of the Russians saw the approaching Abramses now and traversed their turrets and guns left and onto the American force screaming down on them. One Iron Tiger tank went down, lurching to a stop and throwing track across the desert floor. Over a dozen Russian tanks and infantry fighting vehicles exploded, their flames blending ethereally with the strange red morning sky.

"Continue the attack!" yelled Dillon as he saw a few of the Iron Tiger tanks slow down. Shock was an overwhelming multiplier and he didn't want to lose it. *"Mike, keep an eye on the smokers and make sure none of them are traversing to take a shot at our asses,"* he told Stuart as they tore through the remnants of the Russian center.

"Wilco," said Stuart, his face pressed to his sight extension and watching the burning Russian vehicles just in case any were playing possum.

Without being told the artillery and mortars shifted off of the far left. The FSO followed up the shift with a call to Dillon. *"Tiger Three, Lightning . . . shifting fires to enemy command-and-control element to the north. The objective area is now your fight."*

"This is Three . . . good call, thanks."

Now aware of what was occurring, most of the Russian vehicles on the left elevated their gun tubes and put them over the rear deck—the universal tank sign of surrender—as they saw the U.S. force headed their way from the flank. Crews began dismounting, hands in the air. Two of the Russian tanks decided to duke it out; their mistake would be measured in seconds.

Dillon rubbed a grimy hand that smelled of cordite across his face and looked around him. Per unit SOP Anvil and Steel were moving across the objective to secure the far side against potential Russian reinforcements. The fight appeared to be over; still, something nibbled incessantly at his mind, a dark thought that wouldn't go away. The realization hit him suddenly—there were fewer Russian vehicles than he'd first estimated. And unless his initial assessment had been wrong—and Dillon's pride in his tactical savvy told him this was likely not the case—then that meant that some of the Ruskies had displaced. *But where?*

The American major jerked his head to the left as he heard the distant crack of a tank main gun. *Oh shit,* he thought as he saw a T-90 on Knight's flank. Here he had been congratulating himself on what a brilliant maneuver commander he was and the Russians had snuck around the other side. A quick count showed a company-minus of enemy tanks arrayed against Knight.

Without thinking Dillon gave Tommy directions to head at max speed for the Russian force. *"Steel, follow my move. Anvil, you've got security on this objective . . . get the Russian soldiers out, secure them and fire their vehicles."*

Mike Stuart felt the tank next to him blow before he saw anything. He turned in his turret to see what was happening only in time to feel the heat and concussion of one of his 2nd Platoon tanks wash over him. From the way the tank burned Stuart knew that none of the four crewmen in the doomed vehicle would make it out.

"This is Knight Six . . . tanks, nine o'clock! Nine o'clock!"

Stuart began to call for his 1st Platoon—the far left element of his team and thus the closest to the new threat—to reorient their weapons systems in that direction while he maneuvered the other two platoons into a better position. That was when a bone-jarring concussion rocked his tank and flames leapt up from the turret floor.

Dillon saw the red bear on a black background flying from the rear of the lead Russian tank even as it sent a sabot flying into Mike Stuart's tank. Dillon knew by the unit symbology on the M1A1 that it was his friend's tank that had erupted in flames. He also knew from the way the M1A1 burned that the crew still had time to get out if they hurried. He swung his gaze back to the rogue tank that every American soldier in Iraq wanted to smoke worse than any other, for in it rode an inhuman monster. And as Dillon watched, the bear turned its 125mm snout back to Stuart's tank just as the American captain and his loader clambered out of the burning vehicle.

Dillon reached into the turret and grabbed the override, wrenching the gun tube toward the Russian tank. "*Bick* . . . get that fucker now!"

For no small reason did Dillon consider Bickel the best combat gunner in the Army. Sensing the urgency in his commander's voice the young sergeant snapped a shot in the direction of the enemy tank in a split second, worrying more about getting the depleted-uranium-tipped sabot round into flight toward his intended victim than taking his time for a well-aimed shot—he'd do that with the second round if necessary. Dillon stood in the turret and watched the red streak. The sabot round hit the T-90 in the left track an instant before the enemy tank fired its main gun. The Russian vehicle lurched to a stop as its track flopped uselessly to the ground, its own sabot round flying left of Stuart's B-66 tank.

"Pump another round into the son of a bitch!" yelled Dillon.

But even as Dillon issued the somewhat unorthodox fire command a hand waving a white flag appeared from the commander's turret of the T-90.

"Boss?" said Bickel over the intercom. The gunner knew who it was in the tank that sat helplessly in his sights. And it was clear that he was more than prepared to ignore the sign of surrender.

"Stand by," Dillon said bitterly. The Iron Tiger S3 looked over the remaining Russian tanks. Steel had taken out two. That left five or six still operational . . . and there they were. The tanks had found a point of low ground oriented on Knight. Steel couldn't touch them, but for now the Russians weren't engaging Knight. The two forces appeared to have an Iraqi Standoff.

"Move toward the Russian command tank, Tommy," he said coldly. The major didn't need to specify further. Dillon stopped the driver one hundred meters from the T-90.

"Bick, if that tank so much as twitches, fry the fucker."

"Roger that," said the gunner. "Where are you going, sir?"

"For a walkabout."

Before his gunner could protest Dillon disconnected his CVC and jumped from the turret.

Standing topside, Dillon dropped the crewman's helmet next to his .50 cal. As he hit the ground, the Iron Tiger S3 unbuttoned the retaining strap on his 9mm shoulder holster.

Sergei Sedov watched as the American jumped from his tank. He smiled grimly and did the same. *Why in God's name would the man dismount*? the Russian wondered. He'd produced the white flag only in a moment of desperation. It was clear the American force had more than enough firepower remaining to shatter his handful of T-90s. And then he realized what the soldier's shortfall was . . . he didn't want to see any more of his men die. *Well,* he thought, *I can make that weakness work for me.*

The colonel assessed his adversary as they approached one another. The eye patch was his first observation; it occurred to him that for the American army to allow the man to remain in combat with such a condition, he must be a better than average soldier . . . for surely they weren't so desperate for combat leaders that they found it necessary to put handicapped men on the battlefield. Probably three inches shorter than himself but built like a rock. Silver hair shorn to the scalp on the sides and back. And then the Russian felt a shiver run down his spine as he saw the look on the man's face—it was like looking at Death himself as he stared into the man's single cold blue eye.

Sedov shook the final thought off and laughed to himself. What did he have to lose? It was all or nothing. The general had made it clear that his career—probably more—was over if he failed in his mission to stop the Americans.

The men met midway between their tanks, stopping five meters apart.

"What the fuck do you want?" asked Dillon flatly.

"The same thing you want, Major," said the Russian. "And I notice you do not salute me. Do they no longer teach American officers military courtesy?"

Patrick Dillon stared at the Russian. "A salute is a sign of respect. Do I need to say more?"

Sedov laughed. "Ahhh . . . I see my reputation precedes me."

"Your stench precedes you, jackass. One final time, what do you want?"

"As I said, the same as you." The Russian smiled grimly. "I have a proposition for you, Major."

"State it."

"A tank-on-tank battle, just you and I."

Dillon looked over the battlefield situation, ensuring himself he'd missed nothing. "Why should I? I have the tactical advantage. If you push the issue, you and all of your men will die."

Sedov nodded compassionately. "That is true," he said. Then he shifted his gaze from Patrick Dillon to the Knight tanks. "Unfortunately I have already issued orders for my men to open fire on those tanks if I walk away without giving them a cease-fire signal." The Russian smiled now and the sight of it made Dillon's skin crawl. "Not only on their tanks, but also on the crews already on the ground."

Dillon looked toward B-66. Mike Stuart was several meters away from his mount, kneeling in the sand as he worked frantically over one of his injured crew members. "You'd still die, Colonel."

"True," he said and then shrugged. "But it changes nothing. It is your decision, Major."

Dillon felt the Irish in him screaming to the surface. "Pick your tank, Colonel."

Sedov began to turn and then paused. "Will you answer one question, Major?"

Dillon, already moving back to Cyclops II, turned. "What?"

"Why would the American military apparatus leave a one-eyed tank officer on the battlefield?"

It was Dillon's turn to laugh. "I could ask the same of the Russian decision regarding a no-nosed colonel." The laugh died and Dillon smiled wickedly at his enemy. "You want to dance, Ivan? *Let's dance.*"

Sedov watched the burly American as the man turned and swaggered back toward his tank. The same cold fear he'd momentarily felt before struck again, but more pronounced this time. Then it was his turn to laugh. As a good communist he did not believe in God, the devil, or omens.

The signal was prearranged. Once Sedov fired a red flare in the air the two tanks would charge at one another—no further rules were stated. It was the twenty-first-century version of a joust.

Russia's newest and most modern tank and the 1990s-era M1A1 faced each other across less than a thousand meters of open desert, the noise of their idling engines the only sound on the battlefield. Dillon watched as the flare arced into the sky. He didn't wait for it to blossom into a red shower of sparks. "Kick it, Tommy!"

The T-90 and M1A1 sprinted at one another, gun tubes steadying as each of their gunners finalized their target picture. Sedov had chosen to remain in the relative safety of his turret, Dillon had not; *probably because I'm an idiot,* reflected Pat Dillon as he watched the Russian tank's rapid approach.

"Bick, this one's on you, baby," said Dillon. "I'm out."

"I've got it, sir."

Tank main guns roared. A piece of the Russian turret flew in the air. The Russian round missed high. As the two tanks passed one another the gunners maintained control of the turrets, spinning them around in order to keep their quarry in their gun sights. Both tanks kicked in their brakes and began turning. The drivers clenched their muscles, trying to get their machines inside the turning radius of their opponent. When the turns were complete the tanks were only a hundred meters apart, a large distance for a sporting event, extremely small when you manned a combat system capable of engaging a target miles away.

Dillon stood stubbornly in the turret and looked toward the sky. *Whoever's listening, let me take this bag of shit. Please let me send him to the flaming hell he deserves.*

The T-90 and Abrams fired again within a second of one another. There was little doubt of the outcome as the tanks were at point-blank range—both erupted in flames as the gunners found their marks.

"Out!" yelled Dillon. "Everyone out!" Looking down he saw Bickel drawing a bead on the Russian. He reached down and grabbed the gunner by the collar. Drawing on pure bull strength Dillon yanked the NCO from his seat and threw him toward the loader's hatch. "Afraid I'm going to have to pull rank, Bick." Both men scrambled topside.

As Dillon climbed out of the burning Cyclops II he looked to their adversary. The Russian crew was clambering out as well. Dillon smiled. The dance between the Eagle and the Bear was not over. He jumped from the turret to the front slope and to the ground in seconds. "Come on, Ivan," he whispered. "Let's finish it."

My God, thought Sedov. *What have I gotten myself into?* The American was marching, steadily but in no apparent hurry, toward his tank. With nothing left to lose the Russian colonel hopped to the ground.

The two men, over a football field apart, had plenty of time to consider their actions and motives. Neither slowed.

At twenty meters Sedov dropped to one knee and began firing his pistol. Patrick Dillon continued walking. At ten meters the Russian's last round hit Dillon in the shoulder.

Dillon looked down at the wound, momentarily stumbling, then drew his own Beretta.

"Please," said Sedov, falling to his knees. "I surrender. . . ."

Patrick Dillon considered the plea. *Motherfucker,* he thought. He then fired one round into the Russian's left elbow. Sedov spun to the ground. Dillon fired another round into his right elbow. The Russian's pistol fell to the ground and he rolled in pain. The American major stood over him thinking of the 1st Cavalry, thinking of what a flaming asshole this particular human being was.

He fired twice in rapid succession, once to the Russian's right knee, once to his left. He then holstered his pistol.

"You no-nosed *fuck*," he whispered in Sedov's face. "Thank whatever god you pray to that I'm a compassionate man."

Ten minutes later Dillon and his crew, mounted on a tank they'd borrowed from C Company, stopped in front of the Russian headquarters. The major stood silently in the turret. He'd expected some reaction from the enemy staff—resistance, surrender, something. But nothing moved. Vehicles sat around the compound. Tents were spread in an orderly manner, apparently abandoned. Dillon looked to the large tent in front of him. It bristled with antennas.

"Cover me," said Dillon over the task force network. Then he gave Tommy directions.

"Any unit, this is General Colonel Kornukov!" screamed the Russian field commander into the radio handset. *"I need reinforcements at the headquarters! Do you read me?!"*

The staff stood silently by. None of them mistook the turbine engine whines outside as anything but what they were—American armor. What was left of the security force stood arrayed in a semicircle facing the exit, assault rifles ready. The men's orders were clear—give the general as much time as they could on the radio; cut down anything and anyone who entered the tent.

The whine grew louder outside. As they watched a huge gun tube poked through the tent flap and continued moving inward. The guards scattered, throwing their rifles down.

"Oh my God," whispered Kornukov, his hand over his mouth. "It is over."

"This is Major Patrick Dillon, U.S. Army," yelled Dillon into the tent from the front slope of his tank. "I hope to hell someone in there speaks English, because you have exactly thirty seconds to evacuate before we open up." He looked at the SeaWolf. "Make that twenty-five seconds, twenty-four . . ."

Russian staff officers scrambled from the shelter, at their lead a general officer. Dillon looked to his left and saw Boggs trying to decide between targets for his 7.62mm machine gun. The major put his hand on the barrel and directed it at the general's chest. The loader hunkered down over his weapon, now sure of his target.

"I'm afraid I'm going to have to ask you to stand fast, sir," said Dillon with a smile.

General Colonel Kornukov's shoulders slumped slowly; then he raised his hands in the air.

Epilogue

Tom Werner hung up the IP phone connecting him to the U.S. Central Command headquarters in Qatar. "The Russians have thrown in the towel, sir. At least on the tactical level."

Jonathan Drake released a tired smile. "And the Saudis?"

Werner laughed. "Well, with most of the Fourth Infantry now sitting just outside Riyadh, they're being more than cooperative. They really *love* us and are claiming the whole war is a big misunderstanding."

The president snorted. "Like seventy-five percent of the September eleventh hijackers calling Saudi Arabia home is a misunderstanding." His eyes hardened. "Lock that country down."

The chairman nodded. "Done."

Drake turned to Chris Dodd. "What are you hearing from Moscow, Chris?"

"They're scrambling. Apparently they can't locate their president," said the CIA chief with a straight face.

"Will they?" Drake asked in an even voice.

"No, sir," he said evenly. "And without him, and with their military in a shambles, the Federation Council and the Duma will see reason. We'll once more have a happy nuclear standoff."

Werner snorted. "Standoff my ass. The Ruskies now know, after over a half century, that we are *indeed* their daddies."

Drake smiled. "As always, well said and understated, General."

3rd Brigade TOC
Southwestern Iraq

"I'll be back shortly," said Krieger, dismounting from his Hummer. The big scout walked nervously toward the headquarters shelter. He hadn't seen Shelly Simitis in over a week, not since the fateful night of the Spetsnaz attack. He removed his Kevlar as he bent to enter.

"How you doin', soldier?" said a husky voice behind him.

Krieger turned in time to receive a furry white bullet in the chest. He didn't have the opportunity to catch his breath before Phantom began laying doggy kiss after doggy kiss on his face.

"We seem to have a problem, Lieutenant," said Shelly Simitis.

Krieger broke his face loose as he held the Jack close to his chest, stroking it. "What's that, Captain?"

Simitis looked serious. "My dog seems to be overly fond of you. What are we going to do about that?"

Rolf Krieger frowned. "I . . . I don't know, ma'am."

"Do you have anything against dating women who outrank you, Lieutenant?"

Krieger grinned. "No, ma'am."

One Month Later
West of Jackson Hole, Wyoming

The helicopter settled into the mountain valley in a spray of snow. Natasha Khartukov pulled the white parka she wore tight against her as she stepped out into the cold mountain air. The past several hours had been a blur of activity. She'd been packing to return to New York and her job when Angela Bennett had phoned. Five minutes later she was in a government sedan. Ten minutes after that she was picked up from the rooftop of a Manhattan federal building and whisked to LaGuardia for a chartered jet—where the flight was taking her she had not known. Angela Bennett had told her that it was important; that was enough. The woman had proven herself a friend over the past weeks.

When the rotors had almost stopped spinning the pilot hopped out and trotted around the helicopter to open Natasha's door. She looked at the snowcapped mountains and cedars heavy with snow. "Where are we?" she yelled.

The pilot put his lips close to her ear. "Grand Teton National Forest!"

"Where?"

"Wyoming," he said in a quieter voice as the engine and rotor noises died away. "You're in Wyoming."

And then she saw the man standing alone twenty meters away. She took the pilot's proffered hand and stepped down from the helicopter. Slowly she walked toward the lone figure.

"Hello, Luke," she said simply.

Dodd was dressed in jeans, a denim jacket with a wool collar, Ray-Bans, and a cowboy hat. She shivered. He didn't seem to notice the chill. To the contrary, he seemed a living part of the surrounding terrain.

"You look good," he said.

"Luke, what is this about? I thought we'd settled all of this. We aren't . . . we can't . . ."

"Shhh," he said.

"Luke, I know my father's dead. I know . . . I know you . . ."

Luke put a finger to her lips. "Shhh," he repeated. "It's all right."

"Hello, Natasha."

The voice came from her right. Natasha turned toward it and stared in disbelief.

"Father? Father!" She ran forward and hugged him. "You're alive!"

Konstantin Khartukov laughed from deep in his belly. He reflected as he held his daughter close that it had been a long, long time since he'd felt the simple joy of a real laugh; far too long. "Yes, I'm alive. Thanks to your friend," he said, nodding at Dodd.

She turned to Luke. "What does he mean?"

Luke shrugged. "New Russian governments aren't big on failure. When the war began turning against them . . . well, let's just say it was a question of which course they would take with him: a ride to Siberia or a bullet and an unmarked grave."

"So what now?" she asked.

"He'll be taken care of. When we have questions, we'll expect him to answer them. He should prove useful at providing insights into the new Russian leadership. He has his option of several very nice 'retirement' locations, our only requirement being that the world continues to believe him dead."

"Or? What if he comes out in public?"

Luke Dodd looked to Natasha's father and then back at her, but he said nothing.

"My dear, why would I do that?" Khartukov held her shoulders. "Natasha, I have made mistakes—serious mistakes—over the past few years. Not the least of which was almost losing you." Hugging her to him, he whispered in her ear, "I will not take that chance again. Nothing is worth that price."

Konstantin Khartukov pulled back and looked into his daughter's eyes. He saw that she was staring at Luke Dodd. "I approve," he whispered quietly into her ear.

Disney World
Orlando, Florida

"You look funny, Daddy!" squealed Carson.

Patrick Dillon, war hero, sat stoically on one of the theme park's thousands of benches, his arm in a sling, an eye patch across his face, and a pair of Mickey Mouse ears on his head. The soldier looked seriously at his youngest daughter. "Why do you say that, sweetheart?"

"Daddy's silly!" The little blond girl laughed. She then kissed him on the cheek and ran to greet the seven-foot mouse approaching them.

Melissa Dillon sighed and put her head—also adorned with mouse ears—to her husband's good shoulder. "Will it ever be over, Pat?"

She felt her husband tense.

"Honey," he said, "didn't I promise you Florida?"

She pulled back. "You promised a job in Florida where we could spend more time with you. Disney World was supposed to be a stop on the way to our new life, Pat, not a temporary respite from our old one."

Patrick Dillon pulled his wife closer. He smelled the honeysuckle fragrance of her auburn hair. Lifting his head he watched his children cavorting around Mickey, their faces adorned with cotton candy. Unlike so many of his fellow soldiers, he had no illusions. He knew how much of life he'd missed out on because of the siren call: *Duty, Honor, Country*—birthdays, anniversaries, the simple joy of lying in Melissa's arms every night. And he knew that the call was too strong for him to have done otherwise—and always would be.

"Melissa," he said quietly, stroking her hair. "I love you and the girls more than I love life itself. I'd love nothing more than to see you every day for as long as I live, for you to never have to worry again that I'm being shot at in some godforsaken corner of the world as you try to fall asleep at night." He paused. "But when they offered me the Iron Tiger S3 job full-time . . . God help me, but I couldn't say no."

Melissa Dillon hugged him close and felt the tears burn her eyes. "I know, Pat. I know."

TIN SOLDIERS

A Novel of the Next Gulf War

BY
MICHAEL FARMER

An alliance with Iran reinvigorates the Iraqi
military. To prevent a total conquest of the region, a
U.S. Army Heavy Brigade must stand against Iraq's
greater numbers and updated
technology—while the locals are bent on
grinding the small American force into the ancient
desert sand.

0-451-20905-2

S787